THE LOTTERY WINNER

AND THE GUN WITH NO BULLETS

By

Heru Asaramo

Dedicated to

JaJa K. Asaramo
Zora M. Asaramo and Lavoyia T. Miller

TABLE OF CONTENTS

CHAPTER 1

THE DREAMS

The tips of tree branches slapped his bedroom window as gusts swept in from the East. Spindly walls reverberated every few moments, mirroring the gale's uneven heartbeat and mercurial temper. They seemed like they would buckle if the weather got any worse outside. Nature was throwing a fit. Angry winds howled and whistled but did nothing to distract Jacob. His eyes focused on the square clutched tightly between his fingers. Heavens roared and rumbled, claps of lightning and bellowing thunder danced well into the night. The room lit up every time a bolt shot across the sky, then went dark just as quickly. A rickety alarm clock near his bed read 10:52pm. The air was muggy. Humid. It was mid-summer.

Earlier that afternoon a gas clerk received a crisp dollar bill in exchange for this most special piece of paper. Printed on the ticket were a series of numbers. 4,5,8,21,32, and lastly, 33. These numbers weren't random. Each one meant something. Smudged by sweaty hands, the top left corner felt a bit worn. He'd handled it several times throughout the day. Each time, he sent up a prayer. There was a crease running down the ticket's center, from being stored in his dated leather wallet. It's where he'd put every ticket he had ever bought. It was a habit. That way he would never misplace a winner.

As he stood there gripping the prized possession, Maria abruptly swung open the door to the dark room unannounced, to Jacob's surprised disapproval. The ticket quickly found its way into his back pocket. Hopefully she hadn't seen it. His parents didn't approve of gambling. The most they would do is dabble in stocks from time to time. Their son held a different view. Veins in his forehead grew and pulsated as their eyes aligned. The room lit up again as another shot of lightning jumped from one cloud to another. "Mom! What is *so* hard about knocking? I've asked you like a million times!" She flipped the light switch. Dirty clothes lazily tossed on the floor came into view. A jumbled pile of shoes, a few candy wrappers. Before replying to a teen clearly too comfortable, a tense hand whipped up to her hip. "Oh, you mean like the million times I've asked you to clean this dump up? What're you up to in here anyway?" Suspicious eyes surveyed the cramped room as she questioned the rebellious youngster.

Jacob's mother was of the hard-nosed military breed. Her father, grandfather, and great-grandfather were all proud Marines. As were their fathers. Duty and a keen sense of patriotism drew the family to the Armed Forces for seven generations. All the way back, to the days of the Civil War, where her lineage shed blood, sweat, and tears fighting against the demonic wave of sectarianism cresting from the South. Maria's husband, Drake, was also a retired Marine and analytical chemist. This translated to a strict upbringing centered on discipline and sacrifice for both Jacob and his younger adopted sister Myra.

As children, the siblings were not allowed to ask for anything when they went to the store. Their parents weren't having it. The couple always agreed that regardless of income, they would not raise entitled children that saw mommy and daddy as walking ATMs. Jacob and Myra were ensured whatever they asked for, was exactly what they were guaranteed *not* to get.

Additionally, saying they didn't like a certain type of food was forbade. This stemmed from Drake's side of the family. A byproduct of meager beginnings meant he held little regard for picky eaters. Often he could be found chanting, "Waste not want not," as if it were a mantra. Choosiness only guaranteed the unwanted item plagued their dinner plates every day for a month. A tough approach, but it was effective. The children learned quickly.

The family dwelled in an average neighborhood, nothing too fancy. Their apartment was nestled in the southern city of Charlotte in North Carolina. Two minutes from the highway, just off Senna Drive. Humble in nature, it was quite different from the vaunted residence they'd once called home. At least ten miles separated them from the more upscale areas of the city. That life was put on ice once the recession hit. Affluence became a thing of the past.

There was a fifth member of the family, Jason, but his life was cut short. He died before he was old enough to get a license. It was a sad situation. Uncontrollable. His breathing had always been strained, stemming from a little-known lung disease. At first, they thought it may have been asthma, but a few scans and doctor visits ruled that out. It took two hospitals and several specialists to nail down the problem. Once identified, options were limited. The sickness was destructive and chronic, creating scar tissue and irreparable damage over the years. This added crippling doses of stress to an already weakened respiratory system. His dark past was to thank for that. Try as they may, the doctors never found an effective treatment for the frail boy. It was only a matter of time before the lethiferous disease would claim his life.

Jacob and his mother were there in the hospital room, clutching one another for comfort when Jason passed. It was a gut-wrenching experience. The kind that changes a person. Especially a teen. Afterwards, there were nights Jacob would wake with sweat saturating his clothes and sheets. His heart would be pounding, breath racing. It would take a minute for him to come to, realizing death happens just once. It was hell. Like reliving the loss over and over. A nocturnal dolor that clung to him, keeping true slumber at bay.

Although only bad dreams, vividness gave life to their horror and pain. It felt like every moment was real. When he closed his eyes, Jacob could see the hospice sign hanging near the front desk where his sickly brother spent his last days. The sign was always off-center, something that stuck in the grieving boy's mind. He hated it, what it represented, its imbalance and unfairness.

He hated remembering the smell of sickness. And the fog of cleaners and bleach that hung in the air trying to drown it out. Combined, they made his stomach turn. All of it. The faces of those close to their end. Sunken eyes. Withered shadows of themselves. The people on that floor knew they were going to die. The sense of it was everywhere. That day with Maria, it would be one Jacob would never forget. It was branded. Ominous sounds of his mother's sobs lingered, cloaking him in blankets of sorrow.

The rasp of his dying brother's breathing was something Jacob dearly yearned to erase from memory. His ears remembered shallow gasps for air, the faint sounds of a dwindling existence. Jason's eyes were blank and glossed over during his last days. Although open, they were dead. Empty. He couldn't even blink on his own. The nurses had to drip solution on his pupils just to keep them moist. The doctors said he'd fallen into a state of unconsciousness that left his body defunct. Seconds before he died, his eyes regained focus for a few precious moments. It must have taken his last ounce of strength. He looked over at his mother's somber gaze. Then to his older brother. Both had tears forming as his life withdrew into the depths. The seconds ticked at an hour's pace. Then. He was gone...

Those moments would play over in Jacob's mind. They were seared into his fabric. Family was important. Especially to someone with his kind of background. To lose his brother, it broke a piece of him, deep inside. "He knew we were there, and the last thing he wanted before he left this world was to see us *one* more time. He knew." Jacob's thoughts were wrenched back to reality when a loud sound erupted from his pocket. This noise was echoed by the shrill voice of his mother's angry calls in the background.

She demanded he clean his cluttered room and wash the dirty dishes piled sloppily in the sink after the evening's supper. Brown eyes rolled at the notion of yet another chore. His head peered out the door and into the hallway. His phone was still buzzing. As he reached hastily into his pocket, he felt the familiar buttons and shape of a Nokia. Three fingers grazed its smooth surface before pulling it up.

Several months prior he'd set its alarm to go off twice a week at 10:55pm, a reminder to watch the nightly lottery drawing. There he stood, partly annoyed with his mother, partly excited, buzzing with hopeful energy. His attention suddenly diverted to the outdated television in the far corner of the room as the screen lit up.

On it a slim woman of about 25 years of age stood beside a contraption spewing numbered balls into a long clear tube. To some this picture would have seemed quite odd, but not to Jacob, or millions of other people for that matter. Countless hopefuls watched the drawings, praying their time had finally come. For most, it never did and never would.

Every Tuesday and Friday evening he'd stand in front of the television at around 11pm, waiting to discover that night's lucky numbers. This night would've been no different, if not for one tiny detail... Consumed by worry and anxiety, Jacob was accustomed to restless nights. They were as familiar as his own reflection. A part of him. On the rare occasions when sleep hung around, he often suffered horrible nightmares of his brother's death. Jacob was only fifteen when he died. There was also the constant weight of watching Drake and Maria fall further in debt as they tried to keep up with the joneses. He loved his new parents deeply, but often wished *they* would practice the discipline they imparted on him and his sister.

Despite at times bringing in sizable incomes, his adopted parents saved an extraordinarily modest amount of actual cash for much of his upbringing. He often felt responsible for the constant financial woes that plagued the family. These burdens, that typically kept sleep at bay, ceased for three nights straight. It was unusual to say the least.

Absent were the tormenting screams that usually haunted his mind. Gone were the knots of worry in his stomach. No longer was there a cloud of dampening weight resting on his chest. For the first time in years, Jacob enjoyed deep, restful nights. Hours slipped by as if minutes. Not only was his slumber uninterrupted, but he also dreamt.

The dreams were vibrant and picturesque. They all fell upon the same subject. That subject was one which Jacob pondered constantly but never really considered possible. His impoverished circumstance made it difficult for him to believe there was any other way of life his family could live. With parents that couldn't seem to hold debt at bay, the future felt caliginous at best.

The last dream, which occurred on the previous night, was the most vivid and in-depth of all. It began with him standing alone in a nearly empty parking lot. Spring was in full bloom and the sun beamed inviting rays on his back and neck. It warmed his skin and brought a smile to his rounded face. After falling deeper into slumber, he remembered looking around at the beautiful day that lay before him.

A slight breeze carried the scent of honeysuckle and freshly cut grass. It rode the wind in soft waves that splashed against his nose. In this dream, the sun was very bright; it was a spotlight. Jacob remembered having to squint so hard he could barely see more than a few feet in front of him. Clouds dotted the sky. There weren't many people around. A few silhouettes moved in and out of view in a natural feeling way. It was perfect. His favorite type of dream.

His ears picked up the soothing call of a mourning dove in the distance, and there was the occasional thud of a car door being closed. Ahead stood a brick building with slight tints on all the windows. There seemed to be curtains on the ones near the front door. He remembered wanting to know what lay behind them. It felt like something important was hidden just beyond view.

The dreaming teen could tell by the grand entranceway and meticulous landscaping that he was in the right place. It looked just like the picture posted on the company's website. Atop the building lay a sign that read, "North Carolina State Lottery," in dazzling red and yellow letters. His feet carried him forward. Tall double doors. They opened with his approach. He was feeling richer already. "Nice touch."

As Jacob strode into the entranceway, he was promptly greeted by a tall man in an expensive-looking suit. Its pick stitch and polished charcoal sheen was broken by subtle pinstripes of grey. The gentleman wore it well. After being offered a glass of chilled champagne he was accompanied by the man and two armed guards down a dimly lit corridor. Their steps echoed against the hard marble and danced between paintings hanging on display, making the building feel bigger than it actually was.

Had this taken place in the real world, he would've wondered why these people were treating him so oddly. Then he remembered, this was just a dream… Jacob's newly found entourage led him into a spacious office at the end of the hallway. The door creaked open as they entered.

Three women sat patiently inside, conversing quietly among themselves. Everything in this room looked high-end. Tasteful sculptures dotted the area. They added a level of class. A crystal chandelier gleamed light onto every surface in a subtle way. It was turned down low. Other ambient and halo lighting took up the rest of the illumination. The furniture felt futuristic. Like the kind you'd expect to find in some tech guru's home. Jacob was impressed. Whatever the women were talking about got cut short, interrupted by the men's approach. Three sets of eyes peered from behind the mahogany desks separating them from Jacob. The women were seemingly waiting for *him*.

He was beckoned towards the desk in the center, which was decorated tastefully with two framed pictures, a marble trophy, and an orchid displaying vibrant mauve. Without saying a word, the elderly woman sitting directly ahead held out a French-manicured hand. Eyes, sitting behind thick glasses surveyed the man before her. The room fell silent.

Intuitively, Jacob knew to give her the slip that instantly materialized in his pocket. She inspected it with great care, looking closely at both sides and holding it under a heavy magnifying glass for several intense moments. Her almond eyes squinted as they searched for abnormalities. The room's silence persisted. The escorts that had led him in were gone, they seemed to fade into the background.

Not knowing what to do with himself, Jacob stood in front of her with his hands held awkwardly at his sides, waiting for the verdict. His eyes darted around the room. He took in the décor. His gaze drifted up. The warm glow from the chandelier was soothing. It helped slow his heartrate as he tried to focus on his breathing. He was anxious. And rightfully so. This ticket could make all the difference. Not just for him either. For everyone. After what felt like an hour, but was really about two minutes, the woman suddenly stood. Her movement was quite abrupt, especially considering her apparent age. Jacob could feel his body jerk with surprise even as he slept.

She departed the room in silence, a slight smirk forming at the corners of her wrinkled lips as the door shut with a thud behind her. The lady was tailed by one of the larger guards with her every move now under his watchful eye. Something was up. A few minutes later in the dream, a different, younger woman entered the room and approached Jacob with a smile and hand extended. Strands of deep brown hair fell over slim, supple shoulders. The rest sat atop a face that laughed at the thought of make-up. Her pulchritude commanded attention, and Jacob obliged.

There were about four or five other men dressed in casual business attire standing just behind her. Their silhouettes blurred into the background like white noise, leaving only beauty in focus. She felt strangely familiar. Jacob wondered whether they met somewhere before, he thought maybe they attended the same school or something. The woman, seemingly having sensed what he was wondering, decided to answer his question.

"I'm the girl from TV, that's probably where you recognize me from Jacob," she said shyly with the shrug of a shoulder. This realization left the dreamer in utter astonishment. "And how the hell does she know my name?" Even while he slept he could feel his heartrate flutter with excitement. For some inexplicable reason he felt star struck while in her presence. It was like she was famous or something.

She began to blush at his awe-filled stares before continuing with her initial intention. The attractive young woman cheerfully informed him that the preliminary results on his ticket were positive; however further testing would be required to confirm its authenticity. "It shouldn't take more than an hour, two at the most. We should be able to authenticate everything fairly quickly."

After hearing this news, Jacob's heart jumped from his chest and skipped a beat. At some subconscious level, he really hoped this wouldn't be the moment his alarm clock would wrench him from dreamland; after all, he had no idea what time it was in the real world. Dreams had a funny way of ending right when they got to the good part. At least that was *his* experience.

A few minutes passed. A man beckoned him forward. He was led into the hallway and instructed to wait in a lavish room brimming with a plethora of wonderfully odd pieces. It was tucked to the side near the front door he'd come in through. The door to the room was a faded blue. Navy. So understated, most people probably walked right past it. Chipped paint and a rusted handle gave it more of a closet feel than anything else. Its unassuming aura was lifted as the door gave way. There were several plush tufted leather chairs scattered about, which created the distinct feeling of being in some sort of high-end cigar club. Un-expected to say the least.

On the far wall was a painting of a man riding a muscular beast with tones of heather and grey in its coat. The steed's mouth hung open as it galloped at full tilt. A silver spur dug into its inner left thigh. The other side wasn't in view but Jacob was sure it was being stabbed as well. The intense rider had a gun in one hand and the reins in the other, he appeared to be in pursuit of a fleeing fox. Three hounds were also hot on the terrified animal's heels. Their eyes bulged and saliva dangled in the wind, hanging from hungry jaws. They were running down a hill. Hues of shamrock painted undulant valleys and peaks in the landscape. It looked like somewhere on the Irish countryside. Dusk. The lighting was perfect.

He canvassed the beautifully painted masterpiece, musing the time and dedication it undoubtedly took to complete. "This must've taken months to finish. Maybe even years." It was colossal, taking nearly half the space the wall had to offer. There was a signature in the bottom right corner near the frame. Through squinted eyes, it became apparent the squiggly lines etched into the canvas were in fact *not* a name. They instead spelled the number four. Jacob found this quite odd. His curious gaze surveyed the intricate mounting surrounding the stunning work of art. Crafted wood, aged and dusty. There was a sense of charmed nobility about it.

Jacob could feel the presence of several other smaller pieces hanging, but this was the only painting currently in view. He continued to explore, taking time to inspect anything of interest. The room's old floors creaked and moaned from his inquisitive footsteps. As he traversed the area perusing an array of different items, he noticed an African Grey parrot perched on the arm of one of the chairs. Its curved black talons dug deep into dated leather.

Its feathers were long and sleek. Soft. The bird emanated intelligence and wisdom. Round tawney eyes gave it an almost human characteristic. Jacob stood there in silence, peering at the unexpected animal for several long minutes. It sat so still it was difficult to tell whether the creature was alive or a replica. With slight hesitance Jacob decided it would be best to touch the bird ever-so gently.

If it reacted, he would know it was real. As his hand extended out he thought he saw the creature's yellow eyes widen, but decided it was a figment of his imagination. This decision would prove to be a mistake. As his forefinger began grazing over the beautiful animal's feathered back, a sharp, permeating pain gripped him just above his thumb. It felt like he was being squeezed with pliers. Really squeezed. The pain was surprising.

The African bird, without moving from its perch, turned its head a full 180 degrees to face its oppressor. In its beak, it firmly held a shockingly large chunk of Jacob's flesh. Eyes glared intently as it bit with all its might. Jacob could actually see the animal's neck strain from the exertion. When it finally decided to let go, he was left with two painful puncture wounds, a stream of blood connecting them, and the answer to his question.

As he stepped away from the chair, his face wincing with pain, he noticed a low rumble emanating from a window at the far end of the room. Upon further inspection, Jacob watched with concern as a growing crowd of onlookers gathered in the parking lot. Some of the group's participants held TV cameras, and there was an alluring blonde holding a sign that read "Marry Me."

Although aptly intrigued, the scene was still disturbing to the lucid dreamer. He didn't like crowds. Even in real life. He'd always been more of a loner... From seemingly thin air a cup of hot chamomile tea manifested onto the windowsill. Its soothing aromas wafted into Jacob's nostrils and suppressed the incessant dialogue brewing in his head.

How did this growing mass of people even know he was here? Even as he slept, he could hear his mother's voice in his ear. She used to tell him, "Dreams have a funny way of jumping all over the place, but sometimes, you get lucky enough to dream about what you really want in life son." He wondered whether he would be on the news, and actually played a mock interview in his head in which he explained what he would do with the money.

Technically, he didn't really know whether he'd won quite yet. There were cases he heard of. Cases where people *thought* they won, only to later discover they were indeed still poor. The final authentication of a winning ticket was known to be pretty draconian. There couldn't be any damage at all to the bar code on the back of the slip. Scrutinous eyes would be sure to check.

If the signature on the piece of paper didn't match the one on the owner's driver's license, the ticket was deemed void and its value lost. Jacob began to worry maybe his hopes were too high and would soon be smashed to pieces. After all, he'd been in the room for what felt like quite some time by that point. The voice we all have in our heads started speaking. Seeds of doubt began to sprout. "What if I didn't win? Then what?"

Just as he began to relapse into familiar internal dialogue, there was a loud knock at the door, followed by three softer knocks. The first was so brusque it made Jacob flinch. In doing so, he spilled scorching hot tea directly onto his recently acquired bird holes. A plume of steam rose as the torrid liquid seared punctured skin. Squawking with delight at his further injury, the parrot looked on as the door creaked open. Black dress shoes appeared at the entrance. A familiar face.

The gentleman that had greeted him at the building's entrance strode briskly into the room. The heels of his Allen Edmond's clanked against wooden floorboards as he moved. His hand held a sealed envelope. Its paper felt thick and smooth to the touch with a glossed finish. With great enthusiasm, he shook Jacob's hand while sporting a broad grin across his bearded face. The slightly pretentious demeanor wore earlier was erased, and his newfound smile was filled with impish humor.

After an awkwardly long handshake, one word spilled from the man's mouth. "Congratulations!" Without further explanation it became delightfully clear what just took place. Jacob had, he had, "Damn!" He had to wake up from his dream, his bladder was about to explode.

CHAPTER 2

THOU SHALL NOT STEAL

As his mother departed the room, Jacob noticed for the first time how cold the air felt on his skin. Ever wary of too high a bill, Maria would often give the children extra blankets instead of cranking the heat in their three-bedroom apartment. At that point in their lives Drake still clung desperately to the lifestyle they'd left behind. His wife was the only voice of reason. Without her, his tolerance for debt knew no bounds.

The clock read 10:58, and it was just about time for the woman on television to reveal the evening's winning numbers. At the exact moment she uttered, "And tonight's winning lottery numbers are," there was a flash of lightning that lit up the entire bedroom. The weather outside seemed to be picking up. Then, out of nowhere, the TV just completely shut off. The room went ink black.

With squinted, suspicious eyes, Jacob quickly yanked his head around to look over his shoulder. He halfway expected to see his younger sister Myra standing in the doorway with the remote. Turning off the television just as the numbers were about to come up seemed like something she would do. Like many siblings their age, the pair relished any opportunity for mischief.

Upon turning however, no figure met his glare. As he clamored over to press the power button, he realized the entire apartment was dark; there were no lights on anywhere. "Great," Jacob thought. "Not only does God *refuse, I mean just refuse* to let me win, but now he won't even grant me the luxury of knowing I've lost!" His eyes drifted towards the ceiling as his head shook slowly in disappointment. It was the type of disappointment that lingers, crawling beneath one's skin. A lack of Faith.

"No one's listening..." His relationship with God was strained and distant to say the least. Words of prayer rarely left his lips. When they did, they were tainted with negative expectations. Experience taught him that. He felt as though God ignored his every wish. Every desire. Sometimes at night, his head would turn to the heavens and he would plead for a reply. It was rare, but it happened. Usually reserved for only the most dire states, the ones where true despondency had taken root. He would beg for a voice to call out from the abyss. His pleas went unnoticed. At least that's how it seemed. Very much like childhood, that which he asked for, was exactly what he was deprived of.

Throughout life his faith would be tested, an eternal voyage. Taken in solitude. It wasn't that he was void of spiritual belief; it was just, he felt neglected and unimportant to God. It was like God was just standing by, letting whatever happens happen. Somewhere along the way he lost his path. Try as his parents may, they couldn't answer the deep-rooted questions that writhed in his soul. They were the tough kinds of questions. The types a pastor would have trouble answering. Questions like, "Did slaves pray? If so, were any of those prayers ever answered?" His parents had taught him of the horrors his lineage endured. "If *they* prayed, and *still* were *castrated, raped, lynched, burned alive, torn apart, sold away, stripped of history*; and on and on and on... For 400 years... If *they* prayed... Was anyone listening?"

Actually, he felt neglected and unimportant to his own family in many ways as well. There was a period where certain items began to turn up missing around the apartment; and not just money, but jewelry, food, credit cards, all sorts of things were taken. Drake and Maria would always handle these incidents the exact same way.

They would yell out, frustration hugging the tips of every word, "Jacob! Myra! Get your tails in here right now! Now which one of you took it? And don't play dumb, you know what we're talkin' about! Myra was it you?" His sister was sure to deny any allegations thrown her way. She was good at it. Deflection was her specialty. The innocence in her face was Drake's weak spot. Daddy's girl. "Nope, wasn't me dad, I don' even know what you're talking about ta' be honest." Big brown puppy eyes would look up at him, repelling his fury and redirecting it elsewhere.

"Jacob, it *had* to be you then!" The boy's response was always the same. His brow would crumple inward with indignation. Embittered tears would gather, anticipating the familiar journey to Jacob's rounded chin. He couldn't understand how they could take Myra's word so easily and not his own. It made him feel like less of a person. The fact that Drake would say only their enemies would steal from them, and that they felt as though he wasn't part of the family didn't help his self-esteem.

Drake would whip Jacob with a thick brown leather belt, demanding he explain why he continued to steal from his own family. It was so frustrating for him. Maria too. To have a son that constantly stole. A son they had chosen to adopt. To save. It felt like such a betrayal. Jacob was at a loss. How the hell are you supposed to give an explanation for something you weren't even doing? "Why?" It was the toughest question in the world for the boy during those years.

The most emotionally painful and trying times for Jacob were the rides in the car to and from New York City with his father. The family lived in upstate New York for several years before moving to Charlotte to escape the cold. This was before the height of their careers, but they still did well for themselves even back then.

Drake's chiropractor had his medical practice stationed in Brooklyn. Jacob would sit in the back seat peering out the window, knowing his father despised him for crimes he never committed. The boy dreaded the questions he knew would inevitably come his way on these trips. His eyes would jump from trunk to trunk as they wound their way through the wooded mountain that separated them from the city. The questions always came. It was just a matter of time.

"Do you even love us boy? Well? Do you?" It was always asked from lips curled with angered confusion. The question dealt such pain to the young boy's heart. His biggest fear, even beyond Drake's belt, was abandonment. He knew he'd been adopted. To him, they could leave him at anytime. It made that period of Jacob's life particularly difficult. "Yes, I've always loved ya'll, I don' like when you ask that dad." By this point tears would often have swelled to the brink of bursting. Streams of salty water would flow freely. His eyelids were levies. No match for the emotional tide of helplessness.

They would pool, waiting to fall into the lake of sorrow in his lap. It was a journey tears took all too often in those dark days. "Then why do you continue to steal from us? And don't tell me you're not doin' it, cause' if I hear *one* more lie come from your mouth, I'll pull this car over an' whoop you right here on the side of this highway!"

That was the basis of how these conversations would start, and it was a long ride to Brooklyn. Little room was given for anything short of outright confession. Often Jacob did lie, making up some story of why he took that week's item, knowing in reality he'd done nothing. He was made to feel like an outsider by his own family. This burden contributed to the man he would grow into in the years to come.

It was later revealed, after three years of false accusations, that his sister Myra was in fact the thief. A secret stash was uncovered, first found by Jacob ironically. His eyes widened in shocked disbelief at the discovery. Under the floorboard in his sister's closet was a box containing one of the missing credit cards, some money, and half a moldy cheesecake infested by little black ants. He found it by accident. Stumbled upon during a game of hide-and-seek, only coming to his attention when his foot slipped and got caught. It was her the entire time.

After all the emotional and physical stress their son endured, after all the hurtful words and looks, what was their heartfelt response to this shocking discovery? "Sorry son, we thought it was you." That was it. That was his long-awaited day of retribution. Hardly reparations.

In any given crowd he was considered the odd ball out, the black sheep. As a result Jacob grew up lonely. He never really had many friends. It wasn't until college that he was in his first real relationship. Highschool days were some of his least favorite. Torture. That's all he could remember. Unending torture. Every day without fail, he was tormented for the way he dressed. Either that or for the shape of his head. Those days seemed like they would never end.

His cruel classmates, heartless creatures as they were, would say things like, "Hey Beavis and Butthead, when are you gonna' get some better gear? Even your *new* clothes are old, I mean like damn!" While his peers relished the back-to-school shopping season, Jacob utterly despised it. They were right. His wardrobe *was* outdated. Painfully so.

To him, clothes shopping was just another opportunity for his parents to disregard current fashion. They would preach, "I don' care what everybody else is wearing, if they thought jumping off a bridge was cool, would you wanna' go and do that too? We're raising you to be a leader, not a follower. That goes for the way you dress too son." Ironically, both of *them* had nice wardrobes, but then again, they also paid the bills. Being the boss came with its perks. "Until you can afford your own, you'll have to take what's given to you boy. We don' care what those silly kids at school think. None of em' are gonna' be in your life ten years from now anyway." His parents weren't wrong either. Most relationships forged in adolescence rarely make it to maturity. Highschool is like a bubble. Once popped, reality sets in.

They may have not cared, but Jacob did, and so did his sister Myra. It was a tough line to tow. They were at the mercy of parents who could care less about what name brands their children wore. Every school year they would head to Goodwill, the pair dead-set on finding the most horrid fashion items available.

To the best of his ability, and for the most part quite successfully, the boy avoided physical confrontations with his peers as they ridiculed him. The words hurt, but not like a fist would. Sometimes the bouts could get brutal, with several boys screaming opprobrious insults one after another. It was almost like running a gauntlet. Crowds would gather in anticipation of a good laugh. Some hoped for more sinister entertainment, and depending on who the victim was, they sometimes got it.

Jacob, ever wary of going to blows, was involved in only one major fight as a teen. It was during his junior year of high school. He was walking home with Myra when it took place. Luckily there was no crowd around to witness the events of that cloudy day. From the corner of his eye, he could see his assailant quickly approaching from behind. It was a guy that had ridiculed Jacob ever since their first year of middle school. He was a career bully. The worst type.

The thug wanted to establish himself as a force to be reckoned with, and Jacob seemed to be the perfect venue to make an example of. He brought a friend along to relay the outcome to their fellow classmates the next day.

The bully would've preferred picking the fight during lunch, where everyone could see, but he had already been suspended twice that year; one more offense would've meant expulsion from the school. The potential clout wasn't worth the risk. Myra tried to warn her brother, he could hear her saying, "Jacob, you know that guy's following us, right? I think he wants to fight you."

He ignored the warning. It was a mistake. A painful one. He thought if he kept walking as though nothing was about to happen, he would somehow appear brave. The façade was weak at best. A few steps later, a numbing thud rang his left eardrum. His head lurched to the right as his hands went up, seconds too late. Although pain's arm reached out with vigor, the initial blow was just the first of many. More were on the way. His brain throbbed as it rattled around. Piercing. His eyesight went blurry. Weak knees buckled as he tried to regain footing. They were jello.

He'd been sucker-punched from behind, and the impact caused him to stagger off the sidewalk and into the street. Although the strike was dealt with considerable force, Jacob's pride took the brunt of the attack. It only took a few moments for him to regain composure. It was the initial shock that had really thrown him off. He wasn't expecting it. Ego deafened his sister's warning. The looming headache was held at bay, suppressed by anger. Both fists clenched, they rose in unison. This was it!

Instead of running, as he'd usually be inclined; he would stay and fight. This decision proved unwise, a painfully memorable one as well. As the two boys shuffled away from oncoming traffic and into the nearby grass, they began to size each other up. Angry eyes shot looks of fury and distaste in both directions. Jacob, still a little stunned from the initial blow, was dangerously off balance.

It showed clearly in his stance as he hobbled back and forth. He shot his fists and began bobbing his head like he saw professional boxers do on TV. Unfortunately he skipped the part about not using your face as a shield. This would be his first and only major altercation as an adolescent, he wanted to look good for his small yet important audience.

His brash showboating wound up earning him three swift jabs to the face and a sharp knee to the stomach. It felt like they happened all at once. Like he was being jumped. That's how bad he got his ass kicked. The last blow snatched all breath from his body in violent fashion. His opponent mocked him by licking his thumbs and then letting his hands drop. It was a clear sign of disrespect. After noticing the dazed look on Jacob's face he mocked, "Look at this clown, this is gonna' be easy money!" His friend agreed as Myra looked on with embarrassment. All she could do was shake her head.

Fists loose with confidence hung and waited for a reply. As Jacob lunged in on the opportunity, going for his only punch of the fight, the boy leaned hard to the right, ducked low, and clutched his novice opponent tightly by the waste.

Grunts filled the air as their sneakers dug and tore at the grass, kicking up dirt and dust in the process.

With surprising ease, Jacob was lifted skyward, only to quickly come crashing to Earth. He almost felt the tingle of G-force on the way down. He landed with a muted thud. The carpet of grass blunted what would have been a much more painful body-slam. It was at this point that his adversary was pulled from him by the other perp present. The trek home that day was an unusually quiet one, that is, once Jacob was finally able to walk in a straight line again.

CHAPTER 3

LOOKING BACK THROUGH TIME

College was quite a different experience for Jacob. By then, his popularity had grown considerably. Because he was old enough to get a job, and his parents had finally allowed him to, he was able to purchase his own clothing. What a difference it made. Finally unleashed from their subjugation, he let his sense of style run free.

Every week after he cashed his modest yet much appreciated check, Jacob would take the city bus to a local mall and purchase an outfit or pair of sneakers. He did his best to stand out from the crowd, picking rare styles and off colors. It worked. Within a few months he was recognized as the best dressed guy on campus. Everything from his laces to the stitching on his shirts matched, he made sure of it.

This fact quickly drew the eye of a very pretty and notably thin young lady also attending the college. Of course, other women gave attention, but none was offered in return. Jacob's eyes were captivated by only one. She had a dark birthmark on the left-hand side of her forehead, but it did nothing to overshadow her strikingly beautiful gaze. If anything, it added to her uniqueness.

They passed each other countless times in the hallways, each longing for the other to muster enough bravery to make an approach. Then one day it finally happened. They were sitting across from each other on opposite ends of the cafeteria. There was no reason for either of them to have crossed the other's path, aside from hoping to be noticed of course.

Every few minutes one would walk across the room, pretending to get napkins or something silly like that. As fate would have it, the two happened to run in some of the same circles. Many of Jacob's associates were also connected to *her* sphere of friends. It was a who's who type of environment. The best dressed students tended to stick together.

One such person, Peter, was Jacob's best friend at the time. Technically speaking, Peter was his only friend. Although there were droves of people around him during most of his college days, he never considered any of them to be loyal. None of them had his back. He knew that. It was something he'd grown to accept. Fake friends were a helluva' lot better than being verbally shat on, like in his earlier years.

For the most part, they lingered waiting to see if he would spread his wealth around. As with many things in life, his peers based their perceptions solely on outward appearances. It was common practice for students to lend each other shoes and clothing, especially those hard to come by. Often, his male counterparts would greedily eye his vintage sneakers, hoping he would loan them out.

They cared little to nothing about the struggles he faced at home, and even less of the ones dwelling inside. Why would they? As Jacob walked past the pleasant looking woman in the cafeteria for the third time, he was taken aback by her amazingly gorgeous eyes. They were stunning. Prior to that day, he only caught glimpses from afar.

The windows to her soul were deep brown with hints of gold and bronze dotting their surface. They were warm and inviting. Full, lush eyelashes added beautiful contrast to chestnut skin. She was simply intoxicating. Seductive. When their eyes finally met, there was a moment between them. A moment in which time itself held its breath. Bit its lip. For nearly a minute their eyes locked in a romantic gaze of admiration. Ticking at a pace that barely moved, the seconds melted their surroundings away, leaving only them.

Jacob must've looked odd, staring awkwardly at the attractive young lady for several timeless moments. She sat there, smiling and waiting for his advance. He nervously asked if anyone was sitting in the chair next to hers once he collected the courage. She offered a bashful smile at his quivering voice and silly grin before giving her reply. Butterflies fluttered in both stomachs. The ice had finally been broken. Puppy love snuggled the space between them and warmed the water.

When he called her that night, their conversation meandered for hours. The subjects varied from politics to raising children and everything in between. It was absolute bliss. The most engaging interaction he'd ever had. Finally! To meet someone that was on the same page. Within days, they were *together*. Not everyone approved. The months passed by nonetheless. Jacob's mother wasn't too fond of her son's new-found love. She felt the young woman was high maintenance. He was spending too much of his hard-earned money on her.

During their relationship, Jacob blew almost half of every paycheck buying her gifts and trinkets of all varieties. One week he would show up to school with expensive chocolates and roses, the next it would be dinner at some pricey restaurant in the city's uptown or South Park area.

Maria felt Jacob was buying his girlfriend's affection, she feared in due time the relationship would end with her son's heart being crushed. Stepped on, and left to bleed in the dirt. One-sided unions tended to end that way. Her fears were confirmed May 23rd, 2011. It was a perfect lemon-yellow day, and although a little windy, the air was still pleasantly warm. The school's spring semester was coming to a close. Summer peeked over the horizon. Its balmy fingers massaged at his skin.

Two squirrels played gleefully in one of the courtyard trees. It was mating season. The entire campus was well kept, but this was Jacob's favorite place to daydream in between macroeconomics and chemistry. He loved the smell of fresh flowers and cut grass that inevitably greeted him. Benches circled a small fountain where spring birds bathed in the afternoon rays. Aside from it being a beautiful day, he was in high spirits for another reason.

The refund from his Pell Grant was scheduled to be credited to his bank account later that afternoon. A special dinner was planned for his girlfriend since her birthday was just around the corner. It was going to be a big night. For several minutes, he sat on one of the benches, playing over in his mind the events to come. He tried to imagine how surprised she'd be at the gift he planned to present after their meal.

To add to the warm feelings now gushing inside, he looked over to see a couple kiss passionately in the distance. It was that perfect kind of kiss, the type that usually only happens in movies. They seemed to be moving in slow motion, each affectionately caressing and longing for the other as their lips intertwined. The female was quite thin, and he could tell she was beautiful even at a distance.

As Jacob was admiring her long flowing hair he thought he saw something dark on her face. It seemed to resemble the birthmark that *his* girlfriend had. After pondering this for a moment, he realized it was about time to head to his next class. His legs carried him in their direction at a brisk pace. As Jacob neared the couple, he stopped abruptly midstride to take in what lay before him.

The bottle of neon soda in his hand fell silently to the ground. His heart went with it. He knew them; it was his girlfriend, and Peter! When Maria learned of the news later that evening, her eyes crowed "I tried to warn you," but her mouth said nothing. Instead she did what mothers do best. Her son's tears were cried alone in his room, but her soul ached to console her heartbroken boy. A stern face softened, and nurturing arms reached out to hold his pain as their own.

When her and Drake first decided to adopt, they agreed to do their best to raise confident, healthy children. Although a challenge, Maria was a firm believer in not putting them down for the mistakes she knew they would make. Mistakes are seeds. Without them, nothing can grow.

Her heart held a special place for children born to less fortunate circumstances. It always amazed her, the depth and scope of these tragic beginnings. When she first read Jacob's file at the adoption agency, his story nearly brought tears to her eyes. Her heart was pounding that day, the day her forefinger first opened the folder labeled "Jacob..."

September 23rd, 1987, at exactly 12:01am a baby boy at Mecklenburg County Hospital drew his first breath. As oxygen filled tiny lungs his arms stretched out and reached for the white coat collar near his face. He was born with his eyes wide open and deemed "A healthy little fellow," by the doctor in charge. After wiping vernix from his chest and arms with a towel the middle-aged man lifted him up for all to see. Tiny cries filled the room. New life. Little arms shivered, shunning the cold against his skin. The obstetrician tucked the blanket a little tighter and the boy fell silent.

Jacob's mother stared at him as if attempting to imprint his image. Numb with exhaustion, the only thing she wanted was to hold the young life now gazing back at her. The one she had created. He would never even know who she was. It was a blade to the heart. The moments were fleeting. Long before this day, she knew she wouldn't be the one to raise him. The State wouldn't allow it. Her opioid addiction made her unfit to provide proper care. Heroin gripped her with mighty hands and shook all hope from her life.

To make matters worse, the boy's father was sentenced to 50 years in prison just months before his birth. Convicted for the murder of a cop in a botched robbery, his fate was sealed before the jury ever read his file. It was an all-too-common occurrence in that part of town for mothers to give birth alone. The rundown neighborhoods surrounding the hospital were perfect breeding grounds for criminality. Fathers in these households were often incarcerated, both for crimes committed, and some not.

"Looks like someone's hungry for a little milk. Mom?" The doctor and nurse briefly left the room to let the new mother feed. The boy's lips puckered and grabbed at the air, searching desperately for a nipple. After moments that seemed much too short, he was taken from her reluctant arms and placed in a warm bed next to several other newborns, all of which were also up for adoption.

Two weeks later, the infant found himself in a state-run foster home. For the next year and a half this was where Jacob laid his little head. Being so young, he didn't understand he was without a real family of his own. Then without warning, his whole world changed yet again. No longer was there a gaggle of children around. There was only one other child now, a slightly younger girl. The kind foster woman that usually tucked him in at night was also gone.

She was replaced by a different, yet equally caring mother figure. Scents of honeyed davana, black tea, and charred vanilla swept over Jacob each time her warm arms embraced his tiny body. Her perfume always took him to a happy place. All around him, unfamiliar sights and sounds filled the air. Gone was the old brick house with green shutters and gravel filled driveway. It was replaced by sweeping lawns, rose bushes, hardwood floors and a roaring fireplace.

His new home also had much more artwork than he remembered seeing in his last. Although he was too young to appreciate it, he liked looking at the pictures while petting the large, fluffy beast he heard the adults refer to as "Djed."

Djed was a Japanese Akita that became the family pet a few weeks before Jacob's adoption. He was a rather large pup, and when fully mature weighed in at a solid 120 pounds. A tawny coat and curved tail added flair to his step. The proud dog became a popular attraction with the neighbors during his daily walks. Attention and smiling faces appeased the canine well enough, but above all he was a protector. He saw Jacob and Myra as his own and would not hesitate to give his life in their defense.

Jacob's new caretakers were successful at the time they chose to adopt. The couple identified as middle-aged entrepreneurs. They seemed like a convivial young duo, often seen smiling and laughing with one another. For them, life was meant to be enjoyed. The female stood firmly on the short side of average, prancing in at about 5'2". You could tell by looking at her that she was strong spirited. Her face could morph from the calm gaze of a mother watching her children at play, to the fiery glare of a lioness ready to come dashing to their aid in seconds.

Maria loved her children dearly. Unwavering affection seeped through her brown eyes every time she looked at them. The young couple decided early on they would adopt. Nature deemed them unable to bear progeny of their own. Their new-found success within the business world helped to bring that dream to fruition.

Drake started his own scientific research firm a few years before Jacob arrived. He could often be found half buried under pages of notes trying to decipher some new compound in his spacious home office. Many hours were spent in the room's warm light. Drake put considerable effort into making the space comfortable. His work was demanding, it took a lot out of him. He made sure no expense was spared.

He'd often call out to his wife, "Maria I'll be out to put the kids to bed in a few minutes, just lemme' finish this last trial." Nine times out of ten, Maria was the one to see the children off to dreamland. She didn't mind however; her relationship with her husband was one that was healthy. Open.

If she really didn't feel up to the task, which wasn't often, she simply would let him know. He would slowly rise from his desk, slide his glasses down the bridge of his nose, and walk over to hug his beloved wife. Then he'd whisper something like, "I know you're tired honey, I'll finish these notes tomorrow." In those moments, he was able to set his work aside. Nothing was more important than family. It was the kind of empathy and devotion most wives can only dream of.

Maria worked as an art consultant for a private firm in the city. Her employment contract was negotiated so she could dictate her own schedule, allowing her to devote plenty of time to raising her children. Drive and ambition were placed second to the joys and responsibilities of motherhood. She mirrored her husband's sentiment in that regard. Being a parent was an honor.

The proud mother would sell art worth tens of thousands of dollars so often, and with such ease, within months she was offered senior partner. The honor was compounded by the fact that her industry was male dominated. It was something to be proud of. She was an inspiration. Several other women at the firm took her queue. Sales went up. Gaps between ranks shortened. The result was a more prosperous company. Her job security felt ironclad.

Despite bringing in considerably more than many of their neighbors, the newly appointed parents lived an over extended lifestyle. Aside from two luxury sedans often seen posing in their circular driveway, they also owned a third sportier vehicle. It was a metallic-black Maserati Quattroporte, kept in their three-car garage mostly. By this point, Charlotte had been their home for the better half of a decade. Their standard of living increased every year. The city had been good to them.

Drake loved supercars and would frequently rent them out for several weeks at a time. Everything from Lamborghini's to Ferrari's, whatever stroked his fancy. The couple also loved to attend parties, very expensive parties. They projected a facade that exuded "Money's no object to us, if we want it we can have it." Whether by gift or purchase, every piece of clothing the two owned was of the utmost quality. They dressed *extremely* well. Maria's wardrobe contained many pieces handmade in Italy, and her shoes by that point occupied three of the extravagant home's walk-in closets.

Their friends were left with the impression they were

millionaires. It was an intended illusion. In actuality they were falling progressively deeper in debt and had a mere six thousand invested in the stock market. That meager figure hardly reflected the high incomes the two enjoyed. Retirement was at least twenty years down the road. They had time to catch up. Their focus was on living life in the moment. They should've known better.

A month after they adopted Jacob, they decided to take on yet a third child. This time, another boy. They saw the infant for the first time at an orphanage about 10 miles from their home. The case was tragic, like so many where addiction had taken root. To be born into a life of despair. Hopelessness. His mother took her life, leaving the poor child for dead. The rundown building they lived in was a complete dump. Addicts lined the halls and rarely bothered with toilets. When nature called, they didn't hold back. Matter and fluids were everywhere. In addition to fiends, a rat hive, and countless roach nests had also taken up residence. It was one of many such buildings on that block. A rough area.

When police responded to a dispatch for domestic violence by a neighbor, one noticed the door across the hallway was slightly cracked. Upon cautious approach, they heard the child's cries. They were coming from a bedroom in the back. It didn't seem like there was anyone else in the apartment. No one adult at least. No movement. Just whimpers. "Police! Anyone home? CMPD! Hello?" No answer. It didn't take long for the smell to hit them. Piss and shit were one thing. This new scent was an entirely different beast. Putrid and rank, it was unmistakable. There was a body nearby.

The lead officer yelled out again. The only other sound in the apartment was from the child. He was trying to call out, pain seared into the folds of his young voice. He looked over at his mother's dangling body as the police approached the bedroom's doorway. It creaked open as they made entrance, their mouths hung open in disbelief. Drops of water fell from her fingertips and toenails.

Depressed and desperate, the addict hung herself from the shower faucet three days earlier. It was a grim scene. A glimpse into the dark underbelly of society. The side of the city rarely witnessed by those living in nicer ends of town. For children damned to a life in the ghettos, this was just the way things were. This particular hood was nicknamed *Zombie-Land*. The softest drug on any of its corners was coke. Ice, crack, and dippers were easier to come by. Among users, you couldn't consider yourself serious, until you scored here. The orphan's mother had been serious.

Drops of water slapped against her lifeless face as she hung. Her mouth was open. Eyelids cracked just wide enough to show slivers of blood-shot white. She had been determined to die that night. The tub's floor was coated with oil as to not regain footing. No turning back. Autopsy results later uncovered large doses of LSD, methamphetamine, and benzodiazepines in her bloodstream. She was never fit to be a mother. Her baby was rushed to the emergency room for treatment once the officers on scene were able to summon additional units. Among other things, the infant had fallen prey to a severe case of pneumonia. Left to fend for himself after his mother binged on drugs, the boy inhaled toxic fumes until the cops arrived. He never fully recovered from the illness, and as a result his pleurae grew weaker with time.

Many nights Jacob could hear his new brother wheezing as the boy's fragile lungs desperately struggled to fill. They were like balloons with holes poked in them. The more he tried, the more they failed. In addition to respiratory problems, Jason was also highly susceptible to other sicknesses due to a weakened immune system. Almost one third of his short life was spent lying in a hospital bed. The ongoing expenses he added to the family's cashflow compounded their financial woes tremendously.

CHAPTER 4

FOR SALE, EVERYTHING IS FOR SALE

Monday's paper was awash with huge bold letters, **"DOW Starts New Decade with A CRASH, THIS MAY BE THE END FOR THE BULLS!"** The article took up the first two pages and half the third. Black ink brimmed with doom and gloom. Drake canvassed the write-up intently before rushing over to the brand-new flat screen he'd just purchased on credit. His hand brushed aside yesterday's mail. Between the envelopes several bills lay with red writing. The sky outside was grey that day. It hung like a quilted blanket over the city. Rolling clouds were on their way out, pushing to the east, but they took their time. The ground was damp from a recent downpour. Dreary and down; just like the market.

With a shaky hand he flipped the channel to his favorite investment program, then rubbed his forehead as his eyes took in the headlines. "Maria, honey, you may wanna get down here and see this. Maria?" No answer. In the coming years their son would take after his parents in their entrepreneurial spirit. He wanted to earn his own money. For the time being, instead of bringing in the bacon, the youngster would only hear his father complain about the constant losses the family incurred.

The market spared no one. It had come for its pound of flesh.

Finally, she called out. "Yes dear, yes, what is it?" Then her eyes caught a glimpse of the screen. "Wow! Is that just from today?" The previous week's trading session the DOW closed at 7512, the next day's open was 6153. It had been a rough weekend. A few weeks earlier, the yield curve on bonds inverted. An omen of things to come. Red... The market was stained in red. Accounts across the nation bled until their owners were dizzy with losses. There was nowhere to hide.

The anchorman said it was the largest 24-hour point drop since the 1930's. His voice quivered and crackled as he read the horrific headlines to an undoubtedly worried mass of viewers. After staring at the television for an uncanny amount of time, Drake picked up the phone. The hardline's cordage began tangling itself as he paced the room and dialed. A few minutes later he could be heard screaming profanities.

"I don' care about the losses; I want out, have you been watching the news lately? Shit's gone nuclear!" He could barely hear his wife's remarks as she entered the room. As usual, her hand was glued to her hip. "Drake there's no need to yell at the advisor honey, he's got nothing to do with what's happening."

"What do ya' mean he has nothing to do with this? He's the one that told me to invest our retirement money in this worthless stock in the first place! I may not know much about investing, but any klutz could see this company was shit since the beginning, I mean come on!" Beads of sweat were forming at his brow. His frustration seemed to seep into the air. It wafted in his wife's direction as she tried to talk him down.

"If it wasn't for him, maybe we wouldn't have lost $3,400, no, no wait $3760 in one Godforsaken morning! Bill, just get me out that damn company before I lose more while I'm talking to you!" The advisor on the other end tried to interject but was cut off. "I know the whole market's dropping Bill; I'm looking right *at* the television!"

"You do realize since we've been on the phone my account just dropped another $400? If you don't sell those shares right now, I swear ta' God I'm gonna sue your firm so bad, so thoroughly, you'll have to sell that fancy ass suit of yours for groceries!" "Honey, that's about enough! You can stop being irate any day now, besides how do ya' know it won't go back up tomorrow? Just cause' the market's down doesn't mean it's Bill's fault, he's probably lost money today too."

Drake rudely ignored his wife's suggestion. Instead, his rant continued. "Sell the damn shares Bill." He used a hand to cover the phone's receiver before he addressed her again. "Baby! I'm tryna' save us from being wiped out here, the least you could do is support me in my decision!" A menacing look shot in her direction as he spoke. He'd took a moment from berating the advisor to scold his wife but was cut off by her shrill rebuttal. She'd had about enough of him for one morning.

"Support you? *Support you*?" The second utterance held a bit more emphasis. "I do support you! What I do *not* support however, is you being rude to the *one* man who's done everything to keep our best interest at heart!" Drake looked at his wife in utter disbelief. His forehead frowned, lips knotted with incredulity. It was as if she'd slapped him in the face. "How do you know he has our best interest, just how exactly do ya' know that? You don't, do you?"

Maria knew her husband well enough to know once he got started, there was no talking him down. He'd already walked off the cliff. "Sorry to be the bearer of bad news honey, but there's no such thing as a financial advisor that works *solely* in the interest of the client." He had a point. Any job that provides incentive to sell can be exploited if acquired by someone morally flexible. Pinpointing integrity is a skill that eludes even the savviest among us.

"He's gonna' make his commissions either way. Hell, he just made a commission off us today! Our best *interest*?" His voice quivered with anger, it danced wildly on the ends of every word. Sweat dripped from the phone still held tightly in his palm. "Oh you've got some nerve. You dunno' the first thing about who has our best interest; you're always too busy blowing money at the mall all the damn time Maria!"

His wife had heard enough. "So! It finally comes out, you really wanna' talk about *my* spending habits? *My* spending habits? Ok. Let's talk about yours for a minute shall we?" Her arms flailed about as she gained momentum. Now given room to speak, the words seemed to spew from her mouth. "What about all those cars you insist on keeping, or your expensive watches, the two thousand-dollar suits, your stupid grape juice, oops I mean wine collection?"

"What happened to all those things huh? Yeah, didn't think so. Just go Drake, I'll take the kids to school, you obviously need some time alone with your ego." She stormed from the room before she could hear her husband's retort. It was a wise tactic. If she stayed, she'd subjugate herself to an unending verbal assault. Of the few arguments the couple endured, those surrounding money were always the worst.

By the time the family's financial advisor was able to execute the trade, their brokerage account was valued at a mere $2,567.43. It was a devastating loss. One they couldn't afford. The following weeks and months brought more financial turbulence, not only for the Gilferds, but for the rest of the country as well. Things were changing before their very eyes. The signs were unmistakable. And they were everywhere.

En route to and from work, the couple noticed more

and more foreclosed properties and homes for sale. Analysts on CNN and FOX began spewing an infinite stream of disappointing economic data. Even the newspapers, which were often covering some tragic event anyway, seemed more gloomy than usual. Each day brought another scandal or major corporate bankruptcy. The loss of wealth was staggering. Billions were wiped out. Family legacies collapsed.

Some days several of even the largest and oldest firms would fall. Life at home wasn't much better for the Gilferds. Drake and Maria argued more often than before the market's downturn. Within a few short months of the initial economic slump, both incomes were cut by nearly two thirds. What a hit! This only added pressure, compressing the strain the pair already endured. Piles of debt, dwindled savings, and flailing investments. It was the perfect storm.

Maria went from being able to sell twenty to twenty-five high end paintings a week, to barely topping ten a month. As time progressed, even that meager number was reduced to less than five. She just couldn't catch a break. Business for Drake followed a similar course. The contracts once secured with ease soon dried up, and he was left with a company running on financial fumes.

The gravity of their situation didn't truly hit home until they received their first call from John Brown. It was a call they would never forget. Mr. Brown was the vice president of their bank's foreclosure department. By that point, the recession was in its second year and their investments had all but vanished into the ether. It was a story repeated in countless households across the nation. Only one percenters were immune.

The eight-thousand-dollar mortgage so easy for the young couple to afford a few years before, was now almost four months behind. The Gilferds had no hope of bringing their bills current. Ends simply wouldn't meet. Just keeping a decent roof over their heads was hard enough. In hindsight, they'd taken so much for granted. It's easy to do that when things are going well. Complacency is a trap that ensnares many among us.

They were paying more in interest on overused credit cards than most people dish out on car payments each month. Student loans taken to secure Drake's degree added another hundred and twelve thousand dollars of life sucking debt to their burden. And that wasn't even including interest.

They were able to keep their home for a few more months, but the pressure was building by the day. By August of 2001, credit lines completely dried up for the desperate couple. Bill stacks got higher and higher. Final notices were everywhere. The mail became a focal point for all the wrong reasons. Anxiety loomed in the folds of paper. Hidden from view until opened.

Out of ideas and desperate, the pair knew what was coming. One envelope held more weight than the others. When it did finally arrive, its sting was as potent as if it had been completely unexpected. The envelope had the word, "Urgent," written diagonally across its front in all-capped red letters. Many of their neighbors received similar envelopes.

The mail man wore an empathetic look that said, "I'm sorry to have to give this to you." It was the only piece of mail delivered that day. For several days further, it lay unopened on Drake's desk. It was placed face down with a stack of other papers to make as inconspicuous as possible. Out of sight out of mind. He was under enough stress. A few days wasn't gonna hurt anything. He wasn't sure how to approach Maria about the devastating message he knew it held.

Ever since childhood, it was instilled in Drake by his

father that men were the providers and protectors of their family. It was their responsibility. Their duty. Their honor. He was now being stripped of his home. In many ways, his sense of manhood as well. It was the kind of pain only a man can understand. It went beyond ego. It was something deeper. Something carnal. His very essence was being challenged.

One late evening, long after Maria and the children were asleep, he finally built enough courage to break the envelope's glossed seal. A moonlit sky was his only light. The blinds by his desk were open and let adequate doses of ethereal glow soak into the room. Squinted eyes scanned the writing. The letter read, "Dear Mr. and Mrs. Gilferd, it is our regret to inform you that the property located at 4012 Burtonwood Circle in Charlotte, NC 28213 is scheduled to be foreclosed upon due to failure to pay." The wording was so transactional. So removed. Drake's heart slumped. He was at a loss. Despite his best efforts, his eyes moistened as he came to terms with what was happening. It's at moments like these when a man's resolve is tested.

"You have ten days from the date of this letter to vacate the premises or you and your belongings will be removed by use of legal force. Regards, signed John Brown, VP FORECLOSURE UNIT." The postmark was dated August 2nd, by the time he opened the letter it was the 7th. Drake had to say something to his wife and soon. In less than a week Maria would find out anyway, better through him than the Sheriff.

When the day finally arrived, Maria retrieved a bottle of white wine from their cellar and sat out on the English-style front porch. She picked her favorite glass from the kitchen cabinet and poured a liberal amount of what she referred to as over-priced grape juice. She never understood what all the fuss was about. Drake would go on and on about this wine or that one. They all tasted about the same to her. As long as it got the job done. The color of this one was warm yellow. It glistened and twinkled as the light's rays danced across crystal.

Helpless eyes watched on as life was stripped away, one cherished piece at a time. It was painful. Like death from a thousand cuts. Every item packed away was a memory. Her gaze withdrew from her surroundings of despair to watch the golden liquid swirl around in her glass. The first drops of the 1981 Far Niente Chardonnay embraced her lips, and she was swept up by aromas of green apple and Roasted Pear.

Hints of lemon custard, butter, caramelized mango, and pineapple enticed her palate as the velvety liquid trickled down the back of her throat. Several minutes after swallowing, its flavors lingered on seductively; and were just as intense if not more-so. They morphed slightly from tropical fruit, to more complex notes... She could taste citrus peel, and vanilla crème brulee as they drifted across her tongue in soft waves.

For the first time since meeting her husband, Maria was able to appreciate his love of wine. It was sweet yet bitter, it reminded her of life. She slowly closed her eyes, mostly in a futile attempt to hold gathering tears at bay. Her inner voice called out. "How has it come to this? How on Earth can this be?" Her eyes cringed on in disbelief.

A few months prior, the Gilferds saw one of their next-door neighbors being forced from their home, but the ambitious couple always assumed they would find a way to avoid the same fate. They were smarter. Now their indulgences had finally caught up to them. Reality had clenched them by the neck.

There was nothing they could do but pick up the shattered pieces of their life and start anew. "Hey honey, what do you think of this one? The rent's a little high but at least we'll be comfortable. Naw, actually that's a pretty fair price, we could manage this. Honey?" Drake was researching nearby apartments online.

"If I can secure this contract on Monday, I'll be able to move us in with more than enough left over." Expectant eyes looked for a glimmer of light, hopeful for acknowledgment, or at least reassurance from the woman he loved. Her response was less than he'd hoped for. "It looks fine dear." Her back was turned. The words sounded empty. Her attention was elsewhere. It felt like a total letdown, "That's it? That's all you have ta' say?"

Maria let out a tired sigh before responding to her persistent husband. She was on the brink of emotional exhaustion, and he wasn't gonna let up. "What, what is it? What do you want me to say Drake, honestly?" Although he understood her frustration with their circumstance, he still hoped for more. "I'm doing the best I can to give you as many of the comforts we had before, but you need to talk to me. I need your support Maria. Don't you *get* that?"

Drake's forehead frowned a little as he attempted to console her distress. Her body language and tone made it obvious. "Yes, we've made a few mistakes along the way. I can admit that. But we're here now and we've gotta' make the best of what we've got." "I, I know honey, it's just that." Her lip was quivering, and Drake knew what his wife was feeling but couldn't say. The words got lost somewhere in her throat. He was feeling it too. The gloomy day outside did little to raise the family's spirits. It was Sunday, August 12th, their last official day in the home on Burtonwood Circle.

Most boxes were already packed and either in the full-sized U-Haul truck or stacked near the front door. "Wait daddy, we forgot Snuffles!" Myra's voice squeaked as she frantically looked for her beloved stuffed friend. Her eyes darted left, then right. No teddy. “Well where’d you leave him honey? Look, there he is!” He was squatting down so he could be at her level. One of his hands rested on her shoulder. The other was gesturing to an area near the kitchen. “Where daddy?” Her eyes darted in the direction of his pointed finger.

“Right there baby girl, next to that big box that says books. You see him?” Even at such a young age, she could tell something was wrong, her parents did poor jobs of hiding their worries from her curious eyes. After rescuing her beloved teddy bear from a life of abandonment, Myra walked over and hugged tightly on her adopted father’s long muscular leg. Little brown fingers clung tightly to the folds in his jeans. This selfless act of empathy was enough to bring tears to his eyes.

Maria was sitting just outside, but she could see them through one of the windows on the porch. She too found herself tearing up as emotions of despair continued to well. Her eyes drew back to the last ounce of wine in her glass. She poured another helping. Drake let her finish the bottle while he loaded up the last of their things. The future felt dim.

Their new home was very different from the last and came as more of a shock to the adults than the children. Maria and Drake had only made copious amounts of money for a few short years, but prior to that, they were still considered upper middle-class by society’s standards.

Together, the couple pulled in a respectable three hundred and forty thousand on average each year. Starting out, they were able to maintain a comfortable lifestyle living in a two-bedroom condo in uptown Charlotte after moving from New York. Their brief encounter with wealth actually inflicted more damage than it did good. It’s hard to go back once you’ve had a taste of affluence. Standards had been raised. Before being hired at the firm, Maria made around sixty thousand annually working as an accountant.

Her true passion was always fine art, and when one of her clients offered her a position in the field, she took it without a moment's hesitation. Drake worked as a chemist with a large corporation before deciding to open his own lab with a longtime friend. It was a bold move. But it paid off, at least for a while.

Not three months had passed since their increase in compensation before they opted to sell the condominium at a loss. Their hearts were set on a house. They decided to move away from the bustle of the city and into a quiet neighborhood on the outskirts of town. Uptown was nice enough, but the suburbs were more their speed. There's nothing quite like being able to plant your feet on ground *you* own. It draws confidence. Stability.

The six hundred and ninety thousand dollars in proceeds from the condo sale was used as a down payment on their new, one point five-million-dollar residence. It was a hefty upgrade. One they felt was well deserved. With the downturn in the economy, they found themselves on the move again. This time around their surroundings were less opulent. It's amazing how quickly change in fortune can come. One moment manicured lawns and gated communities greet you each morning. The next, roaches are having a cookout two floors down.

Their *new* apartment was tired, badly stained from previous tenants. Paint peeled sporadically along corners. It was as if the walls were shedding, cracking under the pressures of time and negligence. That alone added ten years to the feel of the place. Doleful, tannish brown wallpaper in the bedrooms didn't help. The filth of neighbors living much too close drew roaches and the like. As Drake investigated the so-called master bedroom's closet, he noticed the ceiling had bronze watermarks from a leak that was never fixed.

Unlike the constant sunlight abundant in their last home, this place was tenebrous in every sense of the word. There weren't many windows, and the ones that did exist were small. More of an afterthought than anything else. Their new neighbors played loud music and Maria saw the comings and goings of people she knew didn't live there. None made any effort at friendly conversation. To the contrary they often shot dirty looks at the family whenever the opportunity arose. The Gilferds were considered outsiders. They clearly didn't belong. A stark contrast from the vaunted neighborhood they'd once known. There, connections were actively sought. Networking is usually expected among those with means.

On their second day in the complex, Drake's sports car was vandalized and its tires stolen. They left it sitting on bricks. There were no garages to protect it. Sitting out there in the parking lot at night? On *that* side of town? It was a big no-no. One of many lessons the Gilferds would learn. It was like stepping into another world. The driver's side window was shattered, leaving a bed of broken shards on the pavement, and there was a note slipped onto the seat that said, "Welcome to the neighborhood assholes." It hit Drake hard. Like a shot to the gut.

When he relayed the news to Maria, she just looked away and said in a low, desperate voice, "We've got to get the hell out of here, don't you want our old life back? Look at this place!" She looked back at him, waiting for a reply. He nodded. A deep sigh. His hand was rubbing against his forehead, trying to hold stress at bay. Poverty was so depressing. No matter how bad it hurt, he was the man of the house. He had to be strong, get through it, and figure a way out, back to the life that made sense. "I know honey, this is just temporary, I'm gonna find a way to get us outta' this." To her his words felt like empty promises.

He never did find a way to get them back on their feet. Conversely, Drake pressured Maria into keeping all three cars, which only added to their financial woes. Like many men, he often let pride overshadow priorities. It was a big mistake. Despite now bringing in less than a third of what they did at their financial peak, he insisted they maintain an indulgent lifestyle. It was his way of trying to show he could still provide for his family.

In the end, his ego contributed an additional fifteen thousand dollars in credit card debt. This was acquired during their first year in the shabby apartment. Maria tried to convince him she didn't judge him as a man based on how many expensive dinners he could take her on, or how often they went on vacation. Despite her efforts, a misdirected sense of pride guided her husband's every move.

Drake was determined to give his wife and family all the things he thought they wanted. Needed. He wouldn't take no for an answer. For instance, one afternoon while at the mall, Maria noticed a pair of Christian Louboutin boots on display in Niemen Marcus. They stood out from the crowd with ease, as the brand often did. Fall was just around the corner and the family had decided to get out of the apartment. No big purchases were expected to be made. It was more of a window-shopping trip than anything else.

She was just admiring them, knowing there were other more important priorities like the rent and groceries that needed consideration. There was always a bill to be paid. When Drake noticed her looking at the shoes with such interest, he pulled one of the clerks off to the side. He made sure his wife couldn't see. Surprises were one of his specialties. "Do you see that beautiful woman over there by that table?"

The saleswoman nodded in acknowledgment before

giving a soft smile. "That's my wife, isn't she gorgeous? I think she likes those alligator boots with the strap across the side." His hand made a subtle gesture in the direction of the boots. He didn't want to alert Maria. His voice lowered to a whisper as he leaned in. "Take my card and have em' wrapped up real pretty for her. Would you do that for me?"

The clerk perked up at the thought of a hefty commission. It had been a slow couple of months. The recession hit the retail industry hard. Discretionary spending was way down. This was the sale she'd been waiting for. Her eyes gave him one more thorough lookover. The card exchanged hands. "Would you like to know the price for them sir?" Drake offered a glance marked with disgust. Ego hung on his breath. "Do I look like a man who needs to look at the price? In fact, keep the receipt." His hand waved in confidence.

These particular pair of Louboutins were a whopping two thousand seven hundred dollars. That was before taxes. The manager of the store was called from the back office to present Maria with her unexpected gift. She hesitantly took the bag, thinking to herself, "Here he goes joking with me again." Her cheeks blushed at the gesture nonetheless.

As the smiling middle-aged woman assured her it wasn't a joke and praised Drake's generous spontaneity, Maria's emotions began writhing in conflicted directions. On the one hand, she absolutely loved the new boots. They were perfect! She liked everything about them. On the other, and frankly more important end, rent would soon be due. Responsibilities aside, it was tough not to give in. One little indulgence couldn't hurt anything. Being in such a high-end store felt familiar. It felt right.

The shoes were all black with a sheen reminiscent of patent leather. The only contrast to them were their bright red bottoms, a signature to all the designer's pieces. She knew how much the shoes would set them back. She'd eyed the brand on other visits.

Unlike her husband, the *first* thing she looked at was the price tag. The last thing they needed was another three thousand dollars in debt to be added to their overused credit cards. Many were maxed out. They didn't make the money they used to. This was too much. Before she could offer protest to her husband's indiscretion, he cut in. The salesclerk was out of earshot by that point. He wanted to avoid embarrassment. A hit to his pride was unacceptable.

"I knew you wanted em' honey, so I got them; for old time's sake." There was a pause. "And before you go off telling me we can't afford it... Just know I've got the debt thing under control Ok. I have an interview Monday. The starting salary's right at what I made with Chemco." As he spoke he held her close. His voice was low, as to not draw attention.

"Like I said before honey, we'll be fine, I got this." Her eyes peered up. His charm always struck a chord. She was swooned by her towering husband's tender embrace. Hesitance still lurked however. The twinkle in her gaze was tainted. "That's wonderful news baby, but don't you think we should've at least waited until *after* you got the job? What if they go with another candidate?" Instead of replying, he just kept his fingers interlocked behind the small of her back, holding her gaze the entire time. She shrugged, then relaxed her body and nestled into the cocoon of muscles spritzed with the last of her husband's Clive Christian. Woody Earth, tobacco, citrus rubbed with saffron. This was her favorite cologne. Especially on him. Too bad the bottle's end was in sight.

"I guess I could always return them if things don't work out." Drake declined to mention in his arrogance, he already closed off that option by declining the receipt. They say insanity is defined by repeating the same actions, yet expecting a different result. Others may call that denial. Either way, the decisions Drake made would have an impact in the months and years to come. It was only a matter of time.

CHAPTER 5

THE FIG TREE THAT BORE WINE

Nine months after the Gilferds moved into the apartment the economy showed no signs of exiting the recession. It was relentless. Things were tough everywhere. Crime was up, especially robberies and break-ins. Tempers flared more easily. Unemployment was estimated at an unprecedented 11.7 percent, and that number was growing by the week. The ordeal many citizens faced was accentuated by rising commodity prices; in particular, gas and food were hit the hardest. They knew it was coming. Economists started raising eyebrows weeks before consumers felt the pinch. President Kieden warned Americans that bottle-necks in the supply chain could cause transitory inflation. It was anything but. Higher prices were here to stay. Inflation is like time in a lot of ways. It tends to move in one direction.

A loaf of bread a year prior would've cost $2.50. It now sold for $4.71. Civil unrest added additional pressure. It was a mess. People couldn't even afford to get to work. Gas prices were rising by an average quarterly rate of 13%. Neither Drake nor Maria were able to land a high enough paying job to allow them to catch up on piling bills. There were no jobs. No good ones at least. Most had been downsized or displaced. The few remaining were guarded with fierce veracity. Like many others, the Gilferds were simply unable to keep up. It was like drowning above ground.

The payments and insurance alone on their three cars commanded almost half their combined monthly income. Upkeep for the children, food, gas and rent took the other half and then some. Their credit card spending was left un-checked, and they made only the minimum monthly payments.

“Oh hey Maria! How are you? The ladies and I’ve missed you down at the country club, how’ve things been?” “Oh hi Susan, we’ve been great, I mean, we’ve been good.” Maria was at the grocery store when she ran into an old friend of the family. Back in the day, Whole Foods was a weekly visit. Run-ins were frequent. She looked forward to them back then. Now she only stopped by when a particular item was on a deep discount. It was her way of staying connected to her past life.

“We decided to move to a smaller place, the house was just too big you know?” The indirect lie tasted sour as it left lips tight with deception. “Tell me about it, Maria honestly, I didn’t know how you kept that place so clean, it must’ve been a nightmare for the maids. So did you decide to get another house or a condo?” Maria’s old friend seemed oblivious. Things were obviously still going well for her. It was a punch to the gut.

“Oh no, too many rules with condos, we just went with a nice apartment.” Susan held a look of disappointed confusion at the unexpected remark. There was a slight moment of hesitance between them. “Oh, ok, well, Kevin and I were planning on dinner this Saturday at The Fig Tree, wanna’ double date?” Maria’s heart jumped. It was exactly what they needed. Both her and Drake were desperate for a taste of their old lives. Even if she couldn’t go, it was nice to just think about it. Play along.

"That sounds wonderful! Lemme' talk to Drake and make sure we don't have other plans, I'm sure we can work something out." She knew they had nothing planned that weekend, mainly because they couldn't afford to do anything. When Drake asked how her day was later that evening, she told him of Susan's offer. Susan and Kevin Splinton were longtime friends of the Gilferds. The husbands attended the same college after meeting in the military.

They instantly connected and shared similar political and social views. Both men were deep thinkers who looked at the world through objective, analytical eyes. They took things as they were. After grad school, Kevin went on to become a renowned biologist known for his extensive research on intra-molecular compositions. Several of his pieces were published, one of which received national attention.

They both met their wives while attending a jazz festival in Buckhead Atlanta. The two couples wound up moving to Charlotte North Carolina and within weeks the wives were inseparable. For the last few months however, Maria only talked to Susan in passing due to her family's hardships. She didn't want to be put in a situation like the one she now found herself in. As much as she missed having dinners with the Splintons, there was no way they could afford one now. Especially not after the Louboutins.

When Drake heard of the invitation he sighed and said, "We still have the rent comin' up soon, and I think we're kinda' late on a few car payments." He was right. He readjusted his glasses before reaching out a hand to rub his disappointed wife's arm. She was defeated. It was written deep in the lines under her eyes. Her hand reached up to meet his at her shoulder. He moved to hug her from behind. Both their hearts felt heavy. The weight of life was bearing down.

"I know dear. I know, I just wanted you to know they were thinking of us. Don't you miss our old life? Before all this recession crap! I know *I* do. I mean, we can't even afford a night out, what I would do for a nice bone-in filet right now." Her mouth watered just thinking about it. It had been months since she'd had a decent steak. "Soon honey, soon." Later that evening, after his wife had gone to sleep, Drake silently laid awake beside her. Her light snores were the only sound in the room. His mind drifted.

He was reliving the life they just recently left behind. He thought of the golf tournaments, fine dining, and most of all, the sense of security it afforded. It was like night and day. The difference between then and now was numbing. When he finally withdrew from his mental trance, he decided to take matters into his own hands, once again.

"Good mornin' darling." His beloved wife looked on with curiosity building in her eyes. Upbeat moods were hard to come by in those dark days. "Good morning, what're you so cheerful about, some big interview I'm not aware of?" Drake shook his head. His face was beaming. "Nope, but you can call Susan and tell her we'd love to join them this Saturday!"

"And why exactly is that? We don' have money to pay for a night like that." Her hand rested on her hip, scrunching her dress as she spoke. "You know how the Splintons are. They're still like we *used* to be, spending like there's no tomorrow." She sighed at the thought.

"Actually, you're still that way! You haven't changed a bit." Drake brushed past her comment and continued; his mind was made. "Maria, when's the last time we went out? Life's about the experiences. Now, I know things've gone south for us as far as money lately, but that doesn't mean we stop living does it? Let the creditors call, what more can they take from us? They've already taken everything." He went to the refrigerator and poured a glass of water. After a sip he went on.

Drake knew his words struck a chord. "We can ask your mother to watch the kids. Come on honey, live a little." With a reluctant smile Maria went over to hug her smooth-talking husband. Her mind began to buzz with excitement as she thought of what to wear. Such a welcome feeling. Although most clothes had been sold during their transition, she held on to a few favorites. A stewed-peach dress won the final verdict. It was silk and fell seductively along her generous curves. A gift from Drake for an anniversary a few years back. Hermès. She'd match that with a pair of open-toe heels.

"Good evening and welcome to The Fig Tree, how many in your party?" "Four, we have reservations under the last name Splinton." With a few clicks of the mouse their reservation was found. "Ok great! Your table is being prepared; it should be just a few moments, if you'd like a refreshment in the bar area while we add the finishing touches." The host gestured towards the awaiting bartender wiping the surface of his stage. He grazed the counter one more time as they looked over.

The women decided to split off from their husbands for a moment. "Maria and I are gonna take a trip to the lady's room." Kevin beckoned Drake towards the Burwood bar near the hostess' desk. On its shelves were some of the finest cognacs, bourbons, and whiskeys money could buy. It was a playground for the well-heeled. "We're known for our world class Millionaire's Martini. Care to try one sir?" "Yes, please, Drake what're you having?" "I'll take the same thank you."

"Right away Sir." Before the man could turn to start preparing their drinks, Drake called out. "Say, what's in a Millionaire's Martini anyway?" The bartender eagerly offered a reply as he grabbed ice from a freezer below. A smile crept just behind his lips. Bartending was a passion for him. It showed clearly in the service he provided.

"Well, we start with a 1/3 measure of Remy Martin Louis XIII Cognac, this provides body and depth. We then add a generous dose of our 1989 Veuve Clicquot Brut Rose Champagne to lift and brighten things up. To finish, four drops of the renowned Chambord liqueur Royal." Most of what was said was unfamiliar to Drake, but it sounded good nonetheless. Expensive too. "Wow, sounds amazing, oh here come the ladies, just in time."

"Ladies, what'll you two be having to drink?" "Well I know what *I* want, but Maria may need a menu." Maria gave her friend an impressed look. "Oh, what're you having?" "The French Martini, they have the best in town. I get it every time we come!" Instead of risking picking something she may not like, Maria decided to take Susan's lead. They held similar tastes in many areas of life. "I'll try one as well please." "Right away, I believe your table is ready, would you like me to have those drinks sent over?"

"Yes, and thank you" Kevin replied with a laugh and full grin. The cheerful group strolled through the dining room to a beautifully decorated table tucked off to the corner. The restaurant was at full capacity, yet kept a reserved, composed demeanor. It was classic fine dining. Fresh roses. Candlelight. Suits and dresses abounded. This was home. "Good evening ladies and gentlemen, my name is James Wellington, I will be your waiter for the evening. Have any of you had the pleasure of dining with us before?"

"My wife and I've dined here several times, but this is their first visit I believe." Kevin beckoned a hand towards the Gilferds before recalling, "Actually, I think you may have served us before?" The waiter agreed, "Yes, I was about to ask you that, you looked quite familiar. How've you been since your last visit? Well I trust?"

"Most certainly, my wife and I have been quite well. Let me introduce you to this rowdy young couple." Drake couldn't help but to snicker at the joke. He and Maria were anything but rowdy. Ex-socialites maybe, but rowdy? Three kids made that nearly impossible. "This is Maria and her husband Drake." Kevin gestured warmly towards his longtime friends. They smiled back at him and then nodded to James. "Pleasure to meet you."

"A pleasure to meet you as well." The two men shook hands before James continued with his presentation. "Well, first I'd like to let you know about some of the new wines we are featuring from our cellar. We've recently acquired three bottles of the elusive 1996 Chateau Margaux Margaux Grand Cru. Ladies and gentlemen, let me tell you, what dwells in that bottle is something special." The well-kept waiter stood with his back straight and addressed everyone individually as he spoke. His mien was calm yet focused. You could tell he was in the right line of work.

"This left bank Bordeaux is full bodied, with firm, well-structured tannins. Its nose is reminiscent of dark fruit and wild mountain cherries. Slight hints of Earth and young mushroom hit mid-palate, with a persistent and lingering finish. In my opinion, and I've had many great wines in my day, this. This is the stuff of the Gods." His presentation was informed yet not practiced. Everyone was impressed.

"We are currently offering this gem for $1170. Also, *not* featured on the wine list is a 1987 bottle of the famed Bryant Family Cabernet Sauvignon." James knew the Splintons were the type of clientele that tended to order off-menu. Kevin was a bit of an aficionado.

"This sumptuous offering boasts intense notes of

cassis, blackberry, and complex traces of saddle leather on the back palate. The silky body of this wine..." The thought seemed to bring back memories for James. He held up a hand and rubbed his thumb and forefinger together. Any Italian blood in his lineage was coming through. "Its, it's beautiful, really, it just coats your mouth beautifully." He paused. The table was captivated. He was good. "It pairs amazing with the California Ranch rack of lamb. We're pricing this exquisite bottle at $1650 this evening." Kevin's eyes looked off as he weighed the decision.

"How do they stack up against each other?" James paused for a moment and then replied, "Well, they're similar in refinement and nature, yet, to compare them would be a disservice. The 87' Bryant pairs more appropriately with food. It's more approachable in my opinion, the Margaux likes to stand alone to reveal its true beauty."

"Hmm, sounds enticing." It didn't take long for Kevin to decide. His mind was made up. "We'll take it, and please decant it as well. Make sure you put that on *my* tab please." "Absolutely Sir." James quickly retreated to the wine cellar to gather the evening's highlight. Drake felt compelled to keep up with his friend. He didn't like the feeling of constraint his wallet commanded.

"Kevin you don't have to do that." A hand waved. "Aww Don't worry about it, besides I owe you one for that bet we made back in college." A moment or two later James returned. "Hear you are Sir, a tasting of the 1987 Bryant." The waiter carefully presented the coveted bottle to Mr. Splinton.

"Thank you James." Kevin extended a hand to his sparkling glass and then smiled at his gorgeous wife. She smiled back. Her green eyes twinkled in the candlelight. They rested on her face like emeralds, set perfectly against a backdrop of soft henna skin. "I'm gonna' pour a sample for you to ensure it's not corked, and then I'll decant it." "Ok great." James held the meticulously aged bottle in one hand. He reached for a reserve wine glass that had been placed on the table with the other. After he poured about an ounce of the precious liquid, Kevin took the crystal in his hand.

He began to swirl slowly before lifting it to take in the bouquet. "Wow, that's excellent, it's incredibly complex and approachable. Yet." Another sniff. "A little tight on the nose. Would you mind pouring Drake a taste as well?" "Absolutely." After Drake was poured a tasting Kevin asked, "Isn't that superb?" "That's amazing, the intensity's incredible!" Drake's palate wasn't as advanced as his friend's, but he still knew a great wine when he tasted one.

"I'm glad it's to your liking; we do have a few specials I'd like to go over with you as well if I may." Kevin nodded for the man to continue. "The first up is an amuse of fines de claires oyster butter on a 'Shepherd Loaf' crostini. This is topped with garden herbs and finished with a drizzle of white truffle essence. We're also featuring two entrée dishes for the evening." His hands moved about and drew life to his descriptions. "First is a cold-water lobster cooked confit style."

"Confit? It's actually cooked in duck fat?" "Yes, our chef submerges the whole lobster in a bath of simmering duck fat. This allows the bird's distinct flavors and aroma to permeate the crustacean's hard shell." James spoke with enthusiasm as he continued. Even *his* mouth was beginning to water. The chef was known for his flavor. A true master in the art of culinary pleasure. Anything the table ordered was sure to be a hit.

"This adds a *whole* new profile to the dish. The meat is then carefully removed from its shell and rested in hand-made ravioli pillows; we then fold the pasta into a crushed heirloom tomato emulsion and garnish with young basil shoots." The eloquence with which the young man spoke continued to impress.

"The second featured item for this evening is a meat course. We are slow roasting a Pink Hills Farm lamb shoulder. The animals are fed a steady diet of only the finest organic arugula and alfalfa. This special care to diet contributes greatly to the un-matched quality and taste of the meat."

"The chef serves this over a bed of morel, shiitake, and Hen of the Woods mushrooms." As he went on, the table listened hungrily. It was truly a captivating presentation... "The mushrooms are going to be sautéed with Armando Manni's Tuscan olive oil along with La Bonnotte potatoes and a sweet garlic relish. I'm gonna' give you a few moments to peruse the menu, and then I'll be back to answer any questions." "Thank you so much! And great descriptions by the way!" Maria couldn't help but to congratulate the astute man.

"Wow, those specials sounded amazing! They have some pretty good-looking things on the menu as well I see." "Yeah, say Drake do you wanna' order some apps for the table?" "Um, sure. What should I get?" "Just pick a few out; I believe we're all pretty adventurous eaters here." Kevin waved a hand in confidence as he indulged in another sip of wine.

"Just don' get the snails honey, I'm not *that* adventurous tonight." The waiter returned for a brief moment. "I've brought some chilled Himalayan Spring Water, and the chef is preparing a batch of our house-made brioche for your enjoyment."

"Center-table you'll notice a plate of first-cold-pressed organic olive oil for dipping, and these herbs I'm mixing in are picked daily from our garden outside." While he spoke, the model-like waiter began chopping a handful of aromatic herbs into tiny, almost microscopic pieces on a small table nearby.

It had been set up by a server's assistant while James was speaking earlier.

The helper was so discreet no one at the table even realized how the platform got there. As the sharp stainless-steel knife began to sever young leaves from stems; the air filled with blooms of sage, thyme, spearmint, rosemary, and fresh garlic. The olive oil was a greenish gold and its smell reminded Drake of the quaint town in Potenza he and Maria visited for their honeymoon.

After Mr. Wellington finished carefully chopping the herbs, he placed a small amount into a beautifully crafted ceramic bowl. It was bone tan and highlighted the forest-green paste now cradled deep in its belly. He then added some of the oil and began to swirl the tantalizing concoction. Every movement was precise. It was obvious he'd done this many times. After placing the remaining greenery in a smaller bowl, he assured his guests they were welcome to add more at their discretion.

"So James? Is there anything on the menu you'd recommend?" "Well yes, there are several classics that are personal favorites. Do you prefer something from the land, sea or sky?" Kevin smiled at the thought of the question. With a finger tapping the side of his chin he replied, "Actually I think I'm gonna' let you decide. Send out whatever *you'd* be eating if you were in my seat."

"Really honey? That's a lot to ask of James don't you think? He doesn't even know what kinds of things you prefer, I mean geez, the pressure!" Laughter was sewn into every word. The mood was light. "I'm feelin' lucky baby, hey Drake, remember when I said that in Vegas? It turned out like that movie." Drake snapped his fingers trying to recall the film. Maria beat her husband to the chase, she always had the better memory of the pair. "I know which one you're talking about, um, The Hangover!"

"That's it, that weekend was hilarious. Remember that honey?" "Are you talking about the time we were asked to leave the Mirage? When that cop almost tased you?" "Yep, that's the one!" Mr. Wellington stood there smiling and trying to maintain a professional demeanor as they spoke. These were his favorite types of people.

They were obviously well off, yet they seemed unafraid to have a good time. Most guests that dined at the restaurant felt the need to remind themselves and everyone around them that they were rich. Many were quite rude and seemingly impossible to please. Especially the wives. Entitlement sapped all joy from their lives. But not this table. They were having a splendid time.

"Shall I give the rest of you a few moments to decide, or would you like to order those appetizers now?" Drake saw a dish that sounded interesting, "I think we're gonna' try the Kobe beef Carpaccio and that oyster dish you mentioned earlier." James took note and then hurried off. "So Kevin, how have things been?" "I can't complain, I'm working for Biotech Corp. I actually have a pretty important conference coming up next month. A year ago, my focus was on molecular cell structure, but recently I've kinda' shifted gears."

With intrigue now forming Drake asked, "How so? I always thought that was your area of passion. What changed?" Kevin nodded at the question. "Well, my new focus involves viewing our cellular anatomy from both a quantum and quantum mechanical level. In the lab, we're delving into the correlation between mind, thought, and the effects of consciousness on our biological make-up. It's damn interesting stuff!"

This was exactly what the Gilferds needed. Time away

from the kids. Away from the drudgeries of their apartment. Away from reality. It had been months since they'd stepped foot in a decent restaurant. It was rejuvenating. But like the façade they had lived when incomes were flourishing, it was a lie. In the end, all debts are paid. Living a lie is like living on credit. It may work out early on, but the longer you do it, the deeper the hole.

CHAPTER 6

CONVERSATIONS AND LOVE

"Sounds interesting, so what's your theory?" The ladies smiled admiringly at their husbands while they talked. Their intelligence was so attractive. Intellect can be a powerful pheromone. "Well as you know I started off just studying our molecular biological composition, but, and quite by accident I might add, we took a detour and introduced mind into the equation." Kevin paused. His eyes leveled with his friend's. "Drake, let me tell you, this stuff gets pretty deep. Our research indicates mind, and in particular, consciousness, may actually be shaping reality as we know it."

Kevin had the table's full attention. "We found the very *act* of observing reality changes its compositional essence. The moment a conscious observer looks at something, it changes. It basically points to the fact that we as conscious beings have a lot more power than we give ourselves credit for." With each passing moment intensity quietly built momentum in his voice. "Our research shows that *thoughts* are the things that create reality; and because we can control our thoughts, we may be able to control reality as well. I mean think about that!"

"That *does* sound interesting, so that's what the biologist in you is beginning to believe, what does Kevin the person think?" Drake's wife decided to join in on the conversation. The concept of targeted mind-application had always intrigued her. "Well, Maria, let me approach that question this way, what is a *belief*?" She took a moment to ponder the question. Kevin waited a few seconds and then expounded on his theory. These were the types of conversations he lived for. The entire area of study, the mixing of theology and science. It was so fascinating.

"Take religion for instance; Buddhism, Christianity, Hinduism, whatever system you choose, and dissect it from a strictly objective viewpoint. The only reason any follower of any religion believes in its teachings, is because he or she was *taught* to do so. If you were born in a different part of the world, with different parents, you'd believe what they taught you. A belief is just a thought we keep thinking." As he said this a deliberate finger tapped against the side of his temple. "Think about it."

"Humanity is only just beginning to look at the subject of mindpower. Did you realize we have on average over twenty thousand thoughts a day? Twenty thousand! How many are deliberate? Intentional?" Drake cut in. "Some of us probably have a lot less than that." Maria and Susan chuckled at the well-placed joke. Kevin smiled but didn't let the comment distract him.

"The fact of the matter is; we don't even know what a thought is. None of us can deny that they have a direct and tangible impact on our physiological lives. Just look at what happens to a person if they direct their thoughts towards something they consider arousing." Kevin's arms flailed about as he got into the meat of his explanation. The subject was exciting. On the brink of human understanding. "Without any external stimuli, their bodies will *still* undergo physical changes."

"You know Kevin, you may be onto something. I think I get where you're going." Drake had an aha moment as he digested the concept. James was just arriving back at the table. "I do apologize for interrupting, but your appetizers have arrived. This is the Kobe beef Carpaccio, it's accompanied by a white truffle and fig chutney; and this, the fines de claires oyster butter. A few moments to decide on dinner?" Kevin took another sip of the Bryant before responding. It was maturing beautifully. The decanter had opened the nose considerably by that point. "Well, we can at least order salads, right honey?"

"Sure, Maria, Drake, are you two having any? They make and incredible arugula and strawberry with pistachios, and they actually grill the lettuce for their *untraditional Caesar*. You pretty much can't go wrong with any of the choices here."

"Why don't we each get a different one? That way we can taste each other's." "That sounds like a plan Maria, I'll have the strawberry salad." After they ordered, Kevin continued explaining his findings on thought and its relationship to quantum physics.

"So Kevin, isn't all of what you're discussing kinda, I dunno, out of your field? I mean, few biologists are delving as deep as you are into quantum mechanics." "Well Drake, speaking quite frankly, how can any logical scientist separate the two subjects for very long?"

Drake listened intently as Kevin explained, enjoying a sip of wine from time to time. The candle at their table flickered echoes of light that sparkled brilliantly against the crystal. Burgundy shadows danced across the tablecloth every time a glass was lifted. "They're inherently interdependent. You cannot have life without consciousness, and therefore, one cannot dedicate time to the study of life without eventually transitioning to the study of mind. It just seems like the natural evolution of self-growth for me." Drake didn't look convinced. Kevin could tell he and his friend weren't quite on the same page. He needed to explain the correlation in a different way.

"Here's a perfect example of why I've shifted my train of thought." He took another sip. "I recently read an article by this prominent quantum physicist. This guy's like a, a real thinktank type. In it he discussed the structural makeup of an atom. Get this. It's been confirmed that the distance between the nucleus of an atom's revolving protons and electrons, is proportionately the *same* as the distance between our solar system's sun and orbiting planets. Now what's that tell you?"

Their server James began to approach the table again but was stopped by Kevin's assertive hand gesture. He wanted to get his point across. "Hold off on the salads for a while. Give us a few minutes." At that the conversation went on. Everyone tuned back in. "Well, I guess it could imply that our atoms could technically be really tiny solar systems." "Take it further" Kevin said, eagerness now building again in his voice.

Maria started to interject and then decided against it. "Go on Maria, please go on, give us your input." "Well, I was gonna' say, taking what Drake said and building on it, you could also look at our solar system and say the same thing right? Who's to say our solar system is not just a really large atom, and we just happen to live on one of its orbiting electrons?"

"Exactly, that's exactly where I was going!" These types of discussions were part of the reason the two couples got along so well in the first place... They were on the same wavelength. "There's an old Native American saying that goes, as above, so below. What if when we look up at the stars, we're really looking at what we, and all things in the universe look like at the atomic level?" Kevin made a good point.

As the salads began to arrive, Susan decided to change the subject and asked, "So what made you two get rid of the house? Don't tell me it was the neighbors?" She gave her husband a look and then directed her attention towards Drake.

He shook his head. "Um, no it wasn't that, we just decided it was bigger than we needed right now. We opted for an apartment. At least for the time being." To this Kevin replied, "Did you snag that condo listed in South Park, you know the one honey, what was the name of that neighborhood, Redwoods? They have some great units on that side of town. If we weren't so tied to having a yard, hell, we might've went with one ourselves." He must have thought apartment was synonymous with condo. It wasn't.

Drake shook his head. His fork fiddled with the field greens on his plate. The salads had been snuck into a gap of the conversation, expertly timed by James, as the table was pondering the depth of the universe. Trying to quantify our tininess, our existence as trivial specs of consciousness floating aimless yet true through infinite void. All his strawberries had been eaten. "No we actually moved over to the eastern side of the city, but that's not really important, we just needed a change of pace." What Drake strategically neglected to mention was that they were evicted. It was painfully obvious, their longtime friends were in a considerably more fortunate position. The recession had clearly missed *their* neck of the woods.

To change the subject and deflect, Drake blurted out, "Did both of you hear about that mess going on in the Middle East? The Taliban's taken over the entire country. Looks like there's gonna' be another war, as if we haven't had enough of that already." Anxious eyes surveyed the scene, checking to see if the diversion worked.

His comment was noticeably out of context to everyone

at the table, but Kevin picked up the slack and replied. "Tell me about it, all that ruckus can only mean one thing, higher gas prices for us minions. They'll use any excuse in the book to raise those damn prices. I thought that was the whole point of being over there in the first place?" Another dose of Bryant quelled his nerves.

"Have you seen the way things have been rising? And I don't just mean at the tank. Food, airlines, everything's going up. Everything except my 401k." Susan chuckled. Drake smiled shyly at his wife and then said, "This whole system is corrupt, there're a few old men sitting around in some fancy office that control the world. We mere mortals are basically slaves."

As the men continued to bicker on injustices in society, Susan beckoned Maria into their own side conversation. Their voices were accented by the clink of crystal from tables nearby. Both women were smiling as they spoke. Maria's grin got cut short by a question that brought reality back into focus. "So, Maria how are the children?" "Oh they're fine, Jacob is getting so big, it seems like we hafta' buy new clothes for him every week now."

"And what about Jason? I know he was ill last time we spoke?" At this Maria's voice lowered as she informed Susan of her son's situation. "He's been in the hospital for about a week now, he was having a lot of trouble breathing. The doctor said they've noticed when my baby's sleeping sometimes he stops breathing altogether. Sometimes twenty-five seconds or more! No teen should have to go through that." Kevin overheard them talking and offered assistance. He and his wife were well connected. They ran in some pretty exclusive circles and that meant their access was considerable.

"You know if you ever need anything, Susan and I are here. Just let us know, anything we can do to be of help. We know some truly great doctors in town! We'd be more than happy to provide references." Kevin spoke directly to Drake now, his eyebrows raised with genuine concern. He meant what he said.

The Splintons didn't realize their offer, however kind, was essentially useless to the Gilferds. They were still under the impression that their friends were doing at least *ok* financially. Whatever references they would've provided would have undoubtedly been more expensive than the public hospital their son was currently at.

The kinds of individuals the Splintons were used to referring would make home visits and things of that nature. Home visits from a specialized practitioner, however alluring, would surely be astronomically pricey. For the debt-ridden couple, indulgences like this were a thing of the past.

A minute or two after Kevin made his offer, James approached the table and announced the main courses were about to arrive. Not thirty seconds after he spoke, the food began being ushered in by four serious looking server assistants. They all wore black coats. Dinner was turning out to be an orchestra. Timing on everything was perfect. The execution, flawless. It was classic fine dining.

Each dish was placed in front of its rightful owner at exactly the same moment. Their distinct aromas were absolutely intoxicating. The air around them filled with smells of charred meat, mixed with notes of deep, clean oceanic undertones. Susan had opted for the Pacific salmon filet. A perfect mid-well sear wafted aromatics that played beautifully off the bed of roasted vegetables on her plate. It had been a while since anyone refreshed their wine, and one of the assistants immediately took action upon noticing. He started with the ladies. Carefully approaching from the left. A delicate pour. No formality was spared.

The Bryant was given time to breathe in the decanter for almost an hour, as fine wine should. Its entire profile evolved wonderfully. It was like experiencing wine for the first time, all over again. A rebirth. Its body was rich and chewy, it almost seemed to hug Drake's tongue as he took a sip. Upon swallowing, thoughtful notes of cassis married with cedar and shaved truffle swept across his palate. Neither Earth nor fruit components overpowered the experience. They were seamlessly balanced.

Maria laughed at a comment made by Susan. Drake could sense it had something to do with the face he made while tasting the wine. It was a look of unadulterated bliss. Her eyes fixed on her husband's slim silhouette. The suit he chose for the evening fit him quite well. He looked enticing. Tingles of lust danced around in her belly. The wine only enhanced her attraction. Feeling slightly buzzed by this point, Maria didn't realize her hand in relation to her glass sitting near the table's corner.

Her forefinger tapped it with just enough force to knock it squarely into Kevin's lap. He jumped with surprise as Maria covered her mouth, ashamed and utterly embarrassed at her faux pas. The cherry liquid saturated Kevin's chestnut slacks and managed to splash his new linen shirt as well. It left him looking like he'd just left a murder scene. Red was everywhere. For several moments silence swept the table. When the waiter stopped by to ensure everyone was enjoying their meal, he sped back off with surprising speed, only to return moments later tailed by a small army.

Included in this group was an upper middle-aged man who undoubtedly was the manager. He was the only one not wearing a black coat. His was pinstriped navy instead. Kevin was offered warm soda water and several towels while the man spoke. "Sir I do apologize for this, the *least* we can do is accommodate your dry-cleaning. We can have someone stop by your home first thing in the morning and return them within a few hours."

Kevin's head shook while his hand waved. The manager

was being far too kind. "No, no that won't be necessary. Besides, none of your employees had anything to do with it, it was just an accident." Drake admired his friend's ability to brush off the incident with such ease. It seemed the manager took a kind notice to this as well. He smiled and nodded as if to oblige. Just before turning away he recanted. A dedication to service overtook. He had to make it right.

"Please Sir, I insist, any accident that happens on my watch *is* my responsibility. Additionally, I must insist on covering your meal as well." "You're too kind, everyone here, it's one of the many reasons we keep coming back." The compliment struck home. A smile was coaxed from the man's face. With a nod, he hurried off to comp the meal and make arrangements.

After using the soda-water to remove as much of the stain as possible, Kevin resumed conversing as if nothing happened. He was always able to make the best of any situation he found himself in. The rest of the evening was filled with laughter and fond conversations of memories past. For those few precious hours, Drake and Maria were able to set their worries aside.

Dinner with the Splintons reminded them of the life they once lived. The constant weight of debt that permeated their very existence the day before, now lifted and was replaced with genuine bliss and joy. It was a feeling of ease, upliftment. As Maria laughed at the many jokes told that night, Drake sat there and gazed fondly at his wife. He allowed himself to get lost in her. She looked stunning, and she was his. Only true love could evoke the stares wafted in her direction. They needed this.

It had been months since he looked at her like he did that evening. Temporarily relieved from the stresses of money, he could see her for the wonderful woman she really was. For a moment it felt to Drake as though it was just the two of them at the table. He was falling in love with his queen all over again. He noticed the way her lip curled slightly to the right when she was trying to suppress a laugh. *Such a turn on.*

Her eyes were golden brown and glowed like warm embers in the dimly lit restaurant. Smooth, supple lines on her face gave it character and shape, but didn't take away from her youthful gaze. Maria's hair was pulled up into a bun with two strands hanging down on either side. She exuded elegance. It was her natural state.

She glanced over at her husband and was taken aback by his longing stares. Susan reached for her husband's hand, she saw the way Drake was looking at his wife and it reminded her of her own love for Kevin. For a minute or two no one said anything, there was nothing to be said really. Both couples were in love and happy in that moment. Everything was perfect. At least up until the bills arrived.

CHAPTER 7

DINE AND DASH

When the checks hit the table they were already split according to Kevin's request. Drake's portion was $597.89. He gave a gulp. Kevin chuckled at this, thinking Drake's reaction was meant to entertain. Drake pulled out his American Express Gold Card and placed it in the checkbook, and then snuck Maria a quick look. His eyes cowered, "We'll worry about it tomorrow honey." No words left his mouth. He'd forgotten how expensive a la carte dining could get.

She looked nervous, mainly because he made a point of not letting her see the total amount due. The sensual tension between them dissipated. Reality had set in. Back to the real world. With the tip included they were set back well over $700. The manager that stopped by earlier came by to pick up the checks a few minutes later. He kindly offered Kevin his business card and asked if there was anything else the table needed before he ran the bills.

A few moments later he returned to the table bearing an embarrassed expression. It drug at the corners of his eyes. Everyone could feel the change. His in-charge posture was minified, knocked from the glory it held just 5 minutes earlier.

He shook Kevin's hand and returned the titanium black card used to pay his portion of the bill. Then he approached Drake. Drake held out his hand, expecting to be presented with his card in return. Instead, he was presented with a small black book.

When he opened it there was a hand written note that read, "Mr. Gilferd, it is my regret to inform you that your card has been declined. Would you like to try another?" After giving him the note, the manager hastily skirted away without saying a word. Everyone at the table could tell something was off. The change in demeanor was painfully obvious.

Maria's ears went numb with embarrassment as Kevin tried to assist. "What's wrong Drake? The card expired? That happened to Susan last week at Whole Foods. Just call Amex and have em' re-issue another card, I'll take care of dinner tonight, don't worry about it." Kevin began to reach back into his pocket to retrieve his card again. Having his friend's back came naturally. Drake would do the same for him.

"No, no Kevin, you don' have to do that." Drake got up, trying to hold back debilitating fear as it crept into his gut like a stray cat. He knew what came next. A few tables nearby looked over with curiosity as he fumbled about. In his angst he left his wallet sitting on the table near his empty plate. Once they were safely beyond earshot, the manager began to talk more candidly, as if he'd ran into Drake's type before. The Dine and Dash type. "Look, Mr. Gilferd, your card's been declined, is there another one you'd like to provide?" "Um, yeah I think I may have another card somewhere," Drake said with a shy chuckle. He did his best to avoid eye contact as his body shifted with defeat.

He patted his pockets, looking for another form of payment, but it was clear he couldn't produce one. "Actually, umm, can I spread it across multiple cards? I don' like any of the balances to reach a certain point." The skeptical manager gave a look that said, "I know all your cards are maxed out, I hope you brought cash." Instead of being rude, he replied, "Unfortunately our company doesn't permit that, but I definitely can understand your concern. I'll give you a few moments to procure an alternative form of payment." *That was corporate for fuck you.*

The look on Drake's face said it all, he was broken and beaten. Maria gave a sigh of despair as he re-approached the table with a timid step. His feet drug behind him, anchored down with weights of embarrassment. Sensing something was up, Kevin quickly said, "Don't worry about splitting the check, I'll take care of the bill. We can just tell the manager to put it all on one tab." A hand waved, desperate to save-face. "Kevin that's not necessary, I think I may have another card with me."

Drake fumbled oddly for a few more moments searching in his wallet for money he knew didn't exist, all the while his wife becoming more and more agitated. After the tab was finally paid, there was a long uncomfortable silence at the table. "Next time we'll treat you two, I've gotta' call Amex, that darn thing's been giving me all sorts of trouble recently." Confusion and embarrassment stoked faces at every table on their way out. What a mess.

The drive home that night was silent for the most part. Occasionally Drake would reach over, attempting to touch his wife's arm as if to say "I'm sorry you had to go through that." Her responses to his apologetic gestures were less than receptive. For several days following their embarrassment neither made any real attempt at conversation. Both felt there was little to discuss. The fact of the matter was, they were unhappy and on the brink of bankruptcy.

The realization of their circumstance hit Drake the hardest. He couldn't accept poverty, not after tasting the leisure and comfort his high salary previously afforded. It's funny how life is one sided in that regard. To Drake it seemed extremely difficult to go from being poor to becoming wealthy. Years were spent in his office, building his business up. Same with Maria. It was not difficult to accomplish the inverse however. He knew firsthand the simplicity with which he helped take his family from the top of the world, to the very bottom of the totem pole. It all seemed to happen so quickly. Like it came out of nowhere. Deep down, they both knew what brought them to this point. The math was simple. The reality, harsh.

It was on a gloomy Sunday afternoon that Drake decided to sit out in the family car. Rain teased here and there. A storm was about 3 hours out, slow moving, tugging its way East. Thick clouds of grey lapped against one another, creating darker and darker coils. He needed time to re-evaluate his life; or at least daydream of better days for a few moments. To clear his mind he'd often ponder on subjects of interest. The little voice in his head took center stage. His mind began to wonder. "What are the chances of winning the lottery?" Drake thought on it for a bit. "Probably like one in a billion. The odds are definitely stacked against me."

"Now, what are the odds a man who actually did win would be able to keep the money and his sanity as well? Those odds aren't too good either. That man would have to worry about his family asking for favors forever. Bet there'd also be a lot more family in general to deal with. They'd literally be coming out of the wood-work." He liked rehearsing these types of thoughts over in his head. But every time he tried to imagine winning his mind would insert skepticism and worry.

Drake began to chuckle as he played a scenario out mentally. He pictured some young woman, probably in her late twenties, approaching him in the grocery store. She would exclaim after looking at him for several minutes, "Oh my God, is that you? It's me, Jessica! Don't you remember?"

"I'm your cousin on your brother's dog's sister's best friend's second aunt's side. I was at the family reunion last year and I meant to catch up with you. Listen there's this idea I've been thinkin' bout', and it could make us oodles of dough. I already have a business plan written up. All I need now is the startup capital."

Drake pictured the woman presenting some ridiculous piece of paper with a half-assed plan concocted on it. Probably written in crayon. "That's where *you* come in, with a modest investment of say, $10,000,000 we could be up and running in no time! What do ya' say?" He laughed again at the ridiculous thought he now mulled on. As a father, Drake made a point of informing his children of the wolves the world has to offer.

He would say, "They come in all shapes and sizes, remember that, the wolves are everywhere." Even when pulling a decent income, Drake tended to instill the idea of scarcity into his children. He never wanted them to think things came easy in life. They never do. It was at times like the one he was in now, that he'd wished he'd taken his own advice.

As Jacob grew, Drake instilled in him his own pessimistic nature. On an almost daily basis Jacob would hear his father say things like, "These crooks, all they wanna do is take your money, even if you make it honorably and pay your taxes, they still find a way to get their almighty dollar." He was right in many ways. It became crystal clear during the recession, when layoffs were at their peak. At the end of the day, everything came down to the bottom line. To a business, people are not people. They represent either one of two things. An asset, or a liability. That's it.

"Everyone's in it for themselves; they wanna' nail you to the cross son. Everyone. And you best not forget it. The moment you do, they'll crucify you, I wouldn't tell you these things unless they were true." As an adolescent Jacob believed his father's words. He saw the evils of the world, the injustices bestowed upon his fellow man. He noticed how cruel people could be, chose to be. By the time he was twenty he began to mentally withdraw from society.

Lone walks in the woods were a common way to spend summer afternoons. By the age of twenty-one he still lived at home with his parents, and his sister wouldn't let him forget it. She jumped from the nest at the tender age of eighteen and was pregnant with her first son a few months after that. Several evictions and a few civil lawsuits later, she still found great pleasure in teasing her older brother for his apparent lack of independence.

She would visit often, and although she ridiculed him constantly, she loved her brother dearly. Just in her own particular way. Secretly, Myra began to worry about him, although she would never admit it. He never went out like other guys his age, and when she could get him to step out, he always seemed to be isolated. Even when women made obvious attempts at him, he'd usually ignore their advances and find an excuse to leave the scene.

Aside from walking in the woods with Djed, Jacob really enjoyed spending his days at a local spa in the heart of the city. It was there that he would daydream about stumbling onto some proverbial pot of gold or winning the lottery, or something of that nature.

Jacob took after his father in that regard. He felt good when he was daydreaming, but being at the spa didn't mean he always enjoyed his stay. Sometimes it was just something to do to pass the time. At a mere $20 for a day-pass he could stay the entire afternoon. It was nice for what it was, but he never expected much beyond a little relaxation. One day, he got more than he'd bargained for.

CHAPTER 8

THE SHADOWED FIGURE

"I'm lost in life," Jacob thought. "I'm lost and have no one to tell, no one to talk to." The foaming bubbles in the hot tub swirled around slowly, much like the thoughts in his head, popping randomly as he tried to make sense of it all. At this point in life Jacob was unhappy. Life just felt so superficial. A stow-away vessel at sea, no captain at the helm.

He thought about what it meant to *live* one's life. "Cry as a child, as a teen go to school, then meet a girl, get a job, get married and have kids; and then watch them follow the same cycle, hopefully before you die. That's what life is, that's it? Oh yeah, please, don't forget bills and taxes. There, that about sums it up."

He couldn't explain the feelings welling inside. Feelings of despair, of hopelessness. Feelings that swallowed his confidence. Held it submerged. Part of him wanted to die, hopeful the other side offered something more real, more meaningful. Another part of him yearned to live life to its fullest, whatever that meant. But in that very moment, nothing at all mattered.

He was empty. He had no friends, no girlfriend, and

worst of all, he trusted no one. Life taught him the nature of his fellow man, the deception that dwelled in the shadows of humanity. It was a curse. A virus passed from generation to generation. Now aware of it, he did everything he could to avoid it. He wore a mask of sorts. Shielded himself. "I feel like a stranger in my own body." For several hours he sat alone, sulking in a fog of despair. He prayed for some hint of enlightenment.

Jacob should have been partying and getting wasted with friends at a bar no responsible parent would condone. But instead he sat alone. He should've been lying in bed with a woman blessed with thick hips and sumptuous lips; exhausted after mind-blowing sex that would've put the most hardcore porn to shame.

Instead he sat, motionless. For the previous few years Jacob had tried his hand at meditation. Now a young adult, his mind bore the weight of heavy questions and self-reflection. He read somewhere that happiness began from within. "Easier said than lived, I don't have any happiness left in me. Hell, I doubt there was ever any to begin with."

Just as these thoughts of despair left Jacob's skull he noticed a shadowed figure approaching. It moved silently. The footsteps were light. Almost angelic as they barely touched the floor's surface. As the character neared, its eerie presence was evaporated by the realization that it was just an old man. Coming to soak tired bones no doubt. His height was average. His rounded tan face kind. Deep lines of wisdom etched character into the recesses in his eyes.

"Hello there young man, how are you doing this evening? A little mature of a place for such a youthful lad to be, don't ya' think?" With an indifferent shrug Jacob gave a frank but honest answer. "I don't really have anywhere better to be Sir, and besides, this place isn't too shabby." He began to snicker a little under his breath as the elder looked on with curious eyes.

"Sure ya' do, what do you mean by that? It's a Saturday night; there must be plenty to get into. You know, I was your age once believe it or not. I know I don't look like it now, but I had my day..." The elderly man gazed off for a moment, as if reminiscing on good times. "Aren't you interested in going to a club or something; I believe that's what you young people like to do nowadays right?"

While he spoke, the lanky man removed his cotton robe and sat at the hot-tub's edge. Burbling water lapped against his shins, alleviating stress built from his weekly workout. He rubbed them in long strokes as Jacob replied. "No disrespect Sir, but why're you interested in why I'm here?" The man stopped massaging his legs and looked up with a frank expression. "I am." "You're what?" "Interested."

"You see, we are *all* connected, and your despair is affecting my weekend. I would prefer to enjoy it in glee, especially considering the limited number I've got left. Granted, the doctors say if I continue to exercise I can add a few years to my tab. I dunno' though, these legs of mine are tired." "Excuse me?" "Oh yes, sorry, you see, my body is dying as bodies tend to do when they age. I'm ok with it though, it's sure to be even better where I'm headed anyway."

Jacob sat at the edge of the tub peering at this odd character with a blank stare on his face. The old man paid him no mind while he continued speaking. "Don't get me wrong, this realm is wondrous, but so will be the next." "I'm sorry, what's your name again?" "I am Ming Lao." He was a fragile looking fellow, thin in frame and stature. Slanted eyes reached both inward and out. Hovering above them, grey hairs charred with wisdom rested in two clumps, and raised upwards every time the man spoke. Judging by the lines in his sublime face, Jacob put him at about eighty years of age. A shiny surface sat atop his head; the nearest hair coming from his thick brows.

"So what is it you do for a living if you don't mind me asking?" Jacob decided to oblige the question. "I work in a bank. More specifically a call center. Been there for like a year now. Before that I was a waiter." There was a pause as the man looked over his much younger counterpart. His eyes studied Jacob's body language as the two spoke. "And how is that, working in a call center in a bank I mean?" "To be honest, I hate it Mr., Mr. Lao. Usually when people ask me what I do, I tend to be a little… I guess, misleading would be the best word." At this Jacob sat uncomfortably on the edge of the hot tub, head lowered, feet kicking with a nervous calm in its warm waters. Normally he wouldn't have been so transparent with a total stranger. Something about the old man made him open up. It was like being in confession. Or therapy.

"It's kinda comical really. I tell them I work in wealth brokerage and try to use financial jargon to make myself seem more important than I really am." "Are you not important?" The monk seemed confused by what he was hearing. "Well. It's not that *I'm* unimportant, it's just what I *do* is not very important if you get what I'm saying." A hint of disappointment speckled the end of Jacob's tone. His eyes were pointed south. The elder replied, taking note of the loss in confidence. "I am afraid I do not, please explain."

"Well for starters, people that work in call centers can be replaced pretty easily, we're considered disposable. Our incentive program consists of being able to wear jeans when we do well as a team, and the pay sucks. Just think about it, at my bank alone, our CEO makes roughly eighteen million dollars a year. I make twenty-six thousand, and that's with overtime mind you."

Jacob could see his father's frequent rants wore off on him. He was beginning to sound just like Drake, all that was missing was Maria shaking her head. "Some executives have negotiated private jets into their employment contracts.

Private jets! Meanwhile, when *I* perform well, I get to wear jeans… Fucking jeans. Excuse my French." It felt odd cursing in the man's Zen-like presence. He didn't seem to mind.

The old man just listened as Jacob spoke. "I heard one guy actually refused to pay *taxes* on his four hundred and eighty-five million dollar a year salary, so the *company* paid them for him. Can you imagine, like seriously?" Jacob barely stopped for air as he went on. His list of grievances had been bottled up for so long. It felt good to finally release the pressure. Like popping an abscess. Words spilled out in blobs, and the weight lifted. "And guess whose pockets that money ultimately came from? Mine!" "*You* paid his taxes?" Mr. Lao's voice was drenched in sincere disbelief. "Well, no, not me personally, but people like me." He nodded in acknowledgement to the youngster's point. After a moment, a question came to the monk's mind. "So, Jacob. These executives you speak of, do you admire these people, or despise them?"

"Honestly, I don' care, I just wanna' be happy. I don't need a fleet of jets, but they'd be nice." At this the old man chuckled. "I would like to show you something that may be of use to you young man. I will be at the Greenway Park tomorrow morning at 6a.m. Do you know where that's at?" "Um. Yes…" "Good, don't be late."

Just as ghostly as he'd arrived Ming Lao departed. His gait was so subdued, it was as if he almost floated away. Jacob lingered in the hot tub for a little while longer, contemplating whether he would meet the man and see what he had to offer. Maybe it was a business proposal. The odd man left him curious.

The next morning, he arose twenty minutes before his alarm clock went off. It was set for 5:30a.m. He was no morning person but for some reason, he couldn't go back to sleep. The snooze button had the day off. Cool, moist air brushed at his face as he closed the door to the apartment to leave. His keys jingled a bit until he silenced them with his hand, then secured both the top and bottom locks. He turned to face the sidewalk and then headed towards the parking lot, avoiding the many tufts of Crabgrass along the way. Sometimes fire ants made their homes in those clumps. Heavy dew sat lazily on blades of grass, and the first morning birds were just beginning to stir. Trills, chirps, and high-pitched whistles dotted the tree-line. Robins sang the day's praises with varied tweets and sanguine calls as they headed out, snapping up Earthworms that had broken ground. They had hungry mouths to feed.

Jacob walked up to his rickety heap of a car and opened the door. It creaked and moaned with protest as he shut it behind him after slipping inside. Eyes still flush with sleep, he almost decided to just head back to bed. "What the hell am I doing right now?" As he asked the question to himself aloud he thrust the keys in the ignition. The hunk of metal sputtered to life, rattling from underneath as he shifted to reverse, and then spun the wheel to the left as he gave it gas.

"I don't even know this guy, what if he's some kinda' freak or something. Meet him at the park at six in the morning, who does that?" It was only a short drive, "What the hell," He thought aloud. As he pulled into the nearly empty parking lot he almost started to turn back and go home yet again. His bed was just screaming for him to wrap himself back in its cool sheets. Then he saw him. A blurred figure stood about 50 yards away, distorted by fog that crawled along the ground, nipping its way upward.

"Lemme see what this crazy old coot wants to show me." The wise looking man was dressed in loose white robes that reminded Jacob of a monk's attire. In his left hand he carried five jade beads all held together by a short threaded black rope.

As Jacob approached, the elderly man gave a brief nod of

approval before saying, "Sit." He gestured towards a large stone near where they were standing. With a look of confusion and slight protest Jacob obliged Ming Lao's request.

"Mr. Lao, what's all this about?" The man's eyes were kind, yet his words firm, "Sit!" "Ok, geez, you don't have to be so pushy. What're we doing out here anyway? And at this hour? Jesus isn't even awake yet!" "Silence, sit and learn to be still." His voice remained steady. Direct. That day the two of them sat there on the stone for several hours. Every so often Jacob would try to ask Mr. Lao what they were supposed to be doing, but he would just sit there, motionless and staring into the abyss.

After about three and a half hours of this odd behavior Jacob finally had enough. "Ok, this was a complete wasta' time! I could've been at home sleeping or watching TV. Or anything. I got up and came out here at some ungodly hour. And for what? So I could get eaten alive by blood sucking mosquitos?"

Ming Lao just sat there. Jacob got up and began to storm off, feeling used and deeply annoyed. Just before he was beyond earshot, he heard Mr. Lao call out softly, "I'll see you next Sunday Jacob." His voice was light, as if carried by the whims of the wind.

When Jacob got back home, his father was standing outside smoking a cigarette. Grey coils that weren't quite donuts rose from the Marlboro's tip. They made their way up to just above his head and collected until the breeze carried them off in little clouds. "Dad, you really need ta' stop smoking those things, they're gonna' kill you one day." "They'll only kill me if I *believe* it, otherwise I have your mother for that," Drake laughed. He took another puff. Smoke filled the air around him as his hand swatted, trying to coax the fumes away from his son.

"It's all in your head, mind over matter boy, mind over matter." His father pointed a finger at his temple as he conveyed the lesson. The glasses resting on the bridge of his nose shifted as he did so. Jacob thought about this for a while as it related to Mr. Lao. Maybe the old man was trying to show him something intangible, something about himself. After a few more moments of pondering Jacob dismissed the idea and went about the rest of his day.

Later that week strange things began to happen. He started seeing signs, odd and inexplicable signs. One morning he awoke to a praying mantis sitting outside his window. It was his first time seeing one up close. Before that, the Discovery Channel was his only reference. They looked bigger in person. The insect seemed to have been watching him sleep. Big beady eyes swiveled and took in his every move. It just sat there staring, occasionally stretching its long legs, preening itself like a cat would. Keeping him company while he got dressed and prepared for work.

Right before he left the room Jacob decided to go over to the window and pay the pest a visit. He tried to shoo the bug away but it wouldn't budge. "Shoo, git!" It stood there with its head tilted to the side and looked directly into Jacob's eyes. If it were ever possible for an insect to look curious, this one did. "Fine, whatever, sit in the window all day. Dumb bug."

While at work that day, and for most of the week, people seemed to act strange towards him. Something was off. Different. Jacob absolutely despised his job and the coworkers that came with it. They all seemed so unprofessional. At that point in his life he was working as a waiter in a self-proclaimed fine dining restaurant.

Regardless of what the establishment said, Jacob knew better. The hand-made bread served daily, was really just purchased from a local bakery and heated up in the oven, heck sometimes it would even go in the microwave. Waiters could barely hold back snickers as they watched guests constantly rave about how amazing the "in-house baker" was. It was a joke passed down from server to server. You can tell people anything.

The grain fed Waygu beef, as listed on the menu, was in actuality just regular beef bought from the cheapest butcher in town. And the wait staff? Let's just say they were not nearly as friendly as the guests were led to believe. They were assholes. Funky, unwashed, dingleberry ridden assholes.

Behind closed doors they would curse each other out for the silliest reasons. Jacob could hardly remember a day where he wasn't involved in, or at least within proximity of a verbal assault. He spent almost as much time having meetings with managers about one thing or another as he did actually serving guests. It was a hellacious job. Known to be one of the most stressful in the nation. From the pay to the workload, everything sucked.

This week was different. When he strode through the tall wooden door of the building, he waited for the hostess to point out that he was two minutes late. She loved to remind him of his tardiness. At each workday's onset, the clank of heels against hardened tile would let him know she was on her way to castigate him. Instead, he was given a warm greeting from one of the bartenders who'd always ignored his existence before. The hostess was out sick.

That afternoon, another coworker offered to buy him lunch if he agreed to clean a table that was still sitting and had just ordered coffee. In the service industry one of the most universally shared pet-peeves was a table that wouldn't leave once they'd finished their meal. Jacob didn't mind staying to clean the table however; he was closing so he would have had to be the last to leave anyway. No skin off his back.

When asked why she offered to buy him lunch, her response was simply "I owe you for the table I passed off to you last week, you remember, the one with that annoying kid who kept asking for refills of cherry coke." Although bewilderment crept into his gut from the unexpected gesture, he wasn't about to pass up a free meal.

"Ok, thanks, I just didn't expect you to think about that, much less buy me lunch over it, but thank you." The fat blonde just shook her head and smiled. "No worries, I was thinkin' bout' doing Chinese take-out, that ok with you? I'm so tired of the food in this place."

They both laughed in agreement. "I know right! That's fine, I'm sick of burgers n' truffle fries too." When she returned, the first thing she handed him was her fortune cookie. The squat woman had never been one for sweets. Spice and savory were more to her liking. "I can't stand the way those things taste, here take mine."

"Ok sure thanks, they taste pretty good to me." With both hands he opened it up and immediately read the message hidden inside. The hardened dough split with a crack as he dug the slip out and held it up to the light. It said, "Follow the jade to find your truth." Jacob peered with skepticism at the piece of paper and then at his colleague. "What the hell's that supposed to mean?"

Later in the week he served a young couple that left him a generous tip. They were a chic and spirited pair. On their way out the husband asked Jacob what his religious beliefs were. Jacob was taken off-guard by the question, mostly because he was instructed as every server is, to never discuss religion or politics in the workplace. Management didn't want to risk some loose-mouthed waiter offending one of the guests with an ill-placed comment.

On this occasion Jacob decided to indulge the question. A hand fidgeted with his server's jacket as he replied. It was a nervous tick. The table had been so nice. He didn't want to be rude. "I'm not actually affiliated with any religion at the moment. They all have their merits. You and I both know it's a tough subject. I mean, every religion basically thinks they're right." The position was notable. Unexpected by his guests. "Interesting response, well I wasn't tryna' make you uncomfortable, just wondering. Anyway, here's a stone that may be of use to you, it's always brought me luck. You did a great job tonight by the way." They exchanged a few more words and then the evening was done. It had been a long day, but it was worth it.

CHAPTER 9

A POCKET FULL OF HOPE

Sometimes it's the smallest of gifts and gestures that count the most. They are often the ones that move us. Many times they are symbolic of something greater. In Jacob's case, the gift he'd been given didn't hold much meaning. At least not at the time.

The little stone was a greenish pale that reminded Jacob of marble. Its surface was smooth and clean. It had little white shattered lines running through it, which kind of resembled lightening dancing across a desert sky. An odd gift to say the least. Interesting, but odd. Jacob inspected it with faked interest as he stood by the tableside. The bill had already been presented. His guests would be departing soon.

"It's called a gratitude rock. Put it in your pocket and keep it with you. When you wake up in the mornings, try and remember to put it in your pocket. Before you go to sleep at night, remember not to leave it in your pants. Don't worry, I'm not crazy, there's a purpose to the madness Jacob."

"Ok, so what's the point if you don't mind me asking?" Jacob was confused. The patron could see bewilderment in the server's eyes and offered explanation. "The point's this, every time you touch the stone, try and think of the things you're grateful for. It's as simple as that. No matter how hard or bad you think your life is right now, there is always, and I do mean always *something* you can be grateful to have or to have experienced." It was an interesting proposal. Intrigued, Jacob nodded as he tucked the stone away.

"Seriously, you should try it. My wife and I have had amazing results." The guest spoke with confidence oozing in his voice. By this point there were only a few people remaining in the restaurant, which put Jacob's mind at ease a bit. The entire interaction felt unfamiliar. The less curious ears the better, especially those of management. They preferred the wait-staff not be involved in deep conversation. Bad for business. "That sounds pretty cool, thank you." "No problem, have a great evening Jacob." He was surprised the gentleman remembered his name, it made him feel special for the first time in months.

That being said, he didn't really think the patron's offer sounded cool at all. Jacob was just trying to be courteous, especially since he'd been left such a hefty tip. That night he wound up making over four hundred and seventy-five dollars, the majority of which came from the young couple with the stone.

They hadn't ordered nearly enough food and wine to justify such a large offering, but Jacob wasn't about to complain. On the ride home that evening he began to wonder why they had given him so much money. He hadn't done anything special or out of the ordinary for them.

Upon returning home he headed straight to his bedroom. A smile was on his face. What an odd yet enjoyable day it had been. As he began to unbuckle his pants he stopped suddenly, "Lemme' take my keys out right now, if I don't they'll be hell to find tomorrow." The clink of metal echoed over the distant voice of his mother talking on the phone in the kitchen.

He placed his weathered keys on the small table near his bed. Scratches and dents marked its surface. Careless mishaps. "I can't believe all this money I made, and all in one night!

This is awesome!" He began emptying his pockets, looking for any stray dollars that may have lost their way from the pack. Clumps of lint appeared, but no extra money.

"You dropped something." "Huh, oh hey dad, I'm changing." His father looked away to give his son some privacy. "Look at all this money I made today!" "That's great son, now you can pay for some of these groceries you keep eatin' up." Drake snickered and adjusted his glasses, they tended to slide down his nose from time to time.

"Why don't you reach down and pick up whatever it was that you dropped a moment ago? I know you had to hear it, that's how your room gets so messy in the first place." Eyes rolling and impatience on his breath, Jacob obliged his father. "Geez, between you and mom, you two are such neat freaks."

"Watch it!" "I'm just saying..." "So what is it you dropped?" "Huh, oh it's just some sort've rock this guy at work gave me." Drake made a face and then let out a snicker. "I hope that wasn't one of your tips?" "No, actually the guy that gave me it made my night as far as money. Without him I wouldn't have made half as much."

"Why the hell did he give you a rock though?" With a shrug Jacob replied, "It's a long story; I'll tell you tomorrow, I'm kind've tired." "Ok son, well, goodnight." The door shut with a thud. Jacob had no intention of bringing the subject back up; "He'll forget he even asked by tomorrow anyway."

He finished removing his clothes and then changed into his plaid cotton pajamas. With the small green stone now in his hand, Jacob remembered what the man told him earlier that evening. "So I just hold this and think about what I'm thankful for?"

Just as the words left his tongue a commercial came on the old TV screen depicting horrific hardship in some third world country. They were asking for anyone with a heart to give their support to the poor souls portrayed. It was that classic kind of commercial. The one with the insanely sad child crying. Standing on a porch, or in some desolate field. The type of commercial that leverages human sentiment against you.

"How cliché is that, what a load of crock. I guess I can be thankful I was born in the great US of A." Jacob tossed the green stone into a shadowed corner of the room. It bounced off the wall and landed on the floor next to his half-broken dresser. "I can find plenty I'm *not* thankful for, like this raggedy heap of shit called furniture" he thought.

CHAPTER 10

AN EMOTIONAL REALITY

The next day Jacob was greeted by a sore shin. The pain throbbed and clawed its way up the bone until it nipped at his kneecap. His injury was brought complements of slipping on the very stone he'd tossed into the corner the night before. "Damnit! I knew this piece of crap was gonna' be bad luck!" It was Friday, and Jacob had big plans for the upcoming weekend.

He met this really attractive woman at the grocery store earlier that week and asked her to dinner. To his delight she said yes without a moment's hesitation. She even seemed *eager* to go out with him, as if the honor was all hers. Jacob was excited about what the night could bring. He was 19. Being an introvert, he rarely drew the audacity to approach women in public. This was a pretty big moment for him. They scheduled dinner for 7pm.

As the hour approached, Jacob tried to recall how alluring and curvaceous she'd been in the store. She had the most voluptuous hips he'd ever seen. They were thick and pronounced, leading to a round, feathery soft butt that wobbled playfully as she walked. A thin waist just made it look more enticing. Even those that preferred a slimmer build couldn't help but to sneak a glance. Her hair was long. Her skin flawless. What's more, she seemed ecstatic that he asked her out. He could picture the huge grin that galloped across her face as he suggested they exchange numbers. Her white teeth nearly blinded him. What a perfect smile. "Tonight should prove interesting."

At about 6:32pm that evening his phone began to ring. He saved her number under a specific ringtone so he would know when she called. His voice crackled as he spoke into the line. Butterflies banged against the walls of his stomach. They made their way up his throat and settled on the tip of his tongue. "Hello? Oh hey. Umm, how, how are you doing?" As she answered he did his best to pull himself together. *Don't screw this up Jacob.* "I was just gettin' ready to head out that way. You ready?" As he spoke, Jacob lifted his keys from the nightstand and then grabbed the brown wallet sitting on his bed. He was ready to walk out the door. Being a few minutes late for work was one thing, but to leave a woman like *her* waiting? Never.

There was a pause on the other end of the line. A bad pause. "Um yea, about that. I actually had something come up and was just callin' to let you know I won' be able to make it tonight. Maybe we can hang out some other time. Sorry Jason." Her words were rushed, tainted by undertones of exasperation. He didn't really know what to say or how to react. What a letdown. "Umm. It's Jacob, but ok, so…?"

"What came up if I may ask?" Jacob struggled to hold the disappointment in his voice at bay. It crouched just behind his molars, pushing forward, then retreating, straining against his will to keep it back. "To be honest Jason… My boyfriend and I just had a huge argument and I just wanna' stay at home tonight. I'll probably try and call him later to work it out, but right now I'm kinda' pissed. Don't you hate how selfish guys can be sometimes? Why do we even deal with them?" The line was silent for a moment. In his head, Jacob was trying to piece together what he'd heard. It wasn't adding up.

"Your, your what? You're jokin' right?" "No, I thought I told you about him?" Jacob literally had to stop and look at the phone before he continued. He tossed the wallet back on the bed and ran his fingers through his hair in frustration. "Then what the hell was the point of giving me your number? And leading me on for that matter?" He heard a sigh, as if his questions annoyed her.

"You make it sound like you wanted to make a move or something; we can hang out some other time Jason. I'm sure you have some other guys you can step out with. The night's still young." There was another long pause. It was drenched with awkwardness. "Again, it's Jacob… I'm so confused right now, why do you think I asked you for your number to begin with?" The young lady thought for a moment. Then it struck her. "Wait a minute, oh my God! Shit. This is *so* embarrassing. So, you're not?" "What? What is it? Not what?" "Nothing, wow!" The level of confusion pushed Jacob over the edge.

"Just tell me what it is! What the honest fuck is going on? Seriously." "I'm so embarrassed right now. I'm so sorry Justin." "It's *Jacob* and just tell me, what're you talking about?" "When I saw you in the store, I just... I mean you looked. I thought you were gay..." The ghostly silence that followed was maddening. It swallowed the conversation whole. Jacob was at a loss for words. The unintended insult cut at the threads of his ego. It cut deep.

That night was a lonely one. He couldn't believe what he'd just heard. "She thought I was gay? Gay, really?" It almost made him feel like sitting in his room and weeping. But somehow it felt like doing so would add validity to her view. He stood at the bathroom sink and peered at his reflection. What a slap in the face. Critical eyes stared back at him, trying to see what she had seen. "Do I look gay? Is that what women see when they look at me?" He tried to reenact the interaction he'd had. "Maybe if I retrace my steps, I can see what the hell she's talking about." It didn't work.

For nearly thirty minutes Jacob tried to replay his every movement, yearning to dissect what feminine characteristics he must've given off. "This is retarded; she was just a dumbass girl anyway. Who cares what she thinks?" The words felt empty as they left his lips. They were fake. He *did* care what she thought. Why wouldn't he? Any man would. She, in that moment represented *all* women to him. And she was hot, really hot. That only added venom to the sting.

The next day he arose feeling more lethargic than usual. It probably had something to do with the disgraceful experience he'd endured about fifteen hours prior. His body was made of cement. Aches rumbled through his joints. They mostly settled in his arms and upper shoulders. His back was stiff, and the accompanying migraine did nothing but exacerbate his discomfort.

"Why am I feeling like this?" There was a sort of comical scenario that began playing in his head. "Could I be pregnant? Is it my period?" Jacob chuckled a little at the notion as he threw on a pair of jeans and t-shirt. His footsteps creaked on the worn carpet covering ancient floorboards. "If everyone else is gonna' laugh at me, I might as well get a good one in too."

That day was like the previous in that it did not go well. To start, Jacob looked at his bank account on the family computer. He wanted to see if a recent deposit had cleared. They usually took no more than three days or so. As he clicked login after entering his username and password, his ego took another hit. The homepage screen where his balance usually showed, had a negative number in parenthesis.

Directly below the negative balance there were flashing red letters that said, "Your account is in the negative, please call us immediately to make arrangements or to discuss options that may be available." "How's that possible? Lemme' call this damn bank, these crooks are always trying to get away with charging someone a fee. Probably put their snobby kids through Harvard thanks to em'. Crooks." Jacob picked up his cell phone with a shaky hand and began to dial the number to his local branch.

"We're sorry, but the service for this mobile device has been temporarily disconnected due to one or more missed payments. Please contact your service provider to bring your account current." He almost thought he heard a hint of pleasure in the robotic voice as the message came through. "That's just great, anything else? Like seriously, is there *anything* else?"

He shook his head in disgust and stormed down the hallway of the small apartment leading to the family's kitchen. Mounted on the wall near one of the old wooden cabinets was a landline that was rarely used. "I guess I'm gonna' have to go old-school and use the home phone." The telephone felt awkward and clunky in his hands.

Some buttons had actually accumulated dust from sitting stagnant for so long. Jacob once again dialed the numbers, wiping residue off the buttons as he went. "Thank you for calling HTA Bank, please enter your social security number followed by the pound sign." The female voice was dry and rehearsed. Jacob entered his number, his fingers slipping on the last digit. "We're sorry, but the number you entered was invalid. Please enter your social security number followed by the pound sign." After three failed attempts Jacob's frustration came to a head. It was just one thing after another.

He decided to just press 0 until someone human answered. Such an annoyance. Customer service seemed to be a thing of the past. After being on hold for nearly seventeen minutes he was greeted by a drab voice on the other end. Those seventeen minutes felt like an hour. "Thank you for calling HTA Bank, where we make banking needs and financial dreams a reality. This is Jennifer, how can I help you?"

Her voice drug painfully slow across the telephone line as she spoke. It was like each word was a struggle. Jacob was just happy to speak with a live person. “Yes, I was calling to see why my bank account says it’s over-drafted online? I know I just put like three hundred and something in there a couple days ago. This happened to me like a month ago and I had to get the manag-.” “Sir, Sir, OK.”

Before Jacob could finish he was rudely cut off by the impatient representative. Every client had a sob story. Especially the ones that over-drafted. “Ok sir, before you start I need to verify some information here on my end. I don’t even have your account pulled up yet. Now, what is your social security number?” Before answering Jacob needed to get something off his chest. “That’s another thing; the stupid woman on the automated system wouldn’t even accept my social.” The representative decided to completely ignore his comment. At 15 dollars an hour, she didn’t have the patience to listen to another second.

“What is your social security number sir? And your date of birth? And lastly can you verify the answer to the following security question. What is the name of the street where you grew up?” “Florence Avenue.” There was a pause. “I’m sorry, but your answer to the security question is incorrect.” He could hear a note of malicious pleasure in her tone, tucked beneath the guise of faked professionalism. The worst type. She was really starting to get under his skin. It seemed like the day was just throwing him an unending stream of hurdles.

“What do you mean the answer to the question’s wrong? That’s the answer! That’s the name of the street! I mean I *would* know, it was me who grew up there!” “Raising your voice isn’t gonna’ change the fact that I can’t provide you with any information on the account until you’ve been properly verified Sir. If you’d like, you’re welcome to come into the branch with a proper government issued picture id, we can verify you that way."

Jacob couldn't figure it out. Why things were going so wrong for him lately. It seemed like every time he looked up there was something else to get annoyed with, a constant thorn pricking at every turn. As he walked out of the bank later that day, he thought about how well the week had started off. He made all that money, one of his colleagues bought him lunch, and then things just went downhill from there.

As he was thinking about the money made from that one table, Jacob was reminded of the jade gratitude stone he was given. Its concept reminded him of an experiment he did in one of his science classes. Back in high school. In it the teacher instructed the students to gather several glasses of water and label each with an emotion.

The emotions ranged from hatred to love, and each group oversaw three emotions within that spectrum. Jacob's group got the feelings of love, joy, and gratitude. The instructor told each group to spend twenty minutes a day for a week focusing on the emotions associated with the words written on their glasses. At the end of the week the teacher took all the glasses, labels still intact, and placed them in the lab's freezer.

When the students returned that following Monday, the instructor had them pull their glasses of frozen water out and inspect the icy crystals under a microscope. What they observed was amazing. The crystals for all the negative emotions were deformed and incongruent. Twisted shards and broken shapes met their eyes as they looked through the magnified lense.

The positive emotions told a different story however. Jacob's group held the most beautiful and complex crystals of the entire class. They concluded that projection of emotion directly impacted physical reality, in this case the physiology of the water. Throughout his life Jacob never forgot that experiment and the lesson it taught.

CHAPTER 11

FROM THE STILLNESS

The Sunday following Jacob's incident with the bank he awoke without the aid of his alarm clock. Young slivers of sunlight preceded the day, peaking through cracks in a clouded sky until they seeped between slits in the blinds and tickled at the back of his neck. When he looked over, the time read 6:29a.m. Although LED and digital, it was a bit beat up from one too many tumbles to the floor. The number nine on its screen blinked every few seconds. It didn't matter. He didn't need it that morning anyway. He felt like he was on autopilot. His body was acting without having to think. His sub-conscious decided he would see Mr. Lao again. He got to the park a few minutes earlier than the last time they met.

It was drizzling, but the drops were heavy. Jacob decided to sit in the car for a few minutes in hopes the rain would subside. Bubbles of water splashed against his windshield in intermittent thuds. The car's tattered wipers did little to repel them, try as they may. After five minutes passed, he saw Mr. Lao seemingly appear from nowhere, as the angelic elder tended to do. He was wearing his usual attire of white robes and brown leather strapped sandals. The rain gave way as he approached. It seemed to fall lighter with every step he took.

By the time he made it to the parking lot only a few droplets greeted his glabrous head.

Jacob exited the car and traipsed to meet the graceful man before him. He greeted him with a wave and broad smile that stretched from one side of his face to the other. "Hello Mr. Lao, well, I'm here." Ming Lao said nothing, he just gave a slight smile and led the way towards the huge stone they met at before. A graceful stride added venerational flare to the elder's sublime presence. Kind eyes looked over his young apprentice as they made their way down the short trail. Patches of soft Earth gave way under their footsteps, tracking their journey to the outdoor temple.

Jacob followed Mr. Lao to the large stone and sat a few feet away. The pupil crossed his legs and began to breathe deeply, following Mr. Lao's lead. He didn't know why he was there; he didn't know why the man initially invited him or what he was supposed to be learning. One thing was certain, he knew he was here to learn *something*. That was for sure.

Some part of him was attracted to the thought of silence. Whether due to the constant noise back at the apartment, or a distraction from the chaos of his own mind, he didn't know. Somehow, he found peace in sitting still in the rain, in feeling the drops fall lightly against his face as the weather picked back up a bit.

His breath began to slow along with his pulse. Each inhale seemed to melt into the next exhale. Jacob was no longer aware of time, or the rain, or even of the people that passed by, observing with confused interest. He was unbothered by mosquitos as they eagerly fed. And the crying child that had long come and gone with her mother.

Stillness engulfed the noise, leaving him more in tune with life than he'd ever been. It swallowed him and left him cradled in its throat. A cocoon. The wind no longer brushed stiffly against his skin. Light gusts massaged at his shoulders and rubbed sore joints until placid. The stone beneath him surrendered its hardness. Nature invited him in. It kissed and hugged. Everything was welcome. Rain was sweat. And the call of a hawk's screech in the distance felt as familiar as his own voice.

Jacob noticed his face was starting to tingle. It began in the center of his nose and worked its way outward. After a few moments his entire upper body seemed to be absolutely vibrating with energy, and it scared him. As he became more and more aware of the unfamiliar sensation it began to retreat, as if shooed away. Raw energy resides in the subconscious. The crevasses between thoughts. His awareness was pulling him from its power. He slowly withdrew from his meditative state and became more alert to his surroundings.

His eyes took their time regaining focus. Once they did, they looked over in the direction of his mentor in matters of the mind. Ming Lao was still deep in meditation. Jacob could sense it. Deciding it best not to disturb the old man, he retreated quietly after admiring how sublime and peaceful Mr. Lao looked. When Jacob got to his car the first thing he did was check the time on the radio.

He was shocked to discover it was almost four in the afternoon! He'd arrived at the park before seven that morning. The sun was now out, radiating warm rays between fluffy pillows in the sky. He didn't even notice the change in temperature. The rain had dried up hours ago. "Really, I was sitting on that rock for that long?" Jacob looked at his phone and saw two missed calls and a voicemail. All were from his mother. The voicemail revealed she wanted him to pick up a movie she'd been waiting for on Redbox. Normally he would've been annoyed by a request like this, but after his session with Mr. Lao, he didn't seem to mind as much.

His mind felt lighter, like there was less to worry about. Actually, it felt kind of like there was *nothing* to worry about.

This was despite his recent run-in with the bank, the one in which he incurred almost seventy dollars in overdraft fees. The check engine light on his car activated a few minutes after leaving the park, but even this didn't seem to faze him. He picked up the movie from the nearest Redbox and headed home with a smile on his face. Traffic was light. The drive was pleasant. This feeling of careless freedom was unfamiliar, but he liked it. He wondered what sitting on a rock all day had to do with his new-found state of mind.

"Thanks for the movie Jacob. Do you wanna' watch it with us? We're starting it around six." He shook his head. A hand waved. "No thanks. I'm just gonna' clean my room mom, it's pretty messy in there." For the first time in years, Jacob made the offer without having to be threatened or otherwise coaxed into doing so.

It just made sense to him at that moment. How could he feel good about himself if every time he went into his room all he saw was trash everywhere? As Ming Lao taught him how to clean up his mind, he was simultaneously teaching *himself* how to tend to his physical surroundings as well.

The teen started by sorting the dirty clothes scattered about away from the ones that were supposedly clean. After a few minutes of consideration, he decided they all could use a good washing. There was a funk that seemed to linger, item to item. Maria snuck a peripheral peek as her son took a handful of shirts and pants and headed over to the small washroom across the hallway.

He caught a glimpse of his mother as she whispered something to Drake. The TV was on so he only heard the last few words, "Took our son and replaced him." He smiled and went back to his room to gather another round. As he picked them up a light thud drew his attention. It sounded like a marble being dropped.

Jacob looked down to see the jade stone the man offered

to him in the restaurant the prior week. It was the couple that had showered him in tips. He tossed the clothes into a basket and picked the stone up with a careful hand, subconsciously hoping the fall hadn't damaged it. Without realizing it, he began to ponder back on the things he was grateful for. The ideas that came to mind surprised him.

The first thing that came to mind was Mr. Lao. More importantly, what the old man was teaching him. This had only been his second or third session with the elder, and there wasn't much that was said between them, but the monk was teaching him something nonetheless. The man held a halo. An aura that surrounded him and filled his breath with wisdom. Meditation only amplified the experience for Jacob.

Jacob thought back to how he felt sitting on that stone earlier in the day. He felt, timeless. It was a sensation that was indescribable, its very essence elusive in nature. More than the sense of timelessness was the feeling of being on the precipice of Knowing. Knowing what? He hadn't a clue, but in his soul Jacob could feel that a few more of these sessions on the stone would reveal an answer.

Sitting with Mr. Lao was deeply fulfilling. His first time going to see the man he went in skeptical, and this pinched him off from the connection he was able to experience this time around. This time he knew what to expect and was mentally better prepared.

Jacob still had questions for Mr. Lao. He wanted to ask him why he had chosen *him*? What did both he and Jacob have to gain by them meditating? The most important question he had was also the most disturbing. The question had been on Jacob's mind for some time. It just seemed to make sense to ask Mr. Lao. After all, the old man seemed pretty in tune with himself. Jacob decided the next time he went to the park he would ask his mentor if they could talk for a while before they began meditation.

CHAPTER 12

NOTHING WAS THE SAME

The quickened thud of an unsure heart was echoed by lungs that couldn't quite hold air. His inner voice rambled in chaotic disbelief. Could this possibly be real? Was he having another one of those fantastically scenic dreams he'd come to know so well? No, this was not a dream, this was happening right now! Jacob checked and rechecked the numbers on the slip between his trembling fingers.

"Ok, ok, this is happening, this is happening right now!" Jacob thought, well more like screamed in his head. He felt his legs go languid and his vision blear to a fog. Words formed at his mouth's edge but didn't seem to want to come out. His sister had just walked past his doorway on the way to the bathroom. The creaks in the floorboards announced her approach. "What's wrong with you Jacob, like honestly? You're so weird; no wonder you don't have a girlfriend." She shook her head and continued on her way.

For several minutes he just stood there in a frozen stupor. He must have looked absolutely rediculous, judging by the look his sister had given him. "Could this be real? Did this actually just happen?" When Jacob's legs finally regained vitality he hobbled over to his twin-sized bed and plopped on the edge, nearly toppling over in the process. The old mattress moaned under the weight of his shocked body.

He peered at the numbers on the TV once more. Then back at the slip in his hands. Maybe his eyes were deceiving him. No, no they weren't. The numbers matched. Just to be sure, Jacob decided to call the local office for the lottery and speak with one of their representatives directly. He wanted to hear it come from someone's mouth.

Sweaty fingers reached for his old cell phone and searched for the number in his contacts list. He remembered saving it there, just in case he ever actually won. His optimism seemed well placed. The day had finally come. "There it is!" Jacob scrolled down on his screen to the contact titled, "Lotto Winner." He pressed the button.

"Welcome to the North Carolina Lottery hotline. Our hours of operation are from 9am until 5:30pm Eastern time. For the current winning lottery numbers press, 1. If you would like to speak with a representative press, 2. If you or someone you know has a gambling problem, please call 1-800-HELP-NOW." Jacob pressed 2.

After a few minutes of listening to some uninspired hold music, a young woman's voice moseyed over the line. She couldn't have been more than 25. "Thank you for calling the NC State Lottery, this is Michelle, how can I help you?" "Yes um, Hi." "How can I help you Sir?" Jacob struggled not to fumble his words. He shifted the cellphone to his other hand and drew a deep breath. His heart wouldn't stop thumping. It felt like it was going to fall out of his chest.

"Oh yea, sorry, what um, what're the winning numbers for the jackpot?" There was a short silence on the other end. He could hear the woman sigh with impatience as she tried to maintain composure. She obviously didn't like her job. Most idiots calling in asked questions they could've easily found online. The irony was, if they did, her position would no longer be needed. It was a lesson she, like so many others, would never learn. "What date Sir?" "Huh?" "What date, what date are you referring to?" "Never-mind its ok."

He decided to click off before the rep could respond. He could barely speak and knew the young lady didn't have much patience. He placed the old phone on his bed and just sat there. With inspiration naturally coursing through his veins even as a child, Jacob always imagined that on this day he would be leaping from his skin.

He was sure he would be exclaiming his victory to the world in a situation like this. No outbursts of joy sprung forth however. He was happy, no doubt about that. But the realization also left him speechless. Shocked really. It was like an out of body experience. Unreal. In a matter of mere moments, his life was changed forever. This was real change. Not just a new car or house. This, this was a generational shift.

That night Jacob lay in his bed, sleep taunted him here and there, but never stayed around for long. An occasional thud from movement in the apartment above kept him company. Music could be heard in the background. It thumped at a steady beat. Residents of the complex frequently hung in the parking lot until the wee hours of morning. Their presence was almost always echoed by the smell of weed and the whop of hip hop. Every hour, on the hour, he would pull his blanket from over his head and look over at the rickety clock that was the demise of many good dreams.

"7am, only two more hours to go. And if I take a really long shower, only an hour and forty-eight minutes!" The hot water never lasted long in the tired apartment. At 8:27 his hand brushed the sheets from his body. He sat up and looked around the room. He peered at the jade stone sitting on the dresser. Wobbly legs walked over to the television, a sleepy arm extended. In his excitement he'd forgotten to turn it off the night before and didn't even notice until now. Only one thing was on his mind. The ticket.

His room was dreary, but not even the bleakest Siberian night could bring his spirits down this morning. Nothing except... A sickening feeling overcame Jacob. His stomach churned in his abdomen as his mouth dried up. Where was the ticket? He kept it held securely in his hand all night. Could he have dropped it? Maybe it was buried somewhere in the blankets? No, he looked everywhere, it was gone. "Gone!? How is that possible?" He kept it all night and then it just disappeared? Jacob stormed into his sister's room. No movement. She was fast asleep. "If not her then who?" What had he done last night? The frantic wreck desperately tried to retrace his steps.

He turned his pockets inside out, tearing at the fabric when nothing appeared. After rechecking everywhere he could think to look, he started to worry, "maybe it was a dream." Jacob plopped back on the bed and folded his arms, feeling overcome with grief. "It was a fucking dream! It was so real though?" What a punch to the gut. The feelings felt so real. Even the dream with the parrot hadn't felt that real. His mind was playing tricks on him. "Who was I kidding, I was never gonna' win."

With a sudden outburst he cursed aloud, grabbing the old sheets from his bed and thrusting them violently at the adjacent wall in a fit. Out the corner of his eye he saw a small white image float to the floor after being disturbed by the ruckus. It reminded him of a leaf falling from an old tree after summer's end. He turned his head and sighed with relief. It was the ticket!

Allayed, Jacob placed it safely in his wallet and then

tucked them both beneath his pillow while he showered. The bathroom he shared with his sister was tight and narrow. There wasn't much room to move around, but he and Myra made do. Clutter further constrained the hemmed space. Most of the debris was due to his sister's incessant infatuation with makeup and perfumes. There were bottles of all shapes and sizes. All systematized in chaotic glory. It was a girl's delight. For Jacob, not so much. More of a headache than anything else. There was barely enough room for any of his stuff. Women.

He grabbed his washcloth and stepped under the showerhead. Rubber padding on the tub's floor gave footing. He turned the water to max-heat, and then pulled the little lever so the faucet would come on. For several minutes he just stood there, letting droplets beat firmly against his skin. The steam building in the enclosed room soothed him. It also helped open his sinuses, offsetting the sleepless night he'd just endured.

After about six minutes he began to wash his body. A wet hand grabbed the marbled green bar of Irish soap that sat near the edge of the tub. He began to lather his tattered washcloth and enjoyed the fresh spring scent that followed. He stopped for a moment and mused, "I don' think I've ever noticed how amazing this soap actually smells!"

With a slight chuckle under his breath, the cloth began to rub along his skin starting with his arm and moving towards his shoulder and neck. Blobs of foam washed down his legs and gathered at the drain. After he was finished cleaning he knelt down and squatted on the bathtub floor. His head was held low as the water fell over him. It felt like warm rain. Streams ran down the sides of his face, making their way to his lips and chin. Seven minutes passed by. His gazed turned north. Something had caught his eye. Furry drain flies clung to the walls, hanging on for dear life. They were fighting against the onslaught of droplets spattered in every direction. One had fluttered just above his head. A reminder of how far the family had fallen. Soon, they would be a thing of the past.

By this point the heat was beginning to wear off and Jacob decided it was about time to get out. As he turned the nozzle off, he heard a heavy knock at the door that made him flinch. "Jacob, I thought I told you last night bout' this room of yours?" The floorboards gave away his mother's position. She was headed back down the hallway.

Her voice reverberated through the door and up Jacob's spine. She was complaining yet again about the mess that never seemed to *fully* rectify itself. "I'm washing clothes so I'll take your sheets, but I expect this room to be done by the time they're ready to go back on your bed. You hear me in there? I thought you cleaned up last night?"

Jacob did hear her. In fact her words were more alarming now than ever. If she was washing sheets, that meant she'd be taking the pillowcase as well. That also meant she would see the wallet under the pillow. Surely, his mother would find it curious he decided to leave it there. She was a natural investigator. It would definitely stand out.

Jacob barreled from the bathroom half naked and made a sprint for his room. His still-wet body mottled droplets down the entire hallway. He almost ran straight into his mother, startling her in the process. Disapproving eyes scanned the trail her son had made. "What's gotten into you boy? You been actin' strange these last few days. You're not hooked on drugs are you?" The towel around his waist loosened, nearly falling off until his hand swooped up to catch it. "What? No mom! I'm not a fiend, I just wish you'd respect my privacy. And not go snoopin' around my room!"

She snapped her fingers as if to have an epiphany.

"That's what it is; you've lost your damn mind! It's gotta' be that with you speaking to me like that. Lemme' tell you something you little runt." One hand was on her hip and she used her other to shake a minacious finger in his face. It waved like a sword. Time to reel things back in. "Until your name is on the lease, no room in this house is *your* room." "It's an apartment," Jacob smartly mumbled under his breath. "What was that? Drake get in here and straighten out your son fore' I slap him into next week! Boy dun lost his damn mind!"

Jacob quickly closed and locked his door before he could see what would happen next. He walked over to his bed, lifted the pillow slowly, and held his breath. His wallet thankfully still sat there, safe and sound. The excited and slightly nervous young man put on his clothes and left without saying a word. Even though he'd overstepped his bounds, it didn't matter. The ticket would change everything.

He drove with purpose yet took care not to get pulled over for speeding. At a stop light a few miles from the complex, Jacob decided to take one more look at the ticket. Just to make sure it was real. His mind drifted. He was wondering what the headquarters for the lottery would look like. Eyes stared off into the distance. Seconds ticked by. Then suddenly, a loud thud yanked his attention back, it had come from behind. His car jerked forward and then stopped just as abruptly. "What the hell? What just happened?" The light had turned green and a car with two teenagers unwittingly rear ended him. "Great," he thought, "No biggie I'll just buy another car. Or ten." His clunker was a rolling trashcan anyway.

"Yo bro you gotta' problem or somethin? You know green means go, right? What an idiot!" Under normal circumstances Jacob would have taken a more passive approach. But these weren't normal circumstances. He was rich now. Arrogance sat defiantly on the tip of his tongue, lashing its tail as it saw fit. Anger welled up from the dungeons inside. These guys were beneath him. He let his mouth run free.

"Look dude, you ran into me first off, so that would make you the idiot. Secondly, I'll just buy you a new car, looks like you could use the upgrade. How bout' that?" The angry teen didn't take kindly to Jacob's contumaciousness. Neither did his friend. "Look at *your* car guy. You do know you're in a fuckin' Honda right? This asshole thinks he's rich or somethin. And he's in this busted ass Honda. Ha!"

The passenger exited the car and paced over to Jacob. He was much bigger than his friend. Broad shoulders supported arms the size of tree trunks. There was a frown on his face. Jacob was in trouble. "You gotta' pretty smart mouth dude, who's to say I don't sock you in that hole of yours right now for not showing some respect?" "Hey Guy! Your idiot friend just ran into *me*! Why the hell should I show respect? Respect what? Two broke bitches who can't even look where they're driving? Peons." Looking back, Jacob's ego wished that's how the story ended. As the adage alludes, "You can wish in one hand, and shit in the other. See which fills up first."

CHAPTER 13

GONE WITH THE WIND

Jacob awoke to an incredibly sore jaw. It ached and throbbed with pain. As he came to, the pangs only intensified. It was like having an exposed nerve on a bad tooth and jabbing at it with a rusted nail until your head explodes. He was lying on the side of the road right behind his car. As he sat up in a blurred stupor, looking around, he noticed he was at a small traffic intersection. The light was red and people were staring out their vehicles at him.

None offered to help, but a few began recording with their phones. This was definitely the type of thing that could go viral online. His onlookers wanted to capitalize. Jacob was confused, how had he gotten there? As he rose to his feet and hobbled around his car to the driver's side, it dawned on him. The broken red glass from the busted left taillight brought it all back. "But how did I end up on the ground? On the other end of the car?"

As a numb hand opened the car door he remembered the two punks that confronted him. Jacob didn't think they had fought; he knew the driver didn't do anything but talk. Then like a war veteran having flashbacks, he remembered. The second passenger had punched and apparently knocked him out for running his mouth. He must have been knocked out cold. His attackers were long gone.

Dizziness lingered from a headache looming behind his ears. It's thump left him hazy, eager to get home. He turned the key in the ignition and started to pull back onto the street. Something was wrong. Jacob felt naked somehow. The only time he ever felt like this was when he walked out of the house and forgot either his cell phone or his...

"My wallet! It's gone! Those mother f. They, those assholes really robbed me!" He was in total disbelief. Panic set in, he could feel each pump of his heart as it roiled in his chest. He hadn't gotten any of their information either. In his arrogance he'd forgotten to even get their names! How would he find them? He had to call the police. Do something. "911 Emergency, do you need Fire, Medic, or Police?"

"Police! Please, get me the police, I need help!" "What's the issue sir?" "I need to report a robbery, and a hit and run." "Are you injured? And where are you now?" "No, I mean yes, but not from the hit and run. I just need a cop to get here now ok!" The operator did her best to calm the frantic voice on the other end. "I understand you're upset sir, but you need to give me an address before I can send anyone out. Now again, what's your location?"

After Jacob told the officer that arrived about what happened, he asked how often people like his attackers were caught. The cop leaned against his cruiser while he answered, notepad in hand, only a few lines with ink. With no cameras to sniff the perps out, there wasn't much information to gather. The onlookers had scattered with the light's change. No witnesses either. The notepad flipped shut with the flick of a wrist. The case was over before it got started. "Almost never son, fact of the matter is, there are 2 million people living in this city, and another twenty thousand visit each week. Those thugs could be anyone walking the street. You'd have about as much luck finding them as you would winning the lottery."

Jacob left the part about having the ticket stolen from the police report. He wisely figured information like that might be kept safer in the shadows of ignorance. A low paid and under-appreciated police officer may become tempted if they ever ran into the two assailants. It was a wise choice in discretion.

When Jacob finally made it home he went straight to his room and shut the door. He went to bed that night without eating a single bite of dinner. His stomach would've refuted whatever was offered anyway. It twisted and rung itself until acid made its way up his throat. "That must be the new Guinness world record for rags to riches and back to rags." It took all of a few short hours for him to go from being in shock after gaining everything, to being in shock for the opposite reason. *He had to find those bastards.*

The next morning's sunlight waded boldly through the tree-line surrounding the complex. Rays sapped dew from blades and leaves in short order, quaffing droplets up like they were thirsty. Once the orb made its journey to the halfway mark, the sky really opened up, dousing low hanging Cumulus clouds in waves of warmth that melted them away. A lemon-yellow day. This did nothing to raise Jacob's spirits however. The ticket that was going to change everything had been stolen, and all because he couldn't keep his mouth shut. He was too cocky. And it cost him the world. He began to wonder whether the two guys would realize they were now holding a winning ticket worth over a quarter billion dollars before taxes. The mere thought made his throat tighten.

"Hey Jacob! I'm makin' eggs n' bacon; you want *two* or three eggs?" His mother was in the small kitchen finishing up Drake's two Sunny-side ups and readying the frying pan for another round. He waved her off. "I'm fine mom, I'm just gonna' grab something on my way to the park." Jacob was on his way to see Ming Lao. He needed to clear his head. Food was the last thing on his mind. Mr. Lao would surely know what to do.

When Jacob pulled into the parking lot there were only two other cars there. One was an older Honda, even older looking than his, and the other, an SUV. For some odd reason the SUV looked kind of familiar. Jacob thought maybe it belonged to a friend or something. Then it dawned on him. The hairs on his arms stood up in unison. As he walked along the side of the vehicle towards the front, he saw something that stopped him dead in his tracks. It was like being zapped into the twilight zone. The odds were like one in a million. He had to be the luckiest person on Earth.

Before Jacob's eyes lay a busted headlight. The SUV was obviously involved in an accident. There was burgundy paint ingrained into the car's bumper all around the impact area. Jacob recognized the color of the paint all too well; it was the same color as the paint missing off the back of his own car! Blood revved through his veins as adrenaline began to pump. He couldn't believe it! It was almost like his luck was going through a schizophrenic episode. His first inclination was to scour the park for the perps and teach them a lesson. After recalling his previous encounter with the pair, he thought better of this.

Hurried legs rushed back to his car with newfound life. "This may be the only shot I have to get that money back. They couldn't have cashed the check yet, otherwise they wouldn't be at the park. They may not even know they have it!" Scenarios bounced from one end of his brain to the other like an intense ping pong match. With his body on autopilot his mind was free to writhe with both fury and relief.

He wasn't thinking straight. Jacob's car screeched into his neighborhood and then veered into the nearest parking space. The tail-end was hanging in the next space over. It didn't matter. There was no time. He made a dash for the door but then had to double back once he realized his keys were still in the ignition.

Only one thing was on his mind... The frantic young man knew his father had an old revolver he kept in a safe box on the side of the bed. He also knew it would be incredibly hard to get, with both his mom and dad still present in the cramped apartment. They had eyes in the back of their heads. "How can I get to that gun?" He knew what had to be done. Somehow he would have to get them to leave, and he had to do it fast if he wanted to catch those guys. If they left the park before he got back, they'd be gone forever.

Jacob racked his brain for ideas. What would get both his parents to leave, without any suspicions aroused? He had a thought. He knew their anniversary was coming up soon. It wasn't uncommon for his sister and him to ask them to stay in their room while the siblings prepared gifts. He'd have to try that approach and pray it worked.

"Hey mom, dad, I know I've been acting kinda' strange recently, but there's an explanation for all of it. I kinda' went all out for the two of you this year for your anniversary. That's why I didn't want you to go near my room earlier yesterday mom. And well, there's *one* more thing I hafta' do, but I need both of you to leave for a little bit so I can get it done."

His parents looked at each other and then at him with a shrug. "Ok son, for how long are we talking here?" His plan seemed to be working. No suspicion was aroused. It took everything he had to maintain composure. Inside he was screaming. Every second counted. "Only like ten minutes or so, that's it." "Ok" Maria said. You do know our anniversary isn't until *next* week right?" "Yeah mom, but like I said, this'll be one to remember. But for it to work I need both of you to leave, now!"

"Ok Jacob, just give us a couple…" It was only on rare occasions that Jacob had the audacity to interrupt his parents while they were speaking. This was one of those moments. "I need you to leave now ok! Just take a romantic walk in the parking lot or somethin', please just trust me!" He waved his hands impatiently while Drake and his mother looked on with confused expressions. His parents left the apartment reluctant but compliant, completely dull to the true intentions of their determined son.

He scurried to the back room and opened the door. Jacob could see them walking down the sidewalk through the window. He was sure they would see him if they looked back, so he ducked down and began to crawl on his hands and knees. His face was close to the carpet. The smell of mold was muted, but only by an intense funk wafting off one of Drake's discarded socks. It punched him in the nose as he swung his head, looking around.

When he got over to his father's side of the bed he began to search for the black safe-box. It was usually left unlocked. After a minute or two of rummaging through some clothes left on the floor, he found it. For its size the box was surprisingly heavy. Its skeleton was constructed of compressed steel. Grey and black polymer finishes covered the container's cold surface.

Jacob took a deep breath, "This thing better be unlocked." If it wasn't, he was in trouble. The trip back home would've been for naught. Just wasted time. He extended his arm and tried to lift the lever that held the top latched to the bottom. It opened easily, and he let out a sigh of relief. The box held a vintage Smith and Wesson revolver with a picture of a man riding a horse etched into the metal on one side.

The handle had a Burlwood finish that was smooth to the touch. When Jacob lifted the solidly heavy gun and looked down the sights, he noticed there were no bullets in any of the five chambers. He looked in the box. No ammunition there either. He would have to hope the mere sight of a drawn weapon would be enough. One way or another, he had to get that ticket back.

"Hey Jacob? We're back!" Their son jumped with surprise and tucked the gun into his pants and then pulled down his shirt as he heard the front door close behind them. "Hold on, two more seconds!" It was too late; they were already in the kitchen. Luckily, they were having one of their "romantic hugs" and seemed too preoccupied to take notice of the bulge protruding from his clothing.

He took advantage of the situation and ducked out of the apartment and back over to his car. After taking one more look at the busted taillight, Jacob sped back to the parking lot where he saw the SUV. When he arrived, it was still there along with a few other cars. *Thank God.* Jacob hurried out into the park to search for the bandits. He started near the kid's swing set and worked his way over to the man-made pond. About two thirds of the way through, he saw them.

They were standing near a tree with two teenage girls. All the adolescents seemed to be smoking something. As Jacob approached, the stench of bad weed pinched at his nose. It hung like sweat from armpits. Light breezes fanned fumes over the surrounding area, causing that section of the park to smell like a frat-house. The guy who had been driving the car recognized him first. Their eyes locked. Jacob's gaze was determined. His adversary could see it.

He dropped his blunt and his face curled into a look of both fear and surprise. The perp gestured to his friend and told the two girls to get lost. They left without protest; it seemed they could sense trouble to come. "You! You didn't get enough the last time I knocked your ass out?" The hoodlum took a few deliberate steps forward. His friend followed suit.

Jacob held his hands up as he replied, he figured trying to resolve the matter peacefully would be best. He could only hope the two men held the same sentiment. From the looks of things, it didn't seem like it. One thing was for sure, he planned to get what he'd come for. 250 Million was worth the risk. "I don't want any trouble guys; I just want my wallet back. That's it." Inside Jacob was praying his cool demeanor would have the intended effect. His prayers would go un-answered. He was gonna have to use force. Their body language said it all. Neither of them were gonna back down without a fight.

The lack of fear the larger of the two displayed seemed to give the driver more courage. He laughed confidently, a smirk dashing from ear to ear, "He wants his wallet back! What for? You didn't have any money in there anyway? Oh, wait there was a measly five in there. Big bucks for the big talker." The two guys began to laugh heartily, then the larger one walked up to Jacob defiantly, ready to serve up another knuckle sandwich.

Before the guy could get within range Jacob lifted his shirt to reveal the pistol. He wanted to show he meant business. There wasn't gonna be a repeat of the other day. Not this time. At first, the teen didn't see the weapon. After a few seconds his eyes widened and he began to back away cautiously with his hands raised. The tough-guy façade was gone. A pumped-out chest deflated. He took another step back. "Yo dude, this kid's gotta' piece bro!" Jacob's palm moved threateningly towards the handle. His eyes were trained on the thug.

"That's right, and I'm gonna' use it if you two don't gimme' back my damn wallet. I don't care about the money, I just want the wallet." The perp stuttered nervously as he spoke. You could tell he was scared. His deep voice had given way. Every other word crackled as it left his lips. It was his first time being on the business end of a barrel. "What, what do ya' care? There was no money in there. I mean, well besides that measly five bucks? All this over 5 dollars?"

"I have my reasons. Now where is it?" "It's in the car dude just chill out. Put that away. You're takin' this way too serious." The three of them walked back to the parking lot with Jacob trailing slightly behind. He wanted to keep them in his sights just in case they tried anything stupid.

After a few minutes they made it back to the lot and the driver of the SUV reached in his jeans to get the keys. "Hey, easy there, what're you reaching for?" "Dude, chill out," there was a note of annoyance in the young criminal's voice. "I'm just getting my keys. Believe me, no wallet is worth gettin' popped over." His hands were shaking hard, and beads of sweat gathered nervously on his forehead. His bladder held on by a thread.

The other perp appeared equally perturbed. Before he could give a word of protest Jacob cut him off and barked "What's your name by the way? As a matter fact gimme' your licenses, both of you!" The driver handed his over and then opened the car door. All the while, the pistol trained its mouth in their direction. "I don't have a license" said the other teen. "I get mine next week." Jacob didn't bother investigating whether he was telling the truth or not.

The license given was beaten up and the writing was starting to fade, but Jacob luckily could make out the name.

It read, "Henry Lowens." Lines of distaste crept across Jacob's stern face and sat with demeaning contention. "What kinda' stupid name is Lowens anyway?" Now that he had the upper hand, he figured it was safe to talk a little shit. This time, from a less painful vantagepoint.

Henry didn't answer; he just continued to dig through the junk in the back seat searching for the brown leather wallet he'd stolen the day before. About two minutes later he exclaimed, "Ah-ha! I knew it was back here somewhere!" He handed it to Jacob and then took a few steps back. "This guy's obviously off his meds" Henry thought.

Jacob snatched the wallet and looked inside. The ticket was still there. He could see its edge poking out over a few old receipts. "Thank God. Maybe He is listenin' after all." Henry looked curiously at Jacob, trying to determine what he was looking for. Realizing this, Jacob quickly shut the tattered slab of leather, tucking it into his back pocket, then told the two guys to get in the car and drive off, or he'd call the cops.

Neither of the hooligans held intellect as a strong-suit; otherwise they would've called his bluff. Jacob was the only one in current possession of a firearm, and was himself committing a crime by taking matters into his own hands. Now that he finally got what he came for, the thieves were free to go. He didn't care about pursuing them any further. What was the point?

The SUV veered away in a hurry, tires screeching as they searched for grip. Seconds later Jacob caught sight of Mr. Lao from the corner of his eye. The elderly gentleman looked older than usual. He seemed tired, worn out. Jacob walked up to him and spoke. "Mr. Lao! Mr. Lao! Hey, I was just coming to see you, I just had to take care of some um, some business first." While he spoke, he made sure to hide the gun from his mentor's view.

"Today is not a good day for visits." It was the only thing the man said to Jacob that day. He limped over to his usual stone and began his meditation without explanation. Had he seen the gun? "Whatever." Jacob left the parking lot. For him, the day couldn't have turned out any better. He was back in business.

CHAPTER 14

25 YEARS OF TLC

The drive to the lottery office was a peaceful one this time around. There were no traffic lights that led to accidents, and no guys ready to punch and then rob him. The sun shone bright in the sky. Muggy heat rode wind currents, pushing east at about 5mph. It was around noon. Jacob's stomach reminded him it was being neglected and didn't like it. It rumbled like a dark cloud. Bubbles of hunger popped every minute or two.

He looked at the store signs as they passed by. For some reason, he wasn't in the mood for the usual fast-food delight he would often get from McDonald's. Today he yearned for something a little more... Expensive. The only problem with this new-found desire for a pricier meal, was the money.

Although technically the winner of the largest lump sum in over twelve years, Jacob still was broke, at least for the moment. He decided to curb his hunger with a large order of fries and then get to the lottery headquarters to solve this problem. After ordering his food he made a point of not making any other stops until he reached his destination.

The trek took about an hour and was mostly on the

outskirts of the city. There was scenery along the way he'd never known existed in North Carolina. His fifty-dollar GPS led him through long stretches of road that curved and folded like the coils of a snake. Seven miles later the roadway straightened its back. To his left, lemon yellow. Sunflowers soaked in nature's bounty. Hand-sized bulbs smiled at the sky, tracking the orb that gave them life. To the right, vast green pastures and fields blanketed the land. Beyond them, rolling hills, and the ghosts of mountains. The occasional lone horse could be seen grazing near driftwood fences by the road. It was quite beautiful. White pillows dabbed the sky and waved at the gratuity of color below. He didn't know this side of Charlotte. Even at the Burtonwood property, where his parents were evicted, there were not landscapes like this.

Jacob had high expectations for the look of the headquarters. They would soon be let down. After a few miles of driving on a particularly charming stretch of road, he saw the sign that read, "Next left to NC Lottery." The pressure in his veins began building with anticipation. His life was about to change forever. He could feel it in his bones.

"This is it, here goes nothing." His hands turned counterclockwise on the wheel. The car pulled onto a relatively narrow driveway that led to a half-filled parking lot. Gravel crackled and popped as he backed into a spot near the front. Jacob exited his 1998 Honda Accord and studied it with antipathy. "You do know as soon as I leave this building, I'm gonna' sell you right?" A smirk crept across his lips as he strolled up the sidewalk and towards the building's entrance.

The structure was obviously old; the bricks were worn and dull. Cracks weaseled their way into areas they didn't belong. Whole chunks were missing in some places. There was no landscaping done to the property whatsoever. It almost felt deserted. Bare. To be quite frank, the building looked pretty out of place, especially given the gorgeous backdrop of terrain surrounding it. Jacob almost questioned whether he was at the right location.

"Might as well go in and ask them ta' point me in the right direction, I'm already here," he thought silently to himself. The door leading to the reception desk was heavy and appeared to be built of solid wood. Jacob struggled to push it open, but after a little coaxing it began to budge. The creaking sound it made reminded him of the floors at home. It didn't seem like the place got much traffic.

"Yeah, sorry bout' that. We've been meaning to get that door fixed ever since the Lions won the Super Bowl." Jacob looked confused by the unexpected comment. His brows lurched inward. "Wait, wasn't that like eighteen years ago?" "Exactly son," an old voice said from behind the front desk. Jacob smiled shyly and looked in the eyes of an elderly woman who appeared to be in her early hundreds. He could tell by her raspy voice that she was a heavy smoker.

Her skin was so wrinkled, her wrinkles had wrinkles in them. Despite her apparent age she still had a head full of white flowing hair. It looked as soft and inviting as a basket of fluffed cotton. A few wild strands dangled on their own. The rest were secured into a neat bun. The woman bore elegance Jacob had never experienced. It was like the aura Mr. Lao emanated. Yet, somehow different. He felt uncomfortable making eye contact though her gaze felt warm and inviting, drawing him in. "What can I help you with today son?"

"Yes mam, my name's Jacob; I'm here because I won. This is the place for the lottery, isn't it?" "Lottery? No, son this is a retirement home, what on Earth do you mean lottery?" Her voice sounded sincere. Jacob began to turn and walk out, disappointment forming in his face.

"Aww I'm just kidding with you, yes this is the lottery headquarters! Now what do ya' mean you won? Do you mean the jackpot?" She was peering at the young man before her with curiosity. He had stopped and turned back to face her. A twinkle crept into his eyes. "Yes mam." "Well why didn't you say so?" Her smile revealed a full set of pearly white teeth. "Just got them done, they look good don't they?" "Your teeth?" "Well yes son, you kids these days. Just take everythin' fa' granted. Wait till you get to be my age."

Jacob began to chuckle a little at the woman's odd humor. Her cool demeanor helped calm unsure nerves. "Well c'mon on over here son, do you have the ticket with you?" "Yes I do." Jacob reached in his left pocket and felt for the piece of worn leather between his fingers.

He pulled out his wallet and looked at it for a few moments. "It's not gonna' do you any good sitting in that hand of yours. Give it over and I'll get you started on some paperwork." She took the slip along with his ID. He was then led to a waiting room. There he filled out countless forms. There were forms asking about him, his parents, taxes. They seemed to go on forever. A full three hours after arriving, he finally got his first whiff of excitement.

A tall woman in her mid-thirties exited an office hidden behind the main receptionist desk. He hadn't noticed there was even a door there until then. It blended in perfectly with the surrounding wall. "Hello Mr. Gilferd, my name is Kinyona, I'm an attorney here with the North Carolina Lottery. I'll be representing the Firm and will be here to answer any questions you may have." Kinyona was a stunning woman. Clean cut, refined, absolutely elegant. Jacob gazed with amazement and enthusiastically followed her lead.

She guided him into a conference room quite different

from the dull waiting area they'd just left. In front of them was a long shiny table made of dark marble. Dashes of white and grey gave contrast, spanning the entire length. There were glasses and bottled water at every seat. The chairs were fit for royalty. Black leather roamed their surface, and beneath that, bones of fine wood and metal set structure. A state-of-the-art phone line sat center table. Many important calls were made from this room.

"As you can imagine Mr. Gilferd, not many people get to see this area of the building. This room is affectionately referred to as, "TLC, or The Life Changer." It was named by our founder John Oliver over twenty-five years ago." Sitting at the table were several well-groomed men and a rather plump woman. She appeared to be a little older than the attorney.

"These advisors are now at your disposal." A hand beckoned to the elite staff. "Feel free to consult with any external advisor of your choosing if you like. We find winners tend to fare better when they have a team of professionals to help make the big financial decisions ahead." Each of the individuals in the room arose and greeted Jacob with ardent smiles and healthy handshakes. They made him feel important, more so than he'd ever felt. Jacob was the center of attention for the first time in his life. The experience was a tantalizing window into his future.

"In a few moments the VP of finance will be here to discuss the allocation of funds. May we offer you anything in the meantime? Wine, maybe a glass of champagne? We have a cellar onsite." He shook his head thinking she was joking, then recanted. "No, I'm fine. Actually, do you have anything to eat? I'm starving! All I had were some greasy fries on the way here."

The request was met with warm enthusiasm. "Absolutely! What would you like?" "I dunno, what do you have?" She smiled. "Mr. Gilferd, one of the perks of being

Charlotte's newest millionaire is you can basically have whatever you want. So, what can I get for you?" While Jacob talked with the attractive lawyer, he didn't notice the short stubby man that quietly entered the room through a door near the far end of the table. He hobbled over to Jacob and promptly yet politely interjected. His voice was deep and lumbering.

"Excuse me Kinyona, Good afternoon Mr. Gilferd, my name is Theodore Ferdinand Ellwood. I am the VP of finance. I just require a few moments of your time. I know you've got some food to order from the chef." He'd overheard the tail-end of their conversation. "I'm here to discuss the apportionment of your funds." Pince-nez glasses sat on the bridge of his curved nose, pinching both sides with just enough pressure to stay in place. Very fancy.

"Usually large winners such as yourself like to disperse the money among several different asset classes. The first step is deciding what kind of banking vehicle you would like to use." The blank stare on Jacob's face told the gentleman further explanation was required. Most new winners took the same stance.

"Well. I suppose we should start from the top. You have two initial choices that must be made. The first, take a lump sum withdrawal of the money. In this case there would be fifty percent taken out as a penalty, and then taxes withheld on the remaining amount, both federal and state. Your gross winnings were for, let's see here."

He peered through his glasses at the folder in his hand, "$264,957,747.45." Stubby fingers entered numbers into the calculator app on his phone. "If you decide to take a lumpsum you'll be left with $79,487,324.24. The other choice is to take annual installments over the course of the next twenty years." Jacob did his best to follow along, his head was swimming by this point. Theodore didn't seem to notice. Numbers kept spewing from his mouth. Kinyona had been right. He did have big decisions ahead of him.

"In that case there wouldn't be the fifty percent taken off the top. The winnings would be divided by twenty, minus taxes of course." Jacob suddenly wished he'd brought an attorney, and maybe an accountant. In the end, he opted for what most people choose; the lump sum payment.

It was nearly seven in the evening before Jacob left the building. The sun was on its way to its place beneath the horizon. Rays fought to keep their spot on the clouds. Orange bled to mauve against the backdrop of fluffy cotton. The temperature had gone down. Eyes gazed out. Nature was painting a masterpiece, but it was muddied by a distracted mind. It still didn't quite register with him. The numbers thrown around the room that day were absolutely numbing. He got into his car and drove off after everything was finalized. Mr. Ellwood had informed him that he would not see the credit to his bank account for up to fifteen business days due to the sheer magnitude of the transfer. He'd dreamt of this day for a lifetime. What was two more weeks?

CHAPTER 15

THE SHADOW OF TIME

Nearly two years had elapsed since the day Jacob first visited the lottery's headquarters. Life for him was different after the influx of money, but not the way he'd hoped. In a strange twist of fate, the freedom the lottery afforded put him in a position to lose everything, including the very perceived freedom he once sought.

Luxury hotels, expensive cars, women. These were the pleasures that surrounded him three months ago. Now he was surrounded by a jury of his peers... "Given the evidence provided by the prosecution, and the lack of conviction by the defense, the jury has come to a verdict. In the case of Mr. Gilferd vs. the State of North Carolina, the jury finds the defendant..." The room held its breath. All eyes fell upon the judge's lips. Arguments had been strong on both sides. The cornered millionaire made sure to hire the best. No one moved. Seconds ticked by, an hour at a time. Two months in trial, compelling testimonies, from both ends mind you, and a box brimming with both video and forensic evidence. All culminating in this moment. "*Guilty on all charges*. Sentencing will be one week from today. This court is adjourned."

Jacob nearly lost his balance as the words left the

judge's tight mouth. Murmurs swept the crowd of onlookers and seemed to push against the walls as they filled the room with a low rumble. Cheers could be heard. Cries too. Emotions spanned the spectrum, from sympathizers, to those who wanted his head. "Your honor, I have something to say." His left leg was quivering. It felt like it could give out at any moment. "Yes Mr. Gilferd?" The judge looked at him directly. There was not even a *whiff* of sympathy in his stern gaze. If anything, he looked more bored than anything else. Like he had somewhere better to be. Jacob's lawyer touched his arm as if to warn him not to speak without consulting her first. Defendants had a bad habit of stabbing themselves in the foot when they opened their mouths. He ignored her.

"I've done many things in my life I regret, things I wish I could take back. But murder? Murder isn't one of those things. I was at the scene *around* the time the victim was killed, but I had nothing to do with it! I am *not* a killer. Someone's trying to frame me!" His arms flailed, the jangle of chains echoing through the courtroom. "I know these words may not mean anything in a court of law, but maybe they'll mean something to you. That's, that's all I have to say." He dropped his head, awaiting a reply.

"I appreciate your words Mr. Gilferd, but you are correct, according to the law I am required to judge based on the evidence presented, not mere words. I'll take into consideration that this is your first offense, but you must understand I'm both morally and legally obligated to assign sentencing based on the *facts*. This court is adjourned." The judge's gavel came down with a loud thud. Jacob's fate was sealed. He was going to prison.

The newly minted convict pushed back his seat and was immediately escorted by two court deputies to the back room where his holding cell awaited. "Can I talk to my lawyer for a few minutes Sir?" The officer hesitated. "You have five minutes, then it's back to the cell Mr. Gilferd." Jacob nodded in appreciation, then turned to the woman waiting near his holding cell.

"Kinyona *please*, you've gotta' help me! Get me outta this! Remember when I met you two years ago? You saw this innocent kid who'd just come into money. You didn't see a killer, did you?" She looked away, avoiding eye contact. By this point he wasn't even attempting to hide his desperation. He let it hang out in plain view. "You *know* I'm innocent Kinyona. They're gonna' fucking kill me in there! Hell, the government might even do it." His crackled words were stained with fear. The emotion was well placed. The prison he was bound for was one of the worst in the state. And he'd killed the President's daughter. At least half the country loved the politician. They'd take the slaying personal.

"I know you're innocent, that's why I'm representing you. I know you're a good person. I've seen the good you've done since you won that money. Most people just squander it, but you, you gave back." She gave pause as if to ponder, "You may've squandered a little here and there, but you were generous and genuine. That I know."

"So why can't you get the judge to see that? And the jury for that matter? The prosecutor has me lookin' like Hannibal Lector! Let's appeal!" Kinyona shook her head. He didn't understand how the legal system worked, and who it worked for. She did. "Winning the lottery may be the noose that ultimately goes around your neck Jacob. Someone wants you behind bars. In their place..."

"What the fuck does me winning have to do with this? I told you when they first picked me up I thought that crazy ex of hers did it! Why the hell doesn't someone point the finger at *him* for a change? And why can't we appeal? We have the money?" Kinyona raised a finger as if to stop him from going any further. There were some things he needed to understand. "For one, her ex-boyfriend *comes* from money, *old money*. There's a difference. People like you aren't respected among those circles." Jacob's ignorance stifled his ability to fully appreciate what she was saying. To him, rich was rich. True affluence is a state of mind. It's perspective eluded him. Kinyona did her best to try and bring him up to speed.

"And this is election year, politics are gonna' come into play here. This is the President's daughter we're talkin' about Jacob. Someone has to hang for the crime, and unfortunately you're the only one currently in the system's crosshairs." The wealth Jacob acquired afforded him the opportunity to meet people he would've otherwise not been able to even get close to. At first, it seemed like a blessing. "If I never won, I'd still be free. Money bought me access to, to what? To nothingness."

It was on a trip to the islands of French Polynesia that he first met Kacy. He didn't believe she was the First Daughter when she mentioned it on the beach. It sounded like she was joking. It was only after several encounters that her true lineage became evident. That day on the sand was now just a blurred movie. The memories of Bora Bora felt like they were lived a lifetime ago… Things went so wrong, so fast.

"But what about all the good I've done, and the money I've contributed over these last eighteen months? Does that count for nothing? I mean, I've given more to Kieden's campaign than most people make in their lifetime!" Strands of onyx black hair flopped about as Kinyona's head shook once again. He still wasn't getting it. "That doesn't negate that you were at the scene of the murder. All the money in the world can't sway hard evidence, and the evidence says you're guilty." "That what you believe, I mean based on the evidence, that I'm guilty? Has it dawned on only *me* that maybe I'm being framed? Why doesn't anyone ask that jealous ex of hers any questions?"

Jacob still didn't understand that although he now had money, it didn't mean he had clout. Among the uber-rich, a few million, hell even a few hundred were considered pennies in the bucket. What Jacob needed was something elusive, something earned, whether honorably or not. He needed the power of influence to win this war.

To the families involved in his murder case, only true reverence mattered. They came from generations of wealth. A separate class. If your family name didn't ring bells several generations back, no amount of money could protect you. Luckily for Trent, Kacy's ex, no questions were asked as to *his* whereabouts on that fateful night. That was one of the benefits of being born to affluent blood. It was something Jacob's cheap lottery money couldn't afford.

She placed a hand near the bars and used the other to run fingers through her hair. "Of course I don't think you did it, but what I believe really doesn't hold much weight. You're swimming with the big fish now. Kieden built his career on the selling point of not favoring the newly rich. You know he believes in earning your keep."

"I know you've heard his story by now. That man is a machine, a cold-blooded machine. Two years ago your sentence might've been fifteen to twenty. As it stands with the *new* Administration in D.C., you can expect life if they decide to make an example of you. You need to come to grips with reality Jacob." Her words were an icy river, sending chilled currents up and down his spine. She was right. His fate was sealed.

"Well I'm glad *you've* accepted it. To be honest, it seems like you've just plain given up. Tell me again, what exactly am I payin' you for?" He pointed an angry finger at Kinyona as he spoke. Deep down, he knew the entire conversation was for naught. Convincing her wasn't going to change his situation. No matter how he sliced it, he was headed to prison. "Jacob you don't mean that, you know I've done everything I can, what else do you want me to do? I can't just erase tangible evidence. I mean, they had you on camera going into the building, and your prints were in her room everywhere. I'm a good lawyer, hell, a great one. But I'm not a magician."

His hands swung frantically as he replied to her valid points. He couldn't help himself. He needed to feel like at least one person believed him. "Like I told you, and the jury, we hung out several times after Bora Bora. I went to her apartment like twice. So yeah, my prints were in there. But *that* day I never went up to her floor. I was going to the lounge in that building! That's it."

Kinyona didn't seem convinced of his alibi. "Of all the lounges and on all nights?" An impatient sigh slipped from under his breath. "Just find out who's trying to bury me. And why. That's what I want you to do! The judge is gonna' sentence me next week. Next week Kinyona!" "Ok, I'll talk with one of my connections on Wednesday and see if we can get an appeal started. But even if we get it, it'll be useless unless there's some new evidence brought to light."

Jacob spent the next seven days in the small cell thinking about how he'd gotten into this situation. It was literally like the worst-case scenario. If his life were a TV show, everyone would be tuned in, waiting to see what the next round of drama would be. The guard that stood at his cell door in the evenings would ask him almost daily what it felt like to have won the lottery. He was sure to keep his distance, and kept a hand near his canister of pepper spray. But he was curious nonetheless.

"So what's it feel like? I mean being rich?" It was 6pm

on the fourth night. Jacob was sitting on the bed, arms folded, looking through the bars at the man before him. "Well, I can tell you it was a lot better on the other side of these bars. That's for sure! I dunno' though, the first few months were great." "Did you spend a lotta' money?"

Jacob thought for a moment before responding to the guard. "A lot's an understatement, but, funny thing is, you get used to it much quicker than you'd think. It's only exciting for a while, then you start getting tired of people asking for money. Before you know it you're alone, even in a crowded room. It's almost like you can't relate with anyone anymore. No one really gets what you go through. Nor do they care. That's been my experience at least." His honesty took the man off-guard. It wasn't the answer he was expecting. "Huh. So, if you could go back in time, would you do it again. I mean, win?" He wanted to make sure Jacob knew what he was talking about, given the circumstance.

"Absolutely!" Jacob's voice was full of enthusiasm. "I remember I was at some pretentious dinner party about six months ago, and this woman worth about half a billion dollars was hosting the whole event. Someone at the table asked if she thought rich people should feel guilty for being so well off, you know, while other people struggled. They asked if she would give it all up in exchange for happiness."

"Well, what did she say?" The guard looked on eagerly as Jacob carried on with his story. "She laughed and said no. Instead, she said, I'd much rather be miserable someplace gorgeous, than be happy in the slums." The young guard smiled and rested a hand on his waste. His shoulders relaxed. The good conversation was putting him at ease. He wanted to know more. "And what about you?"

Before Jacob could answer the question, the deputy's supervisor barged into the hallway. He had been watching the slacker on camera. “Dan, you know there’s no fraternizing with the prisoner. Shut your trap or I’ll ship you out quicker than a truck of illegals.” At this, Dan’s back straightened up. “Yes Sir, sorry Sir.” He was a new employee and his wife had recently given birth to their first child.

The last thing he needed was to upset his boss and wind up on the unemployment line. This was the first job he was able to land in seven months. His family’s future was dependent on his ability to keep it. Dan took a few steps away from Jacob’s cell door and stood at attention for the rest of the night. No one else made any attempt at conversation with him for the duration of his stay at the courthouse jail.

On the day of his sentencing the courtroom brimmed with spectators, all clamoring to see what would come of the new millionaire. It was big news for the city. The story was on every network across the nation. Charlotte hadn’t gotten this much attention in years. Jacob’s parents and sister were sitting in the front row, with reporters crammed in the second and third. Cameras were prohibited, but pen met paper wherever the eye wondered.

“This court is now in session. All rise.” The courtroom rose to their feet in silent unison. After a spell of never-ending legal disclosures punishment was finally handed down. The moments leading up were tense. Everyone tuned in, eagerly awaiting the disposition. “In the case of Jacob Gilferd vs. the State of North Carolina the defendant has been found guilty. I will now hand down sentencing.”

“Now, I’ve taken all statements and evidence into consideration and have determined an appropriate sentence. The defendant will receive the following term for his crimes.” There was a deafening silence that choked the room. Not one person could even stand to breathe. This was the biggest case the city had ever encountered. “Life in a maximum-security

Federal Prison, with no chance of parole."

Jacob's heart stopped and turned over a few times in his chest. The news was devastating. A total calamity. He expected it to be bad, but this was utter madness. Life? His eyes went blurry and he saw the ground come rushing up. A heavy thud pounded at the underside of his chin. His head bounced off the thin carpet. A few people in the crowd gasped, others stood to get a better view. He'd fainted. The rest of eternity for a crime he never committed. It was like his childhood all over again, except much, much worse.

When he came about his wits he was still on the ground in the courtroom. Drake was holding Maria. Her screams filled the room and the hallway outside. A mother's pain. Agony. "Don't you touch my baby! Get away from my son! Jacob!" Her voice quaked as she tried to protect her child. The media was in an absolute frenzy. When his family got outside, they were bombarded by a relentless stream of questions and torments. Out there, the flash of pictures taken from every angle was blinding.

"Mr. Gilferd, how does it feel to be at the head of one of the most hated families in this country? You were relatively unknown two years ago, and now your son's just been convicted of murdering the President's daughter. How does that feel?" A news microphone was shoved insensitively towards Drake's stunned face. The reporter cradled a sinister smirk between her lips. Within seconds, ten more mics were within an inch of Drake's mouth. He could've literally bitten one if he'd wanted to. That's how close they were. The broken family just ducked their heads down and kept moving. Maria used her coat to block her and Myra's face. The car felt like it was miles away. Every local network was on scene. It was a mess.

Their questions were crass in classic media fashion.

None got answered. The Gilferds hired two armed guards to ward off the incessant barrage of death threats they received after the verdict was made public. Kieden supporters didn't take kindly to the killing. The country was already polarized, split down the middle between the left and right. The assassination only added fuel to the fire. Aside from verbal assaults, the family was affected in other ways as well. The damage to their name was irreparable. There was no coming back from this.

Myra was newly enrolled in the Harvard Law program. It was a huge accomplishment for her. Her grades had always been good, but not good enough for Ivey League. A 3.4 GPA wasn't gonna get her a full ride anywhere. Before the lottery only partial scholarships to local schools were on the horizon. When Jacob asked her what she wanted when he first won, her only request was to pay for her education. He cordially agreed. Two weeks after the sentencing she received a notice in the mail...

"We at Harvard University pride ourselves with being an institution whose foundation is built on the principles of honor and integrity. We therefore are unable to accommodate your presence in our program as a result of recent developments involving members of your family. This decision is in no way a reflection of our view of you or your actions as an individual, but we must take an aggregate stance and act in everyone's best interest."

What the school was trying to say was, "We are an internationally acclaimed institution, and don't need the bad press your brother's conviction would bring, thanks for the tuition payment, Goodbye." In similar fashion, Drake had started a marketing firm with some of the money he was gifted. Whether from the pressure of the press or other external forces, two of the three partners he was working with withdrew their interest in the venture. Within a month the entire project came crumbling down. There was no doubt about it, the Gilferd family name was marred beyond repair.

CHAPTER 16

WELCOME TO THE DEVIL'S HOME

The bus ride to the prison was a short but uncomfortable one. Massive tires hit every pothole the pavement offered, and the road was generous that day. Heads bobbed up and down, jerking unnaturally as the driver attempted to avoid one of the concrete cavities. Jacob's hands and feet were chained together in something called a Y restraint. His wrists were handcuffed in front of him. There was another chain that extended from the center of the cuffs. It connected with a metal clasp located on his seat between his legs. This forced Jacob's hands to stay in his lap with little room for negotiation. It was painfully vexatious.

The chain continued down to the floor and ended at his ankles. They too were attached to a metal clasp fastened to the floor of the bus. Jacob was the most secure inmate on the transport vehicle; none of the other felons were restrained to his extent. They all took notice. In their eyes, he was the most dangerous man onboard. Everywhere Jacob's eye wondered, gazes of reverence met him. Among killers, violence was respected.

Due to the nature and controversy surrounding his conviction, he had already built a reputation at the prison before ever reaching its algid grounds. Whether this rep would serve him would soon be discovered. The admission process was new to Jacob, and it showed in his constant miss-steps. With every novice move credibility was lost. He awkwardly fumbled through the many checkpoints, each requiring he remove more and more of his clothing. It was like being stripped of his very identity. A transition from person, to number.

In the end he found himself in a small room with two guards. *Every man's nightmare*. The area was no larger than a walk-in closet. Grime and grey adorned the walls. A few old boxes lay in one corner. Aside from that and them, the room was empty. "Drop em con." "Excuse me?" Eyes rolled, fingers gripped a utility belt. "Your britches, drop them! Now!" "I don' think so, I'm not with that." Before he could finish, the correctional officer reached to his side belt and unhinged a large canister of pepper spray. The air grew still as reality sank in. Jacob could feel blood rush away from his skin as he realized what was happening. He had zero control over the situation. Zero.

"Now we can do this the easy way, or the *easier* way, your choice con. I'm gonna' say it one more time, drop your funky draws, we have to search you for contraband." As he spoke, two black rubber gloves appeared from his pocket and he began to slip them on. Just in case things got messy. The other guard grinned, hoping for a show. His arms were crossed, cold eyes fixed upon the clueless fish in front of him. "Ok, I don' want any problems." Jacob pulled his boxers down and let the guards do their job. It was his first-time being strip searched, and he hated every moment of it, especially when made to cough.

After being fully admitted into the system he was escorted to a medium sized room filled with other new convicts, many of which rode the bus in with him. Gunk framed the walls and every crevasse the area offered. Must from sweaty men choked the air, leaking from pits and groins that had slow-cooked all day. It was hard to breathe. A gruff looking guard entered the room and began his speech. You would have thought he was 6'10 by the sound of his voice and the presence he exuded, but gravity held him down, denying him the mark by nearly a foot. His message was just as short. It was one he gave with the arrival of each new bus-load. A welcome of sorts. "Now, I'm sure each of you is eager to build up your street cred behind these walls, so you can gain some perceived respect."

"You may wanna' show them how tough you are." His black cap rode low on his brow. Clearly ex-military. "This is understandable, seeing as how most of you are serving sentences of at least ten years. That's what we CO's like to call, *hard time*. My advice to you is, don't. Every vet inside these walls is gonna test your grit; Believe that. Best thing you can do to survive, is not be the tough guy."

"There've been three deaths in the past two months at this prison. The violence seems to pick up everyday." Murmurs swept the ranks of new convicts. "It's not a statistic we staff are proud of, but if you dare threaten or attack one of *my* men, let's just say the casket won't be for us. It will be for you. We have *zero* tolerance for insubordination. *Zero* tolerance for contraband. *Zero* tolerance for tough guys." His sharp gaze canvassed the sea of eyes. No one said a word. The message was clear.

"We will break you down if you step up, then let you rot in the hole. Moral of the story? Don't cross us." After this inspiring orientation, the men were led to their respective cell blocks. The prison was separated according to the nature of crimes its inhabitants were convicted of. An unending labyrinth of hallways and checkpoints stoked confusion. A maze, meant to disorient would-be escapees. The design proved quite effective. Even guards with years of experience sometimes lost their way.

Jacob was taken to D-block. It was considered housing for the worst of the worst. Only inmates deemed too dangerous to be admitted to any of the other areas lived on that wing. It was located almost directly in the center of the prison, strategically placed as far from the roads and fences as possible. Many inmates on D-block were serving life sentences and were more likely to attempt escape.

The door to Jacob's new home was hanging open as he approached. Chipped paint blotted the bars and surrounding walls. His stay wasn't long. Not ten minutes passed before a guard came around. He was led into general population. It was yard time. This was notoriously the most dangerous time for newcomers. Inmates from all over the correctional facility would be in proximity, and personalities frequently clashed. Fights were inevitable.

Before the guard arrived, Jacob stepped inside his cell for a moment and gave it a look-down. There was a heaviness to the place. He laid his pillow on the top bunk and started to inspect his new home. If there was a hell designated for those with claustrophobia, this was it. He turned to face the doorway with his arms extended out. Fingertips on each hand nearly reached the awaiting walls of grey. As for the toilet? The toilet was absolutely diminutive; so small he could barely fit. Jacob was by no means a large individual. At least not when he arrived. It wouldn't be until months into his stay that he would gain weight. Like most men, working out, especially push-ups and cardio, became a way of life. For now, he would have to hope muscle wasn't needed.

Weighing in at barely a hundred and sixty pounds, he

could only imagine what some of his larger neighbors endured when nature called. It was constructed almost entirely of metal as with everything else in the restrictive space. Aside from the size, there was another drawback to his new bathroom. He'd be using it in plain view of his new cellmate. There wasn't even a curtain. Privacy was a luxury no inmate could afford. Even the bosses succumbed to the demeaning lifestyle the prison demanded. Most got used to it within a few weeks. The ones who didn't would use sheets to cloak areas they wished to remain hidden.

The beds were like the toilet in that they were cramped, metal, and uncomfortable. The mattress was more like a large thin pillow than anything else, and it just barely spanned the bedframe. A far cry from the presidential suites Jacob acclimated himself to over the 18 months prior to his incarceration.

There was also a small sink in the cell. It only ran cold water, with pressure as robust as the cry of a field mouse. Before heading outside, Jacob stopped. For a moment so did his heart. Hairs running along his arms rose from their slumber. A dried stain of spattered blood painted the wall in the back... It ran in streaks and dotted blotches, like an abstract painting. *Drawn by a psychopath no doubt.* He would later learn an inmate was severely stabbed and slashed in that very spot not three weeks before he arrived.

Out in the yard there were all types of men. Most looked like hardened criminals, but a few offered a more approachable appeal. Jacob found a young man of about the same age and went over to try and spark conversation. "Hey what's up, my name's Jacob, what're you in for?" He figured if he was gonna be locked up for the long haul he'd better start making friends early. He remembered watching shows on Spike TV about inmates doing hard time. There was a theme that stood constant on every episode, "An inmate with no allies, is a dead inmate."

The young man didn't say anything at first. He seemed to be deciding on whether to play the tough role or oblige the inquiry. Even Jacob, as new as he was, could see the kid was no veteran. His facade was weak at best. After a few moments the inmate replied, "I'm in for grand theft auto, and no, not the game."

"There were a few drug charges in there too I think." The two laughed and began exchanging stories on how they ended up in such a shitty place. Jacob's tale was much more interesting. "So you didn't do it?" His head shook hard as he replied, "Man hell no I didn't kill that girl, but the prosecutors had their ducks in a row. They hung me out to dry. Gave me life." It was a sobering admission. "Damn, that sucks, so have you met your new celly yet?" The question sounded light, but it held a lot of weight. Your entire experience in prison was anchored on who your bunkie turned out to be. Get the wrong one, and you could wake up with a shiv in your spleen.

"My new what?" "Your new celly, oh C'mon man, you gotta' get down with the lingo in this place dude. The sooner you start talking like one of the vets, the sooner these wolves stop looking at you like a sheep. You pickin' up what I'm kickin?" His lingo was crude and practiced. "Not really, but Ok. So gimme' the rundown then?" Jacob looked him directly in the eyes. This was information he needed to pay attention to. "Ok, so check it, celly means cellmate, shank is a knife or somethin' you get stabbed with." A laugh forced its way out. It was hard to ignore the peculiar definition. "It's interesting you defined it with us being on the *receiving* end."

"Oh yea, I guess I could've worded that differently. Anyways, CO's are the guards, and pod bosses are inmates that call the shots in the yard. You don't wanna' cross paths with any of them. Best thing to do is just keep your head down. Stick to the script." The mentorship was much appreciated. Going it alone was not an option. At first he was sure allies would be hard to come by, but Jacob liked his new friend. The young con was clean cut, down to his freckled, hairless face, and seemed genuine and outgoing once they began talking. Neither traits would get him very far behind the prison's walls. He needed Jacob as much as Jacob needed him. His outward veneer was a weak shield at best, easily chinked to a trained eye. Eyes were everywhere.

"I never got your name by the way?" "CJ, just call me CJ." As the two men introduced themselves they could hear a guard in the distance. His voice quaked across the field, amplified by the UZI MP Bullhorn held in his right hand. "Alright cons, yard time's over! Let's go ladies, move it!" The sun was still pretty high in the sky, it seemed to be taking its time as it moseyed westward. Rays reached down and pressed against the backs of men. It was 6:30pm. Groups broke ranks and began drifting over to the south gate. Within minutes the yard emptied out. Everyone headed to the mess hall for the evening's chow. Jacob was standing in line waiting to grab his tray when he felt a firm grip tug his arm. It was CJ. "Let these guys go in front of you. I haven't been here long, but long enough to know who's who."

Jacob took his newfound friend's advice and let the three men approaching skip. After they got their trays, CJ beckoned him to pick one up. The line cooks serving the food also seemed to know who the intimidating trio were. They gave them an obviously larger portion of food than anyone else. That night, bean mush, hardened cornbread, and mystery meat were on the menu. Most men avoided the beans. The trio were no exception. All their plates brimmed with meat and bread.

Jacob and CJ sat down towards the back of the room

with the other newbies. "So who were those guys anyway?" CJ leaned in, his voice lowered to a whisper. His eyes scanned right, then left for threats. In prison there was always someone listening. "You remember when I told you bout' the bosses?" "Yeah." He beckoned towards the group cautiously. "Well that's one of 'em. The guy in the middle of the other two, his name's Alik. Alik Bravechk." As the name left his lips his voice lowered even further. Names like that weren't thrown around lightly. "He's a Russian mob boss. Got locked up a few years ago for a laundry list of charges. I think he lives somewhere on D-block."

"That's where I am!" Jacob's brows were raised. His arms folded as he watched CJ staring back at him with a look that could only be described as pity. "Damn! They put you over there? You should've just let that chick go man. That's *not* where you wanna' be, damn sure not on D-block. That's the hood. The slums for real." "I didn't do shit, I was framed!" It was a statement repeated by every inmate everywhere. "Yeah, whatever, that's everyone's story at first. Give it a few months, you'll be braggin' bout' what you did so you can get some street cred around here."

"No I won't, I don't care about that shit, I'm gonna' be out soon anyway. My lawyer's working on an appeal." Arrogance sat plainly on Jacob's breath. If anyone had enough money to buy their freedom, he did. "Hmmm, well hopefully that works out for you. So who's your celly, you never did answer my question?" Jacob shrugged and replied "Oh, I haven't met him yet." "Better hope he's an old guy that can't do much damage, otherwise you might have problems. What with being on D-block and all." CJ smiled as he spoke. Jacob's face drooped. His plastic fork poked at the untouched beans on his tray. "Thanks for the vote of confidence." Fifteen minutes later dinner was over.

It was time for the men to return to their cells. Jacob

walked nervously in line towards D-block. He missed the creak of floorboards beneath his feet. The old apartment, once despised, bled bitter-sweet memories. Things were simpler back then, before the money. Now, the clank of metal and bickering men were all that greeted him. Everyone looked angry. Smiles were almost nonexistent. The guards kept a watchful eye on every movement. This was a notoriously dangerous time of day. Attacks were almost always taken out in the windows of time between chow. Easier to blend in.

CJ's warning rang in his ears with each step. He prayed dearly for a good cellmate. He pictured some man that resembled Ming Lao, a fragile figure having a kind, soft demeanor. Then reality set in. He was en route to the most hostile area of an *already* dangerous prison. A Ming Lao was as likely to be his cellmate as a porn star was. "Hey, I won the lottery, so anything's possible. Maybe Mr. Lao got behind on one too many parking tickets." He snickered weakly at the notion.

As Jacob drew near his cell he took a moment and reflected on his wise mentor. He missed his company and conversations. After winning the money he stopped going to the park to meditate. Too consumed with spending his newfound fortune. Although he did go back once to let Mr. Lao know he'd won, he never returned after that. The newly convicted felon wondered if he would even have been sent to prison if he'd continued visiting with the old man. His musings were cut short once he reached his cell doorway.

Jacob stopped abruptly, causing everyone in line to stop in the process. The guard assigned to keep watch didn't take notice. A few of the cons did. They didn't take kindly to the break in routine. "What're you doing newbie? Keep it movin' before one of the CO's see you. I don't need any more attention from those fucking pigs; I just got back from the hole, feel me ese?"

The man behind Jacob held a short, muscular stature. A cascade of veins in his neck and forehead protruded angrily; and he had tattoos all over his arms, chest, and face. He wasn't Jacob's main concern at the time however; it was the person *ahead* that really made his sphincter tighten. He'd been so caught up in his reverie about meditating with Mr. Lao, the newbie hadn't paid attention to who was in line. Inmates were lined up according to their cell numbers. Jacob's number was 51.

As he regained the strength in his legs to move forward, Jacob took the first step into the small doorway. With the help of a rough nudge from the man behind him, he was finally in the confined space with the man he'd be spending eighteen hours a day with from there on out. The realization was terrifying...

CHAPTER 17

ALIK

"Is this your pillow?" The voice carried a deep Russian accent and had a tone of indignation at its end. Jacob's eye drew timidly upon the infamous mob leader. Alik asked the question again, impatience now coming through more assertively. Jacob's lower lip began to quiver nervously, he was at a loss for words. No number of pushups or shadow boxing could have prepared him for this. His luck was going through another schizophrenic episode.

He expected a hardened criminal sure, but not this, this was much worse. He remembered reading stories about what the Russian mob did to its enemies. The tales were chilling. It was almost like they enjoyed it. Killing. Like it ran in their blood. They were known for their use of knives, the gruesome dismemberment of their victims. This was especially true within the prison system where options for weaponry were limited. The Russians were masters in the art of torture. When they wanted to send a message, they let their imaginations run wild. It was a bloody lifestyle.

Alik looked Jacob directly in the eyes; his stare steady and unwavering. He was searching for weakness. Jacob did his best to avoid the grey marbles focused upon him. Piercing and cold, they reminded Jacob of an Arctic wolf's, and he felt more and more like an elk as the seconds ticked by. He knew he needed to answer the man's question, but there were no words in his mouth. They got stuck somewhere at the base of his throat. When he tried to speak only faint sounds and murmurs were offered. Alik could see Jacob was petrified. His new bunkie was a fish out of water. He consequently gave up on expecting a response.

"I'm going to be saying this once, the top bunk is mine. If you are thinking you want it to take, consider how long your life will be." Although Alik's English was broken, the message was clear. The bottom bunk it was. That was the only interaction the two inmates had that night. Jacob laid silently on the bottom bunk, trying to hold back tears of fear that welled just behind his eyelids. They were insistent. In less than a minute the first few broke free and trickled down his cheeks. He was afraid for his life, and he was also angry. At any moment his existence could be extinguished. All it took was one wrong move. The pressure was too much.

He had done nothing to deserve being put in a maximum-security prison. In fact, if not framed for murder, Jacob probably would have been somewhere in Dubai sipping fine scotch and deciding which end of the world to jet off to next. Hindsight was torture. To think of where he could be, what he could be doing. The lottery changed everything for him. There was no mountain he couldn't scale. The world was his playground. It was amazing while it lasted. Intoxicating.

Once in prison, his money had the opposite effect. In society, he was deemed something of a celebrity. All walks of life gravitated towards him to try and get close. Gain trust. In prison, they would also try to get close, but with more menacing, dark intentions in mind. It was a treacherous environment.

The next day when the CO's announced yard Jacob nearly sprinted from the room. He knew the yard was a dangerous place, but compared to his confined cell it was like going to Sunday school, Bible in hand. CJ was in his usual spot near the bleachers away from most of the other inmates and commotion. Jacob jogged over to him, trying to avoid eye contact with anyone along the way. His legs zig-zagged between invisible lines, territories marked out by this faction or that. The strategy seemed to work. His trip across the field was uneventful.

"Well, I have that answer you were looking for. It's Alik!" It was the first thing out of his mouth. CJ was confused by Jacob's lack of explanation. "What's Alik?" At first he had no idea what question Jacob was referring to. Then he thought back to their conversation the day before. "Your celly? No way. I can't believe you're still alive! Did he say anything to you?" His eyes were wide as he asked the question. Relief and terror vied for the best spots on his face. Jacob had his full attention. Upon noticing this, he opted for a little fun. "No, but I told him what the ground rules were gonna' be. I said, now you listen to me you Russian prick."

Before Jacob could finish his narrative the two of them burst into laughter. His story was absolutely hilarious to CJ. "So now tell me, what really happened?" "He basically threatened to kill me and then we went to sleep." "That's crazy, why'd he threaten you? What did you do?" After shrugging Jacob blurted "I put my pillow on the top bunk."

CJ was flabbergasted. The audacity. He couldn't stop his jaw from hanging open. Jacob just stood there. His ignorance lay in plain sight. It made CJ's head hurt. "So Jacob can I ask you a quick question?" "Go ahead." "Yeah so, are you retarded, or just plain stupid? You did what? Did you not see his stuff up there? I mean, are you jus' *trying* to get castrated?" Jacob shrugged. He still didn't see what he'd done wrong. "I didn't know, both of the beds looked the same so I just took one. Neither looked like they'd been slept on."

CJ sighed at the new-comer's luck. "Well the fact that you made it through the night is a good sign, if Alik really wanted you dead, trust me, you'd be worm food. I heard that guy's ordered hits on like fourteen men since he got here a few years ago." The two hung around each other for the rest of their yard time and then headed to the mess hall for dinner. CJ decided to continue playing the role of prison coach. He spent the afternoon doing his best to bring Jacob up to speed. If he was gonna help keep his new friend alive, there were certain things that needed to be taught. Even among criminals there was a code. Adhering to it was the difference between life and death.

At chow CJ noticed one of the men that had been with Alik the previous day. He was peering over at them and beckoning to Alik and other people at their table. "That's never good, they're talkin' bout' you Jacob." Jacob took a discreet look to see who his new acquaintance was referencing. He then quickly drew his eyes back to the smelly Brussels sprouts on the tray in front of him. They were even more infamous than the beans.

"I didn't do anything to him, I dunno' what they're talking about, but he can't still be upset over last night. I gave the top bunk to him for cryin' out loud." CJ just shook his head and turned to give the men at the mobster's table one last look. "You don't *give* men like Alik anything. He takes what he wants. Whatever you do, don't get on his bad side. My ass is on the line too. They've seen us hangin' out." He was right. In the underworld, bad apples rotted the whole barrel. CJ's proximity to the newbie put a target on his back. In many ways, he'd adopted a liability.

Jacob walked slowly back to his cell after dinner. His feet drug behind him. The last thing he wanted was to find himself face to face with Alik again. It was one of a million things he needed to get used to, and fast. This was life for the foreseeable future. The same guy that shoved him the day before was behind him once again. “Look Homes, I’m not gonna’ ask you again, move your ass or I’m gonna’ move it for you.” No matter what he did he just couldn’t seem to stay under the radar. In less than 24 hours he managed to make at least two enemies. It was like trouble followed him around. Jacob quickened his pace but not fast enough. The man gave him a sharp elbow to the kidney before entering the cell next to his. Saliva shot from his mouth as the newbie winced in pain. The strike was well placed.

“Looks like many friends you are making already” Alik laughed as his cellmate entered the room. “Oh no, it’s nothin, that guy’s just a jerk.” He rubbed his side, grimacing as he spoke. He should’ve kept his voice down. His new friend was listening. “Who you callin’ a jerk Homes? We’ll see if blood flows from your mouth as easily as those slick words. I’m gonna’ see you out in the yard, Puta!”

“You have not been in a prison I’m guessing before?” Alik spoke in his broken English to the fledgling. “No, no this is my first time.” The Russian gave a slight smirk. He was lying face up on the top bunk with one leg hanging over the side. Grey eyes were fixed on a picture taped to the ceiling. “Tell me about your family Jacob. You are not seeming like the type bred for prison. What is this like?”

Jacob hesitated. He wasn’t sure talking to a dangerous mob boss about family was the smartest thing to do. Especially considering the organization’s viperous reputation. After giving Alik a timid look as the Russian cocked his head, he also thought better of not answering the question. “Well, where should I start? You're right Mr." He was cut off with a sharp finger. Alik didn't care for formalities. "Alik, just call me Alik." "Right, Mr. Alik." "Are you not listening? I said Alik, not Mr., just Alik." "I'm sorry Mr." Jacob stopped and took a deep breath.

"What are you being told of me? You are afraid of me, no? What are they saying?" The mobster inquired from a place of genuine curiosity. Bosses within the facility rarely heard the rumors spread about them, mostly because fellow inmates were too afraid to speak within earshot. "I have heard you are in charge of, of a group." Alik nodded. A hand scratched at his peppered chin. The sound his nails made against the hard bristles made Jacob's mouth go dry. "Yes, this is true, I am a leader to a group, but why are *you* fearing me?"

Before Jacob could think about what he was saying, the words started to spew from his mouth uncontrollably. "Because you're a murderer, a man that would take another man's life in the blink of an eye. You even threatened me yesterday for a simple mistake. You run this quote-un-quote group, when really all you are is a mob full of thugs looking to intimidate everyone. You're everything a man like me should fear." By the time Jacob got a grip, the damage was done.

The two men sat in silence for a long time after that. Jacob's heart was beating out of his chest as he realized what he'd just said. Alik was sitting up now, both legs hanging over the side. Jacob got up and stood with his back to the bars of the cell door. Space was his enemy. The Russian's face was expressionless, and this scared the shit out of Jacob. He didn't know what to make of it. When Alik did finally speak, the tone in his voice was softer...

"You know, no one has been talking to me in this way, saying these things to me." There was a note of surprise in his voice. The honesty was clearly unexpected. "You see me as a man of evil, no?" Deep lines normally etched into his scarred face dissipated. A more humane side emerged. Although fear still lingered in the marrow of Jacob's bones, he decided to continue engaging the man in conversation. The change in demeanor put his mind more at ease. "I don't know you Alik, I only know what I've been told" he acknowledged weakly.

"Well I am not evil. Despite what they say. I had a God once, but men are bred in my country, they are not being raised." Jacob took a moment to appreciate the statement's impact. It was deep. He couldn't even begin to comprehend the things his bunkie had seen. Taken part in. Ordered. "You mean like, like you're a product of your environment?" Alik's eyes widened, excited at the thought of being understood. His head wobbled with enthusiasm. "Yes, I am producing this!" Jacob couldn't help but laugh at the gruff interpretation. It was the lightest he'd felt since stepping foot in the cell.

"You see Jacob, when you are raised by the lions, being one yourself is, how do you say, natural." There was a nod. "I understand." They didn't say anything else that evening. Their conversation did leave Jacob feeling a little safer. Alik wasn't all demon. The next day it was raining, so Jacob decided to stay in his cell instead of venturing out. A bigger part of his decision was because his next-door neighbor was now an enemy. He also knew he wouldn't be getting a visit from CJ. No need to go looking for trouble. Better to stay inside.

The only people that ever came to D-block were those that had to. Even for prison it was considered the ghetto. About forty minutes or so after the cell doors opened, the short Mexican who lived next door walked past. He was accompanied by a few spectators looking for a good show. Jacob's door was still open. He'd never closed it after his bunkie left to venture out onto the tier. One look in the gang member's eyes showed he meant business. The situation grew more acute by the second. There was nowhere to run. Nowhere to hide. "What's up now Cabrón? Where's that slick tongue now huh?" In his hand he brandished a make-shift shank. It was crude but would get the job done. Melted plastic, molded to a point, acted as the blade. The handle was re-enforced with tightly wound cloth. This weapon had already tasted flesh. Browned blood stained its tip.

Jacob backed into the corner and tried to think of something to say to get the man to leave him alone. His heart thumped as fear closed in from both sides. This was it. He was about to die. Before he could utter a word, Alik walked up from behind and looked the angry gangster straight in the eyes. It was like he appeared from nowhere. His turn up even took Jacob by surprise. Ice was in his gaze. The timing was impeccable. He didn't even seem to notice the guy was holding a knife, and could've stabbed him at any moment. Frankly, he seemed not to care. Without one word being exchanged the confrontation was over. Just like that. Alik stepped into the cell and sat down on the metal toilet after giving the man one last look-down.

"I talked to a cousin of mine. This cousin is on the outside. He told me something interesting about you Jacob." Alik's hand stroked his beard as he watched his bunkie's face contort with unease. "Oh yeah, and what's that?" It was exactly what he'd feared. The secret was out. "He is telling me that you are a rich man. A *very* rich man." "I was." "You are not having money now?" The Russian's brows were raised. Doubt tugged at his face. "Well, yes I still have it, but it's not much use in here."

He could sense Jacob's uneasiness on the subject. "You are not having to worry Jacob, I don't want your money, how do they say in America? Crime pays. I too am having money of this size. Millions." There was no reason to believe he was lying. Organized crime was widely known as an incredibly lucrative business. Tax free as well. The Russians controlled wealth beyond comprehension. Their reach was far and wide. What the mobster neglected to disclose was that his assets had long been frozen. His fortune on the outside was essentially useless. It was a card he held close to the chest. Revealing its face could put his reputation at risk.

"So why do you ask about mine? I mean, if you have your own, then...?" Jacob's voice quivered slightly as he spoke. It was a sensitive subject. He didn't want to offend his Bunkie. But he also didn't want to become a target. What he wanted really didn't matter at the end of the day. He was an ant. There was no way to negotiate with a foot. "You are curious to me Jacob boy. In some ways I am seeing a younger me in you, in other ways not so much, but you are curious. What of your family?"

Jacob smiled at the way Alik pronounced "F-a-m-i-l-y" with his strong accent. He sounded out each letter it seemed. "Are they having money like this to?" His head shook. "No, *I* won the money, my parents were well off at one point, but then things changed." The more tenured convict seemed intently interested in what his cellmate had to say. The questions continued. Jacob didn't mind. Better to have Alik as an ally than a foe.

"What is changing?" "Well, they spent too much, it's as simple as that, they liked to spend money and they wound up spending more than they made. A lot more. In the end it cost them. It cost all of us." Jacob's face was solemn, his head pointed towards the floor. He thought back to the day they were evicted from the Burtonwood property. In hindsight, those were the good times. At least he was still free back then.

"And you are resenting this in them?" "I don't blame them, well sometimes I do. But that didn't matter before I got locked up in here. I had money, plenty in fact, and the freedom to spend it." He was finding the more time he spent with Alik the more he liked him. In such a confined space, this was a good thing.

Jacob didn't see CJ for the rest of that week due to an unusually high amount of rainfall. It seemed as though it would never stop. The clouds were an Olympic pool hanging over the city, dumping bucketfuls at a time. When the downpour finally did subside, the yard was transformed into a vast field of mud. Only those that couldn't stand being cooped up in their cells for the past week ventured out. Most decided to stay indoors until the ground dried.

This gave Jacob and Alik plenty of time to talk with one another. "Can I ask you something Alik?" "Go ahead. What are you wanting to know?" "How did you become a mob boss? I'm sure you didn't say that was what you wanted to be when you grew up? So what happened?" "Jacob, like I said before, I am produced by my home. Mother Russia chewed me up and spat me out. The problem with spitting is sometimes it is landing on your shoes."

Alik could tell Jacob didn't get his analogy, so he tried explaining a different way. "When a man is beaten, the person who is doing the beating thinks he is winning. But unless he kills the other man, all he is doing, is creating a stronger enemy. Do you understand this?" The entire time the Russian spoke, his hands were busy emphasizing his point.

"I think so. So lemme' guess, you were the one getting beaten, until one day you decided to chop the guy's head off and apply for the executive position at the local mob office? That about sum it up?" "Essentially, yes." The two men laughed aloud. They were rapidly gaining a mutual respect for one another. Both were curious about the other's past.

"You know, there is a difference between the millions

we have Jacob. Are you knowing this?" "What do you mean?" "The difference, aside from obvious reasons of legality, is that I got mine slowly." He looked Jacob directly in the eyes. "Yours came all at once." "That's true." "You know, I used to dream as a child growing up in Volgograd that one day, I would find a pot of gold. This is much like what happened to you. And where is the money now?"

Once the mobster realized Jacob wasn't going to tell him specifics on what happened to the money, he decided to move on. He could tell by that point the man before him was careful about personal matters. He wouldn't give too much information too early. Alik brushed a gruff hand through his peppered beard. "Tell me about what you did first, when you were first getting the money." Jacob thought back to that day, almost two years earlier... The day that changed everything.

CHAPTER 18

NEW MONEY

Nineteen months before ever hearing the name Alik, Jacob had just discovered his windfall. The drive home that day took longer than expected. Jacob was still in shock over what just happened. His fingertips clenched tightly to the tattered steering wheel as he tried to pay attention to the road ahead. His mind was swimming. Numb with excitement. "Could this be it, did I really just win?" The clanking sound emanating from under the hood made it hard to believe he was now technically the city's second richest resident. It just didn't feel real. The day's light faded to orange and mauve as he pulled onto Senna Drive, the street that led home.

When Jacob opened the door to the apartment, he decided not to announce the news and just acted like nothing happened. He quietly ate dinner that night with his sister in the living room. Family Guy was on and he didn't feel like watching it on the small television in his room. Not only was the image always fuzzy, but it also had a crack running down the length of the screen.

They both ate in silence, giving an occasional chuckle at the many politically incorrect jokes the show was known for.

After they were finished, Jacob decided to take a stroll through the apartment complex. As he walked, the new lottery winner took notice to the refreshingly cool air and comforting breeze.

The wind blew gently on his face kissing his skin in soft waves. It quelled his racing mind. The occasional hoot of an owl called out in the distance. He'd heard the owl a few times before and assumed it must've lived in one of the many lumbering Oaks in the neighborhood. On this particular evening, he got to do more than just hear the elusive bird. As he approached the outskirts of the complex, just along the tree-line leading to the woods he heard the hooting again. At first muffled, the sound sharpened with the passing moments. *He was getting closer.*

A minute later a ghostly figure floated gracefully from its perch on a low-lying branch nearby. It literally looked like a ghost, silent and powerful. Its wingspan was absolutely massive. Jacob read somewhere that night owls were born with special material in their feathers that absorbed sound. An owl could fly right past your head, and unless you actually saw it, you would never know it had been there. This command of silence was the demise of many unsuspecting rodents.

He stood there and watched as the predator took wind, gliding to the ground below. Its eyes were fixed on something. The air seemed to grow more still. Mother Nature held her breath, embracing the cycle that has unfolded for millennia. The raptor landed in densely bladed grass with a plop, its wings covering the ground around it, as if afraid someone might come steal its prize. Jacob was sure he heard the squeak of some helpless soul trapped between the bird's talons a second later.

The owl stood over its prey for a few moments and then flew off, disappearing into the murky darkness of night; a limp figure clutched tightly in its unforgiving grasp. Nature was cruel. Nature was beautiful. Owlets gave weak hoots somewhere along the tree-line. Full bellies awaited them. Jacob let the breeze hit his skin once more before heading back to the apartment. It was getting a little too cool for his liking, not to mention he was both mentally and physically exhausted.

Nearly two full weeks after his trip to the lottery headquarters, Jacob finally received a call from the bank. "Yes, Mr. Gilferd? My name is Jason Ricci; I am the director of finance here at HTA Bank. I'm in charge of our wealth management department. I was wondering if I could take you to lunch to discuss your future with our firm. Is today good for you?" Jacob looked at the phone before putting it back to his ear. Confusion tugged at his forehead. "Who is this again?" 18 months went by fast. Before he knew it, his address was reduced to cell 51.

"That was how I found out the money cleared my bank account. That guy was all over me, he offered to give me a tour of the city, even though I tried to explain I've lived here for years. Mr. Ricci told me there was a whole other side of Charlotte, a side revealed only to a chosen few." Jacob was sitting with Alik, recalling the first time he'd met the pasty looking banker.

"He did everything in his power to try'n get me to take him on as my new financial advisor." "And was he right, about the city?" Alik was leaning off the edge of his bed looking down at Jacob with intent eyes. He enjoyed listening to his cellmate's intriguing recollections about his oddly interesting life.

"Well, there were a few highlights here and there, nothing to write home about." "Why are we writing home? What is this meaning?" The Russian shook his head with confused distaste while he waited for an explanation. None was given. Instead his celly just blurted, "Nevermind Alik."

Jacob leaned back in his bed, adjusting his pillow to

get more comfortable before letting his mind drift off again. Maria and Drake didn't find out their son won the lottery until almost three weeks after the money was claimed. It was a tough secret to keep. He thought back to their first reaction to the news. "When were you going to let us know? You don' think that's something we'd like to know about?" He chuckled at the thought of his mother with her hands on her hips. The conversation felt like it happened just yesterday...

"Mom! Why're you yelling? We're rich now! I was gonna' tell you, it's just, this is a lot to process you know? If it makes you feel any better, I haven't spent a dime on myself yet. I still don't really believe it's true, that I won and all. I mean this is crazy, like I'm *still* in shock!" Her arms were folded. She wasn't buying it.

"Well you still could've said something, shocked or not. You hear us talking in here about how we're gonna' cover the rent coming up, and you're sitting on 80 million just watching us suffer? Let's go to the bank, and now you can finally replace the TV. You didn't think I saw that crack in the screen, did you?"

That day, Jacob ignored his mother's words and walked out of the damp smelling apartment. He headed towards his car and then stopped dead in his tracks. As his eyes scanned the heap of metal, his face gave a look of disgust at its peeling burgundy paint that seemed to shed with the seasons. The busted taillight. The molded, drab interior and the rust stretching its arms on the hood and roof.

The entire time Jacob was recalling that pivotal point in life, Alik's eyes never left the young man. He appreciated the imagery Jacob was able to convey. Although English was not his first or even second language, his cellmate's detail was much appreciated. With nothing to do in the cell but talk, Alik chose to mostly listen. Interestingly enough, very few questions were asked about what landed Jacob in prison. They usually clung to subjects with lighter weight. Women, money, and family. Jacob didn't mind, he liked to let his thoughts wander, back to the days when things were good... Days like the day he picked up what he would later refer to as "Black Beauty." He had it within weeks of the windfall. It was one of his favorite purchases.

"First order of business, get some new wheels." Maria walked towards the parking lot expecting to be chauffeured to the nearest bank branch, but when she got to the place where his car should've been parked, it and her son were nowhere to be found. Only tufts of Crab Grass lining the sidewalk and a few potholes scattered about met her eye. "Where did that boy get off to?"

The lucky millionaire knew exactly where to purchase his new vehicle. There was a dealership about 8 miles down the road that specialized in supercars of all sorts. Closer to the nicer end of the city. From there it was only a stone's throw to South Park, Charlotte's most affluent area. As far as Jacob was concerned, they were the only game in town. As he pulled up to the fancy car-lot he became increasingly self-conscious about his own vehicle. It was a far cry from the countless Lamborghini and Ferrari offerings on display.

He tried to park as far away from the front office as possible, to avoid being seen in such an atrocity. It was such an embarrassment, even though it didn't much matter now. A salesman with slicked-back hair and a fancy suit strolled onto the lot after allowing Jacob to gawk over a grey Aston Martin DB11 for a few minutes. It looked just like the one James Bond would drive. "She's a true beauty isn't she?" He asked the question rhetorically and held out a hand to introduce himself. A classic icebreaker for someone in his field. They all used the same tired lines. "I'm Jim, what's your name?" "Jacob." "Well what are you in the market for this fine day Jacob?"

The man's conversation was rehearsed and pre-packaged, but Jacob didn't care enough to make an issue of it. "I need a new car, something nice." "Well... As you can see, all of em' are pretty nice." The salesman quickly realized Jacob was a novice at high-end buying and probably couldn't even afford a test-drive. One look at his clothes told him all he needed to know. That, paired with the awe-filled twinkle Jacob couldn't help but emanate as his eyes scanned the lot, it all pointed to a young man out of his league. A window shopper. The excitement in the dealer's body language retreated. His professionalism remained intact for the most part. It waned here and there but he didn't want to judge too soon.

Alik had a frown on his face as he listened to his cellmate continue the story. "And this little sales guy didn't even know? He sounds like a real ass type." Jacob was so mesmerized by the Aston Martin he hadn't picked up on the condescending tone the salesman projected towards him at the time. "Can we go in the showroom so I can see what other cars you have?"

"Sure. Now I'll have you know, they get more expensive on the floor than out here." He gave Jacob one more look-down before beckoning towards the main building. The two men strode into the showroom and Jacob began to inspect the inventory. There was a Rolls Royce Dawn on a spinning platform in the center of the well-lit room. It was the first thing he saw. Bold. Refined luxury.

Its skin was Cornish white, with flesh boasting toasted auburn and woody chestnut. Malabar teak cascaded down a hand-crafted veneer, splitting the rear seats with a sylvan waterfall. The car was a beautiful piece of work, but not quite to Jacob's taste. His head turned left and he saw the one that moved him. The flawless black paint was so clean it reflected every other vehicle in its vicinity. Chills ran up his spine. Then back down. It was immaculate. Stunning. Its curves were seductively perilous. Its posture, dangerous. Deep lines. Wide haunches. "Whoa, what kind of car is *that*?" "That? That my friend is a Night Black CL65 Mercedes AMG equipped with the Designo package." The description was given with pride. The car was a favorite among staff and spectators alike.

"What's Designo?" It was a good question. Only the most well-heeled clientele had ever heard the term. The upgrade came with a hefty price tag. "It's a package Mercedes offers to take its already gorgeous creations to another level. Jim opened the driver's side door and asked Jacob if he wanted to get in. He closed the door behind him and then hopped in on the other side. Jacob gripped the wheel with firm hands and then looked over at the salesman. Jim grinned back.

"You can start the engine if you'd like, go ahead." He looked for a key but was unable to find one. "It's keyless, all you have to do is press the start button and she'll wake up." He found the button in the center console with a little help from the salesman. The engine growled to life like a beast from a long slumber. The sound was absolutely riveting. Snarling, and angry, it was a boy's dream. Jacob took a moment to look at the stitching. A hallmark of the coveted brand. Jim knew he had him. The car sold itself.

"Every stitch was hand-strung by a single craftsman. Look at this." A palm grazed the dashboard. Carefully treated calfskin adorned its surface. Supple to the touch, it was likened closer to skin used to craft high-end loafers than dress a car. With the CL, the designers had raised the standard. "The leather is a special type that reflects heat in the summer and retains it in winter. If you look at the display monitor right here, and press this button," Jim reached around the steering wheel; you'll notice the car comes equipped with night-vision.

May come in handy when the zombies attack." Jacob snickered. "There're also rearview cameras for parking, and look here..."

Jim pointed to fixtures on the steering wheel and throughout the dashboard on the driver and passenger sides of the coupe. "You remember I said this vehicle came with a Designo package? Well this is their flagship trademark. What sets it apart from a traditional Mercedes. This is all granite, yes actual granite, as in the kind used on your mother's countertops. All of these beautiful accents. Look." Jim continued to point out the fixtures in the luxury piece of art.

The granite itself was onyx with white speckles etched throughout, and it was positively breath-taking. Jacob also noticed the leather on the inside of the doors had a wonderful diamond stitch design. "Was this done by the craftsman as well?" His fingers grazed the soft leather. Excitement beamed in his eyes. It felt like butter. This was a level of quality he could get used to.

"You know it! She's a real sight, and get this, this car's from the owner's personal collection." "You mean the owner of this company?" The salesman shook his head. "That's right, and trust me when I tell you, the man takes care of his cars! He spent almost twenty thousand on the wheels and rims alone. I can guarantee you're not gonna' find another car like this anywhere, let alone in Charlotte. It's one of a kind."

As Jacob looked around at the interior of the coupe with awe, Jim looked over him. He was trying to identify signs of wealth. Anything. A watch, designer shades, nice shoes. As far as he could tell Jacob was just an ordinary run of the mill kind of guy. "How much for this?" "Well, you may need to call your boss and ask for a few raises" Jim dis-tastefully joked. "It's MSRP is $189,000." Three seconds could barely zip by before Jacob replied "I'll take it."

Jacob looked the man square in the eyes. Jim could tell he wasn't joking and seemed a little surprised at the assertive response. Thick brows raised, a hand reached to scratch at the whiskers crowning his upper lip. "Um, sure, now how will you be paying for this Mr., what was your name again?" "A bank transfer, we can do a bank transfer, and you can call me Jacob." "Of course, and when you say bank transfer, are you talking about the *entire* amount? I'm just a little confused here?"

His face was wrinkled with utter disbelieve. "Oh, yes, for the whole amount." Jacob wasn't even looking at the salesman anymore. He was still enchanted by the beautiful craftsmanship and skill put into the vehicle before him. Two hours later, and after much fumbling and stuttered sentences on the part of Jim, Jacob drove off the lot, only in much better fashion than he'd arrived. "I know this Jim character, he was feeling stupid no? He thought you were pulling a fast one, like not having the money eh? Mudak." The Russian's native tongue tended to slip whenever he was keen on something.

Alik was intrigued by Jacob's story and urged him to go on. By this time, it was long after lights out but neither Jacob nor Alik were in the mood to sleep. After taking a moment to reminisce on how it felt to drive off that car lot, he thought about what happened next.

CHAPTER 19

MORE MONEY, MORE PROBLEMS

The engine snarled viciously as he urged the acceleration, testing its temper. It was angry. Pirelli P Zero tires gripped at the pavement. A lowered suspension gave sleekness new meaning. It was a shark, swimming with dominance, owning its concrete territory. Other cars were minnows, carps, food on the menu. The feeling of being at the helm of such a powerful machine was invigorating. With the slightest coaxing, the car would lunge forward, ready to please its owner's desire for speed and adrenaline. A V12 made sure of that. Jacob rolled up to a red light and looked out his new window. He couldn't believe it. "This is real!"

Another car pulled up a moment later. Two attractive ladies sat in the driver and passenger seats. They were in a current model Lexus LS. Had Jacob been in his clunker, these two women wouldn't have given him the time of day. The current circumstance earned him an entirely different response from them. He was in a showstopper. All eyes were on him. They beeped their horn and waived. The girl on the passenger side gestured for him to pull over into a nearby parking lot. He obliged. It was his first time being pursued.

When Jacob got out of the car, he was pleased to find both young ladies were interested in seemingly everything he said. It was a huge boost to his ego. Something he needed. He leaned comfortably against the CL65's left hip while they spoke. "So where ya'll from?" "Oh we're from Atlanta; I'm just in for the weekend, but my friend lives here in Charlotte. I come all the time though." She looked him down. Her eyes seemed to peel away his clothing. "You're pretty good lookin' by the way... Why don' ya' have a girl with you in that fancy car?" "Or maybe even two" the other woman chimed in laughingly. The hunter had become the hunted. It's a feeling most men will never know.

"I just bought this car like ten minutes ago. So you two are the first I've met." "Well take our number down and call us later." Jacob did a poor job of hiding his confusion. "You want me to have both your numbers?" "Oh yea, we do everything as a team." The two women blew kisses and then got back into their car and drove off. It was like a dream. Like something pulled right from the beginning of a porn scene. Things like this didn't happen in real life.

Jacob stood there and tried to process what just took place. He looked down at the ground and noticed for the first time how dirty his sneakers were. Mud caked at the soles. Tethered laces hung over tanned yellow fabric that once gleamed white. He hadn't given his appearance much thought. Apparently neither had the women he'd just met. For men, nice cars can be a cloak, veiling even the most obvious of miscomings. "I've gotta' get some new clothes." That's when he decided to head to a mall on the nicer end of town. He knew exactly what store to visit for his much-needed shopping spree.

As Jacob walked into the store he felt the familiar vibration of his phone ringing in his right front pocket. When he looked at the screen he saw one new text from his sister. "You better come home, mom's pissed you left without saying anything." Jacob ignored the warning and approached one of the reps at the front desk of the retail store. The phone slipped back into his torn jeans. They gave him the same reserved look the car salesman had.

"Welcome to Brooks Brothers Sir, Umm, what can I help you find today?" He noticed both the customers and employees all seemed extremely well-dressed. In fact, he was the most poorly clothed person in the store. By far. "I need some new clothes." "Ok, glad to help, what in particular are you looking for?" Jacob looked down at himself and then back at the man. "A new wardrobe" he let out flatly. The older gentleman gave a slight smile that agreed with the assessment, and then beckoned the young-looking patron to one corner of the store.

"Well, if you're looking at creating a new image, you've come to the right place. Before we start, what price constraints are we looking at?" Still in shock at his change in luck, he replied in the same detached manner as before. "I don't have any." Jacob barely gave eye contact to the man. His gaze was preoccupied, scanning the buffet of clothing before him. The fine fabrics on display highlighted his own lackluster attire.

The salesman, thinking Jacob miss-understood what he was asking, tried inquiring in a different way. "I was essentially asking how much money you're looking to spend on this new wardrobe?" "Oh I know what you meant, but I don't have a limit. I just came into some money." There was a pause. Almost as if the man were weighing how to respond. "Ok, well do you have a ballpark figure I can work with?" "How about we just look at what you have, and I will either say I like it or not." The employee could hear a hint of annoyance and decided it best not to push further. "Very well."

When Jacob left the store, it was nearly time for dinner

and he knew his mother would be livid. He left with empty hands as he strode back to his car. This wasn't because he didn't like the items that were displayed; it was because nearly all the employees at the retailer were carrying his bags for him. It was easy to spend money. Too easy.

By the time his appetite for shopping was satisfied he made the company nearly $78,000 richer. It was the single most successful sales day for the store since they opened. Jacob's lust for the clothing line would also later contribute to the salesman's promotion within the company to head of business development. It was a title earned by sheer luck.

To ease his mother's nerves and the wrath that would undoubtedly accompany them, Jacob went to a computer store located in the shopping mall before heading home. He knew the rent could be paid online, so he went to the website he remembered his parents talking about to make the payment. As of recently, whenever he heard the site being mentioned it was because they were fussing about a late fee or sir-charge for not keeping the account current.

The dutiful son decided to pay the outstanding balance on the account, and not just for the month, but for the entire lease agreement. His parents had just signed a new term for the next 24 months and the total balance was a whopping $26,280. "Let's see her complain now." When he finally made it home, it was after eight o clock and everyone was in the living room eating dinner. The sky was painted with mauve and deep oranges. Only a sliver of sun was left, its last glimmers scuttling between the jointed branches of trees. The rest was tucked beneath the horizon.

Jacob swung open the front door and went into the kitchen to wash his hands. After dousing them with soap, he looked up from the sink and over at his mother. She was staring at him with her arms folded. *Just as expected*. "Before you say anything, I'm sorry for walking out on you earlier, and I paid the rent too." Foamy white bubbles splashed his shirt as his mother replied. "Well good, and don' you ever walk out when I'm talkin' to you, ya hear me? You get a little money and think that changes something around here? I'm still your mother and you're still my son, as long as those two things remain true, you *will* respect me. You understand boy?"

"Yes mom." His mother was bringing his spirits down with her complaining, so he decided to change the subject. "Hey dad? Can you check the account for the rent and see if that payment went through?" Drake adjusted his glasses and then logged into the resident portal online. Jacob already knew it had gone through, so he just waited for the reaction. He put a piece of fried chicken on a plate and started to stir the mashed potatoes sitting on the stovetop. They were his favorite. Maria always added chives, cheese, and bacon. All that was needed after grabbing a spoonful was a dab of butter.

"Oh my God! Jacob! Is this for real? Maria, our son just paid the rent!" She rolled her eyes rhetorically. The expression on her face could be summed up with one word. Unimpressed. "Well, he said that's what he did. He's already treadin' in deep water, least he can do is pay a bill or two around here." "No, I mean he paid the rent, for the whole lease!" "Wait what?" The chicken bone she'd been gnawing on fell to the floor near the couch. Her mouth hung open. With a smile on his face and a full plate of food, Jacob walked down the corridor to his room. He knew his trips down this dark hallway were numbered. The fried chicken that night tasted particularly scrumptious; now that financial worries were behind him.

With deliciously greasy fingers he began to tally up how much he'd spent in total. His stomach turned for a moment. The shock was brief. He smiled silently to himself, mulling the satisfaction of knowing he could afford it. The total was still high though, a lot to spend in one day. "I need to make a budget." It was a valuable epiphany. The newly minted millionaire never realized over $260,000 could go so easily.

"I gotta' get those bags out the car in the morning too." Thinking of this reminded him of one minor inconvenience he noticed. Everywhere he went, he had to use a bank transfer to pay for his transactions. A credit card was just the thing he needed. He thought about seeing his father when he would pay for an item with his gold American Express and this gave him an idea.

Jacob wiped his fingers on his shirt, but not before picking out a piece of chicken that had lodged itself in the small gap between his front teeth. Grease bled into the polo's fabric in long streaks. Had he worn any of the clothes he just bought, he may have used a paper towel; but he knew he would be throwing all his old things away. None were worth keeping. He made his way back towards the kitchen and approached Drake.

"Hey dad? What's the number to Amex? I'm gonna' pay off your balance." Jacob's father nearly fell over himself retrieving the number from his wallet. He shot Maria a look of excitement. What he didn't mention to his father was that in addition to paying off the outstanding debt, he also planned on requesting membership to the company's Black Card Program. The payoff would be a nice introduction between the two parties. A lot of business was headed their way. They welcomed him with open arms.

"That was almost two years ago, wow." Jacob looked up from his bed to hear the sound of Alik's snoring. He smiled to himself. At how life had turned out. Here he was, sitting in a maximum-security Federal Prison, and he had just made a mob boss fall asleep by telling him a bedtime story. The memories of his life before prison were as vivid as his dreams from childhood.

Jacob lay with his face up for several minutes before drifting off to sleep himself. During the course of the night he awoke several times. The metal framed prison beds were extremely unpleasant, and thin sheets left him cold and uncomfortable. His new home was either one of two things; too cold, or too hot. Never just right. The next day, Jacob decided to venture into the yard. The mud had finally dried and most inmates were more than ready to get some fresh air after being cooped up for so long. For some, that fresh air would come at the ultimate price.

CHAPTER 20

A SINGLE SHELL CASING

CJ was standing in his usual spot near the bleachers watching a basketball game that had just gotten underway. It was the Whites against the Blacks and the Black team had the upper hand. Almost all their players were taller, faster, and most grew up playing street ball. It was in their blood. One of the Caucasian players gave an opposing team member a swift elbow to the ribs while trying to retrieve the ball. A mistake. Or at least it looked like one. Sometimes hits were carried out on the court. If one wanted their enemy to bleed out quickly, they needed to get the heart pumping. Any strikes that hit a vital area after that would be much more effective. The Crip member buckled with pain. It was a clean shot.

Enraged, his teammates responded in kind. Exactly what the Whites were betting on. Shanks rose from hiding on both sides. They had been kept at bay until the moment was right. You could smell the scent of impending battle in the air. It hung like a heavy musk. One of the larger players grabbed the ball and lobbed it at the offending man's head. It struck him square in the nose, causing it to bleed profusely. Recognizing this had the potential of escalating, CJ decided to put more distance between him and the combatants. As he hurried away from the bleachers he caught sight of Jacob.

"Hey! Jacob!" "Oh what's up man? Why're you not in the usual spot?" CJ looked over his shoulder before answering. "Looks like something's about to go down over there." His observation and subsequent action proved wise. No sooner than the words left his mouth, then a full-fledged brawl broke out on the far east corner of the courtyard. Clenched fists swung wildly in every direction. Most were sloppy and misguided, but some connected. This went on for several minutes. Chaos.

A guard in one of the towers radioed to a comrade in an adjacent post alerting him to the commotion below. Instead of stopping the altercation from escalating they just joked on the transmission about which side they thought would win. It wasn't uncommon for bets to be placed on bouts like this. Fights were the highlight of the day for most guards. Without them, working at the prison could get painfully redundant. Dirty CO's would even go as far as to instigate. Newcomers were their favorite victims. Extra yard time was a small price to pay a con for a good show. For a career criminal, any break in monotony was worth kicking someone's ass over. Throw in a few soups and they may even crack some bones. It was a different world.

The jokes ceased when the initial guard saw a familiar glint reflecting off the oncoming sunlight. It could only mean one thing. He put down the hand-held radio and reached into a long black box mounted horizontally across the tower's balcony. The grin on his face vanished, replaced with absolute focus. His movements were swift and precise. Ten years in the military taught him that. When he raised his arm back up, a high-powered assault rifle was firmly in his grip. A Steiner Optics OTAL-C laser sniffed out its target. This gun was serious business.

The stock had been modified to minimize recoil; and running down its center was a scope that could pick off a man at over 1200 yards. The guard held the heavy firearm steady and began to look down its sights. His left eye was clinched shut as its twin searched for a target. What greeted his eye on the scope's end sent a chill through his spine. Play time was over. He was on the clock.

His gaze met the glint of a blade. Jagged and crude, yet surprisingly sharp to be handcrafted, it was constructed from a piece of metal extracted from a rusty bleacher. The bleachers were well known as weapons factories. Potential shivs abounded near every joint. This one had been sharpened on the pavement slowly over the previous week. Sinister didn't even begin to describe the weapon. Bad intentions were the fires from which it was forged. Hidden from view under a tuft of grass, the blade was now put into action.

Its handle had a firm grip made by wetting individual pages from a magazine and then wrapping them tightly around the base until thick. Magazines were frequently stolen from the prison library. Some were for business. Others for pleasure. Even the silhouette of a woman can get a man going after a few years without. This one like many, had gone unnoticed. Veteran cons knew nearly anything could be constructed into a weapon. Even reading material could be dangerous in the wrong hands.

The guard adjusted his scope, bringing the makeshift weapon into clearer view. He was too late. Thick drops of blood were already dripping freely from its tip. He moved his trigger finger from the safety position and prepared to fire a round down range. A few pounds of pressure was all it took...

A loud crack. Unmistakable. The bullet ripped through the air at 3200 feet per second as it pummeled towards its target, breaking the sound barrier. It tore the attacker's worn jacket collar and pierced through the base of his neck. Inmates nearby could hear the pop of his spinal cord as it snapped violently from the impact. His head swung back un-naturally. The man was dead before his limp body hit the dirt.

The same could not be said for his victim. He lay on the ground, clutching a tuft of grass in one hand and holding his neck with the other. Dust gathered up around him, risen by his frantic movements. A deep, haunting look of agony was etched into his face. His eyes bore the fear of a man not ready to die. Wide. Wild. Red gushed unforgivingly as he tried to keep pressure on the wound. His efforts were in vain. A river poured over his knuckles as life crept away, ignoring his calls to stay.

Everything seemed to be moving in slow motion for several dramatic moments. The single shell-casing from the shot fell from the tower to the pavement below. It flipped four times before hitting the ground, Jacob could hear its clink even from where he was standing.

Moments later the alarm began to whale throughout the yard. It reminded Jacob of the sound he'd heard in movies when there was about to be an air-raid on a city. The last time he saw someone die, it was his brother in the hospital. Seeing this man lose his life to a hot piece of lead, this was something different.

CJ and Jacob could hear the dogs barking as riot squads began to assemble on both the east and west entrances to the yard. The heavily armed men sported dark steel-toe boots, tactical leggings, joint pads and riot helmets. Each of their faces bore the look of a determined soldier.

Some guards held thick leashes, snarling German Shepherds tugging viciously at their ends. Others carried knight sticks made of solid wood in one hand; in the other were bulletproof shields with rectangular sight windows. As they approached from both sides of the yard, snipers began to line the balconies of both towers and the main building. There were always at least a couple on duty, especially during yard.

The warden stormed onto the grass and began speaking into a bullhorn to the inmates now facedown on the ground. His voice rumbled with anger. “We will not accept this type of behavior! From any of you!” His eyes drifted to the lifeless body, then to his victim. Medics were already on-sight, doing what they could, which wasn’t much. “If you’re caught with a weapon, and attempt to use it on another inmate, or one of my men; you will be shot dead where you stand. We’re not playing games at this establishment gentlemen. So either shape up or ship out!”

The stern man gave the convicts a menacing look over before going on. “Just understand, the shipping out comes with a body bag.” Another glance over to the body. A sigh let out as he weighed judgement. “For the next week, none of you will have the opportunity to display your disregard for life. Ya’ll wanna act like savages? We’ll treat you like some. All yard privileges are revoked. One week. And the next time this happens, it’ll be for three!” Angry groans of protest echoed throughout the yard, but no one dare say a word.

That evening Alik and Jacob didn’t talk much about what winning the lottery was like. Jacob sat on the edge of his bed, head hung low, and thought about the violence he’d just witnessed. That popping sound from the man’s neck. His face. “You have not seen this type of killing before?” “I have seen death, just not murder.” Fear bathed in the crevasses of Jacob’s face.

Alik stroked his beard and sulked back, pondering what his celly said. Then he broke the silence, “Where I am from, things like this are common you know.” “Well I’m glad you see nothing wrong with it." He'd grown more comfortable in speaking his mind to the Russian. "I did not say this is nothing wrong, I only say that I have seen much. You think I am this monster? A man with no feelings inside? I know I will pay for the things I've done. We all have a bill to pay in the end."

The shaken convict took a moment to think before asking, "Why, why do you think we're here Alik?" "In prison? This is obvious." Alik knew that wasn't what Jacob was asking. "I mean, why do you think we are alive? What're we doing here? What's the point?" Both men stopped talking for a moment. Their attention was drawn to a shuffling sound just outside their doorway. Footsteps. Midnight had come and gone. All inmates were locked in for the night. The glow of a flashlight briefly illuminated the area a few cells down. Then it left just as quickly. The guards were making their rounds.

"No man is knowing these things; we all have to decide what is important in our lives. Then we act on those beliefs which we hold dear Jacob. This is what I am thinking." "But that still doesn't answer the question. All that says is that we should try to find purpose, what I'm asking is whether we actually have one? There is a difference between *having* a purpose and trying to *find* one."

Before Alik responded, he pondered Jacob's purpose to him. It wouldn't be until months later that his true nature would be revealed. For the time being he saw no harm in conversing with his young cellmate. The more they talked, the more information he was able to gather.

"I guess this is something we will be finding out on the other side." Jacob thought about what Alik said, it reminded him of the kinds of conversations he and Ming Lao used to have. They used to discuss the meaning of life after meditation sometimes. Mr. Lao preferred not to talk until their minds had been cleared of all clutter. He would say, "Before you say a word, learn *not* to." Then he would close his eyes and quiet his mind. Nature would ease into him. Masking, and revealing. Closing the gap between ego, and the heartbeat of life. Jacob laid silent in his bed for a moment, reflecting the serenity of meditation. In prison quietness was an extravagance few men could afford. Just closing one's eyes in peace was a luxury.

That night Jacob started to feel an itch in the back of his throat. It began as a tickle, toying with an uvula in no mood for games. Gradually progressing until it held a firm chokehold on his tonsils. Infection set in. Thin sheets were allowing a draft that created the perfect environment for sickness. Additionally, the food served in the prison was of the absolute lowest quality allowable by law. Most had been stripped of nearly all nutritional value. A balanced meal plan was at the bottom of the totem pole. By the next morning that slight itch morphed into a full-fledged whooping cough. Something was wrong.

"You OK Jacob?" "I'm fine." The concern in the Russian's voice lingered. "That sounds like something we are calling a lockup cough. Are you knowing about this?" "No, you know this is my first time in prison, what does it mean?" As he spoke, Alik's grey eyes scoured the confined room. His gaze jumped from crack to crevasse. Then he looked at his cellmate, at the way he held one hand against his chest, trying to stifle the building pressure. Jacob was in trouble. "These damn cells, they never clean them. Mold is growing in these for several years now. Most of us have been here for a while, so we are used to it you see."

The Russian softened his usually rough voice. "You may want to see the doctor for this sickness." "Is there something I should know? You act like I'm gonna' die over a little mold?" The heavyset mobster shook his head. "You are not knowing this particular strand of mold. I am betting last night you were alright, yes?" "Besides a little sore throat." "Exactly, that's how it started with my last cellmate." His brow raised. "And?"

"Why are you thinking my cell was available when you got here Jacob boy? As you can see, this facility is crowded over." Alik's gaze was solemn. Jacob shifted. He wasn't sure if the question was a threat in disguise. "They told me someone got stabbed, I'm guessing that was your last bunkie?" "No, he is the one who did the stabbing. But he died too, a few days later." "Because of the fight?" Alik shook his head slowly and looked Jacob directly in the eyes. His gaze was dead-serious. "Because of the mold." "Guard! Guard!" "What is it newbie? Your cellmate not playin' nice? Or maybe he's a little too friendly?" There was a sinister smile on the CO's face. "No, I need the doctor, please! I think I'm sick."

"What do ya' think this is? *I* barely get medical insurance and I'm on *this* side of the bars. You cons think this is OnStar? Next time you call me over here and demand something, the only thing you're gonna' get is a week in the hole." The man's brow furrowed with distaste as he spoke. It was a pet-peeve every officer shared. There was nothing worse than a whining, high maintenance convict. They acted like they were staying at a hotel, asking for this, expecting that. Prison isn't supposed to be easy. At least that's how the CO's saw things.

Jacob removed his hands from the bars and looked back at Alik as the guard made his way back to the staircase. "What am I supposed to do now?" "You will have to wait until lunch. Try to talk to one of the guards in the mess hall." "Why exactly did your last cellmate die?" Alik shook his head with distaste as he answered, as if the question drew disappointment. Maybe they had been friends. "He didn't listen to me; I was telling him the same thing I'm telling you. He never is going to the doctor."

The cell doors creaked open at 1pm. They would have

opened earlier, but a fight in another wing pushed everything back. It was a common occurrence. Alik stepped out first, looking back at Jacob with concern. He gave one more glance and then headed to the staircase. By this point Jacob was coughing so hard his chest burned. Heavy wheezing hugged at his lungs. They wouldn't fill. He used his sleeve to cover his mouth. When it lowered, his eyes widened at what lay in its dingy folds. There was blood. Spattered red polka dots with dark green phlegm, grouped in blobs. It was thick and sticky. He stumbled from the cell and did his best to stay in line. Every step was an enemy. A mountain to climb.

Jacob was at the top of the stairs when he collapsed. His vision went dim. And then completely black. He could tell he was rolling but his body was so numb, he couldn't feel the impacts as he tumbled down the thirty-eight steps. He landed at the bottom with a heavy thud, face up, blood pouring from his mouth and nose. The light from the ceiling above was the last thing he remembered seeing.

He awoke to a prison hospital bed. There was an IV stuck in his left arm. A cuff on one wrist. As both Jacob's wits and vision returned, a heavy-set and over-worked looking nurse came into view. Bruises lined his arms. The fall left him pretty banged up. A looming headache palpitated just behind his ears. "How're you doin' there? You were in a pretty bad spot for a while there son." He blinked weakly. She came into clearer focus as the seconds marched on. "How long was I out? What's in this IV?" "Well, this is a combination of Suprax and an anti-inflammatory agent."

"What's Suprax?" The plump woman pulled the blanket closer to Jacob's neck. Once he was tucked in to her liking she replied in a tender voice "It's an antibiotic; Had yaself' one nasty respiratory infection on your hands son. Been tryna' tell the warden for years bout' that mold in D-block. Hafta' doctor up almost every new inmate on that wing." Southern charm weaved in and out of each word. She was much nicer than the guards. Nicer than anyone he'd met.

The still dazed inmate looked on as she continued rambling. "He says the state won't pay since this is a Federal Prison. I think Mr. Keller burned a few bridges in government, so here we are." The guard nearby shook his head. The nurse had a bad habit of talking too freely with inmates. For the most part, members of staff were expected to keep to themselves. It was a hard rule to enforce.

"Good news is, this is the last time you should be up here for this particular ailment. Once treated, your immune system should build up a tolerance fairly quickly. I rarely need ta' treat inmates twice for this. Just lay here'n try to get some rest. The guards'll escort you back to your cell tomorrow morning hun." Unlike so many in the prison, her voice cradled rooted notes of empathy.

Lying in that hospital bed reminded Jacob of the day he and his mother watched his brother die. As he lay there in silence, tears began to pour. He couldn't hold them back any longer. The thin pillow beneath his head soaked quickly against the onslaught. It felt cold on his face. He was crying for his brother. He was crying for himself. For this hell he was in. For everything. "How did I get here?" Jacob sobbed to himself silently.

Maybe it was the fact that his wrist was handcuffed to the side of the bed, but it finally hit him. He was in prison, and he was going to die here. It was a hard pill to swallow. Reality hit him like a Mack truck. He would never have children, never get married, Jacob realized he would never be free again. One of the guards peered into the room through the window in the door, and Jacob tried to hold back the river of despair.

If he was confined to prison for the duration of his life, the last thing he needed was to have it spread around that he was soft; that would make his time considerably more difficult. “What’s that noise I hear in there con?” “Nothin, just coughing that’s all.” Jacob rolled over, hiding his face. After a few seconds he could here footsteps that told him the guard had walked back down the hallway. The one bright spot in his hospital stay was the silence. It accompanied him throughout the night. He enjoyed it while he could. Within hours he’d be thrown back to the raucous slums of D-Block. The wolves awaited.

CHAPTER 21

GO PRIVATE

"Rise and shine." The nurses held a lot more cheer than the CO's. "Probably cause they've been exposed to a lot less" Jacob thought to himself silently. "Good morning. So, how are you feeling?" "I feel like ten pounds of shit in a five-pound bag, which is to say, much better. My headache isn't as bad at least." They both chuckled weakly. The nurse started to check his vitals. She was a different woman than the one from the night before.

"Well there! It looks like your temperature's gone down nicely, you should be outta' here in a jiffy," she said with a chipper voice. Still in pain but grateful, he gave the woman a hearty grin. It was closely followed by a wince. White teeth bared as lips reached for opposing ends of his face. Pain was a shadow he couldn't shake. His wrist was sore and developing a red ring around it from the tight cuffs connecting him to the bed. The metal was digging into his skin. The guard from the night before took his job way too seriously.

After the nurse stepped from the room the new CO on duty unlocked the handcuffs and escorted Jacob back to D-block. Cell 51 opened with its usual creak. Alik greeted him with a burly smile. The old mobster was clearly relieved to see him. Still dazed from the night's medication, Jacob just nodded. "Jacob, I see you are not dying yet!" "Not yet. Wish I could've stayed in sick-bay a bit longer though. At least the mattresses down there only sucked a little." He rubbed his wrist as Alik smiled in agreeance.

"The beds were more comfortable there, even with the cuffs on." "Yea, these beds are so small, my ten-year-old daughter wouldn't fit on them." Alik signaled to his leg as it dangled off the edge. His Bunkie peered up at him with a look of astonishment that straddled the fence, leaning over into disbelief. The Russian hadn't struck him as the paternal type. "I didn't know you had a daughter. When's the last time you saw her?" He should have thought before he spoke. Alik kept silent. The look on his face said it had been much too long. Fatherhood was a knife that stabbed him in the heart, twisting at his flesh with each day. So much had been missed. It was a pain buried deep, a weakness, one that needed to remain hidden.

The Russian decided to change the subject to something lighter. "You never told me whether you got those girls to, you know do the boom boom?" He beckoned with his arms as if to be holding a woman. One limb hung lower, palm gripping and squeezing at an ass made of air. "What girls? Oh, you mean the ones in the Lexus?" A huge grin ran across Jacob's mouth, but then retreated just as quickly. Aftershocks from the headache still stalked the space between his skull. He leaned against the cell wall and thought back to that day, the day they finally met up.

The new convict chuckled at how drastically life could change in less than two years. "I wish I never won that damn money sometimes Alik, I really do. If I never won, I would've never even met Kacy." "Who is this?" "The woman I was convicted of killing." There was something dark about the way the words left Jacobs tongue. Like it was familiar. Death. Murder. "I know you are not a killing type, not until you are done with sleeping." Jacob screwed his face at the odd statement. "Alik you really need to work on your English." "English is such an odd language. It's like you are thinking backwards." Jacob tuned the mobster out. When he started speaking gibberish, that was the youngster's queue to let his mind wander.

As he recalled his first female encounter post-winning, he rubbed a few fingers through sparse strands of hair on his chin. It was a full month before he'd heard from the two women in that Lexus. To be honest, they were the last thing on his mind. At that point Jacob was still getting acclimated to the wealthy lifestyle. It was a lot to take in. A lot to learn.

He decided early on he and his family could use a vacation. He came to that conclusion for several reasons. The incessant onslaught of media personnel played a big part. They gathered around him at every opportunity. It was like having a personal band of paparazzi, all salivating for a chance to interview Charlotte's newest millionaire. Big news. After weeks of having reporters springing from bushes and everyone they knew lining up for a loan, the family needed a break.

Their destination was Bora Bora in French Polynesia. A suggestion by Jacob's new Amex concierge. Even at their height, Maria and Drake couldn't have fathomed such extravagance. When the family arrived at the airport, they never actually had to go inside. Jacob decided they would be flying private. Why not go all out? After all, it was the family's first real vacation in years. Two black SUV's were booked. Both were current year Range Rovers. Men in suits. A follow-car with protection in tow took up the rear. No one would be bothering them, press included. Their chartered jet awaited.

Myra was the first to exit the lead car upon arrival. She modeled a new St. John dress she received from her brother on a shopping spree the day before. As he thought back to that day, Jacob remembered how nice the gown was. It flaunted a burnt tan backdrop with cream petaled flowers and a thin burgundy trim along the neckline. The bottom of the gown was loose and dance gracefully in the breeze as she moved.

She turned around and looked at her brother with a delighted expression. Maria and Drake were in the car behind them. Drake headed towards the back of the SUV to retrieve their luggage and he called out to Jacob to do the same. *Men's work*. His son knew better. He had only been a millionaire for a few weeks, but it didn't take long for him to get into the swing of things.

Jacob just stood by the side of the car and smiled at his father. A second or two later the drivers from both vehicles popped open their respective trunks and started carrying designer luggage to the awaiting jet. Maria laughed as their driver literally took the suitcase from Drake's grasp and said with a grin, "That's what I'm here for Mr. Gilferd." The trip had only just begun, yet the level of service was through the stratosphere. It was a humbling experience.

Aboard the plane opulence was everywhere. The finishes were all African Blackwood; easily the world's most expensive. Craftsmanship and luxury greeted their eyes at every turn. The seats and full-sized onboard couch were furnished with Rose Leather, and there was even a mini-bar stocked with Chateau D'Yqeum, specially requested by Jacob. It was a classy touch that took his parents by surprise. His new life suited him well.

The family was greeted by a lively young stewardess, "Hello and welcome aboard. I'll be taking care of you during your flight. I'm sure you'll find everything up to spec." She gave Jacob a wink that hinted they had made prior arrangements. Her fare skin complimented her bright personality. Well-endowed lashes lightly veiled hazel eyes. They gazed warmly at the smiles reflecting back at her. After noting how her eyes lingered in Jacob's direction, Drake started to survey the spacious cabin.

There was a wooded door that slid up and diagonally to separate the main cabin from the cockpit. It too was constructed from the coveted Blackwood. The area was surprisingly spacious. Drake could stand up comfortably, and he was a full 6'3. In addition to the couch, there were also four reclining chairs and a full-sized dinner table that folded out from the wall.

Everyone found a seat and fastened their safety belts in preparation for takeoff. "Good afternoon ladies and gents, this is your pilot speaking. Thank you for choosing HTA Jets, where we're happy to serve you. The forecast indicates clear skies ahead. We should arrive in Bora Bora in approximately twenty-two hours." There was a pause. Then the voice reemerged. "The first meal will be served around 2pm. Thank you and enjoy the flight."

Jacob could feel goosebumps rising on his skin as the engines roared to life. It sounded like the screams from a thousand golden eagles and then, just as suddenly as it appeared, the sound vanished into thin air. It was like magic. The cabin was as silent as a sleeping baby. Seeing the look of confusion on their faces, the stewardess explained.

"When I closed the hatch the jets electronic sound proofing mechanism was engaged. It's state of the art technology, that's why it's so quiet in here now." She gave a brief smile and then sat near the cockpit in a specially designed chair for takeoff. There was a small window for her to look out of, but the best views were from the couch in the main cabin. Drake took full advantage.

Myra and Jacob looked out at the other planes preparing for departure nearby. The view shifted as the Gulfstream made its way to the runway, picking up speed as it prepared to part ways with the Earth. Then the ground began to draw further and further away, at first slowly and then with sudden intensity. House sized objects looked like toys within seconds. The young woman un-buckled her seat belt and traversed the aisle towards the bar area at the other end of the cabin. Her footsteps were light, cushioned. The flooring beneath her was covered in surprisingly plush carpeting. The kind you'd expect to greet your feet whilst chauffeured in your private Ghost. It was a statement. Something that set the fleet apart, a gift, among many.

She pulled four crystal wine glasses and handed one to each of the gleefully smiling family members. "These desert glasses were handcrafted from the finest Italian crystal. They are imported exclusively for our company." "Excuse me, but I've always wondered, I've just been too embarrassed to ask; how can you tell the difference between *real* crystal and glass?" Maria was inspecting her glass, trying to uncover any obvious clues.

"Oh, no need to be embarrassed, that's actually a great question! There're several grades of crystal, but to answer your question first, the easiest way to tell is to pluck it with your finger." Maria looked bewildered. "You see, crystal is a better conductor of sound, therefore the ding you hear will be more pronounced than with a glass."

"Furthermore, with fine crystal, which is the highest grade available," she held up one of the glasses. "With these the sound can last for over twenty seconds or more." The four of them began tapping their glasses to test the woman's theory.

It proved correct. The cabin filled with an orchestra of musical ringing, the songs of fine stemware.

She smiled and then approached Jacob with a bottle of the Chateau D'Yquem. It was a 1986 vintage. Jacob specifically requested that year because he knew from working in the restaurant industry that it received a one-hundred-point rating by the Wine Advocate. That was an achievement nearly unheard of in the business. To anyone who appreciated great wine, D'Yquem was an absolute must.

"Yes please, thank you." His glass filled with golden liquid. All eyes fixed upon the resplendent light displayed within its depths. "This is one of my favorite sauternes." The word she used was unfamiliar. "One of your favorite what?" "Sauternes" she repeated, patience folded comfortably into her soft feminine voice. A strand of brunette silk found its way over her left eye. Slender fingers wrapped in lightly tanned skin swiped it away, tucking it behind her ear. She made them feel at home. Welcomed. "Sauterne is the class of French dessert wines Chateau D'Yquem belongs to."

Drake was quite interested, "Can you tell us a little more about, how do you say it, Sauternes? I collect, or should I say *used* to collect wine, but most were domestic; so I'm a little unfamiliar with the terminology?" The jet was cruising at 30,000 feet. Sun beams fought their way through clouds and into the cabin's windows. The enclosure was bathed in tangerine light that danced with reticent shadows, playing off the walls in the shapes of fluffy mountains. All was perfect.

"Oh honey didn't we see that at the restaurant that night with the Splintons?" "No that was Chateau Margaux Margaux, it was a Red." The young woman was delighted to expound further to her eager audience. "Well I'd be happy to explain the origins and flavor profile of classic Sauterne. This *is* by the way, one of the finest desert wines on the planet in the eyes of most of the wine world." Enthusiasm stroked at the cords of her voice. "The Vintner really created a piece of heaven." The stewardess poured additional glasses as she spoke, her tone steady and confident.

"The word Sauterne refers to the region of France known as Sauternais. The wine itself is made from a combination of three different grape varietals, all of which have been affected by Botrytis." "That doesn't sound good, what exactly is Botrytis? It sounds like a disease you get from having unprotected..." "Drake!" Maria shot a disapproving look and he cut his analogy short. The woman laughed a little and then continued to explain. His humor amused her.

Before she could say another word, Jacob interjected, "And where's *your* glass? You can't possibly expect to properly educate us on this fine rarity and not indulge in a little yourself?" All too often while serving the rich, the stewardess was offered indifference at best. With money came snobbery. They went hand in hand. It was a line of work suited for those with only the toughest of skin. The Gilferds were a welcome change. Without hesitation she drew another glass from under a hidden counter and poured a half measure. Jacob shot her a wink as his father looked on, reminded by his son of his own younger days.

"Go on, take the rest, we have three more bottles back there." She obliged and then took a seat on the couch next to Maria, but not before giving Jacob a look of sincere gratitude. His bounteousness felt genuine. It wasn't like he was trying to show off. His offer came from a warmer place. It left her with a tingle in her belly. "Thank you so much, and as I was saying, Botrytis is also known as the "Noble Rot" by many wine enthusiasts, and yes you're right in a way. It *is* like a disease, but more accurately, it's a fungus."

"Well what's it do?" As she explained, her fingers

contorted, adding texture to her description. "It actually raisins the grapes partially, sucking water from them. It literally draws the moisture right out. What's left behind is a fruit with much higher concentrations of sugar, thus producing the sweet flavor we're about to enjoy." Maria smiled as she took notice of the French nails the attendant sported. They complimented slender fingers that begged to be modeled.

They all took a sip, then the attendant demonstrated how to properly taste the wine. "When you take a sip, don't swallow immediately. Give it a moment. Try and let it evolve in your mouth first. Better yet, try flipping it on your tongue to really draw out those subtle flavors." She led by example, sloshing the golden luxury between the roof and floor of her mouth. Jacob held back a snicker. He shot his sister a glance. "It wouldn't be the first time Myra's done that." It was a cheap-shot he just couldn't resist. His father gave him a disapproving look before letting it soften to a smile. "What the hell" he thought.

Drake had the most seasoned palate barring the stewardess', and he thoroughly appreciated the richness of the coveted Sauterne. The finish was staggeringly assertive. It just went on and on. Epicureans the world over lived for experiences like this. The D'Yquem was in a class all its own. Nothing else came close. It left his mouth imbued with flavors of seared orange, crème brulee, and honey custard. He was floored by the complexity. There was bitter, like the peel from a Meyer lemon. It was faint. Sophisticated. Sexy. Hiding in the corners of candied sips. The sweetness of the wine was certainly present, but it didn't take away from the acidity or bright tropical undertones permeating the coveted vintage. "Ok, I can die now."

CHAPTER 22

Mount Otemanu

Jacob peered out the window of the Gulfstream G650 and watched as clouds meandered by with lazy elegance. They looked like a thousand fluffy pillows lining the floors of heaven. The jet's twin BR725 Rolls Royce engines roared outside, but the cabin was muted to a peaceful hum. He could see the clouds were starting to clear ahead as he looked out further. What unfolded took his breath away. Words did the view an unforgivable injustice. It was like an orgasm of color and beauty. The jet was in its final descent.

The water below was the clearest he'd ever seen. Sunlight danced across its shimmering surface. White-capped waves lapped calmly as a few yachts waded just off the shallows. Closer to shore he could see vast fields of coral. The reef's valleys and peaks gave it shades of blue and green Jacob didn't even know existed. He admired celeste, cyan, azure, turquois, and around twelve other colors; all in a circumference of about three gorgeous square miles.

"We are now making our approach into the beautiful islands of Bora Bora. If you look to your left you will see the legendary Mt. Otemanu. It's something of a landmark in this neck of the woods." Drake, Maria, and Myra had fallen asleep, but the sound of the pilot's voice coming across the intercom woke them up. In no time they too were drooling over the spectacularly breathtaking sights that lay before them.

Upon landing, the newly wealthy family was pleased to find two Maybach 62s sedans awaiting. The drivers were both natives to the island and gave them a traditional welcome along with placing handwoven flower necklaces around the women's necks. Jacob knew what a nice car looked like, after all, he had recently purchased one of his own; but the Maybach took the notion of *nice* to another level.

Once inside, one of the first things Jacob noticed was the ceiling. It was constructed completely of glass, and it wasn't just any type either. He accidently pressed a button near his fully reclined seat and the glass morphed from see-through to opaque. Myra was in the car with him and she started playing with the buttons in the center console. She wondered about a clear globe she saw sitting near the air conditioner. It reminded her of the Christmas globes she used to adore as a child, only without the snow. Something protruded from its center. There were tiny air vents at its core.

"Umm excuse me, driver, sorry but what's this thing?" The young man couldn't have been older than twenty-three. He turned with a big grin on his face. "That's a personal scent globe miss. If you look in the bottom drawer, right there, you'll find a variety of fragrances. I hope one's to your pleasing." The hired chauffeur was patient while Myra asked several more clarifying questions about the gadget. It was her first time seeing anything like it. Especially in a car.

Electronic curtains lined the rear windows. The Maybach's clientele appreciated privacy. Its designers took every possible desire into consideration. Nothing was left out. Three television screens sporting the Maybach emblem greeted their eyes when they looked forward. Everything in the car either sparkled or shined brilliantly. As the driver shut the door, Jacob noticed the force used wasn't enough to fully secure the car, but the vehicle compensated and automatically closed on its own. "How classy."

Drake and Maria were amazed at the sheer beauty and scale of the Maybach. It was the finest ride they could've ever contemplated, much less dream they'd experience. In both pickup cars bottles of Armand De Brinac Rose awaited, and Sturgeon Caviar chilled in hidden refrigerators. By the time the family started to reach the hotel, both bottles and most of the caviar had been greedily consumed. They had a spectacular time. It was turning out to be the trip of a lifetime. Upon arrival, they were once again in awe of the sight ahead.

"La Orana! Welcome to your home away from home." A small throng of hotel staff began to funnel to the rear of both vehicles to retrieve the family's luggage and other belongings. The front greeter presented everyone with another glass of champagne and then began to escort them to their new living quarters. Jacob hadn't given his family much detail on where they'd be vacationing, only what type of weather to pack for and for how long. Literally everything else was a surprise for them.

By this point in the trip the family suspected their rooms would be extravagant, but nothing could've prepared them for what Jacob had in store. It even surprised him. The greeter that offered the additional libations was also a native to the area. Most of the workers were. She led them through a short hallway that went to the back of the small building. Cream colored orchids and other local flowers adorned every possible surface along the way.

She opened a door at the end of the corridor and suddenly they were outside again. Ahead, a wooden walkway led out almost a half mile into the South Sea. Protruding forth like branches on a tree were smaller paths off the main trunk. Each stem led to its own overwater bungalow. "Wow son," Drake's eyes were beginning to tear up with pride. Another woman was waiting at the door and greeted them as warmly as the first, "La Orana!"

"I will be taking Maria and Drake to their bungalow from here." The excited family started down the path to their respective dwellings, each pair taking a separate branch of walkway. Jacob took notice to the silence on the short trip. No creaks met his ears. "A long way from that dingy apartment and those ancient floorboards" he thought. When Drake and Maria got to their room, the woman opened the door and began to give them a short tour.

"You'll notice when I opened the door, the air conditioner automatically activated. This can be adjusted using this console." She pointed to a remote attached to the entranceway wall. The bungalow was the size of a small home, and it had three full-sized bedrooms all with walk-in closets. A spacious bathroom branched off from the master, boasting his-and-her marble sinks and a shower that could easily fit five fully grown adults.

"This shower doubles as a steam room. There's nothing better after a nice swim off your private deck." The guide showed them how to adjust the setting and enclose the area to allow steam to build. There was also an English-style tub on the other end of the room, in addition to heated marble floors throughout. Everything was of the utmost quality, down to the toiletries.

"You'll find a patio that extends from the master bedroom of course. Champagne's already on ice, waiting on the table in the den, and ooh let me show you this!" Her voice was soft and her English perfect. An exotic accent married each word, dancing between syllables. She walked over to the table and pointed... Its surface was pure crystal. Alone, this wouldn't have been much to write home about. At this point it was pretty much expected. The fact that the flooring *beneath* the table was also crystal, was however.

Drake and Maria watched in awe as a mother turtle and two of her young swam by in the shallow blue waters beneath. They moved in formation, one hatchling under each flipper. "Wow! That's beautiful. Look at them!" The moment was really kind've romantic. Maria drew closer to her husband. His hand reached for the small of her waist. The woman smiled and left them to do a little exploring of their own. Jacob and Myra received a similar tour, the main difference being two bedrooms instead of one master. The bungalows had outdoor decks to die for. Each were equipped with posh lounge chairs and brand-new jet skis waiting on the water.

Later that evening the family got together to enjoy dinner at one of the hotel's several Michelin starred restaurants. Myra noticed earlier in the day that most were open-air themed. Nature provided the best ambiance. Their table was garnished with local flowers, and beneath them was the hotel's signature crystal flooring. It was outfitted with halo lighting, so guests could enjoy views of the reef, even while dining at night.

It wasn't until their second evening there that Jacob heard from the two women that had approached him in Charlotte at the red light. When he disclosed his location over the phone and then held it out over the sea so they could witness and hear the sounds of paradise via FaceTime, their interest grew exponentially. Lust took over. They wanted the lifestyle, to use him. "When will you be back? We have *got* to hang out!"

"I'll call you when my jet lands." He was showing off, he could tell his money impressed them, and he wasn't pulling any stops. He sent them pictures of his room, the Maybachs, and much of the beautiful scenery. His bedroom had the perfect view of Mount Otemanu and he made sure they knew it. Without even knowing his full name both women were ready to bear his children.

Before their vacation concluded, Jacob made a point of windsurfing. It was something he always wanted to do. After a brief class on how to not die, he was off to the water. This is where he first encountered Kacy. She was also taking lessons that day on the beach. Sand clung to their feet as they watched the instructor demonstrate different movements. Rushes of saltwater swept taupe granules away every time the tide reached its long arms inward, massaging the shoulder of beach they were training on. They didn't speak much, but Jacob was sure to make eye contact with the alluring woman before the man released them to the sea.

"Hi. I'm Jacob. I decided to take my family on vacation for a few weeks." He didn't want to sound like he *just* came into money. One look at the guard that never left Kacy's side told him she was from wealth. He knew enough to know women of her class only dealt with upper echelon. New money was repulsive to the truly affluent.

Once in prison, he and Alik would find they agreed on their distaste for this pretentious mindset. Regardless of how he felt, while in Kacy's presence his moral stance on the topic went out the window. He was on vacation, and she was hot. That was all that mattered.

It wouldn't be until several subsequent encounters that he'd be implicated in her demise. In hindsight, he told Alik that he wished they never met. He could have easily enjoyed the day without her in the picture. Women were easy to come by in those days. After the instructional class ended, the teacher gave the small group the go-ahead to have at it.

Kacy agreed to exchange numbers with Jacob against her guard's better judgement. A moment or two later she was just a figure in the distance as she rushed out to sea. A rounded derriere waded behind her. Soft cheeks nearly smothered the cloth supposedly holding them in. Supple flesh swaying from side to side, waving at him, calling his name. Her two-piece was on the skimpier side of sexy. What a view. It was delicious. Aside from a few others enjoying the sun, he had a fair amount of sandy beach to himself. He took a moment to savor the beauty before grabbing his board, then headed in the same direction he saw Kacy go. Towards the light. West.

Brisk gusts met him out on the water. They carried him swiftly across densely inhabited reefs lying just below the surface. It was a front-row seat, a birds eye view into the comfort Nature has within her own skin. Untouched. Pure. The wind nudged him on, encouraging him to embrace being swallowed, entwined into the belly of life. It almost felt like flying. At first Jacob found it difficult to maintain balance on the thin board. Nature seemed to want to knock him off. After about thirty minutes of practice he was basically a pro. As the breeze ferried him around the cove, he smiled and took in his gorgeous surroundings. Behind him were the bungalows, ahead the open sea, and below, baby white tipped sharks and sunfish swam about. Life was perfect.

When they got back to Charlotte the whole family seemed to be in high spirits, and for good reason. Drake and Maria were now officially debt free. A clean slate. Myra asked her brother on the trip if he would pay for her education. Jacob offered to buy her a sprawling house as well, but she declined. She said she could pay for her own things if she could become a lawyer with a graduate degree from Harvard.

"Yeah, yeah, all that is good but tell me about these women you are meeting before the trip, the ones in the Lexus?

I am not needing to hear any more stories of this money. How do you Americans say, I am being there and done these things. I want to know of the girls!"

The Russian had heard enough about nice cars and fancy hotels, after all, they *were* in prison. Jacob sighed, a slight grin forming. "Ok Ok, I'll tell you, as long as you promise not to ask me to tell the story in a feminine voice." Alik reached down off the top bunk and attempted to swipe Jacob in the back of the head. It was a miss. "Easy there tiger, control your emotions damn you!" The young inmate laughed aloud and waited for Alik's reply. "Shut the hell up and tell me about the women you idiot."

"Well, when I finally did call them again I was back in Charlotte. And I definitely didn't hesitate on hanging out." "And by hang you are meaning?" "Hold on geez, you're actin' more like a teenager than a mob boss," Jacob joked. "So anyway, like I said...They invited me to a party at the Ritz in Charlotte. It was hosted by some big-time football player in town. I got there pretty late, but when they saw I showed up, they were all over me."

"Me being the idiot I am, I told them I won the lottery." "So?" Alik looked on, waiting for the punchline. "So five minutes later every chick there was on me." The Russian looked bewildered. "And this is a bad thing?" "Well yeah! When you're at a party where there're twelve quarterbacks pissed some scrawny pipsqueak is stealing all the attention, I'd say that's a bad thing. At *their* party mind you."

"I started to feel, uncomfortable. I guess that's the best word. Long story short, I left early." Jacob could hear Alik murmur something under his breath that sounded like "pushy." "Any intelligent person would've done the same thing, remember, I didn't have the AK47 you brought when you went to *your* parties. Anyway as it turns out, the girls left with me and we hung out at one of their houses, the other chick was visiting I think."

"And?" "And... And we did everything you'd expect a man in a room with two girls to do. I'm not going into detail; you're startin' ta' freak me out. I don't wanna' get you too excited dude. The only thing that sucked that night was when the taller one's boyfriend came home. That wasn't pretty." Alik shook his head in a sigh of disappointment, his right hand pinching at the bridge of his nose. "Please tell me that is not the only sucking that is happening?" His Bunkie ignored the joke and went on.

"Here I am in nothing but some ankle socks and a Mont Blanc wristwatch, when we all hear this banging sound coming from the kitchen downstairs. Everyone stops what they're doing, and trust me, there was a *lot* going on; We decided to send a scout." Alik was silent while Jacob spoke. Most inmates were sleep by that point, a few could be heard talking in cells nearby.

Their voices were muffled, overshadowed by the narrative Jacob gave his Russian counterpart. "Since it was the girl's house, she volunteered. When she saw, get this, her *boyfriend*; she screamed and then ran back into the room. It was crazy! I locked the door and before I knew it I was out the window." Jacob began to chuckle a little at the thought.

"The dude would've been none the wiser had I not landed on a thorn bush with a damn possum hiding in it. Not only did I leave screaming like a bitch, *and* with more holes than I came with; but I also almost died. That crazy guy actually started shooting at me through the window!"

"Well, you were in his house, sleeping with his woman, in his bed most likely. I would have done more than the shooting." Alik spoke frankly, in an almost dismissive manner, paying little mind to his cellmate's reply. "How was I sposed' to know the woman lived with him? I thought the two of them were friends and the one just came to visit for the weekend. I had no idea there was a man in the picture!"

"Well, you found this out. What about the possum? What is this?" Genuine bewilderment lined the creases in the Russian's face. His eyes fixed on the bunk below, neck craned awkwardly. Clearly his American counterpart knew something he didn't. "Are you serious? You really don't know what a possum is?" "We have no such things in Volgograd." With a hand on his chin, Jacob did his best to explain the furry menace.

"Think of the angriest rat you've ever seen. I mean a *miserable* little bastard. Suppose that rat was walkin' down a dark alleyway after a night of binge drinking. Pissy drunk. They stumble into an ambush. Surrounded, the rat gives up without a fight and is gang raped by seven overweight Persian cats. Then water-boarded in a serum made from the sweat of a thousand teenage boys." Jacob waited a moment, allowing Alik time to ponder the description. Then he uttered, "The child of that rat would be a possum."

"And what did this sweaty rat do when you were on its bush?" Jacob looked up frankly. "It bit the living shit outta me, that's what it did!" He lifted his pantleg and showed the scar on his ankle as Alik nearly cried from laughing so hard. "That wasn't the first time I've had to leave someone's house through the window."

"There were other times? Tell me. Please. Tell me boy!" It was the first time Alik had cried in years. Jacob just peered up at the man, he was used to being at the butt end of a joke. "No, not tonight, and stop laughing at me, you're remindin' me of my childhood." His request was promptly ignored. The guard two floors below called up once laughter from the cell reached his ears. “Keep it down up there!” It was three o clock in the morning. Alik’s voice hushed to a whisper. “You are having issues; how do they say? Crazy in the head Jacob boy.”

The next day Jacob got an unexpected visit from his sister. His family usually came to see him on weekends since that’s when visitation at the prison was longest. Fox News was playing on one of the outdated television sets in the visitor’s area. There were several steel tables with chairs attached to them scattered about.

Because of the nature of the crime Jacob was convicted of, he was unable to enter this area. He was confined to a cage-like room where he was forced to talk to his sister through 1-inch bulletproof glass. “I can’t believe you got yourself into this mess Jacob. What the hell were you thinking?”

CHAPTER 23

MYRA

"I told you Myra, I was se." She cut her brother off before he could finish. "Yeah yeah you were set up. You do realize you sound just like an inmate, don't you?" His face grimaced. "What the Hell do you mean sound? I am an inmate! I was set up! And now? Now I'm gonna fucking die in here. I'm innocent. You of all people should know that, look in my eyes. Seriously, Look! I know you can tell when I'm lying." Her gazed shifted to the floor for a moment, a finger tapped at her knee. Then her head shook slowly from side to side. It was tough for her. Seeing her brother like this was a dagger to the heart.

"I, I can't tell much of anything anymore." The two sat there looking at each other for a while longer before she decided to change the subject. Her attempt failed to lighten the mood. A guard nearby took notice and now kept close tabs on the temperature of their interaction. He adjusted his canister of mace, ready to use it if things got too heated. They often did in visitation.

"So how has it been in here?" "Really? That's what you decided to follow up with? That retarded ass question? How do you think it's been?" He shook his head at his sister as she replied. "I dunno, and why're you getting all pissy with me? I'm not the one behind bars for murder!" The guard made eye contact with Jacob. A hand gestured for them to keep it down. Jacob took note and then looked back to address his sister. "Like I told you and everyone else, you know what? You know I was set up. I can't believe you right now." Anger still simmered in his voice.

Myra knew her brother's side of the story. She and the rest of his family read the testimony countless times after his conviction. "So what were you doin' with her in the hotel that night?" After becoming a millionaire Jacob made a point of rubbing shoulders with some of Charlotte's most powerful people. Kacy owned a condo in the charming southern city and would visit a few times each year.

After meeting Jacob in Bora Bora they hung out several times both in North Carolina and in other parts of the country. Jacob knew Trent, Kacy's ex, was jealous of their friendship. They all flew in the same social circles. Most wealthy people did. The air thickened with tense energy every time the three found themselves at the same function. She was a friend the inmate would regret having for years to come. As he continued to go back and forth with his sister, a short man of about 5'4" caught Jacob's eye from inside visitation. He stood next to a woman who looked 5-10 years his senior. They didn't appear to be together.

Jacob swore the man looked familiar. Something about him stood out. Maybe it was his frilly clothing, a three-piece complete with pocket watch, frameless glasses, and Allen Edmonds. All that was missing was a pipe. A moment later he continued with what he was saying. "A murder I was framed for. Look at how suddenly now that I'm down-and-out, you act like you're better than me. I hope you realize it could've just as easily been *you* sittin' inside this cage. You hung out with Kacy too you know." Whatever point he was trying to make, his sister clearly wasn't buying it.

"Umm. Like literally once, and not on the night she died. Jacob, your DNA was in the room for crying out loud!" Jacob started to explain once again, "Because I saw her that afternoon, I wasn't there that night! You know what, forget about Kacy, I wanna' talk about you." He paused to collect his thoughts. She waited, ready to defend any accusations headed her way.

"I remember you asked me to pay for your tuition. You had *no* problem helping me spend money on vacations. But *of course*, lemme' guess, that's irrelevant right?" Myra's eyes rolled sarcastically in her head. Her retort was swift and pointed. "You may also remember my acceptance to Harvard got declined because of this fiasco you're in now!"

Her brother wouldn't let her off that easily. "Well maybe you can also recall that it was *me* winning the lottery that got you accepted to that school in the first place! I really hope you know it wasn't because of your grades Myra. So, the net impact to you was zero. Meanwhile I'm left to rot in this hell hole like some damn criminal!" He had a point.

"Going back n' forth about this isn't gonna' change anything Jacob, and besides that's not why I'm here anyway. I actually wanted to give you an update on the case." His ears perked at the sound of this. It was the first news in months. "Go on." "Well." She took in a deep breath. "It's not good, I can tell you that. We talked to Kinyona yesterday, and she said the appeal got denied, again."

Hopelessness was strewn across his sister's face. It was clear she was struggling emotionally with her brother's misfortune. Beyond its immediate effects, there were more subtle wounds that festered. Something deep down haunted her about his incarceration. Maybe it was her own freedom. That she still enjoyed the fruits of her brother's winnings. Or maybe it was Trent, and the secret crush she held for him. Whatever it was, it weighed heavy in her gut. For now, she needed to pull herself together. Visitation would be over soon.

"So has anyone tried pickin' a fight with you? Have you seen anybody get killed? Has anyone tried to, you know, make you do stuff?" "No you idiot, I'm still a manvirgin if that's what you're asking." Jacob and his sister tried unsuccessfully to hold back tickled grins forming at the corners of their mouths. "So now really, tell me, what's been going on? Mom tells me you didn't call at all this week, or last. Care to explain?" "Not particularly." His gaze drifted. "Well you need ta' get your act together; she's losing her mind, worryin' about you!"

"Me? I need to get *my* act together? Hmmm let's see, umm *I'm* the one who has a mob boss for a bunkie." Jacob could feel himself losing his temper. Myra's comments always had a way of getting under his skin. She always knew what to say, when to say it. Just to piss him off. An effortless talent. "*I'm* the one forced to sleep on a mattress basically made of fucking steel, and *I'm* the one who has to take dumps in front of my celly." "Your what?" "My, never mind." "Already talking like one of them I see. That doesn't help you in court, maybe that's why the appeal got denied."

At this Jacob stood and placed a cuffed palm on the dingy glass. He looked his sister directly in the eyes with quiet anger building in his own. "Yeah you're right, I *am* startin' ta' talk like a convict, and you wanna' know why that is? Cause' that's the only way to survive in this damn place." His teeth ground together as he fumed. Saliva spattered against the barrier that separated them. His voice kept rising. She was commentating from the sidelines, like a couch potato talking to a screen, exclaiming his team should've done this, or should've done that. Until you're in the Game, you really have no clue.

"You have no idea what I hafta' go through in here. You probably don't give a. You know what, never mind." Jacob knew this couldn't be true, his sister loved him and he knew it. Otherwise she wouldn't have come. The pressure of prison was bearing down, it was changing him. He was all over the place. Every time either his sister or parents came to visit, the con, like most, was overcome by both despair and hope simultaneously, almost like being jumped by your emotions. Despair resulted from being cut off from them, from life in general.

He hated that the world was moving on without him. It made Jacob feel the way he'd felt as an adolescent. Insignificant. On the flip side, hope poked its illusive head out now and again as well. Their smiles and tales of the outside world warmed his heart. Fed his soul. With each visit came the possibility of good news. There were some points where Jacob felt so cut off, any news at all would've been welcome. Just to know someone, anyone, from out there still cared kept him going through many cold nights. About five minutes later one of the guards gestured to Myra. "Ten minutes, then I have to take him back in."

"Can we at least see each other in the main visitation area for like two minutes? I wanna' hug my brother." The man shook his head with impatience. His lips tightened to a curl. He wasn't gonna' budge. "I'm sorry miss, but I can't allow this inmate in that area. This is coming straight from the warden himself." "He's not just some inmate, that's my brother you're talking about!"

Myra began yelling at the man even though she knew he was powerless to help. "If I find out any of you corrupt guards have been mistreating my brother I'll have you fired. You know my family is rich, we can make things happen." Her eyes casted a look of distaste in the CO's direction.

At this the guard retorted "Alright that's it, you have to go right *now* young lady. I don't get paid $15.75 an hour to listen to your big mouth blabber. Let's wrap it up!" Jacob's sister indignantly left the room with her arms folded, brow furrowed, and lip puckered after saying rushed goodbyes. As she clamored into her car she began to feel tears of emotion swell. She thought back to the good times she'd only just recently enjoyed with her big brother.

The push start ignition to her new Mercedes CL63 roared to life. With much coercion on her brother's part, she reluctantly accepted the sports car not more than a month before his incarceration. Myra had never really been the materialistic type, and cars were definitely not her *thing*. She was an introvert by nature and would be found off to herself most days.

When she did go out with friends she would usually just have a drink and find a corner to hide in. Rarely was she the life of the party, or even at the party for that matter. For her, home was where the heart was. She was a lot like her brother in that regard. Or at least like he used to be. Before the money.

She was taken in at a younger age than Jacob. Her living situation pre-adoption was a lot worse than his. When the Gilferds found her, she was pre-mature and dangerously underweight. Maria would always remember the day she first laid eyes on her daughter to-be. On that day, the child was lying in a dimly lit room with four other children, all in desperate need of attention. Only slivers of sun made it through the shaded windows. The space was void of color. Stripped of joy. It was a dismal situation. No place for a child.

The bottles they suckled from were disgusting and filled with milk several days old. Rank sourness hung like rotten perfume. Folded into necks that had never been nuzzled. The opening tip of Myra's was so small, when Maria took it and tried to draw milk, even as a grown woman she was unable to do so. There was also the smell. The damp, molded redolence that emanated outward. The stench weighed on the air like a blanket of filth. "This is downright child abuse." "Oh they're fine" said the woman who was assigned to watch the neglected infants. *A real piece of shit.*

Strands of wiry hair distorted weary eyes. The caretaker had been long overworked. A measly salary provided little incentive to nurture. It was a struggle just to do the bare minimum. Maria looked on with disgust as the woman lit a Newport and blew a cloud of poison over the room. "Look they all have milk, how do you figure this is child abuse? Hell, when I was growin' up we didn't even have bottles. We were lucky if we got half as much attention as these little runts." Maria was not amused.

This was around the time her and Drake were both flourishing in their respective careers. When she got home that night she was absolutely furious. Her blood boiled. It was such an insult. To her as a woman, a mother, a person. Who would leave someone like that in the care of children? Seeing their sunken faces, withered shadows of their bright potential, something had to be done. "Drake, you won't believe the woman I met today!" "You mean the one at that art conference this mornin?" He was listening, but not really. It was a tactic many husbands used to impersonate attention while still maintaining sanity. No man could keep up with the constant stories wives are compelled to tell. It was bad timing. She was in no mood for antics. "No! Damn the conference!"

At this unexpectedly sharp response Drake's ears perked

up. His wife was upset. Something was up. "Ok baby, what's going on, what happened?" He adjusted his glasses and straightened his back. She now held her husband's full attention. "Well." Maria wasn't sure how to tell her husband what she'd seen or was now thinking. "I wanna' adopt a baby girl I saw today."

"Ok baby." His response was one of the reasons Maria fell in love with him to begin with. He was always so willing to work with his wife, regardless of the subject at hand. Drake was ready to adopt Myra before ever laying eyes on the poor girl. He trusted his wife's judgement deeply and was confident in her decision-making skills.

Maria plopped down at the kitchen table and began to tell Drake of what she'd seen. He made his way over to her. Large hands rubbed distressed shoulders. Pacified by her husband's empathetic advances, her speech slowed. She took a breath. Her chest rose, then deflated as she let it all out. "It was horrible, just horrible. There were diapers and spilled feces everywhere. Like I told you I was planning last night, I went down to social services to follow up on last week's meeting."

Drake continued to rub. His fingers tugged at knots of tension in her shoulders. They crackled under the pressure. "After I turned in that paperwork to the counselor, what was her name again?" "I think it was Clair or something like that." "No it was Clarissa! That was it, Clarissa asked me if I wanted to see any of the children seeking a home."

Maria began to shift uneasily in her chair. Drake did his best to salvage comfort. "Like I said, there were dirty diapers everywhere, the smell in that room was unbearable! And the babies, oh my God Drake. You wouldn't believe how skinny they were." Her husband looked on. "Where were you at? The *counselor* brought you there?" "That's just it!" She grabbed his arm with her hand and gestured for him to look into her eyes.

"Drake, this was a State-run foster home. Meaning the State is presumably ok with the atrocities taking place in that slum. I actually saw mold forming along the seams of the walls. Like actual mold! There was half eaten food that looked like it had been there for days; and get this, the holes on the bottles were so small a pinhead would've had a tough time getting through!"

Myra was severely neglected and in desperate need of medical attention when they saved her. Her tiny little hands were clenched tightly as if to shake a fist at the world's injustices. For the first month of her fragile life she was blind. The doctors explained this was a sad but all too common occurrence in children brought up under such circumstances. Her primary pediatrician was genuinely shocked when her vision started to return during her sixth week of life. Love had called it back.

"Usually when we see a child brought into the world like this, the odds of recovery are stacked against them. Since her last visit I can see some measurable improvements that're very encouraging." Maria and Drake were standing in the doctor's office, hand in hand as the middle-aged man spoke. "I think we still need to keep a close eye on her, but yes, as far as I can tell, her sight appears to be returning."

At this Drake gave a sigh of relief. He had been trying to mentally prepare for the challenges that came with raising an impaired child. He was ready if need be, but thankful her condition reversed course. "So will she be ok? I mean, is there any brain damage or anything like that?" The doctor paused as if to weigh his response. "Well… As we discussed on our last visit, she'll still have some stagnation in her cognitive function. And there may be some psychological challenges down the road. I would suggest getting her into therapy around age three or so."

The Gilferds chose not to follow the doctor's advice. As Myra got older her physical and mental challenges became less and less apparent. By the time she was a toddler they were under the impression that through attentive parenting, they had effectively eliminated the negative constraints of her dark past.

Time would prove their assumptions quite wrong. During the several years where Myra was stealing from the family, they never connected her actions to any type of mental illness. In fact, the Gilferds had by that point all but forgotten the doctor's warnings. That, paired with the fact that they would always blame Jacob for the thefts allowed Myra to go untreated.

CHAPTER 24

DJED

The name Djed is symbolized in Egyptian mythology as a pillar, a prenomen associated with stability. It is a title held by only the most esteemed. In past years the few who bore it carried it as a badge of honor. That was the name given to the Gilford's family dog, a Japanese Akita. He wore it well. Even as a pup he was massive and had a personality to match. His humungous paws were often the culprits behind many crying children.

One of Djed's favorite things to do was sneak up behind unsuspecting victims as they were about to eat a Red Delicious Apple. He would crouch down low and without making a sound, enthusiastically pounce. Please understand, Akita's are bred as hunting dogs. It's in their blood. Their roots lie in the mountains of Northern Japan where life was often quite harsh. Locals frequently used them to capture wild black bears. In *Djed's* jungle, he was king.

With that in mind it's easier for one to see how even a puppy from this breed could become very efficient at stealing food from mere human toddlers. Their wobbly legs and precarious sense of balance made them easy targets. Jacob could recall one instance like it happened just yesterday.

He was walking outside in the front yard when the showdown took place. It was a lazy afternoon. The seasons were in flux. Autumn crept down stems of Oak trees, soaking through leaves like soft paint, and settled at their tips. Jacob was just about to take the first tasty bite of his bright red apple. He was no older than five and Djed was still considered a pup.

Jacob looked around to make sure the coast was clear; he was used to his apples being taken by the furry menace. Once he thought it was safe, he pulled the apple from his back-right pocket. It felt cold in his small hands and he noticed tiny water droplets on its shiny waxed surface. There was a leaf protruding from the stem and sugar spots speckled its core.

Sweet fresh aromas wafted from the fruit. He'd been looking forward to this all day. *He wasn't the only one.* The apple's flesh felt hard in his hands and he knew even at that tender age this meant it would be juicy and crisp, just the way he and Djed liked it. "The coast looks clear." Jacob stood by the Weeping Willow in the front yard and peered around one more time. Its drooping branches danced in the wind. They were arms that cloaked him in a shade of swaying leaves. Djed was nowhere to be seen. What Jacob did not know, was that the pup was observing intently from a distance.

His head was cocked to the side as he watched his prey. A normally curled tail, indicative of the species, was now wagging incessantly with anticipation. The black and tawny furred pup snuck up slowly behind Jacob, his cute little eyes never leaving the prized piece of fruit. As he crept, Djed was sure to avoid any of the many leaves strewn about the lawn. He knew their crunch would give away his position. Instinct.

"What's wrong baby? Did you drop your apple again?" Just as the words left Maria's mouth she caught a glimpse of Djed's furry butt scurrying into his kennel. The apple was nowhere to be found. "No, no he took it. He took my abble." Snot ran freely and tears began to flow. "Your what?" Maria couldn't help herself, she had to hear it again.

"He took my abble," Jacob repeated, a look of both anger and frustration now forming in his eyes. This was the third time that month. He was tired of it. His mother's amusement wasn't helping. "Aww poor baby! Momma will take care of you. You want another apple?" The boy shook his head, tears still pouring. "No! I want my old abble back! That was gonna' be a good one."

"Well who took it from you? Did daddy take it?" As Maria asked this, Djed poked his black nose out of his kennel, a chunk of fruit resting atop its wet surface. The boy had a love/hate relationship with the dog as a child. When he wasn't being a thieving menace, he was a great playmate. His fur was soft and fluffy, but Jacob's favorite part of Djed were his ears.

They were always pointed towards the sky, likely on alert for food that may have dropped to the floor. In addition to being a quite successful apple hunter, Djed was also an avid opportunist. He would sit patiently in the shadows, waiting for one of the children in the home to drop food from their plate.

It was a well-known fact in the Gilferd's residence, the floor was Djed's domain. Once food left the table, it would never return. Jacob loved Djed dearly, maybe even more so than the rest of his family did. He spent a lot of his spare time with the dog growing up. The canine would accompany him on frequent walks through the woods, and one time even saved his life.

The elegant hound was naturally protective of his owners and would quickly give his life in their defense. He held a special affection for the babies in the household. They were his cubs. At their peak, the Gilferd residence was home to five foster children at once, not all were adopted in the end. During this time there were two young babies in their care. One of them was only three months old; its mother had fallen on hard times when the couple took her in.

On any given weekend, Djed could be found in the living room with this baby. *His baby*. He took his guardianship seriously and would growl at anyone he perceived a threat. On one such occasion he wouldn't let anyone get near the child for a full hour. "Maria, this dog won't let me get the baby! I dunno' what's wrong with him."

Drake came out of his office and slid his reading glasses down the bridge of his nose. "Honey, what's going on?" His wife was chuckling at the teenager looking desperately at her child. Maria did her best to contain herself, but the scene was just too much. She found the situation hilarious. "You better go get your baby." "It's not funny, I think he's actually gonna' bite me." The young woman reached out a nervous hand towards her happily playing child. The baby was just lying there, nestled in the nook of Djed's massive neck.

"Well at least my fuss butt thinks it's funny." Djed stretched out a leg. Opened his mouth and gave a lazy yawn. A pink tongue protruded and curled at the end, rows of white teeth spread out in all their glory. The infant put an ear in its mouth. She was hungry. Once noticed, Maria intervened. "Ok Drake, come get your dog." "Alright honey." Drake knew how to trick Djed into doing what he wanted. This was no easy feat. The canine was naturally intelligent.

The Gilferds insisted on feeding him the best quality dog chow available, and this fact only accentuated his already astute intellect. Drake would swindle him by making Djed think he was about to cook something. He was such a greedy dog, it was one of the things that made him so lovable.

Although loyal and a great companion, he wasn't above selling out his own family for a juicy steak or two. One of Drake's favorite tactics was to use a wooden cooking spoon to hit the side of a pan on the stove. To Djed, this meant delicious human food was being prepared. Whatever mischief he was involved in was suddenly and immediately unimportant. He would come running into the kitchen with his ears perked and his mouth dripping with anticipation. A puddle of slobber was often left in his wake.

One time as a puppy he even knocked Myra over to get to his food bowl, disappointment clearly plastered across his confused face when he realized what was happening. His head was cocked so far to the side it looked like it would fall off. In dog language, that was universal for... *What the fuck*? "Look at his stupid little face; he doesn't even know what's going on," Drake joked affectionately at the time.

Jacob had many fond memories of the canine. During one such memory they were in the woods, as they often were most late afternoons. It was almost an enlightening experience for the adolescent. He would remember it for the rest of his life and vowed to live by the principles learned that day.

It was right at the cusp of winter. The air was cold but not unbearable; fall leaves had been on the ground for some time by then. Their loud crunch against old boots told Jacob they were dry; it hadn't rained in eight days. Evergreens were the only trees that still resisted Nature's bite. Their roots ran deep, leaves built like armor, they were survivors. Much more resilient than their deciduous neighbors. The Oaks didn't stand a chance. He recalled that on this day there was absolutely no breeze whatsoever. It was like Nature was holding her breath. Warm air from his lungs blew out in soft clouds, condensing an inch from his face. The scene ahead drew his gaze.

"Finally, a moment of perfect stillness." It reminded him of the time he spent with Mr. Lao. It had been about a month since he first met with the old man, but he was already starting to take greater joy in the rare moments of silence in his hectic life. "Look boy, you see how beautiful it is out here?" Aside from a few chirps from branches nearby and the heavy pant from Djed's massive chest, all was silent.

As Jacob looked out into the trees he had an epiphany. A cold hand lay upon Djed's head. The sun was setting, retreating to its place beneath the line separating land from sky. Rays peaked shyly through wide cracks in the clouds. Jacob must have stood in the same spot for at least ten minutes without moving a muscle. Djed, being the loyal dog he was, stood by his young master's side. The two of them stared out into the woods and pondered its message.

Mr. Lao would always tell Jacob he should spend more time in Nature. He would say, "Nature will teach you most of life's lessons. It's your job to be a good student." "Alright boy, let's go inside, dinner should be ready soon." Before Jacob turned to head back to the house, a single strand of spider web caught his eye.

It was attached to the trunk of a Pine about two feet from where he was standing. As Jacob's eyes followed the strand from its origin to its destination, he had a thought. At first it only looked like there was *one* line of web, and technically there *was*; at least on that tree. His eyes were acclimating to the twilight and that allowed him to see things previously not apparent. As he gazed into the woods he noticed literally every tree had a strand of web attached to it; each web with a spider lying in wait. Some of the silky strands held tiny droplets on them that glistened with the sun's fading rays.

Most people wouldn't have made any life altering associations here, but ever since Jacob's run-in with Mr. Lao, he was able to look at things in a different light. He could see bugs flying in the distance and noticed some were getting caught in the strands. "Isn't that interesting," Jacob thought aloud. In his mind he likened each strand to one of life's many traps.

For one string he assigned alcoholism, another was drug addiction, and yet another meant having a child out of wedlock... "We are all just bugs, meandering through the woods, hoping we don't get caught in one of life's webs." It was a transformative moment. The insight this simple observation had brought. Throughout Jacob's life he would always remember the lesson he learned that day.

"Be defensive of yourself; make sure you don't fall for any of life's traps. They're everywhere." Now in prison, the lesson haunted the unlucky scapegoat. He was caught in a web. A web with a Russian spider. Alik looked down from his pillow. His younger cellmate was holding a picture of his beloved pet, snuck from his wallet before being confiscated during intake.

As Djed aged Jacob's love for him grew exponentially. Although he would grow to be a fairly shrewd man, Djed was a kind of safety for Jacob. He knew his dog would never lie to him and would never use him, not like people would. He was the best friend you could ever have.

The Akita was a good and loyal dog that was always happy to see him. Even Jacob's own family would cross him in life, and not just once; but not Djed. From the moment he was born until the moment he left this world, his loyalty was unwavering. It was a quality men rarely have. Because of Jacob's love and respect for his canine friend, one particular moment would haunt him for all his days. It was an act of selfishness. Years after Djed had passed away it still bothered

Jacob. It was branded in his mind. Guilt. “I should have been more sensitive.”

Now years later, Jacob was sitting in his cell with Alik thinking about the day he hurt his then elderly canine companion. Although unintentional, it was still wrong, and Jacob knew it. “Jacob, take Djed on his walk, I know you see him looking at the door. The neighbors across the street can probably hear him whining. When did he eat?” He remembered Maria was the one who made him take the dog out. The canine needed more attention in his golden years.

“I really didn’t wanna’ take him for a walk that time,” Jacob tried to explain. “Why not, you are saying that this is your best friend, this dog was he not?” “Yes, he was Alik, and by the way I don’t need your opinion” Jacob snapped at the now intently listening felon. The tension in the room grew.

“If you wanna’ know about what I did, fine! But what I won’t do is sit here and listen to you put me down for something I’ve already been beating myself up about.” At this Alik hopped off his bunk and stood to face his cellmate. His feet hit the hard floor with a thud. He didn’t like Jacob’s tone. “Look,” he was pointing one of his stubby fingers right into the center of Jacob’s forehead. The distance between them dissipated. “Don’t forget who you are talking to, you are understanding me?” His accent was thick with indignation. It hung on the tip of his tongue, dosing each word with venom like an angry viper.

Jacob had become too comfortable with the lifer, and Alik wouldn’t stand for it. The fledgling had crossed the line. It was true, he enjoyed tales of Bora Bora and of Djed and Myra. He liked the conversations. But one’s place could never be forgotten. “Ok, look my bad, I’m just emotional about Djed that’s all, I meant no harm. We still cool?” The Russian nodded. After clambering back onto his bunk he replied. “We are cold still." Jacob gave a shy smile at Alik's interpretation of the question.

"So anyway, like I was explaining, I *really* didn't wanna' take Djed for a walk that day. My parents were having some friends over for dinner and their daughter was this gorgeous girl I had a serious crush on." They were a well-off couple that worked with Maria in the art consulting business. "This was before I won the money obviously, but back then my parents were still doing pretty well for themselves."

The family friends lived in Atlanta GA but were in Charlotte for an annual conference. It was nearly six years before Jacob's arrest. He was just coming of age and girls were the only thing on his mind, although he was still too shy to make a move. "Gwen, why don't you and John come up to the house for dinner?" "That's sounds great Maria, we'll have our daughter Jessica with us, you met her before, right?"

"Oh yes! She was a delightful young lady, didn't you say she was just accepted to Howard? Or was it..." "Nope you're spot on, we're so proud of her." Gwen smiled fondly as she thought of her little princess all grown up. "Well like I said you're more than welcome to bring the family and join us for dinner at the house."

Alik looked confused. "So why didn't you get the girl?" Jacob gave pause to his recollection to explain. "This was long before I won the lottery like I said, so my confidence wasn't all that high." Alik nodded in acknowledgement and gestured for Jacob to continue with the story. He wanted to know what his cellmate had done to Djed. What Jacob did not know, was that based on what he said next, Alik would respond in one of two ways.

Although a convicted killer, *a natural really*, the battle-torn Russian was also a man of principle. If you said you were gonna do something, he expected you to do just that. He also wouldn't stand for certain taboos, and animal abuse was one of them. It was a low too low for him. Just the suspicion made his already imposing gaze go crimson. Homicidal. Only the most reprehensible humans hurt animals, the type that needed to be put down.

"Tell me what happened to Djed, now." Jacob could tell by the tone in Alik's voice he was in trouble. "Well like I was saying..." "Yeah you already said you didn't want to take care of this dog that was loyal to you, so what are you doing to him? Did you *kill* him?" "Wait what? Jesus no! I didn't kill my dog, what the hell do you think I am?" Without even knowing it, Jacob had just saved himself from a long, arduous death. After confirming Jacob didn't murder his dog, Alik tucked away the shank held stealthily in his good hand. One was always within arm's reach.

It took a while of living together for Jacob to notice his cellmate was partially handicapped. The term handicapped is relative. A missing pinky and scarred knuckles, wounds that disfigured, but didn't impede function. Alik was fully capable of doing anything he wanted, including taking Jacob's life with ease. Jacob was aware of this and decided maybe he should let the man know exactly what he'd done. The hairs near his collar-line told him time was running out.

"I didn't kill my dog Alik! I loved him for Christ's sake. I was just a bit selfish that's all." A shift from the bunk above. The bed's metal frame creaked as it strained under his weight. Alik's head peered down. Eyes met. "What are you meaning selfish?" "Well, I didn't wanna' leave the house, knowin' Jessica was sposed' ta be showin' up. Like at any moment. It was Myra's turn to walk him, so I was upset and impatient. He was, he was older then. And, and I remember it seemed as though on this particular walk he wanted to stop and sniff every damn tree in the neighborhood." Jacob was speaking very quickly by this point. His nerves were getting the best of him.

Alik's face was painted with frustration. It ran across his forehead in squiggled lines that dug in deep. His patience was running thin. And stuttered dithering wasn't helping. "Tell me what you did! Stop beating up the bush and finish!" After frowning at the Russian's persistent broken English, Jacob replied. "Stop what? You mean beating *around* the bush? I'm not, I'm just makin' sure you know all the pertinent details before tellin' you what happened. As Djed was stopping at one of the last trees I tugged his leash." There was a pause. "Hard."

"Exactly how hard are you pulling it?" Accusatory eyes surveyed Jacob's face for signs of deception. None were offered. His bunkie opted for truth, as though he could sense the Russian's radar. "Hard enough for his back paws to drag on the ground for a moment." With utter distaste for his American counterpart Alik replied. "You monster! You drug your dog home so you could see some silly little girl?" "Well, hold on a sec, let's be clear" Jacob said with a finger raised in his defense. He could tell he'd pissed Alik off and was trying desperately to think of something to appease the imposing gangster.

"I didn't *drag* him, but I remember seeing his hind paws slide a bit as I tried to hurry him along. They scraped on the concrete for a second or two." "And how are you feeling about this?" Still cautious, Jacob paused for a moment to reflect. "It still haunts me to this day. It reminds me of the nightmares I had about my pet iguana." "What is this?" "What's what?" "Iguan, Ig, what is it you were calling this?" "An Iguana, it's a type of lizard."

He thought twice about going into too much detail on the story of his other pet. Already treading on thin ice, there was no need to crack it further. "So why'd you want to know about Djed anyway?" The response was frank. "I have no respect for a man that is hurting animals." This was not something Jacob had expected of the mob boss. He adjusted his pillow and leaned back in the metal bunk. The meager cushion was wrapped in a towel to give it bulk. It did nothing for comfort. Alik had two pillows.

"So, you're like one of those PETA people?" "A what?" "Never mind, but yeah that's basically it with Djed. I never forgave myself for how I treated him that day. It was just so inconsiderate of me. He was old and tired and all I cared about was seeing that girl."

To this Alik sighed, "It is good that you are feeling guilty about this. I will not have anyone in my organization that is abusing animals, you are understanding?" "Umm. Not really." Jacob thought maybe he just miss-understood the Russian, after all, Alik had a weird way of saying things. "I'm not in the mob." "I know Jacob boy. Not yet. You are like a sleeping child. Too clueless to be with us." Confused by the reference, he caught a glimpse of his cellmate off the reflection of a small mirror taped to the opposite wall. The mobster was looking right back at him.

CHAPTER 25

FAMILY TIES RUN DEEP

The Russian mob was a well-organized conglomerate. Vodka soaked fingertips touched every continent on Earth and funneled both information and wealth back to the mainland. Back to Moscow. With ties to the KGB and a reticent group known only as GRU, espionage and counterintelligence were just two among many strengths in their wheelhouse. Income streams were, and still are, diverse in both scope and depth. Their financial reach was unmatched. When Alik was initially indicted, his bank accounts were frozen in the US and abroad. The authorities knew with access to money came power. Power to influence. Power to coordinate. To escape. Once word of Jacob's wealth leaked, the Russian began devising a plan to use this knowledge to his advantage. Behind the prison's cold walls, he was forced to regrow the Family business.

Although many old connections had long dissolved, the society still held contacts on the inside. It was a longtime Russian motto, "Never let the money stop flowing." Their income streams were derived from varied and sometimes starkly contrasting origins. In this world of caged men, only a few individuals ran the micro-economy's drug trade, among other things.

There were several key factions controlled by these people, and each group specialized in its own niche of the prison's money movement. The African Americans were broken down into four bodies. They held both Blood and Crip presences in the institution. Additionally, there was the Muslim population and lastly the D-Block Boys. The Muslims tended to stick to themselves. They were a quiet group. Most days were spent in prayer, lecture, or group themed readings from a prison issued Koran. The D-Block Boys were another story...

Their distinct graffiti tags could be seen all over the prison yard. Try as they may to gain economic rank, the lion's share of profits still went to the Aryans and Russians. Everything ultimately came down to them. *They* were not really considered gangs, but more, militant corporations. Both groups ruled with an iron fist. Crossing either was like begging to be slaughtered. Even the D-Block Boys paid homage.

The next day in the yard Jacob looked for his friend CJ. He hadn't seen him in several days and was concerned something might've happened to the newbie. In prison, your time could come up at any point. All it took was one wrong move. "Jacob! Jacob! Over here!"

CJ beckoned his friend to a shady spot near the bleachers. On the side of the rotted wood read the letters, DBB. The scribbling hadn't been there before. It was new. A sign. As the pair canvassed the prison graffiti, a figure approached from behind. Weighted footsteps gave him away. "You can't be around here anymore homeboy." The man addressing CJ was a stocky, muscular gang member from D-Block. He was built like an English bulldog, and had a face like one too. The type you'd think twice about messing with. Low and squat but heavyset. Broad, hilly shoulders. Jacob had never spoken to this person, but he did recognize the man as a fellow block inhabitant.

He couldn't have been more than 5'5", but minatory eyes more than compensated for a lack in vertical longevity. "We're not tryna' cause any trouble, we come to this area like every day man." "Well this is DBB turf now. So if you know what it is, you'll step, ya' feel me?" He was looking right at CJ, his dead stare seemingly sucking any trace of confidence from the diffident convict.

"What's both your names by the way? I recognize you." His sight now set upon Jacob. CJ seemed to melt into the background. He wanted nothing to do with the killer. His friend held a different sentiment. A defiant gaze looked over the gang member. "I'm not afraid of you, we didn't do anything, and besides, you're DBB right?" CJ nearly peed himself at what Jacob was saying. His eyes went wide with fear.

"Dude, you really shouldn't be talking about stuff you don't understand." He wanted to have his new friend's back, but this *was* a DBB member after all. They were known to beat the living shit out of their own members for even minor infractions. It was a group built by violence. Maintained with brutality.

"The fuck did you just say to me?" "I said I'm not afraid of you, or any of your little cronies. That's not exactly word for word what I said, but that's what I'm sayin' now." Both CJ and the gang member stood speechless, their mouths wide open. Only untouchables spoke like that.

"Where do I know you from? Wait... Aren't, aren't you Alik's celly? In 51?" Jacob chose not to answer with words. Instead he just walked away. It was a blatant form of disrespect, but no retaliation was given. "How the hell'd you just do that? Do you know who that was?" CJ was nearly jogging to keep up with his friend as he stalked off. Jacob didn't slow his pace. His eyes were trained ahead. “It doesn’t matter; if I’m gonna’ be stuck in this shithole, I’m not gonna’ back down from these clowns anymore.”

“Ok, that sounds great, but you *do* realize who that was right? That was Rico, he’s crazy dude, not to mention a lifer, so you know what that means! You need ta’ watch yourself. Seriously.” In prison, inmates serving longer sentences were more likely to assault and even kill their peers. A man with no hope, is a dangerous man. Rico had been docked for money laundering and drug trafficking before adding on a substantial extension for offing two CO’s the year before. His fate was sealed.

“I’m not worried. Like I said, I don’t even belong here. I’m not gonna’ be anyone’s punk. Besides, from what I hear, all the gangs, well at least all the ones on D-Block answer to Alik.” In one way or another he had his mangled hand in every transaction that went down in that wing.

This fact gave Jacob strategic leverage over his peers, and he was starting to capitalize. Death threats held less weight against him. His confidence was building. The fledgling newbie was no-more. “Alik and I’ve been having a lot of conversations. That’s all there is to do in here, you know?” The look on CJ’s face said it all. He wasn’t convinced. “Talking with Alik doesn’t just automatically give you immunity in a place like this dude. Shit gets deep quick, feel me?”

They had moved near the basketball court. Spattered stains still marked its rough grey surface. A grim reminder. Only a few men were playing. Others were spread across the yard, grouped up in clicks. Traffic around the area had lightened ever since that day the fight broke out. It was like people didn’t want to be around the memory. The same guard who’d been on shift was in his tower. His long-gun was tucked in its case, but always a millisecond from activation. Everyone on the yard knew it.

"To be honest, I don't really give a fu." Before Jacob could finish he was interrupted. Alik's authoritative approach, along with two other men, cut things short. CJ was signaled to leave. No room was offered for negotiation. The command was given from king to serf. The timid convict bowed out without protest. "We are needing a conversation, now. I am meaning now Jacob." There was a sense of urgency and Jacob could sense it. "Didn't we just have one this morning?"

Alik had seen the DBB member approach the two less tenured convicts and he wanted to know what their conversation was about. The Russians never liked the DBB's and tensions were on the rise. Meanwhile the Aryan's watched in the shadows, waiting for their opportunity to strike. They hated everyone, everyone not born American and white. Whichever group fell first, it was all fair game to them.

"What is that guy having to say?" Jacob looked over the two men that stood with Alik. They were taller and more muscular than their boss. The pair sported elaborate tattoos depicting both angels and demons. Jacob didn't have any of his own, but he'd always admired them. Alik had ink, and a lot of it. On his thick neck crawled a black widow. Venom dripped from one of her deadly fangs. The garnet-red in her hourglass covered a scar from Alik's past. Whoever the artist was, they were talented. Their use of shadows across Alik's skin gave the arachnid life and depth. If not for the magniloquent size of the rendition, one could easily mistaken it as real.

Long pencil-like legs extended down his shoulder and onto his chest. He also had two five-point stars on his elbows, and what looked like upside-down words etched into his chest and stomach. Jacob could tell by their faded color they were very old. As he pondered them a question popped into his head. "How old are you Alik?"

"Old enough to know." "To know what?" Alik looked at the young man with his usual deadeye stare. He wasn't easily distracted, and his question still hadn't been answered. "I want to know what that DBB member is having to say to you?" "He just said CJ and I can't be over here anymore. I think he mentioned this being their turf now."

Alik turned to the man standing to his left, Jacob saw the two of them together often during chow. He didn't recognize the other person, but he could tell both were clearly members of the mob. Murder hung on their spirits with curved talons. Their hawkish eyes pierced through armor and egos alike. They were born to intimidate. "Looks like it's happening boss." "I know, tell the others, and make sure we are ready, I wanna' send our friends across the hall a message. A clear one." At this Jacob started to ask "What the hell is going," but Alik signaled for him not to speak, silencing the newbie with the wave of a tatted finger.

The DBB's were preparing a hostile takeover of the cell block. They knew to never cross the Russian mob or anyone the mob associated with. The fact that one of their high-ranking members said something to Jacob and CJ told Alik they were becoming bolder in their endeavors. The entire facility was a pressure-cooker. It was only a matter of time. War was inevitable.

Jacob didn't connect the dots and was confused as to how he was tied to any of what was going on. "You're unfortunate in that you are arriving as my cellmate now. There is a war about to begin." "Well whatever thing you have going has nothing to do with me. I just wanna' do my time, that's all." Alik scoffed at the comment. "What about what you are saying to your little friend when I walked up, something like you will not be backing down?" He waved a dismissive hand at the hypocrisy.

"I meant what I said." Jacob didn't know Alik had heard what he and CJ were talking about. "The fact is, you are my cellmate now, and that is making you connected to me. You are knowing that I am, how do you say, running the block?" Jacob gave a nod of acknowledgement and then readjusted his stance. "I know when you come into a room everyone pays attention to what you say and do; so yeah, I'd say so." "This power I am having over these men is running across traditional lines. You see?"

Alik could tell by Jacob's blank stare that he didn't. "What I am saying is my power extends beyond the reaches of mother Russia and our family." "What do you mean *our* family? *Your* family, right? You *do* know I'm not Russian? Don't you?" The gruff man gave a brief smile before continuing. His head shook as he spoke. "I am not talking about you, silly boy. To be honest, you are like a small bug to me. A tool." "Ok? I guess so." Uneasy and slightly offended, the new con was sure he didn't like where the conversation was going.

"When I am saying the Family, I am meaning the mob. We are having, how do you say, a strong bonding." Jacob pondered for a moment before speaking. One hand was tucked under his elbow as the other scratched at sparse hairs on his chin. "I think I understand. In the streets we call that having family ties, you know; being married to the mob." He began to chuckle a little at the sound of hearing himself recite the popular phrase. "I sound like Lil Wayne right now, married to the mob."

His Bunkie wasn't amused. His authority was under threat. It was a threat that had to be dealt with. There were many things at play. A bigger plan was about to be set in motion. "That is not the point I am making, it is true, we are fiercely loyal to our own; but we are also controlling the other groups in here. Each of these," he waved his hand in disgust, swatting at the air, “little gangsters as you call them, they are paying me. You understand?” Jacob nodded. “Yes. I get it Alik. What I don’t get, is your point?”

By having their hands in all the proverbial money pots within the prison, the Russians had become both the most feared and respected group not only on D-Block; but throughout the rest of the penal system as well. Their access to wealth was but a fraction of what was once enjoyed on the outside. But in prison, it was enough.

This had a direct impact on the number of enemies the mob incurred on a seemingly daily basis. Nearly every faction clamored for a spot at the top. They all knew whoever was at the head, controlled the money. Controlled the drugs. “They are wanting to take this power from us, but what they are not knowing is, we are prepared for them. Our plans are bigger, bigger than this place. We alter outcomes.” It wasn’t what the Russian had said, it was how he said it. Whatever outcomes he was talking about sounded important. Global.

Behind the mob, the next most influential crime family within the prison was the Aryan Brotherhood. Unlike the Russians, the Brotherhood would only do direct business with inmates of Caucasian descent. This thwarted them from most deals that went down in the wing; however, they had an ace up their sleeve.

The Brotherhood’s income stream was comprised of a singular source. Liquid Meth. It was all they needed. Contrary to what the warden believed, over nine percent of staff, and a full fifteen percent of inmates were hopelessly addicted to the deadly concoction. From the outside looking in, the place seemed under control. It was a façade. A façade so convincing the city’s Mayor actually believed the prison was one of the safer variations in the State. He was mistaken. Gravely. Violence happened in the shadows. Masked from view and never spoken for. LM, as it was often called, was usually the culprit. Other drugs were abused too. LM was the institution's most influential.

Cohorts on the outside often sprayed the poison onto the endless letters sent to the Aryans. The guards that checked the mail for contraband were left none-the-wiser. A perfect cover. Its deathly grasp claimed two lives in Jacob's first month. It was only a matter of time before it would take more. OD's were a common occurrence. Guards usually just swept them under the rug. The less bad news they had for the warden, the easier their jobs were. The abuse was allowed to fester.

CJ tried to save one of the victims once. He found the man, an inmate who had been in-and-out of the penal system his whole life, slumped in a dirty bathroom stall. He told Jacob the convict had green and brown vomit running down the length of his shirt. From the smell; it appeared the man defecated on himself. By the time the shocked inmate could notify the guard waiting in the hallway outside, the addict was gone. His shell lay on the ground, waiting to be swept away.

To CJ, the experience was wrought with trauma. The CO held a different view. To him it was just another day at the office. Many grew numb to the sight of suffering. On both sides. It was a survival tactic. The ability to adapt is our greatest strength, and greatest weakness. While locked in their cells the men incarcerated found many ways to distract themselves from the monotony of daily life. For the majority, illegal activity abounded. Whether hustling or selling dope, prison was in many ways just like the streets. Idle hands will always be the Devil's playground.

What made it even more difficult for Jacob was that he once lived a much better life, even before the lottery. Bittersweet were the fading memories of those brief moments of bliss, those precious years where his parents were thriving. "If life could have just frozen back then..."

CHAPTER 26

4012 Burtonwood Circle

"The next house we're gonna' look at is a true gem. It's nestled in a beautiful cove over on the East side of town. Wait till you see it!" There was an abundance of excitement in her voice as she took a left onto Monroe Road. Fifteen minutes later they pulled up to the paved driveway. "This property has over 1.7 acres of immaculate lawns, garnished with all the trimmings. There are fresh roses in the front yard and the back has about a half-acre of wooded area." "Not quite enough for hunting," Drake joked. The young couple had been viewing homes for the past month and were growing a little weary. It would be years before their son would end up in prison. This was when life still made sense to the Gilferds.

"I dunno about you honey, but after this house I'm about ready to check out for the rest of the day. I'm tired." Fatigue lingered in the corners of Drake's eyes. The day's heat hadn't yet reached its peak, but rays seared their way through the sky nonetheless. Summer was two weeks away. "Ok darling, it's been a long day." The realtor politely cut in at hearing this, she didn't want to lose the sale. "Well hopefully this will be the *one*; I know the two of you are particular when it comes to specifications, so, I saved the best for last." Drake secretly wished the agent would've shown it first.

The traditionally styled home bore a healthy dose of southern charm. The front porch spanned the entire length of the house and was by far Maria's favorite feature. There was a Magnolia tree in the front yard near the road. Glossed, dark green leaves cradled buds that had given way. It's aromatic flowers were in full bloom. Ivory petals soaked in rays, giving off the sweet smell of spring fruit washed in champagne. A real treat. Jacob took note of the slight trench that formed along the edge of the lawn's border and inquired about it.

"Oh yes, rainwater sometimes collects in that little ditch area, its nothing to worry about." Maria was paying no attention to what they were discussing. "Drake look! They have the perfect little area in the back for that garden we talked about." It would be Jacob that would clear the patch of land and sow the first seeds about 13 months later. He would plant tomatoes, bell pepper, even squash. His introverted nature made him a natural horticulturist. The dark soil was calming. Massaging the Earth. Pruning her. Petrichor rising with each fold and tug. Nature was the boy's safe-place. She always gave him peace.

"Oh yes and before we actually enter the home let me show you two one other thing." The short, frumpy woman waddled past the three-door garage on the side of the house. What lay ahead was definitely one of the home's selling points. "Take a look at that and tell me that's not cool. Not every day you see a walking trail this gorgeous." She was referring to the stone path that led through the woods and ended with a quaint seating area towards the back of the yard.

"You can walk right out your door and enjoy Sunday brunch in nature. It's really relaxing." Drake liked the idea. "What do you think Maria? We could even have a little pond put in with a few fish; I think you'd really enjoy that. You could probably even set up an area out here for your art business. Who knows, you may get some inspiration from the fresh air."

Drake knew his wife was rarely outdoors, and when she was it was definitely not in anyone's woods. A little too dirty for her taste. He thought she would find some comedy in his commentary but to his surprise, she was onboard. "No Drake, I actually like that idea! I could use a little fresh air in my life. Can we see the rest of the house?"

"Absolutely! let me show you my favorite part!" As Maria and the agent started to move towards the side door Drake called out, "Hold on for a sec' here." He had walked around to the back of the residence and was inspecting the area of grass directly over the septic tank. "This spot's damp too." He shot Maria a weary look. "Let's at least see what the inside looks like, we're already here." Drake followed after his insistent wife, reluctance in his stride.

A moment later the three of them were standing on the side porch looking out at the paved driveway. "Wait till you see the master bedroom, it's literally the best room in the house." She was spot on; the room was magnificent. It was large enough to fit a California King size in the center and still have plenty of room for a full furniture set. Drake was impressed with the size of the bedroom, but his real highlight was its adjacent private bath.

Its layout was spacious and open, with his and her sinks across from each other. As Maria stood at the entrance she pointed to the deep soak-in tub at the opposite end. That was her idea of heaven. She really liked the fact that it was right next to the front porch window. Its toasted tan hue matched the creams, chestnut, and other earth tones the restroom boasted.

"This would be perfect for an evening soak with a good

book, girl please. Send the husband away with the guys and pamper yourself a little. Lord knows we women deserve it with all we hafta' put up with." "Yes honey. Relaxation with a view!" The two laughed and looked at Drake's eyes as they rolled at what he often referred to as *girl talk*.

His smiling young bride was sold. "And for you Drake, I know it's not an actual lab, but I have a little surprise for you upstairs. I remember you mentioning something about your line of work. A scientist was it?" His head shook. "A chemist actually but close, I'm an analytical chemist."

Drake gave a smile at her keen skill in sales. Attention to detail. It bode well in his eyes. "Well every professional needs an office; I think that holds true regardless." The short woman led them from the master bedroom and on to the staircase by the front entrance. Fat ankles filled the open-toe heels she sported. She stopped briefly to point out a guest bath and then turned to head upstairs. They spiraled clockwise to the second level where there were two additional rooms for the children. Her heels clanked against hardwood steps as they made their way up. Maria followed in second while her husband took up the rear.

"I'm not a huge fan of this balcony area baby. This fan's a little too low and close for comfort." Before his wife could respond the agent quickly cut in, a hand waving, "Oh no need ta' worry about that, you're thinking about the children right now? Right?" Drake nodded. "Yes, we have a rambunctious group, and I can just see them swinging from this in no time."

At this contention the realtor replied, "No worries there, the last couple raised three small boys and never had an issue. They had the rails lifted six inches to accommodate any overzealous occupants. Now, let's head to the office, shall we?" Her dress snapped smartly as she turned to face the room ahead.

They all strolled across the short balcony in unison. The bedrooms were understandably smaller than the master downstairs but were still quite impressive. "The children's bedrooms are pretty standard, this one has a nice view of the driveway." Jacob would later use this window to stand guard over when his parents would arrive home from outings.

Mischievous children meant there was always a job opening for a good lookout, and strategic guard posts were in high demand. There was a door across the room from the closet. Their tour guide beckoned towards it. "This is the entranceway to your new in-home office. It takes up a full two thirds of the top level of the residence." "Drake look at this storage space!"

The saleswoman took notice to Maria's observation and was quick to chime in. "Yes, you can fit plenty of stuff in that area, and there's even more space over here." "I can put basically all my art up here, look Drake." "I see honey, but I'm pretty sure she said this office was *mine*" he joked. In actuality there was more than enough space for them both to comfortably conduct their respective businesses.

"Tell us a bit more about the neighborhood. You almost forget you're in Charlotte, I really like that." The realtor nodded in eager agreement. She appreciated the pair's engagement. Especially this late in the game. Most would've checked out days if not weeks ago. "Yes! I'm so glad you noticed Maria, it's one of the main draws of this particular property. Because of its location you really have the best of everything at your fingertips."

As Drake and Maria were turning into the neighborhood an hour earlier, they'd noticed a full-sized park across the street. Its sign read, "Mason Wallace Community Park." "Myra and Jacob would love that." Now at the end of the in-home tour, Drake brought the park back up in casual conversation. It was something that had caught his eye.

"Can you tell us a little about the umm... the recreational area we saw on the way in? How much and what kind of traffic does it get?" The woman shuffled a little and then responded. "Well I'm kind've restricted in what I can disclose as far as the type of clientele." She paused. "For obvious legal reasons; but I can let you know this park sees a lot of great action on weekends."

"Local parents usually have baseball games out in the field on Saturdays and the kids absolutely love the basketball courts after school." "Our son Jacob loves basketball! He would love this. And look how close it is." "Absolutely, and they also have a lacrosse and soccer field over there, and if you go about 3 minutes past the tennis courts there are additional walking trails." Girthy Pines lined the entrance to the wooded pathway. They created shadows that enclosed the area, shading hikers and the like from the worst summer had to offer.

"As far as education is concerned, we have some of the best public schools available in the area." Maria politely interrupted, "Now what's that statement based on, what criteria are you using?" The woman was impressed by the well-spoken couple. "Great question, I love how thorough you two are." They were standing outside, huddled by the cars. The realtor sat the folder she'd been carrying on the hood of her Nissan. A few pages shuffled lightly as the breeze picked up. This was her shot to close the deal.

"The main metric used in assessing a school's success rate is its pass to fail ratio. Basically, they use a standardized testing algorithm that determines student turnover rates, SAT scores, and graduation rates and then ranks each institution against its peers." *She'd done her homework.*

"Sounds intense!" Maria was a stickler for education. She was all ears during this portion of the tour. "It is! The local middle and high schools are ranked in the city's top five best educational programs." This was salesmanship at its finest. What the real estate agent chose not to mention was that the city only had six schools at those levels anyway. Being in the top five wasn't much of an accomplishment.

CHAPTER 27

UNTIL SOMEONE SAID YES

Jacob was about eight years of age when he made his first dollar. Sure, he'd been given money before, what with birthdays and the occasional loose tooth, but none were like the one he earned. "Maria, did you tell Jacob he could go bike riding today?" Drake was working in the home office all morning and was only half listening to his son. Little arms fidgeted as the boy tried to draw his dad's attention. He hated being tuned out.

"Dad! You're not listening, I don't wanna' go out and ride my bike, I wanna' go make money." Jacob was standing at the entranceway to the office peering in at his father. His face was frowned in defiance. The boy's mind was made. When his dad finally looked up over his glasses, it was to address Maria as she entered the room. She ruffled Jacob's dark brown hair as she brushed past.

"Honey have you heard this boy, says he wants to earn a living." Maria could hear the pride in her husband's voice. "Well talk to your son, he takes after his dad you know." Drake pushed his reading glasses back up the bridge of his nose and put away the notes scattered heavily across the desk. "You wanna' earn some money boy? That true?" "Yes sir" Jacob said in a low but firm voice. "I wanna' buy some new clothes for school." He shuffled nervously as he awaited his father's reply.

"You already have clothes." "Drake. Let the child make his own money, he wants to buy some of that name brand stuff these kids go crazy about these days." Despite being well off, the two militants-at-heart never understood parents who splurged on children's clothing. It was so temporary. "Well how do you plan on making it, you know you're too young to work?" "Mowing lawns. I can make money doing yard work in the neighborhood."

Drake looked at his son, his almond shaped eyes full of pride. "Boy has a plan." The Gilferds were a driven couple, and it meant the world to them that their ambition rubbed off. "Well *I* don' have a problem with you riding around the neighborhood trying to drum up some business. Maria what do you think of all this?" Drake already knew his wife was in full support.

"Ok, down to business; we need to set some ground rules before you head out. First rule. Nothing in life is free, including the money you earn." Drake could tell by his young son's blank stare that he wasn't following. He adjusted his glasses and began to explain. "If you wanna start making money, I don't have a problem with it. But that also means you'll start paying towards the house as well."

The boy's face frowned in disagreement. His father's position seemed a bit harsh. "But I know kids at school doin' the same thing, and they don't hafta' pay *their* parents," he protested. His little arms were still tightly wound. Disappointed eyes pointed south. "We're not those other families, and what did I tell you about comparin' us to other people anyway?"

Drake and Maria determined early on, if they ever had

children, they would teach them the value of money. As is often the case with parents they wanted a better life for their progeny. They knew they had a spending problem, but that didn't mean Jacob and Myra needed to follow in their footsteps.

"If you wanna' start making money you will have to pay the house 40% of all your gross earnings." Jacob was young, but not too young to know this was a steep price. He eventually agreed to the terms with a little coaxing from his mother. She always had a way of softening harsh lessons. His father was less accommodating. He believed in tough love. Fair though. When the children needed consoling, he allowed his wife to take up the reigns. Nurturing was in her blood.

"Baby I know you don't wanna' pay any money to us, but you need to understand how life's gonna' be when you're on your own. Nobody *out there* is gonna' say you no longer hafta' pay rent, right? Life's tough, we have to prepare you for it. That's our job son." Her eyes conveyed love as her lips released the wisdom. He was sitting on her warm lap, looking off into the distance in a fit. The corners of his mouth pulled their way towards his chin. It wasn't fair.

Jacob couldn't see how taking almost half his money was in any way supposed to teach him something about life; it seemed less like a life lesson and more like highway robbery. "I will give you the 40%." The boy was reluctant, but really given no choice in the matter. It was either accept the terms of the contract or stay in the house and make nothing.

The Gilferds also held leverage in other ways. Aside from sheer dictatorship. "Do you have the tools you're going to need to be successful son?" The boy wasn't sure what his father meant. What else did he need? He had a bike and himself; and he was perfectly capable of working. After all, they already had him mowing the lawn and he wasn't even getting paid for it. "You're just planning on going out there and knocking on doors? What if someone answers?"

Being young, Jacob hadn't thought much beyond riding down the driveway and just jumping in. It wasn't until he spoke to his father that reality emerged. "You're gonna need at least a few different items before you start. For instance, one of the most important things you need before starting to mow lawns, is a lawn mower."

Drake wasn't trying to discourage; he was simply preparing Jacob for the realities of the world. "Don't be too hard on him Drake, can't he just use ours?" He threw Maria an impatient glance. The lesson was important. It was a father's duty. His wife's overstep wasn't appreciated. "You don't think I know that honey? I know he's gonna' need startup money and materials. I just want *him* to think like a businessman. That OK with you?"

"Ok, well I am just gonna' leave you two men up here to figure it out." Maria left the office and closed the door behind her. She started to walk down the short hallway towards Jacob's room. As she got about halfway there, she heard her husband's all too familiar call.

With an eyeroll she turned back around and replied "Yes honey, I'm headed back downstairs to clean the kitchen up." "Before you do that, I have a question for you. Jacob why don' you wait outside the office for a minute. Your mother and I need to talk again. It'll be just a moment. Go on. Git."

He and Maria were the best types of parents when it came to raising their children. They always kept open lines of communication. Drake wanted to bounce a few ideas off his wife and get her take on things. "Always good to get a little motherly input before pulling the trigger. How do *you* propose Jacob obtain the materials he needs to start his new business dear?"

"Well, first thing he should do is create a list of what he needs, that way he doesn't forget anything." Maria was a stickler for a good list. She would often employ them on frequent visits to the local Whole Foods. "Good thinking honey, you heard your mother, now go on, get to it. I saw you peeping around that corner." Jacob didn't feel like he was making much progress towards his business. Instead of actually making money, he found himself with pen and paper in hand.

"Ok, I need a lawn mower, a leaf blower, my bike." About ten minutes after Jacob started his list his father popped in on him. "How's it coming in here? Do you have your checklist done yet?" "I'm almost done dad." The boy looked over the piece of white loose-leaf paper one last time before presenting it to his newfound venture capitalist. A few words were misspelled but it was the effort that counted. The lesson.

"Let's see what we have here. Looks good. Now where're you planning on obtaining the materials on here you don't already own; which is to say most of em?" Drake could see his son was confused by the question. "But we have all this stuff?" "We? *We* don't have any of this, *I* have these items. *I* paid for these materials. The only thing you own is the bike you got last year for getting good grades in school. Remember?"

"So, what am I sposed' to do then?" His goal wasn't to demoralize; it was the opposite. He wanted him to think as a person of business would. "I'll make you a deal, since this is your first business I'll supply the mower and leaf blower, but you're responsible for the gas. How's that?" After the two negotiated agreeable terms, Jacob set off on his Huffy bike.

In order to bring the lawn mower he tied it to the back of his seat with a piece of threaded rope. It had a full tank of gas Drake fronted in anticipation of his boy having a successful day. He was expected to pay it back. He used another piece of rope to tie the leaf blower diagonally across his chest. The makeshift sling tore at his left shoulder, making it sore and tender to the touch as the day wore on.

When he returned home that evening Drake was waiting with expectant eyes. A glass of scotch was in his hand, he took a sip as his son road up the driveway. "How'd it go?" Jacob didn't say much to his father, "It was ok." "So how much money did you make today?" He'd earned a crisp twenty dollar bill an hour prior for weeding the herb garden of an elderly man in the neighborhood. The job only took forty minutes or so. The boy had originally asked for $25. He decided it was worth taking a pay-cut to secure the job after realizing the man wouldn't budge on price. This would be his first lesson on the law of supply and demand. If he hadn't taken the deal, another boy would've.

"Oh wow! Look at this Maria! Our son just earned $20 by working hard. Great job son!" "Look dad, I have more too!" Jacob was planning on keeping the rest of the money for himself but decided against it at the last moment. He wanted his father to be proud and was elated at his response over the first bill.

"What do ya' mean you have more?" Drake's face looked like it was about to crack from smiling so hard. "I took some trash out for Ms. Wilson too and she gave me seven dollars." Jacob pulled the rest of the bills from his back pocket and handed them to his father. There was a half torn five-dollar bill and two intact, yet severely crumpled ones. It was Jacob's first time truly earning anything on his own. It was transformative.

"Ok, so now let's talk about how this breaks down." Maria cut Drake short and grabbed her tired son softly by his left arm. She could see his clothes were dirty and there was a small cut on his index finger. Her maternal instincts kicked in.

"Why don' you let the boy get comfortable and eat first fore' ya'll get into the numbers? I'm sure he's hungry by now."

It was true, Jacob was starving; he was out for a full six hours before returning home that evening. "Why did you wait so long to get back baby?" "Cause' after I helped Ms. Wilson with her garbage everyone else kept on saying no. Most people weren't even home."

His father looked bewildered. Curious eyes peered over glasses riding halfway down his nose. That level of pertinacity was unexpected. Admirable. Fulfilling in every way. "So you rode around for six hours?" "I rode until someone else said yes. I didn't go out of the neighborhood, well not far at least." That night Maria and Drake stayed up late in their office and talked. "I can't believe he stayed out there for all that time. I mean, the perseverance!"

"He had to have been out there for a solid five and a half, if not six hours. That's like a full day's work!" "And at his age? Well, let's let him do it, Lord knows I'd rather him out there earning instead of gettin' in trouble." "I agree. What about the money he made?" To this, Drake responded frankly, shrugging his broad shoulders. "What about it? He earned it; he can spend it how he wants." The boy had already paid his household dues.

At this Maria gave pause. A finger whipped up to her chin as her brows cockled inward. "I don' think I fully agree with that dear. I think we should make him save at least a little of every dollar. Just like you're teaching him work ethic, we also need to focus on his ability to make money work for him. We don't want him growing up to be another worker bee. Lord knows *we* spend too much, you know he watches our every move."

"One step at a time honey. One step at a time." Adoption taught them many things. Most importantly that parenthood is nothing to be taken lightly. A lifetime of tough decisions lay ahead. They wound up compromising on the issue and decided to just have him save the money he was putting towards the house. "Let him spend the rest, you see how hard he's workin? This weekend *and* last. He's workin' overtime!" "I know! I'm so proud of him!" The two of them enjoyed the rest of the bottle of wine Drake uncorked to keep him company while he worked.

"Dad! Dad!" The next weekend Jacob was up an hour earlier than usual. He couldn't wait to get on his bike and make more money. He was hooked. "Dad! Wake up!" Drake had a trail of drool seeping from the corner of his mouth as he tried to gain focus. He looked around the room with red eyes. Everything was a blur. "What? What's goin' on? Jacob?" "Dad I'm ready!"

Drake completely forgot that he promised to put gasoline in the mower for his son. He didn't like the idea of letting the boy handle the incendiary liquid on his own. He was known to get himself into a pickle on many occasions, especially with no adult supervision. "Maria I'll be back in a moment, lemme' go put some gas in the mower for this boy." A loud crack popped in his back as muscles stretched for the first time in hours.

"Jacob from now on you need ta' ask me about this the night before. I didn't get to bed last night til' 3am." His son *did* remind him. He had just forgotten. His mind was elsewhere. Drake looked over at the alarm clock sitting near a lamp on the dresser. His vision was still a little blurry, but he could just make out the red numbers on the small black screen.

"7:28 a.m., this boy's gettin' me up at 7:30 on a Saturday." Maria wasn't listening. Her light snores confirmed it. He sat up reluctantly and looked at the door leading out into the hallway, Jacob's eager eyes peered through the crack right back at him. "Alright boy I'm coming."

Before getting out of bed Drake gave a well-deserved yawn and twisted his torso counterclockwise until he heard his back pop again. Sleep tugged at his eyes. But responsibility tugged harder. “Alright let’s do this.” He wasn’t fully paying attention when he got out of bed. His toe smashed painfully against its edge. “Ouch! Damnit! You’d think there would be *one* morning, just one, when I don’t hit that stupid thing.”

With a limp he hobbled over to his son and placed a loving hand on the boy’s head. That day Jacob asked if it was ok if he went further outside the neighborhood. He felt like he’d already exhausted the local market and needed to expand his territory. It was a savvy assessment. “That’s fine son, just check back in every few hours.” Even though he felt apprehensive about letting his son stray too far from home; he knew he had to let him grow, and allowing Jacob to be out of sight sometimes was a part of that process.

The only way the boy was to mature was to let him have his own experiences. So he could gain exposure. “Have fun Jacob, and remember to check back in. I want you back here every two hours.” “Ok dad, I will.” The sound of her husband’s voice brought Maria to the door. A hand held her blouse closed. She preferred sleeping unclad, but the neighbors didn’t need to know that. “Goodbye baby, make plenty of money! And stay safe!” “I already told him honey, he should be checkin’ back in every two hours or so.”

She gave Drake a nod and started to head to the bedroom but then doubled back. Her blouse opened slightly with the abrupt about-face, exposing a nipple. Drake smiled at the treat while his wife asked “But don’t we have that art show today?” His eyes lingered for a moment longer before finally drawing up to hers. “Oh yeah! We do have that, it completely slipped my mind. So what are we supposed to tell Jacob? What time is that event again?” He was scratching his head as he asked the question.

"I think it starts at 2pm." Sometimes Drake would accompany his wife on her shows for support. Since this one wasn't until the afternoon; it gave them enough time to at least speak to their son, his first and second check-ins would have been due by that point.

Jacob rode for a full hour and a half before anyone even answered the door. The first house he knocked on was about a mile away from his own. He already had asked everyone in the neighborhood the week before, so he decided to start out in an adjacent community. It too was quaint, secluded, and boasted well-manicured lawns. A plethora of fresh rose bushes were scattered about.

"I'm probably not gonna' find much business here," Jacob thought with disappointment. There didn't seem to be much demand, all the properties were already taken care of. *Yardwork's a tough business.* As the notion left his head, he heard the grumble of a truck's engine idling behind him. He turned to see where the sound was coming from, and was met with both his answer, and competition. "John's Lawn and Garden Care," was displayed on the side door of the oversized pickup. The letters were painted in clean, sharp lines, with a professional looking logo placed dead-center right beneath them.

Even at that age Jacob was able to comprehend the concept of competition. He decided the best course of action was to learn from his adversary. "Hi, can I ask you a question really quick Sir?" The man who exited the vehicle was stocky in build and had a full and lush beard. Irish red. His jawline protruded slightly. Broad shoulders rounded him out. He was a man's man. "What can I do for you son?"

"I just wanted to ask you a few questions. I just started

my business and I wanna' learn from the best." The man gave a brief chuckle before indulging the young entrepreneur. His voice was deep yet kind. It was a pleasure to lend a helping hand. Especially to a younger version of himself. "Well I'd be happy to answer a few questions. What would you like to know?" He could tell by the ensuing silence the boy wasn't sure what to ask.

It was around this point in Jacob's life that he learned a valuable lesson in business, "Never ask someone for help if you don't know exactly what it is you want from them." "Well lemme' make it a little easier for you, I can just tell you a few pointers and best practices. How's that sound?"

Jacob gave a nod of acceptance. "First, I'll say congrats on getting a mower, Lord knows I didn't have one until like three years into the job." "It's not mine; both of these are my dad's." "Well that's still more than I had at your age. Are you licensed and bonded?" The boy's head shook as his eyes shifted lower. "No. I, I actually just started, this is my first weekend riding this far from home."

This was exactly the scenario that prompted Drake to have his son do periodic check-ins. He was concerned he'd be vulnerable as a young Black man riding around knocking on people's doors. There were a lot of recent headlines in the news about racist police and civilians killing innocent people, and Drake was not about to put his son's life at risk. Like it or not, Supremacy held roots that spanned the entire country, especially in the South. People are like roses. Roses are beautiful, strong-stemmed, thorned. Imagine the personification of a flower. That it could feel. Love. Hate. The petal's hue has little consequence. A Rose is a Rose.

Aside from the run-of-the mill idiot racist, there were other threats that needed to be accounted for as well. One such threat was standing right in front of Jacob. Strangers. They were something to be avoided. Starting at a young age, Maria and Drake instilled a defensive mindset into any children they encountered.

All too often a child would come into their home that was abused in some way. A few of the young women that passed through the loving foster home had been sexually assaulted; almost all instances were at the hands of a stranger. "Now Jacob, you know what we've told you about people you don't know." He could hear his mother's stern voice in his head as he spoke to the man. "If we're gonna' trust you to go out and make your own money you hafta' give us some assurances. Firstly, do *not* under any circumstance go in anyone's home. You don't need to set one foot in their home if you're doing yard work."

"Secondly, if anyone tries to give you any food, don't accept it. They can give you something to drink as long as it's in a sealed container; but I don't want you eating any of that garbage I'm sure they'll offer." The last rule was the most important. The prior night Maria had given Jacob a brand-new flip phone. Drake insisted the boy should pay for it, but in the end, she convinced him otherwise.

"What if something happens? He needs to have a way to get in contact if he needs us. Just think of how we'd feel if something were to happen?" It was a valid point. She was right. It didn't take long for Drake to give in. "Ok Ok fine, he can have the cell phone." It was Jacob's first phone, and the only reason he got it was so he could stay in contact with his parents. During the week he had to turn it into his father until the following weekend.

It was silver in color and was one of the first of its kind. Cell phones had only been on the market for a few years, which actually made Drake more inclined to say no to Maria about the device. "Well if he's gonna' have it he can only use it on the weekends, and I think we should add in parental controls as well."

The phone's screen was green and was only capable of basic functions. The LED lighting it displayed when flipped open amused the young man. He liked pressing his finger against its screen and watching the imprint spread across its smooth surface. There were only three numbers saved, the police, Drake, and Maria. Even though the phone only came with limited internet capabilities, those were also restricted by the protective parents. They weren't taking any chances.

The man that had gotten out of the truck asked Jacob a question he hadn't thought of. "Have you ever considered getting business cards? They're a great way to drum up new clients. That way if someone tells you they don't need your services today, you can hand them a card. They may need you tomorrow."

It was a great idea and one Jacob hadn't thought of. In total, he was able to complete four yards that day and was feeling pretty amazing by the time he started the long journey home. Two and a half miles separated him from a hot meal and some much needed R&R. A couple stops before getting to his neighborhood, Jacob paused to tally his earnings. The bills were folded in half and placed in his left back pocket throughout the day. It hadn't occurred to him to keep track of his cashflow until then.

"One, two, three," In total he counted $115. One of the new twenties felt a little different than the others. Upon further inspection he realized it was actually three newly printed twenties stuck together. "Oh my gosh!" It was the most money he'd ever held in his ambitious hands. "Why should I have to turn over 40% of this to them? They didn't even do any of the work?"

As the thought swam through his young mind he came up with an idea. “Why don’ I just tell them I only made like $60?” He knew there was no way they would know the true amount anyway. In the end he decided to just take two of the three crisp twenties and slide them into his right back pocket. It wouldn’t be the only time he chose to pay himself first.

CHAPTER 28

THE UPS AND DOWNS

Jacob was glued to the television for the past two days. The headlines on the old screen all covered what was going on abroad. It was several years since he last mowed a lawn. Now a young adult, he was in the stock market. The money he'd skimmed from each yard job was now his start-up capital. The young investor needed every dollar he could find, a storm was brewing.

"The DOW's currently down over 1200 points and the S&P is not fairing any better. All indices are down for the day. Wait, something's coming through here." A new wave of bad news had just been announced. "We're just getting word, the Brexit *has* taken place." The news reporter covering the story began to stutter as they helplessly watched the turmoil unfold.

"Son you don't need to be looking at that all day, there's nothing you can do to change a thing." Maria loved that her son was investing his money, after all, she was the one who had negotiated that he save in the first place. She wasn't a fan of the constant stress her son now endured however. His decision to invest had turned sour. Every day it seemed as though he was doing one of two things. If not working a double shift at his restaurant job, he was glued to the family computer, scouring information on the market, and what impacts that info may have on his portfolio.

After years of saving small amounts, like he'd done the time he went out mowing; Jacob was able to amass a nest egg of over 11 thousand dollars! Even though at one point in his parents' life they brought in more than a third of a million dollars annually; they never effectively self-implemented the principles they'd instilled in their son.

At its height, *their* portfolio only stood at about seven thousand dollars, at least outside of their holdings in the horrendously performing hedge fund Drake insisted they buy into. One can see how this number was hugely disproportionate based on income. Where they fell short, Jacob found a way to excel. He made about 4 percent of his parent's taxable combined AGI yet managed to save almost twice as much in the same amount of time.

Jacob could remember when he first opened his brokerage account. It was with a company called TD Ameritrade. He asked his mother if he could use the family car at the time. By that point the Gilferds had already lost the Burtonwood property; and with it eventually their fancy cars as well.

Drake held on to his prized automobiles for as long as he could during the economic downturn. After months of relentless roadblocks, he succumbed to the pressure for a capital infusion. He hated to argue with Maria about anything, especially money. After several heated conversations about where they could get the cash they needed for things as simple and essential as rent, Drake finally realized he'd have to give up his beloved toys.

The couple wound up settling on a burgundy mini-van. It sported sliding doors and everything else functional for a large family. It didn't help much in the imagery department however. Both Drake and Jacob hated getting in and out of the oversized van. Maria didn't seem to mind as much. Cars were never really her thing anyway. "Men are not supposed to live like this."

It was clunky. Shaped with the finesse of a potato. Potbellied and wide. If cars were people, this one would be the drunk uncle everyone hates being seen in public with. There was a large section of paint missing on the back from a previous hit and run. Absolutely nothing about the car said "money." To the contrary it whaled helplessly, "The struggle." It was this rolling refrigerator that ferried Jacob to the bank to make his first brokerage deposit. As he pulled up to the branch he drew a deep breath. It was a big moment for him. A big risk.

He held a recently printed cashier's check in one hand, in the other, his old flip phone from his lawn mowing days. "Hey mom, I made it to the brokerage house, wish me luck." Drake wasn't aware of what was going on until later that night.

"How much did you start with son?" "I put five thousand in today." Jacob could see his father's eyes widen with surprise. He never asked his son exactly how he was able to save that amount based on his income. This was a fact Jacob would always appreciate. He didn't want to have to explain to his parents that he was skimming money off the top before giving them their so-called 40%.

"Wow son, go far with it! I'm really proud of you by the way." That was all he said before retiring to his favorite living room chair to relax. After making his initial deposit, Jacob began to make regular smaller additions every time he was paid as well. His mother grew concerned he was missing out, wasting his young adult life.

He was so wrapped up in trying to help his family get

out of debt that he rarely took any time to himself. It seemed just yesterday he was trying to impress people on the college campus. Just a few months after graduation, stock quotes and cash flow statements consumed his determined mind.

His attitude towards money would change more than he could imagine after the windfall, but that wouldn't be for a few years to come. At this point in Jacob's life, he saw the market as his only way out. Myra was quite the opposite when it came to money. She took after her father and loved to splurge on items she couldn't afford. As she grew, her attitude changed drastically, but as a teen, the world was her oyster.

When she turned eighteen her parents let her get her first credit card. It was a VISA and carried a limit of $300. Myra maxed it out within two days. As Jacob saw his sister begin to ruin her credit, he vowed silently to steer clear of this trap. Debt can be a terrible thing. It's like a gun in many ways. It can be used as a tool, but can also ruin your life.

Try as they may, his parents were unable to convince the ambitious youngster of the merits of credit. "If you use it wisely and to your advantage, it can be one of life's biggest blessings. A force multiplier." It wasn't until years later that he would even consider getting one of the cards; but when he did, he went all out. He and his sister moved in opposite directions as they aged in that respect.

At *this* point in his life however, taking on debt was the last thing Jacob was thinking about. For the previous year he had only brought in a gross amount of $14,000. Of that amount, he was able to save $5,200. This was considering he was still obligated to *pay the house* 40% of his income. The feat was profound.

"Why're you always reading those stupid books Jacob? Are those even for school or are you just being a nerd again?"

His sister could never understand why he was interested in the stock market. She took a lot of other people's viewpoint when it came to investing. Ignorance was bliss. "I dunno anything about finance or money, so I'm not touching the market." It was a thought process that would prove costly. Unfortunately, she wouldn't realize this until much later in life. Despite growing more conservative with her spending over time, her business savvy remained stagnant.

She recalled one of their many arguments, it should be noted that these were rarely about money; the siblings were just like any other brother and sister in that they argued about literally any and everything. The subject of this particular bout revolved around whether it was better to buy a vehicle in cash or make payments.

Like many of their disagreements this topic was completely fabricated, neither of them were actually about to purchase a car. The pair simply enjoyed being on opposing sides; each ready for a fight. Their verbal tussles were commonplace in the Gilferd household. "Why would you make payments on a car if you have the money to just pay for it outright? That's so retarded." Jacob began his reply with a sigh of disappointment. His finger tapped at his knee. "Look you idiot, just because you have the money doesn't mean you should use it all."

As Jacob continued his retort, Drake and Maria walked into the room. Raised voices had drawn them in. "What's all the commotion in here? You two are always yelling at each other about something." "I'm trying to explain simple math to this girl, so you know she's not getting it. They haven't created math simple enough for her tiny brain yet. Do you have any crayons I can borrow?" Myra shot her brother a dirty look before offering protest.

"Ok genius, please, explain then. No go ahead, the floor's

yours Einstein!" She waved her hands as if to give him the stage. He accepted with a condescending bow of the head, his arm extended into an absurdly stilted curtsy. "Thank you peasant." "Hey, watch it Jacob, what'd I tell you about calling your sister names?" "I didn't even start it, she's the one who doesn't know what she's talkin' bout." The now interested father allowed his children to continue. "Well go ahead and explain your point of view son, just omit the name calling."

Drake and Maria liked to use opportunities like this to help their children sharpen conversational and debate skills. "Well, as you know I've been reading a lot of books on finance." "Yes, we know, you are *so* lame, no wonder you don't have a girlfriend yet." Her comment struck its mark like hammer to nail. Jacob shook his head and started to go off on his sister, but was stopped by his father's stern voice.

"If you two're going to have an intelligent conversation, make it just that. Don't demean yourselves or each other. Remember, at the end of the day we're family. We hafta' stick together." He reached for Maria's hand as he spoke, emphasizing the point with the gesture. "Now, go on Jacob." "Well like I was saying, in one of the books I'm reading they talk about using OPM." "What does that mean?" "OPM, it's an acronym for Other People's Money. Instead of tying up your own cash, why not use the bank's?" Myra cut in, "Because then you'll owe the bank stupid, aren't you the one who was totally against credit? Well that would be credit genius."

"Oh you silly, simple little creature. Stupid little thing." "What did I say Jacob? Watch it!" He ignored his father but softened his tone a bit as well. His face was still screwed in disgust. Willful nescience was so annoying. He was gonna have to break it down for her. "Ok. Walk through this logic with me. Try to think of each of the dollars you currently own as if they were employees working for you. You wouldn't wanna' give those hard-working employees to someone else, now would you?"

Myra pondered her brother's question for a moment, "Well, depends on whether those employees were hard workers. Lord knows I have some people at my job I wouldn't keep on." "Exactly! I'm glad you bring that up, that's a perfect bridge-way into my next point." Both Drake and Maria were now paying full attention to the young scholar. His intellect was shining through.

Although it was Maria who initially got her son to both save and invest, that by no means indicated her own aptitude on the subject. The Gilferds had been many things; high income earners, homeowners, evictees, business owners, and on. One thing they hadn't been however, was savvy at investing. They were more interested in what their son had to say than Myra would ever be.

"If a car costs 100k and you have the money in the bank, you essentially have two options. You can either pay for it outright, or have the bank come out of pocket instead. That way, you still have the 100k you started with." Drake sat down on the couch and continued to listen. The scenario was painfully familiar. A hand stroked at his chin. This wasn't something he had taught his boy. This knowledge, it was learned from taking initiative, from doing the work. His son was growing into a fine young man.

"Going back to the analogy I gave of the employees, you still have all your original workers, plus..." He held up a finger. "You've been loaned the *bank's* employees as well. Now let's say you have decent credit and can secure that loan at a rate of say, 5%. Which is kinda' high to be honest. Even still you come out ahead." "How's that, I don't follow?" His father thought back to the many luxury cars he'd owned...

"You come out ahead if you choose to not let those 100k employees just sit around doing nothing. Put em' to work." Maria gave a look of curiosity, "And what would you suggest?" "Well historically you can expect to make anywhere from 6% to 9% annually on average investing in an S&P Index fund. So what's that tell you?" Jacob could see the light go off in his dad's eyes.

"I think I know where you're going with this." He snapped his fingers and looked at his son. "You're eluding to the fact that if you can pull off gains in the market of let's say 8%, even after you give the bank their 5% interest, you're still up the 3%."

"Exactly! It's like leaving free money on the table." Myra had lost interest long before her brother could finish his explanation. Numbers were never her forte. While Drake was talking, she pulled out her iPhone and began to browse Instagram. Varied images of art, nails, hair and puppies slid up the screen as she scrolled lazily. As Jacob reached into his own pocket to get his phone a thought popped into his head.

"Why the hell do I still have this old flip phone?" Unlike him, Myra was quite capable when it came to getting what she wanted. As they grew up, she used that fact to make sure the lion's share of gifts went to her. "Ha, that is *so* funny!" She'd gotten up and headed to her room. For the foreseeable future her eyes would be glued to whatever posts were popular that day. Social After everyone left the scene Jacob redirected his attention back to the television. It was still on the channel covering the financial markets.

The volume had been turned down for their discussion. But now that it was over it was back to business. Since they'd been talking the market dropped again and many of his positions were deep in the red. "Maybe you should sell out before it's too late." Jacob decided not to heed his father's advice. He'd stepped back into the living room to grab his glasses. By market close, his account lost 70% of its starting value. It reminded Drake of when he too lost money.

His son's first investment was in Ford Motor Co. He purchased the block of shares when it was trading at $7.05 and held them for about a month before selling at a steep loss. Just his luck. Multiple recalls and several hefty lawsuits for a rear axle weld issue left the company on the brink. The news came from nowhere. One day, things were fine. The next, headlines dashed across the screens of every major network. A fatal crash uncovered the problem. Another fatality two weeks later broke the camel's back. After that, the young investor switched strategies to something even more aggressive. Pennystocks. The choice would prove costly in the short term, but provided priceless experience for Jacob later in life.

When he first began investing, he was the classic type of day trader. Emotionally tied to his money and as a result unable to make rational decisions. At one point it felt like every trade he did was guaranteed to be at a loss. It was like the market would wait for him to buy into a position, and then immediately drop that share's value just because he was now in it.

Although many losses were incurred, the thrill of the ride was intoxicating. It was so exciting to watch his money move up and down with no physical exertion on his part. One of his favorite things to do while at work was talk with guests about recent events in the market. Not only did Jacob enjoy the content of these conversations; but he also felt with each interaction he moved farther from being a waiter and closer to finance. To him, the grass was greener on the other side.

CHAPTER 29

A LITTLE FAMILY ADVICE

Before the market swept away their savings and home, the Gilferds lived a comfortable life. The recession was a year and a half out. Incomes were still high. All was good. It wouldn't last, nothing in life ever does. "Hi, that's a great car you have there! Maserati?" The man who gave the compliment was short and well-kept with a heavyset build. His clothes fit comfortably. Tom Ford shades blocked rays that made their way through wide cracks in the branches of nearby trees. He tried to make eye-contact, but his efforts were refuted. He sensed annoyance in the gentleman before him. Drake and Maria had just gotten out of an argument an hour or so before, so Drake wasn't in much of a talking mood.

"Thanks, and yes, it is." Drake started to walk towards the building's entrance. He was headed to the sandwich counter. After their altercation he decided to get out of the house for a little while. One of his favorite escapes was a little deli called Dean and Deluca in South Park. They served hand crafted sandwiches that drove him up the wall.

"Hi welcome to Dean and Deluca, how can I help you?" "Yes, can I have the Rosemary olive bread?" Drake tried not to sound annoyed with the small woman manning the sandwich counter. He knew she had nothing to do with what was bothering him. She'd served him a few times before. Never made a mistake.

"Can I have half and half meat? I want both smoked turkey and the Black Forest Ham." The woman looked slightly confused, which only added to Drake's discontent. "Wait, so you want double meat? I'll have to charge you twice for that." He shook his head and sighed. "No that's not what I asked for, just put half as much of *each* meat." She still wound up charging him an extra $5 but he decided it wasn't worth bringing up to the manager.

After reluctantly paying for his overpriced sandwich and a beer, Drake retreated to his usual table outside on the patio. It had just drizzled an hour or so before. The downpour cleared the air of pollen. A beautifully clear day was the result. The perfect setting to relax and take a breath. Reassess. The man he saw a few minutes earlier was still outside and tried yet again to spark friendly conversation. He picked up where he'd left off. "Yeah I used to have a Mercedes before I got that Lexus over there."

A finger pointed to the black sedan parked a few feet away from the sidewalk. Drake seemed uninterested and made little effort to entertain the odd fellow. Instead he chose to watch two sparrows as they nibbled on crumbs spilled under a table nearby. His mind was elsewhere. The argument he and Maria had that morning was over him spending too much money on his cars. Its tinge still stuck in his mouth like bitter fruit. She had valid points, but ego clouded him.

Even though the couple made plenty, Maria felt like the money should have been more evenly distributed between them. Most of the time the two got along fine and would often be seen having a great time together. When they *did* argue, the bouts were usually brief and would typically resolve themselves within a day or two.

This subject was one they repetitively bumped heads on however. It escalated once the economy began its descent, but even in good times would occasionally rear its head. Between car payments, insurance, and maintenance they were spending money she felt should be used on things like family vacations. “You use more than your fair share of our monthly budget, why do you get to make the rules?” Drake didn’t think he was being unfair at all. Both he and his wife used all the cars, although she rarely drove the Maserati.

“Why shouldn’t we drive like we make good money? After all, we work hard for it?” The bout that day was before the first blows would reach their portfolio. What he didn’t understand, was that he and his wife had differing and sometimes conflicting priorities. They both enjoyed the finer things in life, but they diverged when it came to the *allocation* of funds.

One important factor to Maria, stemming from childhood, was the need to save. She didn’t care how much they put away, she just remembered what it felt like to have no money growing up; and vowed to always have some measure of safety in adulthood. She was applying pressure to her husband, demanding at least some of their monthly income go towards savings.

“You look like you have a lot on your mind.” Drake nodded in agreement. “Believe me when I say I do. My old lady went on a rampage this morning; tore me a new one. She says I need ta’ stop buying these cars. According to her I’m wasting money. This woman doesn’t know the first thing about investing or saving, yet she’s trying to lecture *me*?”

He shook his head in annoyance as the man concurred. “Well as fate would have it, I happen to be a financial advisor.”

Even Drake had to laugh at the irony. “My luck exactly. What’s your name?” The well-dressed man held out a hand. Drake took note of manicured nails and of the wedding ring resting on his finger. Married men always seemed more trustworthy. Maybe it was their ability to embrace commitment. Men of stature usually held matrimony in high regard. It was a symbol of stability. No amount of soignée could compensate for that. “The name’s Bill, pleasure to meet you.”

“Likewise. So how long have you been in the industry?” Bill raised his eyebrows at the question. “You speak like you’re an advisor?” “Oh no, not me, I’m actually an analytical chemist. I just started my own firm, well let me correct that; my partner and I started a firm.”

Drake was an avid believer in giving people their fair due. He felt that if people are made to feel valued and not like they’re taken for granted, they’ll perform better and remain much more loyal. Although he’d financed most of their company’s start-up costs, he knew his business partner was an integral part of its success.

“I give credit where it’s due,” he laughed. “Well I can definitely appreciate that” the advisor enthusiastically agreed. “So tell me more about this disagreement you and your wife were having?” He heard the words as they left his mouth, “I’m sorry, that came out wrong.” Bill saw Drake as the perfect prospect and wanted to capitalize on the opportunity. The last thing he needed was to start off on the wrong foot. Impressions lasted. He knew that.

“What I meant to ask, was whether you currently have a financial advisor looking after your interests?” Drake couldn’t stand to be sold or pitched anything, a fact all too many high-end store clerks learned the hard way. This man made him feel different. He knew what Bill was getting at, but what he appreciated was the approach taken. The slip-up didn’t bother him. Its acknowledgement meant more.

Most financial advisors the Gilferds encountered would try to dictate terms without listening to their needs at all. They were just in it for the sale. He could at least tell that this person had taken interest in him and *his* situation. That was appealing. New for a change. "We don't have an advisor at the moment. What firm do you represent?" His sandwich lay untouched, still in its white paper wrapping.

By this point Bill got up and was moving to a table closer to his potential client. "Oh please, take a seat here." Drake beckoned for the kind looking gentleman to sit in the chair next to his. The man sat down. "Well I actually followed your lead from earlier and started my own company. Here's my business card."

As the advisor held out a hand, Drake took note of a few subtle yet important factors. Bill was wearing a white button-down shirt that had been freshly laundered. Pressed slacks covered his legs and ended with a pair of well-made Verona loafers. Drake looked closely at the man's collar line and the ends of his sleeves.

He respected a gentleman that took care of himself. The most basic form of that was making sure one's shirt was void of stains. Drake came across many salesmen in his day, most of which wore dingy clothes and shoes with worn soles. What this said to Drake was, "I'm just here to collect a paycheck and go home." He wanted nothing to do with the type.

"So, if you don't mind me asking, are you currently investing?" Shortly before meeting Bill, Maria and Drake decided to get into a hedge fund Drake had been reading about for the previous few months. They received articles and publications all the time attempting to solicit their business. The fund they decided to go with was primarily focused on the pharmaceutical sector and subsequently carried a fair amount of volatility.

After many late-night discussions Drake was able to convince his wife to place nearly all their wealth into this single investment. Almost 100k. A smooth tongue eased over any reluctance she held. He felt he'd conducted an adequate amount of due diligence and was confident in his decision. She wasn't so sure. In hindsight he'd wished he would've empathized more with her position on the matter. Maria was always the more cautious of the two.

The fund manager that worked with them reminded Drake of Bill in some ways. They were both articulate, polished individuals that could build a strong rapport within a short amount of time. Both were well dressed. They diverged a bit in personality. The manager had been more aggressive. Bill was strategic. Only time would tell if either would be good for the Gilferds. "Oh wow, so you're an accredited investor?"

Bill's eyes sharpened as he came to the realization. Drake only recently became acclimated with the term. The hedge fund had certain checkpoints in place to ensure only a specific class of investor walked through their doors. Their process pulled back the curtains on every client wishing to do business with them.

The firm was legally obligated to ensure any clients they took on fell within one of three categories. They were either required to have a standing net worth of 1 million dollars, make 200k as an individual, or 300k annually as a couple if married. At this point in their lives Maria and Drake fell into the latter category.

"So how's that investment working out? If you don't mind me asking of course?" "Of course not, well," Drake drew in a deep breath. A swig of beer later he spilled the beans.

"We're actually losing our shirts at the moment. Down 78% last I checked." "I'm sorry to hear that, I know hedge funds can be pretty risky." "Yeah! Tell me about it, we've lost most of our life savings to that damn investment." "Have you ever considered any other forms of investing? There are more conservative ways of building wealth you know," Bill laughed.

Now that he was not as tense as before, Drake couldn't help but join in the humor. "I'm sure you're right, the problem is, like I said we've already drained our nest egg down." Before responding, Bill took a moment to think. Drake drew a couple more sips of beer. It was beginning to warm a little in the sun. "Well based on the joint compensation you indicated you should still have a decent amount of disposable income at the end of each month, am I right?" Drake shifted uneasily in his chair at the question. It was getting a little too personal for comfort. They'd only just met.

Bill, reading his body language, decided to back off a bit. He could sense if he continued to push, he could lose the potential cash cow. Savvy salesmanship. "I usually don't take on new clients with less than 100k to invest, but I think we can work something out. I think it's worth at least talking about." It didn't occur to Drake as to why this advisor was taking such an interest in him.

Over the course of the next few weeks Bill would take both Maria and Drake on several dinner dates. It was common practice within the industry for an advisor to court a prospective client for months at a time. This gave both the advisor and client adequate time to properly assess each other. Bill would be the same advisor that Drake would scream at months down the road, a fact that ultimately ended their professional relationship.

The seasoned vet didn't mind taking the Gilferds out for another reason. Now that he was aware of their income, he knew their potential. Just because they didn't have a large chunk of money on stand-by didn't take them out of the game. Bill knew any of the other financial advisors in the area would jump at the opportunity to speak with such highly compensated clients. If cash was king, cash-flow was still prince.

After about a month and a half they decided to hire the man. "Where are we gonna find another advisor that'll take us on with such a small starting balance? We can't withdraw any money from the hedge fund, remember?" Drake was partially correct in that it was true; most consultants did prefer a much higher nest egg to work with; but what he underestimated was the power of earning a high income.

In actuality the Gilferds were the best types of clients from Bill's perspective. Because they would constantly be adding to their investments to build up their balance, they'd also be incurring transaction costs. For Bill that meant a steady stream of commission checks. Most of his pre-existing clients were older and only made their initial investment with no annual additions. The Gilferds would be his newest and youngest clients. If he'd stuck around long enough, he may have been Jacob's advisor too one day...

CHAPTER 30

I NEVER WANTED TO BE WARDEN

Years later, once Jacob was incarcerated, money lined the family's bank accounts. Jacob's main bank froze the lottery assets after his conviction, but within weeks they released the funds. Although still technically his, his parents took custodial power over the account. They were able to secure the deal with the help of Kinyona, their son's lawyer.

Not long after entering the prison's walls, word of his vast wealth spread among interested ears. A few fantasized of extorting him by holding loved ones hostage on the outside. Their dreams were quickly shattered with the knowledge of who shared his cell. None dared interfere with whatever business the Russian held with the young inmate. It was a line not to be crossed.

This was the kind of power that worried Mr. Keller, the correctional institution's warden. He never wanted to be in the prison industry. In fact, as a child Keller aspired to become a parole officer. There was a time in his life when things made sense. Even after becoming warden, he had a sense of direction. All that changed with the arrival of Billy Stanler. The con was a cold-blooded killer. No mercy. Void of morality. Evil. On the streets he was known as "The Enforcer." The name stuck.

Mr. Keller attended a four-year college in the windy city of Chicago before studying law at the University of North Carolina. He was heavyset and walked with a slight limp. Two tours in Nam were to thank for that. Shards of shrapnel burrowed deep into his right hip, a reminder of the frag that should've killed him. He wore the metal with honor. Although his eyesight was fading, he held a gaze that could intimidate even the toughest of men. It usually softened in the presence of women and children however. He would often visit local schools in the area to talk to youth about making the right choices. Mr. Keller lost his path somewhere along the way, but still believed if he could touch even one child, it would mitigate the wrongs of his past.

He was married to a good woman, but because of choices he made along the way; his marriage was in constant jeopardy. It wasn't that he had committed adultery or anything like that. Keller's problems began to arise with the arrival of "The Enforcer." Try as he may, his work life inevitably slithered into his home. It was a mistake many men with rank fall victim to.

It was his third year in the leadership position and he felt confident that he had a firm grip on the convicts under his care. The facility was nominated the prior year for being one of the safest super-max prisons in the state. It was a long road to that victory. The penitentiary's past was stained with stories of darkness. Murder. Clusters of violence often sprang from seemingly nowhere. In truth, control of the drug trade was usually the culprit. Everyone wanted to be King, and drugs were the only way to the throne. It took an iron fist and relentless eye to get things under control. But Keller was ambitious. Knew what to look for. He received a trophy for his efforts along with a bonus check for ten thousand dollars compliments of the city.

On the day he was to give his acceptance speech he met the Mayor for the first time in person. They'd spoken many times on the phone. The politician opted to lead from a distance. Let the warden show what he was made of. It was a big day for the tenured lawman. "I never wanted to be warden; in fact, it was the opposite of what I wanted..." He could see confused looks beginning to spread throughout the crowd. Candles flickered on each table, reflecting the glistening sea of eyes staring back at him.

Mr. Keller was standing at the wooden podium onstage. Governor Sims had thrown a grand dinner in the warden's honor. His work helped to get the hard-lined politician re-elected, and that put him in high graces. It was a good place to be. The warden now looked directly at the Governor as he spoke.

"It's true, I actually wanted to be a parole officer." The crowd began to chuckle a little and he could hear the clink of champagne glasses as he continued. They thought he was joking. "I mean it. I wanted to be a parole officer, because, well I guess I thought maybe I could reach these people before they wound up incarcerated."

"The work we've done over the past few years to rehabilitate these convicts, it's a direct function of the expertise and dedication of our city's leadership." To that he rose his bubbling champagne glass. Pride beamed through his brown eyes, his chest poked out, bathing in the moment. "I'm proud to say that I now run one of the safest prisons not only in the state, but also nationwide. I'm just, I'm honored to accept this token of appreciation from the city and from you, Governor Sims." The Governor gave a smile and then called out, "Now get down here and let me pour you another glass, come on!" The room erupted in applause and laughter.

For the most part, Keller was a happy man at this point in life. He had been married to his wife for nearly 25 years and they had three children together. All were off to college. Two were out of state and one studied 30 miles from Keller's home at the only School of Law in the State. Everything made sense. His life was simple yet fulfilling. It wasn't until the Brotherhood arrived at the prison that things took a turn for the worst. He first noticed their presence during a routine shakedown of the D cell block not long after Jacob showed up.

"We're ready when you are Sir. I have team 1 covering the ground level, and teams 2 and 3 will search the upper decks." Mr. Keller left his office a few minutes earlier to oversee the shakedown personally. Before he closed the door to his work area he went over to the bookshelf at the far end of the room. Literature on criminal psychology and law abounded. He was an avid collector. A scholar at heart.

It was there that he decided to place the prized trophy from his recent honorary dinner. The keepsake was small yet heavy, the Governor mentioned it was encased with 18 carat gold plating. Probably worth more than the check he'd received. His administrative assistant caught a glimpse of him as he left to meet with the head correctional officer to review logistics. "Congratulations again Sir on a job well done." "Thank you Susanne, can you make sure I don't have any other appointments for the day? I think I may head home to the misses after this."

"You're all clear, oh wait, you have that 4pm conference with the chief of police. Do you wanna' reschedule?" He gave her a nod and then reached for his blazer, throwing it over one shoulder. "If you could. I'd appreciate it. If I don' see you on my way out, have a great rest of the day!" "You too warden." He wouldn't know until hours later that he would not be getting home early. In fact, from that point on there would be many grueling days to come; for inmates and staff alike.

The lead CO instructed the three C.E.R.T teams to begin their search. The units approached the block in silence. Once at the doors, they rushed the tiers in unison. Surprise was an important force multiplier. It narrowed the window to ensconce illicit material. These periodic raids were a key factor in the prison's safety. At first, they uncovered all types of illegal items, everything from drugs to cell phones were commonly found. As the convicts acclimated to the new warden, less and less was discovered. That didn't mean the underground market was dead. Wisdom was a friend to those with time. Behind bars, time worked against the staff. Crime among inmates also declined drastically; this was due to harsh punishments Keller would impose for even the slightest infraction.

There was one time an inmate was caught with a blunt tucked in between his pillowcase. Where other wardens may've sanctioned a one week stay in the hole, Mr. Keller ordered the man to thirty days before he could even give an explanation. On top of that, once the inmate was released back into "gen pop" he received an unexpected visit from the stern lawman. This instance took place a few months after receiving the award. Had it happened before, the punishment would've likely been considerably more severe. Keller loosened his grip ever so slightly after the accolade. After all, he was top dog now. At least in the dark world of the State's prison system.

"I know you've heard stories about me, and you may have your opinions about my methods; but I do what I do for a reason. Your unwillingness to follow the rules is inhibiting me from doing my job." Keller used a hand to add emphasis to his next words… "As you may or may not be aware, *no one* stands between me and my profession. I've worked hard to get here. Hard. I'll be *damned* if I lose ground on the workings of a degenerate druggy."

"You get *one* opportunity. Now, where'd you get the weed?" The warden knew about the unspoken code among inmates. It was a code that originated deep in the ghettos and slums all across our great nation. "Snitches get stitches." It was as simple as that. Most inmates would rather have additional time placed on their bids than go against the code.

They knew if word got to the other convicts, once they were returned to gen pop they were as good as dead. Talking just wasn't worth the risk. To combat this the warden devised creative methods of coercion. With this individual, who happened to be a repeat offender, he had something special in mind. Not one day after getting out of the hole the man was given two options, tell the warden where the drugs came from or...

"Do you know how the Chinese conquered some of their greatest opponents during the Imperial Age?" The prisoner shook his head, his eyes wide and bloodshot after spending the last 30 days in complete solitude. His brain was rattling. Keller allowed adequate pause before continuing. "They used the power of perception."

"They would make their enemies believe they were somewhere they weren't. Deception can be a compelling motivator. Sometimes they would lead them to believe there were thousands of soldiers ready to march on a city. It was genius really. Especially for the period. Often the locals would just up and leave in anticipation of the pending onslaught." The warden knew he was speaking above the con's head.

"Look boss, I don't know nothin' bout' no Chinese or nothing like that. All I know is I aint no snitch, simple as that." The warden was standing right outside the man's cell as they spoke. "Is that so now? I figured as much. Most men in your position would take a similar stance." He clicked his heels twice. Then, leaning back on them he blurted, "Unfortunately for you, I'm a man of little time, and even less patience. So here's what's gonna happen."

"You're gonna tell me exactly what took place. Actually, before I say that, did it ever occur to you why I'm standing here? In this spot?" The inmate shifted on his cot and shrugged, "You want a snitch and I aint it." "No, I mean do you know why I didn't have one of the guards bring you to my office to talk in private?" No reply was given. A sneer hid behind his lips, wanting to come out, but Keller held it back. He had the convict cornered and he knew it.

"Let me simplify this for you. Where am I standing right now?" With a look of bewilderment the inmate replied. "Right outside my cell." "Exactly, right outside *your* cell, in general population, on D-block. You don' think your peers have taken notice to our conversation?"

As he was conveying this, Alik walked past the cell door. A moment later another few inmates strode by. They were DBB. Now that the warden mentioned it, he could see how his situation was precarious to say the least. The warden's presence was drawing attention. It looked bad. There was no doubt about it. "I'm screwed either way." Keller nodded, shifting his weight to lean against the door. "Well you're partly right. If you don't start talking, and I mean right now," his voice hovered just above a whisper, a finger pointed menacingly in the con's direction.

"I'll walk away from this cell, but not before thanking you for finally cooperating after a month in the hole." The nervous con screwed his face with indignation, twisting it until his freckles got lost in the folds. Satisfaction sat on Keller's. He smiled as the inmate offered protest to the dangerous lie. "But I didn't cooperate with you. I haven't told you a damn thing! And I won't!"

"Well. That may be true, but the others don't know that. To them it'll look like you sang louder than Rihanna at the super bowl last year. Oh yeah you didn't see that did you? What with being in prison and all." The con just stood there, in shock by what he was hearing. He knew Keller could be a tough S.O.B., but this was crazy. If he didn't tell who had given him the blunt, he was sure to die; but then again if he did he was doomed as well. "What if I tell you...?" *Checkmate.*

That is how Mr. Keller first learned about the Aryan Brotherhood. In the days and months to come he would hear and see disturbing evidence of their influence throughout the prison. Their propensity towards violence shifted the entire ecosystem. "Susanne, can you get me on a call with the Governor? I've been noticing some changes going on out there I don' like." He was standing by the window in his office, hands in his pockets, gazing out into the yard below as he spoke.

It wasn't until the next afternoon that his assistant of three years was able to secure the conference call. As Mr. Keller walked into work that day, she stopped him midstride. "Oh warden, I got you down with Mr. Sims today at 2:00pm sharp. He sounds like he's having a bad day, so there's that too." "Wonderful, thanks Susanne." The door to his office creaked closed once he was on the other side. He pressed two fingers against the bridge of his nose and inhaled. "I can already tell this is gonna' be a long day." The week wasn't even half-way through and he was already getting a migraine.

The call that afternoon went exactly as the warden hoped it wouldn't. "What do you mean trends you don't like? So change them, you *are* the warden after all." "Yes governor and thank you again for taking time to speak with me, all I'm saying is that this Brotherhood, they're; they're different. They follow a different set of rules than I've typically seen among the others. They kind've remind me of the Russians in a way."

"I literally had to threaten a guy's life yesterday over some marijuana, that's the kind of influence this group has over the other men Sir." There was a pause of silence on the line, after a moment the Governor spoke. "What sections of the prison are under their control? Where's HQ? I've found in my experience the best way to approach situations like this, is to separate foot soldiers from leaders. Cut off their chain of command."

"That's just it Sir, these guys are smart, and from what I can tell, they have no discernable system of hierarchy." The warden could hear a sigh before the Governor responded. An impatient sigh. "Groups like this always have a leader. Now it's your job to find out who that person is." The line clicked. Keller eyed the clock on his desk. "Time to get to work."

CHAPTER 31

THE TEST

About a month or so after the discovery of the blunt within D-block, the warden got another call from Governor Sims. It too was an unpleasant conversation. By that point the Aryans had established a foothold within D-Block and were spreading their influence to some of the other wings as well.

"Governor, we're doing everything we can to determine the causes of these incidents, but none of the convicts are talking. They seem scared, even on the yard, where you and I both know the hardest criminals are. There're some new players in town, I can tell you that." He took a breath. "They've created a drug market we're trying our best to kill." It was true, the prison did ratchet up its efforts in crime prevention. Raids came more often. Guards worked overtime. Tensions were high. Keller's back was nearing the proverbial wall.

The Governor's familiar sigh slithered through the line before he replied. All he heard were excuses. No results. "And what market might that be Mr. Keller? You know, when I handed you that trophy something told me it was premature; I just *knew* I'd regret it." Another impatient breath. "Look, I'm gonna' level-set with you here. If you're not capable of getting that prison back under control, I'd be more than happy to find a more competent leader. I'm not gonna' be made a fucking fool of in front of the entire city. Just because you're unable to do your job!"

"Governor, I appreciate your concern, but I assure you this meth problem is only temporary. I have teams out there daily searching; no stone is left unturned." Keller's voice quivered as he spoke. His career was on the line. His recognition for a job well done was now a noose. The rope was getting tighter by the day. "Meth? I don't care if you hafta' start searching the damn guards; *someone's* bringing these drugs in. Meth you say?" At this Keller closed the door to his office. The room wasn't soundproof, but at least it would buffer his voice a little.

The last thing he needed was for his assistant to hear where the conversation was headed. She was a loyal colleague, but also held a bit of a reputation for being loose at the lips. If the CO's caught word of the Governor's accusations, many would have undoubtedly quit that same afternoon. Low pay and heavy workloads already weighed on the men. Luckily for Keller, he made it through the day with the same number of staff as he'd started with. Where the ride home in traffic used to be something he despised, it was now embraced. Yearned for. Anyplace was better than the pressure cooker his workplace had regressed to. His office felt more and more like a cell as the days drug on.

What was just recently one of the safest super-max prisons in the country, now relapsed to its old ways. A cesspool for drugs and rampant corruption. It was like the place had a mind of its own, a twisted, dark mind. Mr. Keller knew he needed to do something, he worked so incredibly hard to get where he was at; and he wasn't about to give up his throne to the Aryans.

That night when he got home the weary warden skipped supper and went out onto his front porch. His mind was absolutely dizzy with the whirlwind of thoughts now swimming freely. "Tomorrow I'm gonna' take a different approach" He thought to himself silently. Mr. Keller was the type of warden that led his prison by the book most of the time. Sure, there was a little law-bending here and there. It *was* prison after all. But he believed in order. Respect.

To the best of his ability, he made sure both staff and inmates all adhered by the same base set of rules. The first and most important rule was if you conducted yourself with dignity and respect, you would be treated in kind. Reciprocity held considerable weight in his book. Whenever he did step outside the guidelines, it was only a tip-toe. And it was always for the greater good. Never for personal gain.

He wasn't aware of the illicit relationships being formed right under his nose. When it came to the convicts, he expected a certain amount of dishonesty; it just went with the territory. What he was not prepared for was the sheer magnitude of drug paraphernalia that somehow made its way over the prison walls. He knew they couldn't be getting the meth from inside, unless there was an actual lab within his facility!

"I dunno' what would be more embarrassing, if I find out one of my staff is behind this mess; or if we're really that bad at our jobs; so much that these men built a functioning meth lab, *in prison*!" Anxiety banged against the walls of his skull. It felt as if it was about to crack under the pressure. So much had gone wrong. And so quickly.

His wife had just come outside to check on him. She stood by the front door, swatting away a cloud of cigar smoke. Keller picked the habit back up as things at work began to tailspin. That and the occasional scotch. “Are you ok honey? You didn’t even touch any of your supper? I made pot roast and it turned out excellent, it’s even better than before.” Along with his reply, he offered a dismissive hand-wave. “I’m fine honey, I picked up something on the way home,” he hadn’t. The last thing the warden wanted to do was tell his wife about his problems at work. This was a weight best bore in solitude.

The next day he met with senior staff to discuss their action plan. In the end they opted to use leverage held on inmates like the one caught with the blunt to flush out culprits. The primary target was liquid meth. Sure, there were plenty of narcotics flowing through the system, but meth was the only drug causing people to die.

Having inmates under your care overdose on a drug as sinister as meth was never a good thing; even less-so when you’ve just been publicly nominated Warden of The Year. “Good morning warden.” It was his secretary. She was wearing a bone white blouse and slacks. Remnants of an Everything Bagel lay near her neckline. “Morning Suzanne, you have uh, you have some crumbs…” He gestured towards her collar.

She swiped away the embarrassment with a slender hand and then got down to business. “Oh, thank you and sorry Sir. I have a request for a meet and greet with a Mr. Splinton this afternoon?” “Um, that doesn’t ring any bells, he from the Governor’s office?” Susanne shook her head, “No, I think he’s some type of independent contractor. He said something about testing some chemical?” “Oh Yes!” The meeting had slipped his mind.

In his frustration the warden left no stone unturned. He heard about the work Mr. Splinton had become famous for through a contact and decided to give the biologist a shot. “Ok thanks for reminding me, I definitely forgot about that.” As usual, he shut the office door and then took a seat behind his cluttered desk. Paperwork from the day before still lay untouched. Among the piles were letters from inmates listing unending grievances, staff requests, administrative forms from the State. The work never ended. And the day had just begun.

Later that afternoon, Mr. Splinton arrived at the prison gates. He was right on time. The guard at the front inquired as to the reason for his visit. He wasn't the type of person the guards were typically used to seeing. Too clean cut. "Mr. Splinton is it?" Kevin rolled his eyes with impatience. His arms fidgeted at his sides, then drew near his chest in a fold of defiance. "That's what my ID says doesn't it?"

He was saved from further questioning by Mr. Keller. "He's good, Kevin, right?" The two men shook hands and spoke for a few moments before walking down the gated pathway towards the warden's office. "So please, tell me more about what's going on here? I understand you have a bit of a controlled substance problem?" "Yes, that's kind of an understatement, but yes. You have the gist of it."

"So what is it you're hoping I can help you with warden?" Mr. Keller once again closed his office door before continuing. He also shut the wooden blinds. Then he turned to face his guest. "I've heard from a few trusted contacts of mine that you're *quite* the star when it comes to intra-molecular compositions. That true?" Kevin shuffled a little at the unintended compliment.

"Well I wouldn't say I'm *famous* or anything, but yes, we've had a few successes within our firm. But, I'm a little confused at the connection between my research and your prison? I received a hand-written letter requesting this meeting, so here I am."

The warden paced the length of the room while Kevin

remained near the door. Susanne was stationed just outside. Her fingers were busy at work finishing up a letter Keller had asked her to write-up. Muffled clicks on her keyboard seeped through the walls and echoed the wardens voice as he addressed Kevin.

"Well I can understand how us being here today can be confusing, but I have a situation on my hands that requires an unorthodox approach. Something with a little finesse. As I'm sure you read in my letter, there seems to be an influx of drugs passing every safeguard we have in place. One of my inmates recently lost his life to this. We *need* to know where the meth is originating. That way we can stop it at its source."

"I totally agree with you, but I'm still not seeing the connection here? What exactly are you looking for from me?" As the words were leaving Kevin's mouth, his answer knocked on the door. It was the inmate the warden had threatened earlier. He was escorted by two CO's into the office and instructed to sit in a chair most men avoided like the plague.

This chair was usually reserved for convicts with a history of violent interactions with authority, but given the circumstances, the warden wasn't taking any chances. The last thing he needed was an incident to go down in his office. Especially not with a guest present. "Sit down son. Go on, take a seat. Do you know why you're here?"

Wary, the inmate shifted his head to get a better look around the room, first at the two guards and then at Kevin and the warden. "You still want me to snitch on my celly." Before he realized what he'd said it was too late. His eyes dove southward to break contact with Keller's keen gaze.

The warden grinned before saying, "I see your tongue's quicker than that tiny brain of yours. So, you *do* know where the weed came from." Kevin gave a look that could only be described as confusion and said, "Wait, is the issue here weed or meth? Because I thought we were talking about *meth*?" After getting up from his desk and pacing a few more times, Keller went over to a drawer at the far end of the room. His steps were slow and deliberate. He opened the cabinet and pulled out a grey folder heavy with case files. With his back to the convict he shuffled papers until he came upon the one he was looking for.

"It says here your legal name is Chad Jenkins, but you go by CJ. Is that correct? Looks like we moved you over to D-Block a few weeks back. Thefts, write-ups, and now drugs." Mr. Keller was peering over his half-moon glasses at the man, confidence oozing from his eyes. "Yeah that's right, and I told you before, I aint no snitch. If you're tryna' scare me right now, it aint workin. What else you gonna' do to me you haven't already? Hell, I kind've got used to the hole." It was a lie. No one got used to that place.

"That's not what this is about, this is about you saving lives." At this, everyone in the room gave a look of skepticism, even Keller's staff. "And how exactly am I sposed' to be doin' that?" "We need to know where these drugs are coming from, I know you're in possession of that information. Instead of being enemies, wouldn't you rather be allies?" It was an interesting proposition. Being on the warden's good side came with its perks. Big ones. If played right, it could be life changing. On the other hand, any misstep could leave you marked for death. The only question was, was the carrot worth it?

CJ was raised to have a deep distrust of law enforcement, and that included any type of authority figure as well. "Why the hell would I wanna' help you? You *do* remember you stuck me in a fucking cage for a month, by myself; and then you basically threatened my life!" At this comment one of the guards placed a firm hand on the convict's shoulder. He got the message.

"Your cellmate, what's his name? No need to play games, I can easily look up what I need to know." "His name's Marc." "He the one who gave you the joint?" CJ was starting to get annoyed by the intrusive questions. Uneasiness swam in his gut until it made its way to the muscles near his jawline. "What does this have to do with anything? It was just a stupid blunt; I don't even think it was real weed. It hit kind've weak, course I would've liked to finish the rest of it."

"You're not here to talk about the weed." While they were talking Keller had pulled a chair from near his desk and placed it in front of CJ. He now sat; his eyes locked with determination. "Then why am I here? I'm missing my time in the yard right now. You know I just got out the hole, the last thing I wanna' do is be indoors." The warden paced his breath as he spoke. "I understand, however," a finger raised into the air, "I need you to do something before I let you leave."

"Oh yeah, and what might that be?" CJ was sure whatever it was, it wouldn't end well for him; it never did. "I need you to get some more weed from your cellmate. We found trace elements of methamphetamine in that blunt we confiscated." "You've gotta' be kiddin' me; Marc tried to get me hooked on meth? I knew something was off about that weed." The con recalled the twitches he had an hour or so after hitting the joint.

"So why do you need my help? Isn't there someone else who can do it?" The warden gave a sigh. His patience was wearing thin and it came through in his tone. "You're the only one con, and don't think of it as being a rat; after all you're not actually telling us anything. Think of it more as a drug run than anything else." The young inmate gave a laugh of skepticism, "So you wanna' get high huh?" "Just get the damn product" Keller snapped impatiently as Kevin looked on with confusion.

While the guards escorted CJ back to his cell, the warden and Kevin picked their conversation back up. "When he gets back we'll have our answer. I need to know where this meth originates. Once we have a larger sample, will you be able to at least find out how this stuff's produced? That may help us pin-point the culprits."

Although Kevin had little experience interacting with chemicals in the capacity being asked, he saw the merits of the request and agreed to help. About three hours or so after they sent CJ on his assignment, the convict finally returned. Again, he was escorted by an ever-present guard, although this one was different from the last two. Shift change at the prison happened at 6pm and the night crew was now on duty. The CO held the inmate outside the office until the two men inside finished talking.

Mr. Keller knew that of all his employees, the night crew were the most corrupt. But they were also the best at getting things done. Many held close business relationships with some of the worst and most powerful characters in the prison. If anything, having them on board was a necessary evil. Everyone couldn't be as by-the-book as Keller. To clean up the muck, one had to get dirty.

Now placed at a cross-road, hate it as he may, the warden had to call on these individuals for help. "Why don't you just get rid of the scumbags you have on staff? Clean up from the inside out." Keller's head shook in tandem with his reply. "It doesn't work like that. Not behind these walls. One thing I learned early in my career, is you can't eliminate evil. You can only try and use it to your advantage." It was clear Kevin held a differing view based on the look he gave Mr. Keller.

"For your purposes, Kevin, all I need you to do is tell me how the meth was manufactured. If we know the materials used, we can probably stop these bastards." "Do you really think they have a lab, like I mean, is that even possible?" From the warden's experience behind bars, *anything* was possible.

In his tenure he saw firsthand the lengths a man would go through to get what he wanted in prison. Many of them, especially on D-Block, were lifers. This didn't necessarily mean they would spend their entire lives incarcerated; but it *did* mean they were required by the state to serve a *minimum* amount of time.

For most this would be at least the next 20 years. Tack on extra time for incidents bound to happen while locked up, and 20 could morph to life within the blink of an eye. The inmates knew this. Now imagine for a moment the psychology of an addict. You know you're cut off from your normal supply. How do you cope? Wanna know the answer? You improvise. It's what man was born to do. Convicts are no different. "So, you think since they can't get what they need from the outside, they're manufacturing it? What if you're looking at the wrong people? Instead of the addicts, why not look at the people supplying them?" The warden silently thought to himself, "That's what I just said genius."

CHAPTER 32

MARCO POLO

CJ's cellmate was a rather fat man of about 6 feet. He lumbered around the prison like a Mountain Troll. Most other inmates tended to stay away. Imposing tattoos spanned his massive torso. Bolts, devils, skulls. Skinhead etched in cursive ran from one shoulder to the other. The ink was dark. Shadowed. It drew life to otherwise leathery weathered skin. On the streets CJ had been a low-level drug dealer who'd done his best to stay under the radar. Now bunked with a three-time killer, playing grey-man was more difficult. The youngster was outgunned. Upstaged in both street smarts and size, he was food. Before his arrest, CJ's life wasn't great; but it wasn't horrible either. It was like anyone else's coming up on his end of town. It wasn't until he tried his first line of cocaine that things took a turn for the worst. He couldn't remember all the details, but he remembered being under a mound of stress at the time. The powder was a temporary out. A release.

His child's mother was pressuring him to come up with overdue rent. On top of that, the lights had been off since the day before. He also had another baby from a separate woman on the way. It was just too much for him. He remembered being admitted to the prison nearly three years before meeting

Jacob. One of the first things they asked was whether you were on drugs of any type.

CJ declined to mention his newfound habit to the authorities and was admitted into the facility without incident. It wasn't until after he was introduced to Marc that he had his first relapse. With so many drugs flowing through its walls, it was only a matter of time. The prison itself was massive in scale, even compared to others in the state. There were five main buildings not including the warden's office and three guard towers.

Marc was transferred from a penitentiary up north and was a longtime resident of the penal system. He was in and out of jails since the age of sixteen, and was no stranger to the use of narcotics behind what the inmates un-affectionately referred to as the "Big Wall." It was the only life he'd ever known.

"Open on cell 31." The night crew rarely handled prisoner intakes, but the facility was severely understaffed. The day crew was able to complete most of the processing but left actual cell assignments to their nocturnal partners. "I can't stand this job. The pay sucks, the convicts don't know their place and the warden gets all the glory for the work you and I put in."

"You know, there're ways to make a quick buck, especially in prison." The two guards were walking towards the intake room to bring in the next batch of scumbags. The older one continued, "I know you've only been here for a few weeks now, but at some point, you're gonna' see how things work round' here. Just wait."

CJ held up residency in cell 31 for about a month and a half before he got his first bunkie. In such an overcrowded place this was a luxury few convicts would ever enjoy. As he looked out, beyond the confines of rusted steel bars spattered with the miseries of men and time, he could see the guard's desk that sat center-building. It was surrounded by a circle of four floors, each housing up to 80 inmates. Most of the residential buildings were designed with the same basic layout, with the occasional variance here and there.

Being one of the largest buildings in the compound meant C-Block also had the highest concentration of guards. The inmates knew this and would use the information to their advantage. Just like the warden and his staff kept tabs on the convicts, the incarcerated also ran counterintelligence on staff. Observant eyes were everywhere. Waiting for any opportunity to bend the law. Sometimes crimes would be petty. Other times not so much. It was like a city in many ways, there were good neighborhoods and bad ones. But no matter what area you were in, recon was always at play. Convicted spies if you will.

They would often communicate with each other using a complex system comprised of both coded messages or *kites*, and a modified version of sign language. The tactics proved effective. Only the most tenured staff were able to interpret these messages. Being able to decipher these codes was at the forefront of the institution's priorities.

When asked in an interview with the local news as to why so much of the prison's resources went towards recon and intelligence efforts, Mr. Keller's response was simple and straightforward. "The prison's population conducts extensive research on my team, why should they know more about us than we them?"

He was right too. Many times inmates actually had a more accurate depiction of the prison's staffing than the prison itself. They knew what shifts had the least supervision, which guards could be bought, and who could be extorted. Up until the arrival of the Aryans, the drug problem within the compound was so minute it wasn't really on the warden's radar. Within weeks all that would change. The guard that sat at the central desk pressed the red button marked 31. "Opening on 31" he shouted out to his colleague in a southern accent, his eyes rolling at yet another redundant day. His job could get incredibly boring. Until it wasn't. The door creaked open.

As Marc approached the small 8 by 12-foot cell, he looked at CJ and then back at the guards. He seemed surprised. A sneer crept down his jawline and settled in the folds of his chin. He began to protest and shouted "I'm not bunking with one of these fuckin' darkies. I thought the lady in bookin' said ya'll would place us with our own?" The cuffs he'd just been wearing jingled. They were begging to be reunited with his wrists. The fight was futile. It was either here or the hole. He looked back into the room with disgust before the lead CO ordered him in. They didn't have time to play prison politics.

It was true; under normal circumstances the prison did make every effort to separate inmates by association. But their criterion wasn't based on race as many of the white supremacists hoped. It was Mr. Keller's policy to keep like *gang* members together. Gangs tended to recruit from within, but that wasn't always the case. Black sheep popped up from time to time. Each pod was an ecosystem. Keeping the peace was a challenge. An art. There would always be predator and prey. Keller's job was to create balance. Sometimes sheep had no choice but to share space with the wolves.

It fell under a set of truths he liked to refer to as "The lesser of two evils." The warden and all the guards knew placing direct rivals in a cell together, or even on the same block could have catastrophic ramifications. To avoid an all-out riot, many of the highest-ranking members were placed on blocks they weren't technically supposed to be on. An effort to keep them from calling out hits on neighboring factions. Such was unfortunately the case with CJ's cellmate.

C-Block wasn't known to have a high population of killers within its ranks, much less than the average for many other areas of the prison. So when they moved him to D-Block, the news was devastating. It was like being evicted. Once incarcerated, every man eventually became a rolling stone. When Marc finally, and after much protest stepped inside the cell, he didn't say a word to CJ.

The younger con could tell immediately he wouldn't like his new celly. Everything about him was wrong. The man that stood before him was muscular, but not in the sense of a bodybuilder or anything like that. His strength just seemed to emanate from within, despite a gut that more than hinted at a lust for beer. His eyes were cold and blue; CJ could sense an eerie tingling on the back of his neck as he looked his new neighbor over.

A few moments after the door shut and the guards who escorted Marc had left, the man spoke. His voice was deep and had a rasp. The no-nonsense type. "I'm gonna' say this once and once only, don't talk to me, don't ask me anything, and if I tell you to do something, do it, or I'll kill you." The greeting reminded him of the one Alik offered Jacob. *A Killer's welcome.* CJ was no stranger to death threats, he came across them constantly and even dished out a few empty ones of his own over the years. This was different however.

Something told him the man he was now eye to eye with wasn't someone he wanted to test. He decided to give a nod and heed the lifer's warning. It wasn't until Marc heard of CJ's addiction that he began to warm up to the young man. He too was an addict. "I know you asked me not to say anything to you, but I have one question."

"What is it Darky?" Marc looked down from his bunk

at his celly before throwing his legs over the side of the bed. The bars running down the front of the room were rusted and stained with speckles of dried blood. Shades of grey and dingy white were all that met the eye. It was a dreary existence.

As you faced the cell the first thing you would notice was the comically small metal toilet. After the two men were on speaking terms it would be this toilet that would be the focal point of the cramped enclosure. Neither correctional officers nor the warden were aware of how important of a tool the toilets were to inmates.

Aside from obvious uses, there were other functionalities the cold chunks of metal fulfilled on a daily basis. One such use was in the making of a longtime jailhouse favorite, "hooch." The alcoholic concoction went by several different names. Some of the other references both Marc and CJ were familiar with were Raisin Jack, Brew, Jump, and Buck. Both preferred "hooch" however.

The first time Marc went to the toilet and started making the prisoner's version of wine CJ knew exactly what he was doing. He could tell what was about to take place by the materials laid out. At first it looked like his cellmate just smuggled some extra food from the mess hall. CJ could make out apples and a few oranges; both considered prized luxuries among inmates.

There was also a small paper bag of sugar, some milk, and a piece of molded bread, which provided the yeast. The heavily tatted man placed the ingredients into a plastic bag he snuck into the cell the day before. Much to CJ's surprise, Marc actually handed the drink over to him after he took a few sips. From that point on, the two were not necessarily friends, but they weren't enemies either. No matter who you were, in prison, an enemy was never a good thing.

About two weeks before Jacob arrived; Marc offered CJ his first prison blunt. He'd smoked several times before in the small cell, but only offered his young cellmate hooch, the weed he kept for himself. "You wanna puff rug head?" By that point CJ was just about used to Marc's racist comments and rarely took offense.

"Hell Yeah, I'll take a go at it." The dope was rolled in a piece of magazine paper and its ink laden smoke burned CJ's lungs with each draw. However harsh the makeshift blunt was, it was nonetheless greatly appreciated. What an escape, even if just for a moment. It had been some time since that first encounter, but now he needed weed for a *different* reason.

He had known Marc now for 24 months and CJ was also becoming close friends with Jacob as well. As he walked yet again back to his cell from the warden's office he ran into Jacob. "Hey Jacob! What's been up man?" The two only got to speak for a moment before one of the CO's intervened. "Let's go cons! Break it up!" Their conversation needed to be quick. The staff in this area didn't like cons fraternizing too much. It kept drama down. The farther from Keller's office you went, the lazier the guards became. "Where're you headed?" CJ's voice got low enough for only his friend to hear.

"Warden's got it out for Marc, my celly." "Looks like you may have the place all to yourself again then?" CJ shook his head. "I doubt it, he just wants me to do some recon and get some bud." "Really? The warden asked you for weed?" It sounded odd, and Jacob's expression showed it. CJ didn't miss the look on his friend's face. It said, "Bullshit."

"It's not what it sounds like. I think they're playing a game of cat n' mouse, tryin' ta' find the kingpin in here most likely" CJ mused as he let out a chuckle. "Well in this case I'd say it's closer to Marco Polo." After thinking about Jacob's observation for a moment CJ agreed, “Well said.”

CHAPTER 33

BROTHERS IN ARMS

The warden was under incredible pressure to control rampant drug use taking place inside his prison's unforgiving walls. Accolades bestowed by Governor Sims were a distant memory. He was less concerned with the many forms of weed and alcohol, and much more interested in the liquid meth taking hold. Overdoses were more common. The bodies were piling up. Family members on the outside drew in the press. They wanted answers.

On D-Block, tensions between rival groups did nothing to alleviate the stress Mr. Keller endured. It wouldn't be until the next week that the results from Kevin's lab would arrive and he was in desperate need of a break. Sims had him under a microscope. In all honesty, the burly politician could care less of the dead bodies. Strung-out degenerates that had no future anyway.

For the Governor, it was the potential political fallout that held real weight. With every casualty the prison incurred, his public image was equally tarnished. Among men of ambition, bad optics are unacceptable. Voters wouldn't take kindly to stories of a prison out of control. All eyes were on him, his were on the warden. At the end of the day it was Keller. His head was the one closest to the blade. So close to the action, if shit hit the fan, his lips were sure to catch a few chunks. The warden needed to fix the drug problem. Fast!

The solution presented to him provided anything but relief however. The truth was, there was no real solution. At least none viable. The paper that morning read, "After the slaying of the President's daughter, the death penalty still hasn't been adopted by the State?" Jacob caught a rare opportunity to read this headline during visitation with his father later that day. Rain outside drizzled at a steady pace. Clouds lumbered and rolled in coils of grey. Sunshine hadn't brightened the sky for nearly a week. The weather matched the mood.

"You know son, we think about you all the time. Your mother and I love you very much. We always have." Visitation was only an hour that day. Everything was cut short by a disturbance unfolding over in Ad Seg, the area of the prison reserved for punishing the unruliest of residents. Jacob was lucky enough to avoid the place by staying under the radar. No easy feat considering there were several convicts with greedy eyes set on his wealth.

The only thing standing between Jacob and the caged wolves was Alik. His tactics were subtle, and his intentions remained elusive. Once incarcerated the Russian's assets were seized by the state, leaving him to rebuild his empire from scratch. He kept close tabs on the flow of money moving throughout the prison's hallways.

Having a cellmate with such vast wealth waiting on the outside presented opportunity. Alik bided his time. Waited for the right scenario to present itself. Life had taught him to be patient, observant. When the moment was right he would act. For now, he settled for friendly conversation. Jacob wasn't going anywhere. Compared to other correctional institutions he'd attended, this one was a breeze. He easily established a foothold and began collecting *rent* from the other cons. There was only one area the mobster didn't control, and that was Ad Seg. No one controlled that area. There was nothing worth claiming.

Once placed in the hole, you were doomed to an existence of solitude. Prisoners were only allowed an hour of sunlight per day; and given very little by way of personal items. If the food in general population was bad, it would've been considered dinner at the French Laundry compared to the offerings of Seg. Inmates living here often dreamt of death. They welcomed it. The darkness taunted them, swallowing men into its belly and melting away life in a stew of acidic misery. Voices called out that weren't there. Men grew wild in this hell constructed from steel and concrete. But nothing, nothing drew them crazier than the food. Every meal was an insult. An open-palmed slap in the face. Choking down repugnant mouthfuls cradled the fetus of resentment.

It was the horrid smell emitting off the spoiled Brussel's Sprouts that drew the poor man mad. The con was a resident of this seclusive, crepuscular place. He was confined to a room that was completely steel; there were no blankets, no bed, and no pillow. The one visible light, only teased and prodded, never offering comfort. It flickered sporadically in the hallway and created shadows for the demons of men to hide in. Six such cells were stowed at the very bottom of the prison. Rarely did any man leave this place the same as he'd arrived. Most would lose at least some aspect of themselves to the silent darkness. It sapped all will. A black hole from which hope lost its way.

This inmate was locked up for possession of two gallons of "hooch," but more importantly a vile of meth was also found hidden in a crevasse at the foot of his bed. The guard who discovered it was known for his thoroughness during shakedowns. He was one of the few staff members that could not be bought during the night shift.

"Warden look, it's some of that stuff," the CO escorted the convict straight to Mr. Keller's office once he realized what he was looking at. After a brief and unsuccessful interrogation, the warden decided to just throw the stubborn criminal into the hole. "Let the darkness have him." And have him it did...

After being locked away in solitude for over a week, the man lost it. "Chow! Now you enjoy that." The CO thrusted the beat-up metal tray into the slotted door sloppily, rancid food spilling over onto the floor in messy globs as he did so. The prisoner lifted a handful of sprouts and looked them over. They were ridiculously overcooked and felt so soft it reminded him of holding a blob of slimy fat.

By this point, his sanity was already clinging by a thread. When the CO tried to add injury to insult, the thread finally snapped. "How's that food in there? Would ya' like a glass of wine to go along with that?" The guard positioned his face near the slit in the door, taunting the man now crouched in the shadows. "You stupid cons think you can out smart us CO's? I wish I could throw all of you in a hole to rot." For the guard, it was personal.

He absolutely despised criminals and joined the prison system more from spite than anything else. He'd had a dark childhood. This was payback. In his arrogance he hadn't considered the lengths a man will go to once pushed. While too busy tormenting the prisoner, he didn't notice that his throat was exposed near the door's opening.

His adversary was more observant. The convict used the darkness to his advantage and stood just out of view. His murky silhouette blended perfectly with the room's dim surroundings. Dirt dulled the paleness of his skin and made it tan. White teeth and a sneering smile greeted him at the door's slot. The guard was bent over to ensure his insults were heard loud and clear.

Once the officer was within striking distance he sprang into action. The CO seized up and his eyes went wide as he felt the wild man's hand grip tightly around his windpipe. Uncut fingernails dug into skin, piercing and tearing, ripping until they broke the surface and burrowed into flesh. Carnal hysteria set in. The squeeze tightened. He could barely draw a breath, let alone call for help. It took all his might to remember his training. Every second counted. He was in trouble. Crouching, trapped in the con's grasp, he reached frantically for his keys. They jangled in loud clinks as his fingers tried to multi-task, darting back and forth between his belt and the door's slot. "If I can get this door opened maybe I can dose him with some OC. That'll get him off!" The plan sounded good on paper. Execution was another matter.

The guard had underestimated the strength of a man in desperation, and paid dearly for it. The "minor disturbance" announced as the reason over the intercom for short visitation? Well, that was actually a full-on and well orchestrated assault. The first in a sequence of attacks. Leading to an ultimatum. The correctional officer was unable to open the door in time. He collapsed to the floor in front of the holding cell, drool seeping slowly from a slightly opened mouth.

Before his victim fell to the ground and out of reach, the inmate hastily grabbed the keys attached to the limp guard's utility belt. His eyes were wide with craze as he fumbled to unlock the heavy door from the inside. The keys clanked together as his arm strained through the confined opening. There wasn't much space.

After a few failed attempts, he could feel the small chunk of metal find its mark. The steel door creaked and moaned as it opened cautiously. The escaped con swung his head around, looking back and forth several times before trying to locate an exit. He paced frantically down the dimly lit hallway, searching for a door to the outside world.

Within five minutes the escapee found his way to the prison yard. Breath heavy, it was finally starting to dawn on him what he'd just done. There was no turning back now. If apprehended, another 20 years would be added to his bid. The stakes were high. "Hey you? How'd you get out here?" Even with plenty of cons in the yard at the time, all of them were in their prison blues. Inmates sentenced to Ad Seg got assigned bright orange uniforms. That way they were easier to spot for both inmates and staff alike. He stood out like a sore thumb.

The prisoner tried to act like he didn't hear the guard, but then the man called out again. "How the hell'd you get out here? Hey Josh, get over here, and open this gate!" As the guard approached the felon he noticed the distinct tattoos of an Aryan Brother. The CO was also a part of the group and had maintained a silent yet active connection.

This was also true of many other Correctional Officers, especially ones working during later shifts. In actuality, nearly 40% of every criminal enterprise within the facility was represented by at least one staff member. The payoffs were just too high. Salaries too low. The environment bred corruption on both sides.

This guard had been made aware from someone within the Brotherhood that *something* would happen. He wasn't told what, just to be ready to support the cause. The sight of the tattoo beneath the escapee's left eye gave him away immediately as a Brother. Beneath his eyelid in black ink were the numbers 1488. Within the Neo-Nazi organization these numbers were significant for a few reasons.

In this individual's case, the *14* symbolized the number of words used in a slogan the group stood firmly behind. It was their mantra. "We must secure the existence of our people and a future for white children." The Great Replacement Theory was seared into his brain. A long line of fathers had passed the notion from son to son. It was an ideology bred by fear. Powered by violence. Although his mental state was on shaky ground after his stint in solitary, the con remained true to the movement.

As the guard recognized the inmate as a "Brother" he ceased his questioning and beckoned the other guard he'd called for to return to his post. "Good luck Brother," the guard said as he snuck the convict past two other colleagues. He was instructed earlier in the week to ensure all Brothers were granted safe passage through the yard. This would not be his only visitor that day.

The nearly exhausted escapee didn't have such good luck after leaving the yard. Playing Grey-man was out of the question in his current attire. He just barely managed to slip past two other CO's on his way to his final mission. Moving around was like dancing on a minefield, one mis-step and that was it. Atrophied muscles weighed him down, but like his comrades, his focus was unwavering. His escape was a small part of a much larger effort by the organization.

The final objective was deep within the bowels of "The central zone" near visitation; an area of the prison foreign to him. He received his orders via kite, a sophisticated network of internal mail lines between convicts. This messaging system was illegal. Yet like so many things at the facility it happened regularly anyway.

Incarcerated or not, the men found ingenious ways of communicating with both friends and rivals alike. A kite, as it was commonly called, was essentially just a small rolled piece of paper with coded instructions hidden in the text. The inmates would also talk to each other through what they affectionately referred to as *the telephone*.

Sure, they had access to the regular payphone, but this was limited and expensive; not to mention it allowed for zero privacy. Every call was recorded and intently reviewed by a team of prison analysts. Within the confines of their cells the men had more freedom from prying ears. First, they would look to make sure the coast was clear. Once confident, one cellmate would walk over to the toilet and empty its contents.

Having been built in the early 1900s, the prison's piping was outdated and allowed cons to talk through the toilet to neighboring inmates. The "phones" basically functioned the way you'd expect two cans tied to a thread of string to work. It turned out to be an integral form of communication in a population where a simple conversation could mean the difference between life and death.

The Aryan Brother who maneuvered through the yard was only able to do so because of one such exchange. He was in solitary for nearly two weeks before he got the call. It was from one of the highest-ranking members on D-Block and the instructions were clear. "Kill the babysitter, initiate Phase 1." Final details were sent through the mail. The objective was set.

The call ended in less than five seconds, but it was an integral step in a larger initiative already under way by the Brotherhood. "I will complete my mission Sir. Waffenbrüder." This term, *Waffenbrüder*, was a term the Brotherhood used regularly when communicating; it was German for, "Brothers in Arms..." A chess piece moved across the board. The Aryans were in play.

CHAPTER 34

BLOOD IN THE STREETS

Alik was irritable from a phone call he received that morning from the outside. Although no stranger to incarceration, he also ran a profitable business on the other side of the big wall. Back in the Free World. It took him several long years to rebuild old connections. The cashflow he received on the inside paled in comparison to the wealth he controlled before his indictment.

Ties to the Russian mob afforded Alik the privilege of exposure. Of the few people that called or visited the hardened man, most were business contacts in some respect. "Hello Alik, I hope you are well my friend." The voice on the other end of the line held a tone of concern.

Alik was standing outside at the one payphone near the edges of the yard. It was something of a landmark to the locals for many reasons. It was in this area that one inmate had been shot when the prison first opened its doors. The felon was attempting to escape, and used the phone as a ploy to get near the barbed fence. He actually made it to the outer wall before being discovered.

It was a story told often among the prisoners, all of

which shared in the dream of eventually escaping. "I am well brother, today I got the kite you are sending, what are you meaning by what is said?" The person on the other end was also a part of the mob, but not through blood. They were adopted into the family after completing the nearly two-year probationary period.

During that time, the prospect was expected, and in some cases forced to carry out all sorts of assignments. Only a privileged few, those born into the mob, could bypass what members jokingly referred to as the "half-blood" period. Many people wanted the access being *affiliated* could provide; a few were accepted into the program, and even fewer ever became full-fledged members.

Once a member of the mob, it was for life. There was no such thing as going back. Most other gangs in the prison acted as though they fell under the same stringent guidelines, but they would rarely kill a defector. In many scenarios it would mean a severe beatdown, maybe even demotion of title, but seldom did it end in death. This was not true with the Russians.

"Alik..." The man paused over the phone and Alik could sense the apprehension he was trying to conceal. "I have some bad news for you my friend. We are under an organized attack. Our opposition is still unknown. Who, whoever it is, they want war, and they're well funded." The member's voice quivered as he spoke. Alik was glaring at the gate, his eyes red with anger as he listened. He knew his organization was under siege, but to hear it was also being penetrated on the outside, this inspired a level of rage only a mobster could muster. "I see."

Alik stalked back across the field and headed towards D-block, there was a lot of work to be done and little time to do it. As he neared the center of the yard he saw the Aryan who escaped from the hole. At the time, he didn't know who he was seeing; he only caught a glimpse of the crazed supremacist before the man disappeared into a nearby building. As he opened the door to the building, the guard who he saw give the Aryan clear passage stopped him. "Alik, get over here. You remember what I said to you the first day I met you?"

The CO was standing with his legs slightly opened and his arms crossed. They covered his broad chest and flexed as the man shifted weight. His eyes were fixed on the Russian. "I am remembering, why are you asking me this? And now?" Alik carried a look in his eyes that said, "I know something you don't." The guard thought for a moment and gave a smirk of contempt. "I'll be seeing you real soon Alik."

The two never liked each other. They were often seen exchanging words. None were good natured. It wasn't until almost fifteen minutes later that the alarm began to ring out. Every inmate in the prison knew what the incredibly loud siren meant. It wailed and screamed. Relentless, deafening. It reminded Jacob of the sound cities would make when under an air raid.

He and Drake were in the visitation area when it first began. They could hear a voice patch through on the nearby guard's radio. Static garbled the line, but you could still tell what was being said. "We need assistance in B-wing now! CO down! CO down! I repeat we are a code 4!" The officer addressed Drake first. "Um Sir, I'm gonna' have to ask you to leave. We have a disturbance." The guard raised his voice so everyone in the room could hear him as he spoke. He was careful to remain calm. It was essential to maintaining control.

"Alright, everyone I need your attention please, if I could have all guests on this side of the room." It was standard protocol under those circumstances to check each and every person who entered the building that day. Whenever there was an inmate uprising, the first thing the prison would do was initiate a full-scale lockdown; the less free-roaming bodies, the better.

This involved searching every man, woman, and child that was not a current inmate or staff member. Mr. Keller learned early in his career that the most common time for either contraband to be smuggled in, or convicts out, was during situations like this. Criminals loved to capitalize on distractions that allowed them to slip past their enemy unnoticed. As the other visitors began to leave their seats and congregate at the corner of the room, Jacob too rose from his seat. The CO's still wouldn't let him have visitation in the general meeting area. According to them he was a flight risk.

Before he could say goodbye to his father he was whisked away. Chains jangled. Cuffs tore at his wrists. "What's happening? Why's that alarm going off?" Drake could barely hear the words as they left his son's mouth. The siren screeched on as the now single correctional officer tried his best to control the increasingly annoyed group of on-lookers. His colleagues were summoned elsewhere in the commotion.

One visitor, a small boy no more than ten years of age, stood alone in the center of the room. In the frenzy of moving bodies, he'd lost his older sister and was now crying for her. His small hands were shaking as they clutched tightly to one of the metal table legs. Luckily, there were not many people in visitation. It was only a moment or so before she found him.

From the looks of her youthful face she seemed to be in her early twenties. Jacob could tell by the way she interacted with her brother that she loved him very much. He'd caught a few glimpses of them before the alarm sounded and her affection was obvious. Now he could see them from the holding tank they placed him in. They were only separated for a moment, but she hugged her brother as if it were an eternity. It made him think of his sister Myra and the life he was missing on the outside.

"I hafta' check everyone again, when I call you, if you can please follow me back to the metal detection line." The visitors had already gone through a thorough search on their way in. Many weren't happy to hear they'd have to endure the process yet again. Disgruntled mumbles thickened the air. The guard could feel his skin warm with anxiety. This wasn't what he signed up for. There were a lot of bodies to manage, and no help. To everyone in the room, he was the bad guy.

Whatever discomforts experienced by this group, they were nothing compared to what the convicts on lockdown were about to endure. Their security measures were considerably more intrusive, and involved demeaning violations that culminated in cavity searches. Sure, metal detectors could be inconvenient, but they weren't humiliating. Having to remove one's shoes and belt? Keys? Prisoners often said civilians didn't know how good they had it. At least they kept their dignity. Their sense of worth. Confined to their narrow point of view, the group in visitation complained nonetheless.

The small boy who'd been frightened was two people away from being called by the guard when he saw a flash that caught his eye. It reminded him of one of the characters he would often watch on television in the mornings before his older sister would send him off to school. "Look!" He pointed a small finger in the direction of the thing that had drawn his attention.

The guard was the first to hear the child. His eyes widened as he realized what the boy was looking at. "What the? How the fuck did *he* get in there?" The man that stood before him was about six feet tall. His arms were muscular and dense. They filled the sleeves of his jumpsuit with ease. The guard could see thick veins as they bulged in the felon's neck and forehead. Then he noticed the tattoo. Numbers that identified the killer's faction.

He was not standing in the visitation room, but everyone could see the man through the glass window separating the two areas. Jacob was already being searched in an area designated for inmates only. He'd just been pulled from the holding tank a moment before. Standard protocol.

With his heart rate rising exponentially, the guard stopped checking the visitors and got back on the radio, "I need backup to visitation! Now!" The warden was in his office and could hear the disturbance over the intercom. He sprung from his desk and rushed to the door. The secretary had just hung up the phone as the wooden frame swung open.

"Susanne, tell me this is a drill?" A weight lingered in her eyes he'd never seen. Fear tickled at the creases of her chin. Something serious was going down. "No, I think this is real. One of the guards is with the visitors, and we have men gearing up in the armory now." "What do you mean *one* of the guards? Why's there only one guard in visitation? Where's his backup?" The question was rhetorical.

He knew Susanne had nothing to do with the prison's staffing problems, but he needed someone to yell at and she was the only one there. His job was on the line. Experience taught him how quickly things could go south. Complete control was his only real weapon. Without it, a single spark could see the entire prison over-run. Tensions were already high. The place was a tinderbox. Things were just begging to spiral into chaos. Keller knew what he had to do. "I want this place locked completely down. No one gets in or out until every prisoner is accounted for! And *every* visitor searched!"

There was a moment of silence before Susanne got to work. She switched the main intercom over to her line and began to speak; her words were clear yet urgent. Green eyes darted in Keller's direction every few moments. "This is not a drill, we are code 4. Any CO's not currently in the armory please report to your designated post immediately." Her voice amplified over the loud system and was muffled only by the whaling alarm.

As the CO in the visitor's area heard these instructions he glanced at the entranceway, hoping to see the familiar navy-blue uniforms issued to all guards at the facility. He was growing nervous for a few reasons. Not the least of which was the muscular man he now looked directly in the eye in the room next-door. A tremor crept up his spine and rested in his shoulders. Beads of sweat broke the surface of skin on the guard's forehead. They looked like little marbles of fear.

"I should've stayed on the damn police force; I don' even have a fucking gun for shit's sake." The only real weapons he had were a night stick and some pepper spray. That wasn't going to be enough. "I sure hope that glass is thick," it was the only barrier separating the guard and more importantly the visitors from an almost inevitable attack.

He couldn't stop shaking. His hands grew slick with sudor as the seconds ticked on. Nerves were getting the best of him. His right hand gripped his club. It was lifted from its sheath and put to the ready. He couldn't keep a good grasp, the sweat on his palm was like oil on the stick's smooth wooden surface. Grip or no grip, he had a job to do. Lives to protect. It didn't seem like the Calvary was coming... He planted his feet, standing firmly between the visitors and the killer on the other side of the glass; his chest thumped, barely holding his heart in place as combat loomed. The baton was held waist-height, poised for action. *This was it.*

With a steady stream of blood flowing freely from an unseen wound, the escaped convict looked around frantically.

His eyes bulged and darted as he took measure of the room. At first it seemed as though he was looking for the exit, but after he walked right past it, everyone knew there were other plans at play.

Visitation was stationed close to the central control room. No more than 50 yards or so separated the two areas. This was where the prison's mainframe and virtually all access points were monitored and controlled. Only a few of the prison's residents knew about a kink in this room's proverbial armor. From where the Aryan now stood he could see the fire alarm, his key to a flaw in the system.

Back in the early 90's, the warden at that time was too cheap to properly fortify several weak points throughout the prison. One such point was the control room. For starters, the engineer who designed the place didn't properly calculate the potential risks of having the room in such proximity to visitation. It was a tactical mistake.

With enough planning, any civilian could penetrate the weakly secured area. If they knew the schematics; within an hour they could have complete control over the facility. The inmate knew if the fire alarm was pulled, the room would automatically go into its own form of lockdown. Its three-inch steel door would close from the inside and seal shut. There were only two ways to open it after that; one option was at the hand of someone already in the room.

The other was to have the door opened by the police. There was a security code not even the warden knew, only the chief of police was in possession of the numbered combination. This was one of the first things Mr. Keller protested when he arrived at the penitentiary. "How am I supposed to be in control of this prison and the monsters here, if I don't even have all the keys to the kingdom?"

The Governor wouldn't hear another word of it; it wouldn't be until later down the road that Keller would have his ear... The escaped man lunged for the alarm, blood dripping from his forearm as he reached. Within seconds the sprinklers were on and the two men inside the control room could hear the large deadbolt lock as it clicked into place. Red fog lights sprayed beams across the room. It gave the hub a military war-room feel. The system locked down. No one was getting in. Or out.

"I dunno' what's goin on out there, but they won't be gettin' in here, that's fer' sure." The two men were looking at an oversized monitor showing live feeds for every camera in the prison. The third screen up from the bottom spotted the culprit first. "What the hell's this guy doing? Doesn't that look like the prison gowns they use down in Ad Seg?" "Sure does. Well I hope he wasn't planning on gettin' in here." "Sucks for that guard and those visitors though." "Naw, the troops are probably ten seconds out..." They weren't.

As they were talking, they didn't take notice to what was happening on the cameras in visitation. One of the visitors, an older woman, pulled a small bottle from her purse. The container reminded Drake of the jars used to fill prescription drug orders. She gracefully limped up to the guard on duty and asked if she could use the restroom.

"I'm just here visiting my grandson, but I need to take my meds. I have a heart condition and have to take these wretched pills every day." After giving her bag a quick look over he directed the woman out of the room and into the hallway. She seemed innocent enough. By this point the sprinklers had been shut off by the two men in the control room. This wasn't until nearly everyone in the prison received a brief but cold shower however.

"I'll wait by the door to let you in." The lone guard stood in the doorway with one foot wedged sideways to prop it open. "Oh you are so sweet my dear, you remind me of my son. You don't have ta' stand there, I know you have a job to do, I don't mind knocking when I'm done." She motioned a wrinkled hand, swiping away droplets that had gathered on her forehead, and turned to cross the doorway. He watched the old lady as she snuck a look back at the visitors.

Her demeanor seemed odd. After pondering this for a moment the guard obliged. "Ok, just try and be quick, I'll get ya'll outta' here as soon as possible. Sure'd be nice if I had some help in here though," he thought silently to himself. He glanced behind him to see what had caught the woman's attention.

The escapee had already left the other room and was nowhere to be found. "Doesn't matter, he won't get far." Up until this point, staff were only made aware that someone being held in Ad Seg was attempting to escape. It would be in the moments to come that the true intentions of those involved would be brought to light. For now, a lot remained hidden from view. Smoke and mirrors were the order of the day.

The elderly woman with the medication had been gone for several minutes by this point. At first the CO didn't notice. He had his hands full. After checking three more people his spidey senses started to go off. "Where is she at?" He was just about to go looking for her when she returned. Her face looked different than before; something carnal had etched its way into the deep lines around her cheekbones.

"Were you able to find the bathroom ok miss?" She completely ignored his question and started in the direction of the building's exit. The CO, thinking the woman was just having a senior moment, called out after her. “Miss? Miss? I still need you to come back over to this area.”

“I haven’t fully searched you yet.” She hobbled along, continuing to ignore his calls. “I gotta’ get home son, I have some food heatin’ in the oven. It’s time for me to go. Bye now.” Something sounded off about the way she said it. As she limped away he noticed streaks of blood trailing behind her. “What the fuck? Where did that come from?”

CHAPTER 35

WETTING THE SHEETS

About a week before Jacob got the visit from his father he and Alik were deep in conversation. Their debate was sparked by a comment Jacob made during dinner that evening in the mess hall. By this point he was finally able to eat basically wherever he wanted. It was rare that anyone would try to pick a fight with the cellmate of Alik.

The two were standing in line waiting for the evening's chow. "How're you able to sleep at night Alik? I'm not tryna' be funny or anything. I'm jus' sayin. Don't you have family on the outside? I *still* have nightmares about my brother." Jacob spoke too soon. He tried to cut the words short but they'd already left his mouth.

"What brother are you talking about? I am not knowing any brothers you are having?" Jacob stopped and thought for a moment. "Wait, that's right, I never told you about my brother Jason, did I?" The look on Alik's face indicated he thought the question was rhetorical. "You are knowing you have not told me these things. So tell me about him? Wait a minute," He was using his mangled hand to stroke his peppered beard. Wiry strands clung to the nails on his fingertips. "This is the one you are talking about when you are sleeping?"

Jacob looked confused. “I don’t talk about anyone at night. Wait, *do I*?” Alik gave a hearty laugh before replying, “You talk about him almost every night. I thought you were, you know, doing the love with him.” “What? No! Ok, let’s get one thing clear,” he stood so everyone in the mess hall could see and hear him. Now that he had a little seniority in the prison, his confidence was beginning to build.

“Let it be known, throughout the halls of this wretched place that Jacob Gilferd is no punk, I’m no sissy, and no bottom-bandit.” The group erupted with laughter at his descriptive words. Other inmates started to chime in with a few of their own. The room’s collective mood shifted. Even killers needed a good laugh from time to time.

“Are you not a Bum-driller then lad?” an Englishman called out. “Nope.” “What about a Batty Boy?” The voice sounded Jamaican. Deep. “Heck no!” It was a form of bonding between the men, a moment rarely shared behind the big wall. If the other inmates liked you, they gave you hell; if they didn’t, they might take your life.

“Hey Jacob, are you a butt rustler?” Even Alik had to laugh at this. “No I think the term you are looking for is butt pirate, butt pirate is what you were lookin’ for.” It was in these rare and precious moments that gang affiliations, race, and other differences between the men heeded to the call of uninhibited laughter. Alik even thought he saw a few of the Aryans give a chuckle.

The three guards assigned to that shift’s dinner allowed the jokes to continue for several minutes and one even decided to join in the humor. “I’m surprised you haven’t mooned us.” Jacob leaned back in his seat and interlocked his fingers behind his head before responding to the wisecrack. “Why the hell would I do that, you’d enjoy it too much. Look, he’s about to do a cavity search." "Ha Ha, yeah he probably would love to find "contraband."

The guard was quick on his feet after years of dealing with the rowdy men, "No I actually just figured you forgot your helmet." "What?" "Well aren't you an anal astronaut?" The room burst with a new wave of laughter. "All right cons, keep it down. Warden should be making his rounds soon." Another CO had just entered the room. He was more of a stickler than his coworkers. The mess hall lulled to a murmur. Funtime was over.

After dinner that night Alik and Jacob walked together back to their cell. The building for D-block was placed center-compound, making the journey long and tiresome. By the time they made it back it was almost time for the nightly count. The two lined up in front of their cell doorway and waited for their names to be called. Of all the things to hate about prison, count was probably the most redundant. Just when some semblance of normal was achieved, count would snatch the feeling away, reminding you of where you were. Never letting you forget. A thorn that pricked the skin three times a day. Five during lockdowns.

After getting checked off the evening's list, their door closed and they were left alone for the rest of the night. "That was pretty funny, I mean what happened at dinner. Anal astronaut?" Jacob began to laugh out again. He lowered his voice a little at Alik's direction. The Russian's eyes were fixed on something below. There was a guard's table on the ground-level of their building. The man that was assigned the night shift was different than any of the CO's in the mess hall; for starters, he was an Aryan Brother.

He sat in an office chair that reminded Jacob of the ones you would see used-car salesmen try to screw you over in. It was all black and had stains on the armrest and back. The desk wasn't in much better shape. It was really two smaller tables pushed together; there was also a plastic water jug sitting on one end. The CO spent most of his time talking with fellow Brothers housed on the block.

This evening he seemed even more hostile than usual. Something was under his skin. Maybe he had problems at home, trouble with the Misses. Who knows. "If I hear another peep from *any* of you, the rest of your night'll be in Ad Seg. Shut your traps!" His angry voice rang through the night; all fell silent. He worked for a while longer at his desk before making his way over to cell 4 on the ground level. Steel-toed footsteps announced his approach.

This was home to one of the prison's most dangerous residents. The individual here was not a threat because of what *he* would do personally. Grunt work was beneath him. It was his influence that was the real death sentence. Legion stood behind him. "How are you doing Brother?" The guard called through the bars, his voice almost at a whisper. He could see the cheap blankets on the top bunk begin to stir.

The man on the bottom turned over but didn't say a word. His face was stained with blood. The right eye was nearly shut. A fractured socket the culprit, swelling had set in. When the CO squinted down at the floor he saw what looked to be a tooth laying near the sink. He shook his head with a smirk. It wasn't surprising. His friend was famous for his temper. "I had to teach him some manners, these young guys ya'll send in here don't understand the art of pleasing a man; sometimes you have to teach em' the hard way. I'll soften him up soon enough."

The guard nodded. His sneer lingered. "I hear you Brother, Marc mentioned you needed to get a message to one of our guys down in Ad Seg?" Even from where he was standing several floors up, Alik could see the two men talking on the ground floor below. "You are remembering what I said about the balancing of power?" Jacob was a little thrown off by what his celly was saying. "What're you talking about?"

He was over at the toilet, trying his hand at a batch of "hooch." It wasn't going too well. "Do you mind coming over here for a second? I need a little help with these oranges." The Russian's attention remained focused on the men talking two floors down. His head turned a little to address Jacob, but his eyes never left cell number 4. "Throw a couple of these fruits to me, I will show you how to make a drink worthy of Mother Russia."

The two already had a batch done from earlier in the week and decided on a little quality check while they waited on the new brew. "This stuff's like jet fuel, but I think I'm getting used to it." "Wait until you taste this batch that is coming," Alik's voice was distant; he was distracted by what was going on between the two skinheads. They were definitely up to something.

The Aryans continued to speak, oblivious to prying eyes watching from above. "You are right, the time has come. I need you to make sure the phone lines are open down in Ad Seg. And John, make sure our guy down there is moved to cell 7." Cell number 1 in Ad Seg was really just an interrogation room. "We need to be patient Brother, but our time is coming. Soon you will own this prison, and all its profits. We're with you." The CO took pause before he went on. This was his shot to really prove his worth. There was nothing more valuable than having an ally in prison. Especially an ally with keys. "I'll do my part."

Before the Aryan turned to walk back to his desk he asked, "How are the LMS's going?" Dirty staff and prisoners alike needed to speak in code, especially when in public areas. They never knew who was listening just around the corner, or even in the next cell. It was like operating under a spy's nest. Every wall had an ear pressed to it.

For the Aryans, the acronym LMS stood for Liquid Methamphetamine Shipment. "They're fine, but we're getting some pressure from the warden, one of my contacts in sanitation let me know there may be a raid comin' soon. You heard anything about that?" The CO thought for a moment before answering, his head shook in tandem with his reply. "Administration won't be a problem; warden still thinks the lab's on the grounds. What a twit."

The two men laughed at Keller's expense. The poor warden was completely in the dark. Clueless. "He's a fool. Everything's panning out. Good." The inmate in unit 4 was standing at the bars by this point, his sharp grey eyes now fixed upon Alik's cell. For what seemed an eternity, the arch enemies locked in an intense stare-down. It ended when Jacob spilled the hooch.

"Watch what you are doing boy!" "Sorry Alik, maybe if you weren't so busy making googly eyes with your friend down there you could be more useful helping me!" By this point in their relationship, Jacob was really starting to like the Russian. They talked nearly every day; well, every day Alik was not confined to the hole.

Alik too was taking to his neighbor, often granting him access to high level meetings usually only reserved for members. He was one of the few people Alik would tolerate outside the mob. Even the COs thought twice about messing with the borderline psychopath.

"Tell me more about this brother you are mentioning at dinner?" He needed a change of pace, the only thing that consumed Alik's mind as of recent was the impending war. The mob had many enemies. A conversation of a different nature was a welcome thought to them both. "Well what is it you wanna' know? There really isn't much to tell."

"Sure there is a thing you can tell. You are talking about him all night while you are sleeping, sometimes you are even crying. What is happened?" His thick Russian accent used to annoy Jacob, what with his bad puns and ill placed analogies; but as of recently Jacob had come to enjoy the simplicity of it.

"At least he doesn't speak in riddles like Mr. Lao used to." But then again, if he could choose to be either there talking with Alik, or out in the real world sitting on a rock with the monk? Jacob would take the damn rock, "Even it's got to be softer than these hard ass beds." Alik was now staring directly at Jacob with a look of impatience in his eyes.

"What? What Alik, what did I do now?" "You are not answering my question about this brother." He didn't really like talking about his dead sibling, but he knew that when Alik focused on something it consumed him; and right now his focus was on Jason. "He died ok. He's dead. My brother Jason is dead. It happened like six years ago." "Who is killing him? I have people on the side of the wall you know."

This was one of those moments where Jacob wasn't quite sure what the Russian was trying to say, but it sounded like he wanted to help. Jacob could hear the sincerity and concern in the middle-aged man's deep voice. "No, no one killed him. Now what was that other thing you said?"

With a few more attempts Alik finally conveyed his message. "I was saying that I am with you on this. You are understanding? I can hear you some nights down there, sobbing and things like this. I know how it is feeling, this death thing." Jacob stared blankly, "You've died before?"

He knew what his bunkie was saying. "Thank you Alik,

I hope one day I can stop having those nightmares, I'm tired of waking up with sweat soaked sheets." "Don't worry Jacob, I am understanding this, and once you are a part of the family you will see there are many like you, men suffering with the past." Although he appreciated the gesture, he didn't like it, that this would be the second time the mob boss referred to him "joining" the family. Once in, it was for life. He was already serving one sentence. Another would be too much to bear.

CHAPTER 36

AD SEG

It was considered by far the worst way to die in prison. To be left to one's own mind was hell. For most the voices would start within a week or so. At first, men described them as feeling like thoughts, but soon they would realize they were speaking out loud. It was usually downhill from there. Within a month, even the strongest would succumb to the tortures of solitude.

Jacob remembered overhearing one of the older prisoners talk about *the hole* with a CO one frosty afternoon. November's end was a week away. He was out on the yard, hands stuffed in thin pockets, mouth shut. His teeth wouldn't stop chattering. The day's high would barely break 40 degrees and sporadic gusts of brumal air from up North didn't make things any warmer. A cold front had moved in overnight. "It's so interesting, ironic even. We get basically the same punishments as children do." The guard was an old friend from the outside. A friend that chose a more lawful path. It had been years since they hung out. A few felonies later they picked up where they left off. It was a surreal experience for both parties. The choices we make can have a profound impact on which side of the fence one ends up on.

"How do ya' figure that? I'd say punishments on adults are far more severe?" "You didn't hear me, I wasn't questioning the severity, merely the nature of the punishment itself. Think about it, what's the difference between sending a child to "the corner" for a time out? And dragging a con to the hole for fighting or whatever?"

The guard thought about it for a minute, "I guess you're right in a way, both people get sent to time out." The men knew there were stark differences. For starters, the child would likely be confined to the corner for 15 minutes at most. There were men that spent *years* in the darkness of Administrative Segregation. Decades. Down there, minutes took hours. Time was a statue. An ominous, mind-numbing statue.

It was located literally underneath the prison, and to make matters worse, directly under D-block. The stairwell leading down was dark, creaky, and cold. It led to the land of misery. There was a constant draft that carried the stench of despair on its breath. If the beds and sheets in other areas of the prison were considered cheap, they would still be a vast improvement to what was offered to the unfortunate souls confined to this place.

Each door protruded from the wall and had a slot in the center to exchange food and water for buckets of feces and stale piss. Everything about the place was designed to break a man's spirit. Slow. Deliberate. A tunnel with no end. There was no natural light in the enclosure, and the only contrast to the metal, was the cement. The sole saving grace of Ad Seg were the rats. On one hand, the detainee determined to keep his wits about him could *talk* to the furry rodents.

It was not uncommon for men to make up names for the animals, some longtime residents went as far as to even give them individual personalities. A rat was like a companion dog, just smaller. And rattier. There was another reason an inmate could see the infestation as a plus. A much darker one. Early on in his career, Keller caught a lot of heat over the rodents, and not for the obvious reasons.

Alik and most of the other lifers had heard the tale. "They are saying that a prisoner had befriended the rats, that he is feeding them." Jacob was sitting on the bottom bunk listening to the Russian's depiction of the horrors taking place below D-Block. "You mean *was feeding them, right*?" Alik learned to ignore the young man's corrections. "He is feeding them, but not himself."

To the warden's utter shock, one man had actually used the rats to try and starve himself. He knew the CO's would take notice if they saw he wasn't eating. In extreme cases, they'd force-feed unwilling detainees. Reluctant mouths were wedged open with a closed pair of cuffs, restraint chair at the ready, tasers out. It was like being water-boarded by your dinner, which was likely pig-slop anyway. To get around this hellish experience, the inmate would feed a small army of rats his daily rations. Within two weeks the individual lost half his body weight. *His plan was working.*

By week four one of the guards finally opened the door to the disease infested room. He had to immediately leave the area due to the overwhelming stench. It wasn't just the sickness, but also month-old feces, both human and not, that really added depth to the fetor. Enough to make the CO cough as he tried to catch his breath. In addition to offering the rodents his food, the deranged man also allowed them to gnaw hungrily on parts of his body as his strength faded. Tiny teeth tugged and tore at exposed tendons. Feeding frenzies were common. It was a grim scene.

Medical professionals arrived almost a full day after the severity of his condition was discovered. All of them left work before that night's shift started, so he was left to fend for himself until the next morning. After cleaning filth and rot from his body, they had to stitch an infected gash dripping with green and tan puss. The wound was over-run with gangrene, and the smell emitted by the infection was profound, it was a miracle the man survived. The same could not be said for his arm. After the rats had taken their fill of bicep meat, maggots set in, building a nest in the nook of his elbow. The will to live had retreated, leaving a feast for whatever was hungry. They had to wheel him from Ad Seg on a gurney.

The holding-cells themselves were not so much rooms as they were large closets. There were no windows whatsoever. The walls were made completely of fortified concrete and there was no bed. Instead, Mr. Keller said if inmates enjoyed living in the slums, they could sleep there as well. Everywhere the eye wondered, grey, rust, and layers of grime met its gaze. In winter, they were freezers. In summer, ovens, baking men on a low broil that rushed from cell doors every time a slot was opened.

Alik would tell horror stories of this place. He called it the place where "Minds are being lost." Although Ad Seg was an absolute and in-escapable hell for prisoners, CO's assigned there didn't fare much better. It wasn't uncommon to lose one's mind to the sounds of incessant screams. Incoherent conversations abounded. They would tell their wives of madmen arguing with themselves. One man lost an intense disagreement with himself and wound up evening the score with a noose.

Staff-on-prisoner abuse was also common. The warden would rarely hear of these due to the strict code all inmates lived by. "No Snitching." It was a concept known by guards and prisoners alike. Using this knowledge to their advantage, CO's would often sexually assault vulnerable newcomers, especially young first-time offenders.

They would not however take liberties with the likes of Alik, or any of the other heavy hitters throughout the facility. Every CO knew all too well that when they were behind those stone walls; the hunter could become the hunted at a moment's notice. So could their families. If there ever came a day when the entire population rose against the staff in unison, it would be the end. Inmates outnumbered staff 50 to 1. Divide and conquer, that was Keller's motto. Segregation was an essential tool. An effective deterrent.

One of the only forms of entertainment while in Ad Seg was to write. Inmates were allowed one piece of chalk twice a week, on Mondays and Fridays. For the unfortunate individuals who found themselves here, there was nothing to do but write. The men found all manner of ingenious ways of expressing themselves. Profanities spattered the walls, floors, a few even made it to the ceilings. Shit buckets made great stools.

Some did it from spite, for others it was just a release. Many completely lost their minds over time. For them scribbling gibberish would suffice. Anything would do to get rid of the incessant silence; it was the silence that could kill. A man could be sent to Ad Seg for any number of reasons and for any amount of time the warden saw fit. There were no State laws restricting his authority in this regard.

Although Mr. Keller did his best not to abuse his power, this did nothing to negate his iron-fist leadership style. The inmates knew infractions didn't have to be big to be sent here. Even a single day in the hole was enough of a deterrent for most men. Alik's least favorite part of the all too familiar dwelling were the "beds."

Ad Seg really didn't have beds per se. What they did have were small sheets of metal connected to the cement wall with screws and bolts. Each "bed" also had chains securing it to the wall. These chains only added to the already eerie feel of the place. It was like being in a dungeon. Sleeping in hell. On rare occasions Mr. Keller would allow the local "Scared Straight Program for Youth," to use the hole as a tool to get troubled adolescents off the streets. A very effective tactic indeed.

CHAPTER 37

PHASE 1

The guard should've never been placed in Ad Seg to begin with. He wasn't nearly experienced enough to be assigned such a dangerous post. It was an oversight the warden would later regret. A more tenured CO would've known to never expose their neck to the door's opening. Because of this mistake, this young man lost his life that day. He woke up that morning just like every other morning. The poor man never had a fighting chance; once the crazed inmate got a firm grip on his windpipe, it was over.

Detainees in neighboring cells looked on as life was snatched from the recently hired employee. The Aryan assigned to cell number 7 had received the message intended for him. Phase 1 of their plan to overthrow the Russian Mob was now underway. There was no turning back.

After escaping Ad Seg, the prisoner sounded the fire alarm near visitation. Upon completing his mission he would be apprehended and sent back to the hole, only this time for a much longer stretch. This didn't faze the seasoned extremist however. During his brief "phone call" while in Ad Seg, the dedicated Brother was told to set the alarm off at all costs.

He was also instructed to kill the guard. No loose ends. The stakes were too high. He knew if he *violated*, or disobeyed orders, he would surely be killed himself. High level violations such as this would require more than just death. Each group had its own special system of justice. Almost all would sanction *beat-downs* for minor infractions. These beatings could get incredibly savage. Broken cheek bones, fractured jaws, cracked ribs. The list of gifts bestowed was endless. Most survived, but sometimes things got out of hand.

In scenarios where the entire future and possibly even the group's survival could depend on a single mission, punishments could get incredibly severe. Barbaric even. Family was often targeted. Luckily for the Aryan tasked with initiating Phase 1, he was fully committed to the cause. As he felt the last breaths of life leave the guard he was ordered to kill, he whispered "Waffenbrüder" into the dying man's ear. It was a cold gesture. "Brothers in Arms."

After completing his mission, he just kneeled on the floor and put his hands on his head, blood still dripping from his fingertips. His segment of Phase 1 was complete. "Heil Hitler!" he shouted before interlocking his fingers as he waited for his inevitable apprehension.

"You're telling me he killed one of my men so he could ring an *alarm bell*? A bell? Is that what you're saying right now? Who was it, who did we lose?" The warden was furious once he received the news. "It was one of the younger guys, I think he just started a month or so ago." There was sure to be bad press. Reporters always followed up on stories like this. Bold headlines were great for ratings. Not so much for Keller. He was trying desperately to rack his brain for ideas.

"The Governor know yet?" Susanne shook her head no. While Mr. Keller was receiving further details on what took place, the guard in visitation was finding out he too had his work cut out. He was attempting to get the elderly woman who'd just used the restroom to take a seat in the waiting area.

Up to that point he still didn't know where the blood was coming from, but he suspected the old woman probably cut herself in the bathroom somehow. Maybe on a loose pipe or something. When he went over to inspect her, he noticed the blood didn't appear to originate from her body. There were no visible wounds he could see. His eyes scanned arms and legs, then her torso and neck. Nothing.

"Miss, are you hurt? I can see some blood trailing from the hallway, and I really do need you to stay in this area." The visitor refused to listen and had to be repeatedly escorted to the wooden bench where everyone else was waiting to be checked.

After an eternity of coaxing, she finally hobbled over to the only available seat next to the young boy who originally spotted the escapee. A moment later another guard stormed into the room. "What the hell's going on down here? Where did this blood come from?" His questions were heavy with agitation.

This man wasn't nearly as accommodating as his colleague. Before signing on as the head Correctional Officer at the prison, Lieutenant Price led a team of 7 US Navy SEALS through four tours overseas. He was a man few chose to cross. After receiving word one of his men had been killed by the Aryans he was in no mood for games.

Before the other guard on duty could even respond, the man was off. Price stormed back out the visitation room and began to follow the trail of blood down the hallway. To both his surprise and dismay, the thick burgundy puddles created a path leading directly to the control room. The saliva in his mouth dried up as his eyes fell upon the scene ahead. There was no movement. The door was open.

"Hey! Get in here! And call for a medic! We have two men down!" The words rang through the hall and within seconds the younger guard came running. His eyes went wide with shock as his colleague came into view. "Oh my Gosh! I didn't even see them, there was no one out here! Is he still alive?" Lieutenant Price was holding two fingers on the neck of one of the victims. The veins had sunk deep beneath his skin. It didn't matter. Any blood still in them was on its way out. Most had already found a path down the man's shoulder and onto the floor. The other individual was also non-responsive. Thick white foam congregated at the corners of his lips. His skin was pallid. A puncture wound on his left breastplate was in plain sight. The attack had been vicious. A skillful killer was on the loose.

"Were there other cons that got out?" Before a response was given, Price was already on his radio barking orders. "I want this place locked all the way down, and someone get me the damn warden! I think we have another runner on our hands." The slightest hint of fear could be heard in his voice. It wasn't audible through the com-line, but the guard near him caught it. The shit had hit the fan.

What the men had not thought of, was exactly what the Aryans were betting on. The younger of the two guards pressed the red button on his walkie talkie and began to speak. His words were frantic. "Yes, this, this is Correctional Officer Dan Little in visitation. We need. We need immediate assistance now! I have two men down."

Dispatch on the other end asked what kind of injuries were sustained. "I, I don't know, I just see blood everywhere! It's all over the place back here." While Dan talked, Lieutenant Price began to more closely inspect the man whose neck he was holding. As far as he could tell, there were no other wounds aside from the professionally carved gash near his jugular. It was almost like a rogue surgeon had gotten to him. The flesh was split with a single vicious slice. Each time his fading heart pumped, another spurt of blood shot out, soaking his collarline and eventually painting the tile beneath. He was doomed.

"How many do ya' think got out?" Like most prisons of that size, accurate communication was rare. In each area of the prison everyone knew something was going down, but few knew all the specifics. This was exactly what the Aryans were hoping for. "I'm gonna' go back into the visitor's area and get these civilians outta' here. In about 30 minutes this is gonna' be a shit storm with the media."

He stalked from the control room and headed a few yards down the corridor. As he walked, it dawned on him, where was the elderly woman from earlier? She could've saw what happened, after all she *did* have blood on her. Maybe there was a connection, and besides, it was the only lead he had. He figured he would start with her and then ask the others if they saw anything. When he got back to the room, a look of utter confusion struck Dan's face.

"Where did the old woman in the red blouse go?" No one answered his question. The woman was gone. Upon review of the cameras she was seen walking right out the front door. She was picked up by a dark blue van, and Mr. Price pointed out that she seemed to move a lot easier on the video than what the younger guard described.

"I'm sure Sir, she walked with a, a wobble or something. Like a limp. It was different than she's walking on this tape I can tell you that!" He was sure of it. "So, she wasn't a civilian." Within less than ten minutes the entire prison was on lockdown and everything appeared to be under the staff's control. All prisoners were locked securely in their cells and additional CO's were being called in from their days off for overtime.

"Let's clean up this mess, I need to make a call to the Governor, Susanne, can you have someone call the wives of the men we lost; once you get them on the line let me know. I wanna' offer my condolences personally. And..." He wiped his forehead, "Let's provide any assistance we can to the families." Keller and three of his staff were standing in the control room. By this point there were also several police officers onsite as well.

"Warden? You may wanna take a look at this." Price beckoned him towards the dead body of the man he was trying to save earlier. "What is it?" "We found a letter on this one." Mr. Keller gave his lead CO a look of indifference. There were too many things to do and reading a letter was at the bottom of the totem pole. He had three dead bodies to deal with. "So what? Just put it with the other evidence, come on we've gotta' get this place cleaned up and get this situation under control. Put it in the bag and let our friends downtown handle it."

"Sir, the Governor's on line one for you, he sounds pretty pissed." "Tell him I'm stuck down here in visitation, I'll hafta' call him back." As the words were leaving his mouth he could hear the correctional officer interject. "Um Sir, you really do need to look at this letter." Keller felt like he was being pulled in a million different directions. Everyone needed something. "They don't pay me enough for this crap," he thought silently. "Mr. Keller!" "What?" "Sir, your, your name is mentioned in this letter Sir."

"What do you mean *my name*?" With a bit of hesitance the guard handed over the folded piece of paper. It looked like it had been torn from a CO's notepad, half the top left corner was missing. "I mean, well just read it for yourself." The note found in the man's left pocket was stained red with blood and part of the writing was illegible, but the message was clear.

"Mr. Keller;

I appreciate your leadership style and respect your values. However, as I'm sure by now you are aware; I hold the *true* power at this institution. Three of your men are dead. Two of them at the hand of an old woman, (we have people everywhere Mr. Keller.) Now, I'm sure by this point you've apprehended our man from Ad Seg. We're gonna need him placed back in gen pop. We miss him dearly, and he hasn't had a decent supper in ages.

Additionally, I would like a face to face meeting. We have much to discuss dear friend. One Hour. D-block, cell 4. Come alone or we take another life.

Toodles for now.

Keller was reading the letter aloud, his eyes growing wider with each word. The entire premise was baffling. "What the hell does any of this have to do with me?" He plopped into a nearby chair and put his arm on the desk in front of him. In his carelessness the warden's elbow accidently touched one of the buttons, setting off yet another alarm. "I've gotta' regain control, what the hell'm I gonna' tell the Governor?" Mr. Keller knew his stern boss would be on the grounds within a few hours.

What started as a fairly contained onetime event down in Ad Seg, was quickly spiraling out of control. "Alright, let's put a plan together, I want the heads of each block in my office in 15 minutes!" He stormed from the room and hurried back to the main building with a few of his subordinates trailing a few feet behind. Once safely within its walls he began to break down. He could feel tears beginning to well up for the first time in years. "Either way I handle this I'm screwed. Regardless of what happens from here, those people are dead. And it happened on *my* watch."

The warden slumped back in his chair and shut the window blinds. Slivers of light from a lamp outside his office slipped through the cracks. They provided just enough illumination to see the room's layout. There was a revolver in his desk drawer that had been lifted off a visitor earlier that day. Normally items like this would've been secured in the prison's vault, but this piece drew his interest.

It was meant to be delivered to someone on D-block and the warden wanted to know who. Maybe it was for whoever was in Cell 4. Maybe not. "All of these pieces are linked somehow, I just know it!" As he sat there, a thought crossed his mind. It was more of a fantasy/nightmare scenario than a mere thought really.

"I have three options the way I see it. I can go down to D-block, find out what this idiot wants and then make him think he's gonna' get it. We could easily lock him and his cohorts up in Ad Seg." This prompted the warden to recall what just took place in the dark hellhole. "Which leaves me with my other two choices."

"I can take this revolver, walk down to this guy's cell, and put a bullet in his fucking head for killing my men." Mr. Keller wasn't thinking rationally. He felt like his career and everything he worked for was beginning to disintegrate. It was so recently that he'd received the trophy for his good works; but now that he really looked at his resume there were some serious doubts.

"Law enforcement's the only thing I know. What'll my wife think when I lose my job?" Warden Keller sat in his chair and reached for the drawer at the bottom of his desk. In it he kept a bottle of whiskey for those truly hard days at the office. It was already half gone. After taking a healthy gulp or two, he tightened up his pants and tucked the gun in his belt under his shirt.

Keller didn't say it aloud, but option three was to use the gun on himself. He knew if and when he lost his job, he would also lose his hard-earned reputation and the pension that came with it. His entire savings was in that pension. Everything. Life's cruel hands would no doubt take his wife with the coming turmoil as well. The murders would likely be viewed as negligence. Keller knew all too well if someone had to go down for the wrongful death, the Governor would surely hang him out to dry...

CHAPTER 38

CELL NUMBER 4

After a few short minutes of solitude, the warden opened the door to his office. He was greeted by his secretary Susanne and several other men, some of which were law enforcement. Instead of stepping all the way out, he just peeked his head. "Susanne will you send them in groups? I'll start with the guys in blue and then we can put a plan in place for our friend down in D-Block."

The deputies on scene entered the office one after another and began to speak. "First off Mr. Keller we just wanna' say we're here at your disposal. I, on a more personal note, wanna' give my respects to your fallen." The fellow lawmen shook hands as they spoke. The officer was sure to keep eye contact the entire time. He meant every word. "So, with that being said, tell me a little about what's goin' on here? Was this an orchestrated event? What do we know?"

"Well, we're all still a little in the dark. The inmate that took out my CO down in Ad Seg is in custody, but he isn't talkin. Now granted, that's to be expected, what with him being a skin-head and all." The police officer raised an eyebrow at the remark. His arms were folded. "You have an Aryan presence?"

Both Keller and Susanne began to laugh at the question. They couldn't hold back. She chimed in, "To say we have a *presence* is a bit of an understatement. They basically run about a third of the prison." She pointedly spoke directly to the inquiring officer and ignored the suppressive look offered by her boss. He didn't appreciate her comment.

"Um, Susanne, last time I checked, *I* ran this prison." Mr. Keller cut her a sharp look before addressing the officers again. "Like I said, we haven't gotten much out of him, but we're on it." The cop nodded. "Ok, now can you tell us anything about this letter? Why would they ask to meet with you, and alone at that? Is there some kinda' history you have with this inmate?" No response was given. Just a timid look.

"Mr. Keller, I need to level-set with you here. We're at a juncture. The decisions you make now could be critical down the road." The way the officer was speaking reminded Keller of the way he would speak to convicts. He chuckled a little at the irony.

"We have reason to believe your life might be in danger." The female officer spoke for the first time. She was a pretty blonde with blue eyes and a face that looked much too kind for her line of work. "What do we know about the woman that took the men in the control room?" With an uneasy shift Keller responded. "Nothing really, the guard said she appeared to be in her early sixties. Nothing came up on her file. We believe she used an alias to gain access to the building."

"Do we know how she was able to escape? Did she have anyone on the inside, like the security guard, or maybe someone at one of the checkpoints?" While the officers were musing scenarios, Susanne tried to appease the Governor on the phone. Her efforts yielded little fruit. There was only one person Sims wanted to hear from. "Sir, he's asking for you again, line 1."

Mr. Keller shook hands with the responding officers and left them with his lead CO. Against his better judgement, he decided he would heed the instructions in the letter and attend the meeting alone. The walk to D-block seemed to take longer than usual. He had a lot to think about and little time. *The clock was ticking.*

Up until this point, the warden still had no idea what awaited him. All sorts of things ran through his head. "Was this a set-up? Otherwise why would they have asked that he come alone?" Before opening the heavy metal doors to D-Block, Keller sent a silent prayer to the *Woman* upstairs.

"Lord, if this is gonna' be my Day, please make it quick. Look after my family. Please God, I beg you. Hear my prayers. Just this once." He knew if his life was meant to end, it was unlikely to be anything other than slow and arduous. If the convicts couldn't stand the CO's, and would gladly kill one in a heartbeat; what did they have planned for him?

Mr. Keller walked up to the make-shift guard's desk located on the ground level. He looked the CO on duty in the eye before speaking. "Do me a favor n' watch my back while I'm in here, can you do that for me?" The man said nothing. His hand went out, gesturing towards cell number 4.

The warden looked confused. He raised a finger before turning to ask, "How'd you know what cell I needed to go to?" Silence. Then a cold voice called out. It was coming from behind. The tone was like the photophore on an angler fish, luring him in, towards the devil's lair. "Warden! It's me you need to talk to. Come, let's chat." By this point, D-Block was a madhouse. Word ran rampant through the prison that there'd been an escape.

This got the inmates going for sure, but the real kicker came when they found out about the bodies. They were yelling and screaming profanities, some even threw rolls of hard-to-come-by toilet paper from their cells in celebration. Within minutes the block was an absolute mess. "Some pigs got cooked today boys! I smell bacon!"

Mr. Keller walked slowly in the direction of cell number 4. His palms were slick with sweat and the hairs on the back of his neck were beginning to rise. Then he stopped and thought to himself. "Yes, they had the upper hand about two hours ago, but this is *our* prison, not theirs." The fact that he was afraid to speak with a prisoner locked in a cage made the man feel silly. With courage now rekindled, he walked with more confidence.

"CO! open on cell 4!" As the warden strode in the direction of the steel cage, he took notice of the way the other inmates were looking at him. More eyes drew in his direction with every step. It felt like they knew something he didn't. *Like they expected something.* Despite his best judgement he continued on. The cell door finished sliding just as he was arriving. Metal ground against metal and then stopped with a clink.

"Good evening Mr. Keller. I'm glad you got my message. I was beginning to get worried." On the way to D-block the warden had rehearsed what he would say to the thug. He'd tell him who was boss and speak clearly and with conviction; as to ensure the other convicts could hear the example he planned to set. When he finally did speak however, his reserved voice set a different tone.

"What is it you want? And why'd you feel the need to kill my men?" The inmate assigned to cell number 4 was none other than Billy Stanler, aka "The Enforcer." Aside from Alik and one or two other men, he was considered the prison's most dangerous inhabitant. A thin man in stature, his dead stare and eerie voice added demonic undertones to his presence. It was like looking at the devil's cousin. You could tell at a glance he was no one to be messed with. There was a wildness he gave off that put you on edge almost immediately.

"It has come to my attention warden," he spoke slowly, the arrogance in his inflection told Keller the night was still young. "It has come to my attention that you've hired a Mr. Kevin Splinton. Is that correct?" Billy could tell by the ensuing silence that he was dead on target. Nonetheless, the warden wasn't about to admit anything. He had to be strategic. Billy was no dummy. "I dunno what you're talkin about, maybe you needta' check your sources." The Aryan gave a smile. It didn't come from a good place. "My resources span far beyond the reaches of these walls Mr. Keller, as I'm sure your friends down in the control room can attest to."

The warden held back the urge to respond, he knew this Billy character was holding all the cards now; that was becoming quite clear. "You never answered my question, what do you want?" "Mr. warden Sir," the man said mockingly, "I want you to recognize us." "Us being? What, the Aryans? We know who you are."

"No. Mr. Keller, you know we're occupants in this prison, yet," he wiped the corners of his hairless mouth with mocked disappointment on his face, "you still act as though you're the one who's in control. This cannot be allowed to continue." The warden couldn't believe his ears. "What *exactly* are you getting at con?" Before he could say another word Billy cut in. "Rule number one, you will no longer refer to me as con, inmate, or any of the other derogatory names you idiots call us. Rule number two. When I ask you a question, answer it." For each rule, Billy held up a finger.

"From this point forward, if I want your opinion, I'll

give it to you." "Just who the fu." The cocky killer cut the warden off just in time. "Rule number three." With the snap of a finger one of the neighboring cell doors creaked open. An inmate of about 200lbs walked out and stood behind the warden, a grin on his war-scarred face. "How the fuck? Guard?"

The CO on duty said nothing. He just sat at his desk, a sneer hidden behind tight lips, eyes fixed on a magazine he'd been reading. Mr. Keller was on D-Block alone for the first time in his life. "So *you* were a part of this the whole time?!" He was addressing the silent officer now staring back at him from behind Billy's guard-dog. "Ya' know they killed three of our men today don't you?" Acting as though he hadn't heard anything, the undercover Aryan continued to look back across the room in complete defiance. His face was a stone.

"As I stated earlier, we have people everywhere Mr. Keller, so as you see, that's not *your* CO. He's mine. Now there's one other thing I have to ask of you." Keller was just standing there, glancing over his shoulder every couple moments in utter disbelief. He felt powerless. Exposed. "So why haven't you escaped yet? If you have my staff in your pocket, why the hell don't you just have them open up all the doors?"

What Mr. Keller didn't know was that the Aryan's only had a small percentage of the staff on their payroll, but each person held key powers the organization wished to exploit. "I understand I'll spend the rest of my life behind bars. I get that. Now, it's *you* that needs to come to grips with something. We control everything that goes on in this prison. Everything. You're merely the babysitter."

"So you felt the need to kill my men, just to tell me that?" "No. Gosh no! You're such a simple man Mr. Keller. I envy the empty space in your skull. Must be quite commodious up there... I brought you here to offer you an *out* to this madness." The warden began to laugh nervously; he now knew fully what this man was capable of. "Tell me more about this Mr. Splinton you've so efficaciously placed to flush me out? Yeah, we know about him too warden."

Kevin's findings on the drugs bore a plethora of evidence. In addition to being a large enough quantity of meth in the laced blunt to test, the harvest also hinted at the drug's origin. From his years in law enforcement the warden gained experience linking criminal organizations to their crimes through forensic screening. When Kevin reported traces of lithium, Mr. Keller suspected the Aryans. Lithium came from batteries the group frequently used in their meth cooks. He chose to keep the suspicion private until he could confirm, but Billy beat him to the chase. Once word of Kevin's arrival at the prison reached cell 4, phase 1 was already underway.

"By the way, did you ever find out where that lab was located? I heard you were lookin' for it?" Billy and the man now standing directly behind the warden began to laugh. Keller's eyes drifted towards the floor, "There was never any lab was there?" "See, there you go asking questions as though you still run things around here." Billy shook a finger as if to admonish a child.

By this time the warden's patience had been worn to a nub, Billy was clearly having fun and felt like he was in full control. "You were correct to hire Mr. Splinton about your meth problem, you definitely have one." They laughed again as he continued to mock the entrapped lawman. "However, and on a more serious note. I think you and I can come to an agreement about how we can move forward."

"What the hell're you talkin' about? I'm not *moving forward* with you! When'd you forget that you're the prisoner, and I'm the warden?" Billy's rebuttal was swift and well placed. "I think that may have been around the same time the pig we killed in Ad Seg took his last breath. Or maybe it was as we watched your friends down in Control bleed out; at the hands of an old lady by the way." Billy looked at his comrade standing behind Keller. "Patty was always good with a blade wasn't she brother?" "You got that right Sir. Damn good."

"You're in the business of hiring old women to do your bidding?" Billy scratched his chin and began to pace his cell as a general would, strategizing for war. "This is our proposition. Allow us to trade meth freely throughout the system. We want full access. And I don't just mean here. I mean across State lines. Pull whatever strings you need to. This is your only way..." Before he could go on the warden let out a grunt in protest, "That'll be the day, in my own damn prison." "You didn't let me finish warden. Just wait, it gets better. I even threw something in there for you."

Keller had been in D-Block for quite a while and the rest of the staff were starting to take notice. They knew he went alone. One of the deputies on scene ventured out into the yard to check on the lone man. It was the end of November. A crisp gust nipped at the skin on his face. It stung. Winter was nearing. His breath condensed into small clouds that trailed behind him as he traversed the yard. The officer's fingers tensed and cramped in the air's frigid bite.

As he approached D-Block, he could see the warden through one of the few windows in the building. "No! Stay back! I have this under control officer!" The warden could see the advancing man and beckoned him to stay away. He wasn't sure what to make of what Billy proposed, but Keller knew he had to be cautious. His career was at stake.

The deputy reluctantly backed away from the side entrance, but still made sure to keep Keller in his sights. "If they lay a hand on him, I'll send them a little something, courtesy of the State of North Carolina." The officer placed a tense hand on the Glock 34 on his waist, ready to use it at a moment's notice. 17 Monolithic hollow points rested in its clip. 9mm. Another sat eagerly in the chamber. If things went south, the metal pitbulls were just begging for a meal. A convict's chest was a steak dinner.

Billy continued his demands without missing a beat. He wasn't the least bit concerned with the threat outside. "In exchange for your cooperation, we will not only help you get outta this mess, which, let's be honest; I mean well the Governor's on his way." His face was masked with a sinister grin that bore surprisingly white teeth for a criminal. "You're in a mound of shit warden. Knee deep I might add. I just don't see you owning the right pair of boots to fit the job. But that's alright, you can buy some, cause' we'll also compensate you as a part of our deal." Mr. Keller was not in the business of making deals with the devil, but under the current circumstance, he didn't see where he had much of a choice.

"What exactly are you proposing?" Billy smiled and clapped his hands once in a fit of satisfaction. Maybe Keller was finally ready to play ball. "Now we're talkin, see I knew you weren't as stupid as you look. That wasn't so hard, now was it?" He paused for a response but none was given. "In exchange for you allowing the Aryans free trade and distribution rights, we are prepared to pay you 10% of all net profits. This can add up to a substantial amount Mr. Keller. We're talkin' thousands of dollars a month in tax free, untraceable money."

The warden would not be bought that easy, and definitely not by a criminal within his own prison. Without giving the notion a second thought he replied candidly, "No deal." "Wait a minute Mr. Keller, you didn't let me finish." There was something sinister about the way Billy said it. It was like he expected Keller's response. "If you choose to refuse our most generous proposal, we may be forced to more direct methods of persuasion. And when I say we may, I mean we will." A smile tailed the threat.

Surprisingly enough, the warden seemed un-phased by the inmate's offer. "I highly doubt you'd have the balls to kill *me*, and besides what good would that do anyway? I'd be dead, which in a way, I kind of am already." He paused to think about this. Billy nodded in agreement, his face stuck in its usual sneer. "You're absolutely correct Mr. Keller." He didn't like the way Billy kept calling him by his last name. The Aryan's tone was condescending, arrogant, and restrained all at once, as if he knew the warden would end up in his pocket, but the journey was yielding as much pleasure as the ultimatum.

"Killing you would serve absolutely no purpose whatsoever. No money would be made, by either party I might add. There would be pandemonium in the streets." Billy's voice emitted almost unbearable sarcasm. Every word was doused in it. "So, rest assured, you'll sleep safe n' sound tonight Mr. Keller... Now, the same cannot be said for your staff."

"That's right warden. If you don't allow us to move our product freely, we will kill each and every husband, father, son, uncle. Well you get the picture, one by one. Blood that'll be on *your* hands. All disposable. All except the ones currently on our payroll of course. But you have no idea who'se who, *do you*? We are well organized Mr. Keller, so make your decision. You have Fifty-eight minutes to decide."

CHAPTER 39

THEODORE FERDINAND ELLWOOD

Six minutes after leaving D-Block, the warden was still rushing to get back to his office. His usually slight limp seemed more pronounced. Stress had settled comfortably into his bones by that point. It rested in his hips and tugged at the will to move forward. "What happened down there? I saw one of the officers went looking for you? Everything ok?" Mr. Keller didn't hear his secretary as she spoke, his mind was too consumed by the choice that lie ahead.

"That woman, the one who killed those two guards, what've we found out about her?" Susanne began to say there wasn't much more information available, but he cut her off mid-sentence. "I don't think she was hired as a one-time contractor. The guy down there, this Billy character..."

"He talked about her like they worked together before. I wanna' know the connection, and give me everything you've got on the Aryans and our guest in cell 4." His voice rose as he spoke, culminating at a near screech-like pitch. Sims wasn't onsite yet, but his arrival was only a matter of time. Keller needed answers. A way out. He was under the gun. The minutes ticked by.

"We're trying to track her down as we speak Sir; it seems she used an alias to get in the building. Her name never checked out. Not on a single database." "Of course she did, and how are we coming with that information on the other people in visitation?" The main office of the prison was in a frenzy. By this point, it was completely over-run by both law enforcement and staff alike. Papers fluttered, voices murmured at a low rumble, orders were being thrown about. Information flowed in a river of organized chaos. It was the kind of environment that could make one want to hide under the shadows of a desk. Utter madness.

One of the analysts onsite strode up to Susanne and asked her a question. "Hi there, I'm Christie, I'm with the Charlotte Police Department's Drug unit. I hear this incident may have been drug related? Do you know anything about that?" Before she could answer she was rudely interrupted by her boss. His patience was wearing thin. There was a chain of command.

"Please, if you don't mind leaving all policy and legal questions to me!" The inquisitive cop gave one of her partners a look as Keller went on. His defensiveness didn't go unnoticed. 10 Years on the force told her he was hiding something. "I'm still the warden of this prison, at least for one more night." He looked at the clock near a stack of papers on his desk. Time was an enemy, plaguing its victims with the certainty of insomnolence. He only had ten minutes to give Billy his answer. "I've gotta' head back down to D-Block for a minute. I have some business to attend to."

He left the main building in a hurry, early in his career he learned that when the Aryans said they were gonna do something, they did it. "I see you're back Mr. Keller, come to cast me into the deepest darkest hole you have?" No answer. "Didn't think so." Billy stood leaning by his cell door as he spoke. He seemed to have been waiting for the warden to return.

"Yes, I'm back, and I've thought about your proposition." He also thought about the gun in his beltline. It was still there. "I accept your proposal. But, that does nothin' ta' get me out of the situation I'm in. I still have three dead bodies on my hands. I'm held accountable for what happens on my watch."

"It seems you've thought this whole thing out in great detail Billy, but you may've missed a spot." Mr. Keller gestured as though pretending to wipe something. "Did it ever occur to you that this deal you're tryna' strike with me can't be executed?" He waited for the supremacist to respond.

Billy smirked. "How so?" "Well, for starters, you've basically killed my career, I never got to thank you for that by the way." Out of nowhere Keller clenched his right fist and launched his arm as hard as he could. His first two knuckles were the only that connected, but they were enough to do the job. Billy landed squarely on his back. The punch took him by surprise and his expression did a poor job of hiding it. He almost looked indignant.

"Are you crazy? Didn't I just show you what I can do? Did you *not* get the message?" "Oh I got the message, loud and clear! Now that I got that out my system I can finish what I was saying." Keller's hand was shaking from the impact, but it was worth every moment of discomfort. "You've ruined me, you know that? Everything. Everything I've worked so hard to build, and for what? Drugs? Money?"

"How do ya' figure that?" Billy was holding his swelling jaw, nursing the pain as he spoke. Keller had caught him good. "By this time next week, I won't have a job, or a pension for that matter. Best case scenario I get fired and have my title and retirement stripped. So your little plan of basically blackmailing me into compliance isn't gonna' work. I won't be here asshole."

The Aryan leader thought about this for a minute and then responded. He was still on the floor when he replied. "The only reason you'd be implicated for the loss of life is cause' it happened on your watch, correct?" He spat a glob of blood into a corner of the cell. His eyes never left the warden's. "Exactly, how am I sposed' to explain that to those men's wives? To the Governor for that matter?"

As he thought of the hole he was in, it only seemed to get deeper. "Now that I think of it, I may even be charged with murder by way of negligence." Billy could see the validity in what the warden was saying and shot back, "Don't worry about the bodies. Now that *we* work together, we'll take care of your problem. Just take care of ours." Keller needed further explanation, so Billy elaborated. "Have you ever heard of the Russian Sleeper Cell program?" It was an odd question. What did the Russian's have to do with this? Sure, they were enemies. But meth was ran by the Aryans. He didn't see the connection.

At the lawman's blank stare Billy said, "Not many have." Before he went on, he made his way to his feet and dusted himself off. The two men were now eye to eye. "It's a program started in the early sixties. In Volgograd Russia. Dark shit. They'd send agents to the US, deep across our borders." He shook his head, as if disgusted by the thought of foreigners tainting US soil. Aryans were the worst hypocrites. They hated the idea of migration, despite their own horrifically colonial roots. *Imagine what the Native Americans must think every time they hear someone say, "Get out of our country." Empathy can be transformative*. Billy took a breath. Regrouped. "The best way to destroy a nation is from within. Many addicted mothers in this country's worst cities needed money to support their habits, and those crazy Russians saw an opening. Poverty's a motherfucker. Even today jobs are hard to come by. Back then it was the wild west. The program flourished for decades. Decades warden."

Mr. Keller listened to the inmate, trying to determine where his story led. He drew a bit of satisfaction from the pain still lingering in Billy's features. The con's occasional rub to the jawline warmed his belly. "These agents would pay fiends to enter their little rug-heads into what the Russians called a simple medical experiment." His story was laced with supremacist undertones. He couldn't help himself. The Aryans despised everyone not white and held no qualm with the occasional slur. "The agents were allowed one month with the children. It was all the time they needed."

"I still dunno' how those damn Russians pulled it off, but it worked." The Aryan leader thought for a moment and ran a hand over his face. "Wanna' hear a joke?" Keller didn't answer. "Here's one for you. What do you call it when a chip, a few microwires, and some crazy Russians have a party?" A pause was added for effect. The skinhead was enjoying himself. "You get America's worst nightmare. That's what you get! A living, programmable nightmare." The story seemed far-fetched. Keller wasn't buying it. Billy didn't seem to notice. "Those bastards really pulled it off. Well at least for the most part. You could send orders right into someone's brain. Teach em' to fly a chopper, learn Krav, whatever the fuck you wanted. They created their own army of sleepers. They have an army. All ready to do their bidding. Just upload new code with new instruction, that's all it takes. Or at least so the legend goes."

"Great bedtime story con. What the fuck does that have to do with me?" "Good question. The Russians didn't stop with the many slums this great country offers. After a few years they expanded. Orphanages, foster homes, State-run institutions, all ripe with young minds, ready for the taking. You know they have a few of their sleepers right here in this cozy little prison? Yeah, right here at home..."

The warden tried to put the pieces together, his hands found their way into his pockets as he leaned back on his heels. "Are you suggesting we blame today's murders on the Russians? That's absurd, and it doesn't take me off the hook!" "Oh but it does! How can a simple-minded warden combat the full might of unknown agents who set siege to his kingdom? I can see the headlines now!"

Mr. Keller frowned as he listened to the pale man paint his distorted picture. "Or maybe you want me to say that just to put the Russian's on the hook! I know you two're enemies. How do I know this isn't just some elaborate scheme to take out the competition?" Billy turned his back with a sigh. "I guess you have a choice to make..."

"We still have a problem here." The warden was looking at his sore fist and testing his ability to tighten it. Bolts of pain shot down each metacarpal with every attempt. "Oh yeah, what's that?" "One of the men you killed, I was close friends with him and his wife. Now I have to get on the phone with her and let her know the husband I was best-man for, will not be coming home."

"He was a good friend of mine. You don' get many of those in life. Being the soulless piece of shit you are, I doubt you understand. Nonetheless, you took him." Keller's eyes glistened. Tears of anger were pushed down deep. Held against their will in the depths of a man whose life was a lake of aching currents. "I want you to know you're gonna' pay for that. Before you die, you *will* pay." The Aryan leader looked off into the distance and sighed, "In the end we all pay." Potent snapshots of his violent life flashed like lightning in his mind.

On his way back from D-Block, Mr. Keller nearly stumbled into the police officer that had come looking for him earlier. “Have you been outside this *whole* time?” The warden knew the young cop had good intentions, but knowing too much in a place like prison wasn’t always a good thing. Experience taught him that. “Oh no Sir, well, yes. I was just looking around the yard for clues to help us piece this whole thing together.”

Mr. Keller didn’t know what the Aryans had in store for him. Billy knew he needed the warden to make his plans to gain control work. “I don’ want this young punk out here snooping around my house. Last thing I need him to do is find something that could stop Billy from steering the spotlight off me. I need that pension” Keller thought.

He knew he had to act. A diversion was needed. “I think we have this area pretty well covered. We could use a little help in A-Block.” It was all he could think of. The young cop looked puzzled. “A-Block? Did anything even happen over there, I looked at the building schematics, that’s on the other end of the compound isn’t it?” Bewildered eyes looked at the warden, waiting for explanation. He’d backed himself into a corner.

Keller knew there was no turning back. Not only had he made a deal with a Neo-Nazi, but he was also willfully inhibiting an investigation by sending this officer in the wrong direction. Life seemed to be getting more complicated by the minute. When he opened the door leading to his office, he was nearly knocked over by the stack of files shoved into his arms.

“Here’re the documents for everyone that came in an’ out the building within the last week. I figured maybe we should expand our search a little wider, you never know what might turn up.” He nodded. “Good work Susanne.” Along with a few other dedicated staff the warden and Susanne scoured through the mountains of information. Manila folders nearly busted at the seams.

Within the pages were the names and addresses of all visitors, who they'd visited, and for how long. There were also video feeds to review and interviews to conduct. The one high note of the day was that Governor Sims had given up on seeing Mr. Keller earlier that evening. He knew the warden had enough on his plate, and the only thing Sims had for his subordinate was an earful; he could give that at any time.

"Here's something you may find interesting. Look at this guy, he graced us with his presence twice this week." Her low-bridge glasses were halfway down her slender nose as Susanne pointed out the odd character. "Since when do you know an inmate to get two visits from the same person in the same week?" Keller had to agree, it was uncommon indeed.

"Who is that guy? And find out who he was here to see, both times." After exhausting all the prison's resources, the warden decided it would be advantageous to involve the police in their search. "We want this under wraps as quick as possible, the last thing I need is a media storm. I already hafta' figure out how I'm gonna' navigate through the typhoon of profanity Sims is conjuring up."

It wasn't until the wee hours of the next morning that they were able to locate an address for the odd character. "Send a team down there to pick him up." It was after three O' clock in the a.m. when the unit of Special Tactics CO's made it to the residence earmarked on their GPS. They were locked and loaded, vests and all. Keller wasn't in the mood for surprises.

The large home was gated, and it was easy to tell its inhabitants were quite well off. It reminded the men of a haunted house in some ways; there were vines on the gate. Some were thick, others slithered over the metal, moving with the shadows. The most gnarly ones clung to the home itself and seemed to hold it in place. Ghostly silhouettes from trees resembled ghoulish figures stalking the night.

One of the unit members walked cautiously up the front steps and began to knock on the heavy wooden door. It was too thick to kick in if things went south. His colleagues decided the most effective way to back their partner up, was from a distance. They hung back but kept their barrels trained on the front entrance. "We'll cover you, see if he answers."

After what seemed an eternity, there was a disturbance at the window. At first, they thought it was just a breeze that stirred the curtains, but when it happened again the highly trained CO's knew something was up. *Someone was watching them*. "You see that? Window on the left, one bogie in sight."

Once the team made contact with their target, their tactical training went into effect. With amazing efficiency, and without inflicting an ounce of damage, they were able to extract the stubby old man from his noble home. He left indignant but didn't put up a fight. "We need you to come with us for questioning."

"Questioning about what, and at this hour? What's all this about and who're you men? Wait, those are prison badges. Surely you cannot think *I* had something to do with that fiasco at the prison yesterday?" The CO that was holding his arm just replied, "We just need you to come with us Sir." Shock stuck to the old man's face as he was whisked away. Two SUV's escorted the transport vehicle back to the prison.

"Mr. Theodore Ferdinand Ellwood, is that correct?" An hour later he was sitting in a room that reminded the small man of the interrogation areas he had seen so many times in movies. No windows. A single steel table. Two chairs. The classic setup. "What is this? I've done nothing wrong. Nothing at all!" His fat wrists were bound by the links of curved metal used to restrain criminals. Their sharp edges drew deep in his skin.

Mr. Ellwood screwed his already severely wrinkled face. His voice lumbered as he addressed his captors. "I'll have you know I am a very prominent member of this community, you've brought me back here *against* my will, and I demand an explanation at once!"

He spoke with the eloquence of a man well heeled, something the prison CO's found great humor in. "Mr. Ellwood." The warden addressed him directly as he entered the prison's makeshift interrogation room. The door shut with a click behind him. His footsteps echoed against the cold floor's surface as he plodded over to the table with confidence in his stride. You could barely tell he had a limp. "Do you know who I am?" After a moment of looking the man up and down the detained gentleman replied, "Well of course I do. I was at the dinner in your honor a while back; in fact, now that I think of it, I'm pretty sure we sat at the same table! Yes, it was with Sims, I remember now!"

"Well I didn't bring you here to reminisce about good times past Mr. Ellwood. I brought you here... Because you're now considered a person of interest." "A person of what? On what grounds?" At this, Susanne chimed in, "Our records indicate you've visited the prison multiple times this week? Any particular reason for that?" The vertically challenged man leaned back in his chair in total disbelief, the accusations being thrown around the room sounded absurd.

"I was here visiting an old friend, and last I checked, there was no law stopping me from doing so!" Everyone in the room could tell he was beginning to get upset. Resentment was firmly baked into every word. It was becoming clear. Keller had made a mistake. "Furthermore, I will be speaking with my legal team first thing in the morning, this is ridiculous, I will *not* have my good name tainted."

"Yikes. Well that went well. Did you hear when he said legal *team*, this guy hires lawyers by the team." It was about an hour and a half before they released Mr. Ellwood with their sincerest apologies. He was the only real external lead the prison had, and their investigation was quickly running cold.

The Aryans now held the warden under their thumb and all hope of recovery seemed lost. Mr. Keller sat back in his chair and looked at the clock again. He was back in his office. He usually left the old chronograph on the table off to one side of the room, but as of recently he kept it on his desk where he could see it. Time seemed to be more precious nowadays.

"Something about Mr. Ellwood seemed off Susanne. Susanne!" He called out two more times before she heard him. "Yes warden, I heard you and I agree. He didn't act like he was guilty, but he was definitely hiding something..."

CHAPTER 40

THE GUN WITH NO BULLETS

The very last thing a man has to lose, is his mind...

MING LAO-

After the three killings, the prison remained on total lockdown for nearly a week. By day four Jacob and Alik were growing restless. And they were not alone. The wave of cabin fever was cresting, patience wearing thin for both convicts and CO's alike. Two floors beneath them, Billy's frustration was building as well. His plan worked but it came at a cost, and the cost was being locked in a 6 by 8-foot cage for twenty-three hours a day.

During the daylight hours, many convicts would find solace in hand-made board games and other primitive forms of entertainment. Alik and Jacob used this time to strategize. "This is not a random you know." Jacob knew what he was trying to say.

"I know, I remember you sayin' there was a war coming,

just had no idea it would be so soon." "These murders, they are a message from the Aryans I am thinking, they are showing a might of power." His disfigured hand was stroking through strands in his beard. A greyed stare overtook the Russian. His eyes fixed on the bars ahead, seeking out and then highlighting chips in the rusted metal. Much like his adversaries, finding the weak points. "I'll never get over the way you talk Alik," Jacob joked. "This is not the time for the jokes, this is serious Jacob." Neither of them knew about the deal already underway between the Aryans and Keller. But they would soon find out. Billy would make sure of it.

Alik knew whatever they had planned, it was sure to culminate with his demise. He couldn't let that happen. The Aryans were notorious for what they referred to as *severing the head of the snake.* It was an ideal shared by many students in the art of war. His survival wouldn't be possible under the current circumstances. There were too many enemies. The first hint of trouble came with the incident Jacob had with the DBB member.

After that, Alik knew the other gangs were testing the chinks in the mob's armor. The wolves smelled blood, and the Aryans were gaining control of the money through extortion. With all his millions in drug money frozen or seized, buying more muscle was out of the question. The Russian was out of options. Or so Billy assumed.

"There is more going on than is meeting the eye Jacob. Soon you will see who you are really being and what your purpose is, both to me and the mob..." This made the younger inmate uneasy. "Alik, I've been meaning to ask, why do you keep eludin' to that? Are you tryna' recruit me?" Alik just smiled and asked, "How are you knowing you are not already recruited?"

The next day Alik received what convicts referred to as

a kite. Many times, these makeshift letters carried orders, but when they were being sent to high ranking bosses they were usually of a more informative than instructional nature.

"It looks like they have a person of interest in this." They'd just returned from mid-day chow. "What do ya' mean?" Alik was struggling to read the tiny writing etched onto the unrolled piece of paper. "Here, lemme' see it," Jacob reached for the message with a clammy hand. Moisture smudged the writing a bit, but not to the point of ruin. He wiped his fingers on the edge of his pillowcase and then picked the slip back up. His eyes squinted.

Normally, kites were only read by the person it was intended for, this was especially true for those meant for a boss. Alik decided to bend this unspoken rule for the moment, "I cannot read these little words." He shook his head and laughed at the youth of his American cellmate. His age was catching up to him.

"Yeah, you were right, based on this it seems," Jacob squinted again; it was his first time reading a message that small. "The warden thinks some guy that was in visitation has some connection to what happened with the Aryans." As Jacob thought back, he remembered taking note of one particular character he saw in visitation. Now, granted, he was behind a dirty glass cage at the time; but he did recall the man standing out. Something about the way he held himself.

"I do remember seeing a guy down there; I thought I knew him from somewhere. His face just looked so familiar." It wasn't uncommon for Jacob to feel as though he recognized someone. During the nearly two years *post* winning and pre-imprisonment, he encountered literally hundreds of different individuals, all from various walks of life. Many times, people would come up to him and ask where they knew each other from.

These encounters held little weight, since most were ulterior motives in disguise. Almost anyone would claim they knew him, just to try their hand at a piece of his wealth. He and his Russian cellmate held these types of experiences in common. Money drew attention. However, Alik never told Jacob his own vast fortune was inaccessible.

"So what do ya' think comes next Alik? I mean once lockdown's over?" "I am not sure about this, but I am thinking the time is coming to activate." Jacob threw his hands up and said, "Alik, please, what the hell does that even mean?" His question was ignored.

While the inmates continued to groan and complain about their harsh restrictions, the warden had his own problems to deal with. For the past several days he spent long hours trying to conduct damage control. Some of this time was spent with CO's like Lieutenant Price and his men. The rest was consumed on conference calls with both law enforcement and the ever-watchful Governor.

Although he didn't lose his job, which was in part due to the agreement he now held with the Aryans; Mr. Keller did feel like he lost something much more valuable. His freedom was held captive. The warden had made a deal with the devil. His gut churned with guilt and defeat. The irony was classic, "The head of a prison, imprisoned by a prisoner."

He walked into the office that Monday morning with a heavy heart, a dumbbell in his chest. All weekend he had time to think about the men who lost their lives. About his job. About Billy. Even Susanne wasn't her normal self. On an ordinary morning she would typically greet her boss with a hot cup of black coffee, two sugars and a smile.

"Susanne, unless it's the Governor, or the matter's

pressing, please, just put it on my calendar for tomorrow." His office seemed darker than usual. Despite never holding much luster to begin with, there was a definitive change to the feel of the space. The air was thick with the stench of worry for starters. It stuck to the walls like sweat.

Mr. Keller had never been the alcoholic type, but once again he reached for the cabinet where he knew the bottle was located. As he opened the drawer, he remembered the gun one of his officers confiscated from a civilian the week before. The person came to the prison as a visitor and left in handcuffs; within months they would return, only this time for a much longer stint.

He found the type of gun they brought with them to be kind of curious. Already two drinks into his morning, Mr. Keller was now looking down the rear sight of the old Smith and Wesson. The front sight jutted from the silver barrel's tip, pointing skyward like the horn of a rhino. "Why the hell would anyone try to sneak such a clunky revolver in? They *had* to know they would be caught."

Without thinking about it, he gripped its curved handle firmly and slipped the heavy piece of metal and wood into his beltline yet again. It made him feel like a cowboy. A big-shot. "Susanne, I'm headed out to the yard for a bit. I need some fresh air." None of the cell blocks were scheduled yard time this early in the day, so the warden's walk was a quiet one.

As he moved he tried to adjust the gun in his pants. Having a live weapon in this area of the prison was strictly prohibited, but hey, who was looking? "And besides, this is *my* house" he thought to himself confidently. The half hanging sign above the Ad Seg building had completely fallen during the days following the string of murders. The warden shook his head as he saw it and thought about the prison's ever-dwindling budget. His house was in shambles.

"Yet another thing that needs to be done around this little pocket of hell." With that thought Keller stopped walking for a moment to ponder the events that led to where he now stood. "I remember when I used to wanna' be in law enforcement to try and save these guys before they got here. Now I'm about to go into business with 'em."

The thought angered him, and before he knew it, he was storming over to D-Block with a quickened pace. The dirty guard that opened the door for Billy on the day of the killings wasn't on duty for another eight hours, he usually worked the evening shift. "Mornin' warden!"

The young guard greeted his employer with an eager voice and stood up when Mr. Keller entered the building. His boss was moving so quickly the air seem to whoosh around him. "Mornin' young man." He didn't miss a beat as he kept stalking towards cell 4. Before he could reach its rusted bars, Alik called out from above.

"Warden, the morning is good, yes?" Keller glanced up with distaste but didn't say a word. "Guard, where's the inmate assigned to cell 4?" "Um, Sir he's in the infirmary, I think he came down with something bad last night." Even from three floors up, Alik could see the wooden handle protruding from underneath the warden's polo shirt.

He backed away from the bars to address his cellmate for a moment. "You are remembering what I am saying earlier in the yard?" Jacob thought back to the DBB member he'd stood up to. "Yes Alik, you were tellin' me somethin' bout' a war about to start." "It has begun." The Russian called out to the warden again, "Hey pig, I asked a question of you, why are you not answering me?"

Mr. Keller didn't know whether it was the power of

knowing he had a gun, or the four glasses of the Devil's Nectar for breakfast, but the comment set him off. He stormed up the thirty-eight steps that led to cell number 51 instead of going to Billy's cell. The trap was set.

"I don't think today's the day you wanna' get smart with me con! Open on 51!" This was the moment Alik had been waiting for. It would be pivotal, not only in Jacob's life; but for the rest of everyone around him as well.

While Mr. Keller marched up the stairs Alik whispered something under his breath about the gun, then he quickly addressed Jacob. Grey met brown as their eyes aligned. "I am only having a moment comrade. It's time to wake up." "What the hell's that sposed' to mean?" The air grew still as the warden drew near.

Alik broke eye-contact and gazed down at the tattoos etched on his stomach. He'd waited a long time for this day. Nearly 23 years. He canvassed the faded ink. The words were spelled upside down by design, making them legible when Alik looked from his viewpoint. Jacob didn't understand what they meant, and wasn't even sure they had a meaning. Many things the strange man did made no sense.

As he pondered what would happen once the cell doors opened, Alik began to read the words carved into rough patches of his skin. "Four, Parrot, Polynesia." As he spoke Jacob looked at him with utter confusion. "What the hell're you doin?" The Russian's voice was steady. Focused.

For some reason the words felt familiar, as if a stitch in the fabric of his being. Jacob could feel muscles in his arms begin to twitch involuntarily. His stomach went queasy. Something was off. "I hope I'm not about to have a stroke" he thought as he noticed the changes invading his body. As seconds progressed, a looming power engulphed his very *will.*

Alik continued, “Meditate, Jade.” With every word the Russian spoke Jacob could feel himself losing control. Of what? He didn’t yet know. What he *did* know was that whatever was happening, it scared the shit out of him. He saw flashbacks that seemed to last milliseconds and an eternity all at once. As if time itself was confused.

There were scenes from the dream he’d had as a child, of Ming Lao, of the lottery ticket. Each word uttered took self-control from Jacob, and gave it to the man beside him. As Jacob lost command of his mind, his life flashed before his eyes. Most scenes were familiar, but others seemed to appear from the ether. The experience was terrifying. Then. Everything went black. Deep, ink black. Darker than Ad Seg. Darker than night. Vacuity swallowed him whole. Jacob was gone.

“Tainted...” Alik looked up from his stomach. The words in his tattoos were hidden in larger pictures and were hard to find to the untrained eye, but Alik knew his work was done. His bunkie’s transformation was immediate. “How are you feeling comrade?”

A thick Russian accent came through clearly as he greeted his fellow soldier. “Agent 51 activated, ready to comply.” Jacob’s voice and demeanor were completely different than they had just been not ten seconds prior. It was a total transformation. “You’ve been under for many years comrade, your time has finally come.” As Alik looked into his cellmate’s eyes, he saw evil reflecting back. The cell door had just finished opening and Mr. Keller was rapidly approaching; anger in every step. Little did he know of the monster that awaited. Alik took a moment to inspect the Nurolink embedded in the top of his bunkie’s skull. It was tiny. Aside from a half millimeter indentation, there was no sign it even existed. It had been there for the last 22 years. A monster hiding in plain sight. The Russian gave his first order.

"Take his weapon comrade. We are leaving." Jacob's pupils dilated at the sound of his *handler's* voice. It felt like he was observing himself from the outside. His mind no longer held control over his body. His heart rate rose ever higher with each of the warden's steps, and then. Silence overtook.

"Now what was that you were sayin' inmate? Something about me being a pig?" Under normal circumstances the warden would have never approached the cell doorway without at least one CO at his side, but he wasn't thinking straight this morning. Liquid courage coursed through his veins. Hung on his breath. Protocol went out the window.

"Do you want me to come up there with you Sir?" The guard below was calling out to see if he was needed. "Do I look like I need your help kid? I been doin' this longer than you've been alive." As he spoke, the warden reached into his waistline and felt for the cold piece of metal. He wasn't sure if he would've pulled it out or not, and it really didn't much matter. *He never got the chance to decide.*

As his forefinger began to graze the edge of his brown leather belt, Jacob sprang into action. With one hand gripping tightly to his opponent's wrist, he used the other to send a vicious strike straight into the unsuspecting warden's chest. His timing was perfect. The force and speed with which Jacob moved was like nothing the other prisoners had seen before. Many had come to their cell doors in anticipation of a show. They knew something was about to go down. You could smell it in the air.

Mr. Keller tried to call out for help, but his breath was stolen by the blow; it was a clear shot to the solar plexus. He would later find out the cracking sound that came from his chest was a rib being fractured. Before he knew what was happening, he was looking down the barrel of the very snub-nosed revolver he'd just held.

Even with adrenaline now pumping and pain causing his eyes to tear, he could see that the pistol had no bullets in it. "Thank God," Keller said with a sigh of relief. Meanwhile, Jacob knew what he was doing but was unable to stop. If his body was a car, he was no longer the driver. All he could do was sit back in a corner of his own mind. Watching, praying that any moment he would regain control of the wheel.

He didn't even know *how* he was moving the way he did. He felt faster, stronger, even smarter somehow. He could see the gun in his hand and felt its smooth wooden handle. What Jacob could not do, was control himself, or anything around him. A newfound power surged through his body. And yet, he was powerless.

His vision was incredibly sharp. It picked up intricate details he would have never noticed before. The old pistol, still clutched in his hand, held a familiar face etched into its side. Jacob stood in disbelief as his eyes remembered the image from years ago.

"I remember this cowboy. And I remember that horse!" The animal's muscular shoulders flexed in a show of might. "I know this gun," he whispered in terror to himself. Confined to a dark room of his mind, he watched helplessly as Alik took the reins of his body. "Welcome back to the family comrad." It hit him like a Mack truck. He was a sleeper. A slave.

It must've shown in his eyes. Inside he was screaming, whaling out, trying to fight free. Jacob was stuck in a dream. The kind that leaves you in a pool of sweat and shaking long after you've woke. He looked into Alik's eyes. *What horror's have I committed? How many? How long?* A thousand questions ravaged his brain. Then, his eyes widened. One word left

Jacob's lips. It was all he could muster. "Kacy?" The Russian looked away, eyes set on the exit. "A necessary evil...We have to go. Our window is closing."

If you enjoyed this work by Heru Asaramo, please leave a review by clicking the link below! I'd love to hear from you...

www.amazon.com/review/create-review/?ASIN=B086GFPMSZ

Note to the reader: I put my heart into this work. For the past 13 years I have worked day in and day out, trying to make this dream a reality. I will never stop working for my family. This is my pain, my love, this is my work. Follow your passion everyday.

Cry for it.

Fight.

Persevere.

Overcome.

I truly hope you enjoyed. Look forward to the sequel...and please encourage other readers to enjoy my work!

Follow your dreams...Dream Big!

Made in the USA
Middletown, DE
18 August 2022

71656957R00231